Ever Since the Ball

by

Kate Ellington

Ever Since the Ball

Cover Art by *Teddi Black*

The Wild Rose Press, Inc.
PO Box 708
Adams Basin, NY 14410-0708
Visit us at www.thewildrosepress.com

Publishing History
First Edition, 2025
Trade Paperback ISBN 978-1-5092-6172-7
Digital ISBN 978-1-5092-6173-4

Published in the United States of America

Dedication

Thank you to everyone who helped and supported me along the way. You know who you are.

Chapter One

It couldn't be dawn yet. Miranda Harlake turned on her side to read the mantel clock by light of the dying fire. Two-thirty. Still unsure what had awakened her, she curled up and tried to get back to sleep. Almost on the verge of a dream, she heard the noise again. It was coming from her balcony.

Miranda looked over just in time to see a figure, bathed in moonlight, climb over the railing.

"Peter…" she muttered and closed her eyes.

She stayed in bed. He knew the way in.

Sure enough, the French doors opened and closed quietly, followed by footsteps creeping across the floor.

"Miranda," Peter whispered, shaking her shoulder lightly.

"I'm awake," she said, turning onto her stomach and pulling the blankets over her head.

"Miranda. Get up."

She pointed vaguely toward the balcony. "Come back tomorrow."

Peter walked over to the hearth and stirred the embers until the fire glowed, then went around the room lighting candles. "We need to talk."

Blearily brushing the hair out of her eyes, Miranda sat up just enough to lean back against the pillows.

Peter perched himself on the edge of her bed. "We have to get engaged. Tonight." He pulled a ring out of his waistcoat pocket.

Miranda was tempted to pinch herself to be sure she was awake, but since this wasn't the first time her best friend had come to her bedroom in the middle of the night, she didn't bother. Still, it had been some weeks since Peter had done it and he'd never proposed before.

"What are you talking about?" she asked through a dainty yawn.

Peter took her hand and gazed steadily into her eyes. "Your parents are betrothing you to Ebenezer Rockford tomorrow."

"Ebenezer Rockford! He's almost old enough to be my father!" Truly awake now, Miranda shot out of bed.

"He *is* old enough to be your father."

After a few moments Miranda stopped pacing and looked at Peter, trying to determine if he could be sleepwalking. Not that he ever had before, but it would make much more sense than what he was telling her. "I think you were dreaming, Peter. Where else would you get such a ludicrous notion?"

"It wasn't a dream. I overheard your parents talking earlier. Accidentally, of course." Peter flushed slightly and ran a hand through his hair. "Mr. Rockford's seeking a bride and your parents want her to be you."

"You must have misunderstood. Perhaps you should start at the beginning." Miranda cast a longing look at her bed. "Or come back in the morning?"

Peter rose and joined her beside the hearth. "The morning will be too late. Your father's going to speak with Mr. Rockford first thing tomorrow." He glanced at his pocket watch. "Well, later today."

"But he hasn't even proposed. Are my parents going to…to *offer* me to him?" Miranda asked, letting her arms fall to her sides.

"From what I heard, yes."

"Then why are you proposing, if indeed you truly are, when you know my parents want me to marry Mr. Rockford?"

"Because if you're betrothed to me you can't marry him." Peter tried to slip the ring onto Miranda's finger, but she balled her hand into a fist.

"This is absurd!" Miranda hadn't said more than two words to Mr. Rockford since that night he'd come to dinner three years ago. As she'd been barely seventeen and still in school at the time, she couldn't have made much of an impression on him.

"Absurd or not, your parents apparently can't resist trying to make a match. He's wealthy, lives close by, and comes from a good family."

"We don't need his money. We aren't paupers." Miranda walked over to the sofa and sat down. "My parents can't have been serious," she said, looking up at Peter.

"Your father's lawyer was with them. They were going over your marriage settlement."

Miranda was almost speechless. "An arranged marriage? It's so old-fashioned! This isn't the eighteen hundreds."

"It was the eighteen hundreds ten years ago," he said with a slight grin.

"Oh, what can I do?" Miranda had never been the type to run away, but the idea had its merits at the moment.

Peter sat beside her and took her hand. "If you accept Mr. Rockford tomorrow, you'll be married by harvest, but if you're betrothed to me it will buy you time. You'll be able to think what to do." His eyes shone as he held up the ring again. Miranda recognized it at once as his grandmother's.

"You're sweet to offer, Peter, but who would believe it?"

He looked affronted. "Your parents won't see me as a proper suitor since I'm only the housekeeper's son?"

Miranda tutted. "Don't be ridiculous. Nobody cares that you're the housekeeper's son. But don't you think people will notice that we've never once behaved as though we're in love?"

"You don't wear your heart on your sleeve like some girls, Miranda. We'll tell your parents we kept it secret because we didn't think they'd approve."

"But what about you? Don't you…have someone?" She hated to mention Ann, but she had to.

Peter looked away. "That's over. Long over. I don't think I'll ever marry."

"You're too young to decide that. Besides, we both know you aren't the type of man to live alone your whole life."

He met her eyes, looking torn between amused and irritated at her assessment of him. "This isn't about me. It's about you. We won't actually wed, so you can rest easy knowing you aren't coming between me and the woman of my dreams."

"But how will it work?" she asked, shrugging. "We simply go downstairs tomorrow morning and tell my parents we're engaged?"

"Considering that I haven't been allowed in your bedroom since we were ten years old, coming downstairs together probably isn't the best way to announce our betrothal. It's more likely to get me banished from the house. I'll arrive at the front door and ask to see your father, and you will look ecstatic when I later emerge from the drawing room with his consent."

Miranda rose and walked to the window, still barely able to believe her parents would arrange this match—*any* match—without consulting her.

"There must be another option," she said. A pretend engagement seemed not only drastic but complicated.

"There is. Tomorrow morning you promise to become Mrs. Ebenezer Rockford."

Miranda stared at the dark, starless sky. She'd always known she'd marry one day but had assumed she'd love—or at least like—her bridegroom. She definitely wouldn't have chosen someone twice her age that she barely knew and had never had a meaningful conversation with. As ridiculous as Peter's idea was, it might be the only way. Unless…

"What if I simply refuse to go along with my parents' plans?" she asked, turning to face him.

With a sympathetic yet exasperated look, Peter crossed the room to take her hand. "When have you ever been able to refuse them anything?"

Since Miranda couldn't argue with that, she tried another tack. "Perhaps Mr. Rockford won't want to marry me. He could have his pick of any young lady in town. He doesn't even know me."

"First of all, yes, he does. He's been to your house before. Secondly, who wouldn't want to marry you? You're pretty, amusing, and intelligent. And Mr. Rockford greatly regards your father."

"I don't think his admiration of my father's work is enough to make him want to marry me."

"I'll be frank, then, shall I?"

Miranda raised a brow. "When aren't you?"

"You'd make him an excellent wife and he knows that. Just trust me, Miranda. Mr. Rockford will say yes. So you've got to say no, and unless you feel the time has come to finally stand up to your parents…" He showed her the ring again.

"But if we say we're betrothed, my parents will expect us to actually get married. Soon."

"We'll say we want a long engagement, but simply cannot bear another day of not being promised to one another."

Though Miranda had misgivings, Peter's plan appeared to be the best, and the only, one they could devise before morning. "A *very* long engagement," she said. "Otherwise my father will start planning the wedding this afternoon."

He broke into a wide smile. "Is that a yes?"

Miranda was about to speak, but Peter held up a hand. "No! Wait." He went to his knees and took both her hands in his, staring up into her blue eyes. "Dearest, most beloved Miranda, wilt though doest me the honor—"

She covered her face with her hands, overcome with laughter. "Oh, do get up."

Peter rose and, taking Miranda's left hand, slid the ring onto her finger. They stood in silence, watching the diamond sparkle in the candlelight. After a moment they met each other's eyes.

"What now?" Miranda asked, taking her hand back.

"Now I go home," Peter said and let out a huge yawn. "You go back to bed, and I'll call on your father in the morning. Try to act desperately in love when you see me."

"Then we'll decide what's next. Such as how to extricate ourselves from each other when the time comes."

"That won't be a problem. I'll do something scandalous that gives you second thoughts, or you'll be caught in a compromising position."

Miranda's cheeks turned pink. "I absolutely will *not.*"

"I'm only joking," Peter said, laughing. "We'll think of some reason to call off our engagement, but we'll wait until Mr. Rockford marries someone else. Then you'll be free to fall in love with a lad you meet at a picnic or a dance."

Miranda put a hand on his shoulder. "Thank you for this, Peter. If my parents had told me tomorrow morning that I'm to marry Mr. Rockford, I would have been so shocked I'd have said yes."

He started toward the balcony. "You need to learn to stand up for yourself. But that's for later."

"Wouldn't you like to take the stairs?"

"Oh, no. This is much more romantic. Goodnight," Peter said as he climbed over the railing. When he reached the ground, he blew her a kiss and ran into the darkness.

Though only an hour had passed since Miranda woke up, it felt like a lifetime. Her mind raced with questions and doubts as she extinguished the candles and climbed back into bed, the ring on her finger heavy as a stone.

****

The next morning Miranda childishly hoped she'd dreamed Peter's visit. But no. There was the ring upon her finger. Sighing, she got out of bed and walked out to her balcony.

Miranda's great-grandfather had settled in this quiet New Hampshire valley and built the house from the ground up. He'd named it Majestic Oaks though it was only a two-storied home. Still, it was large enough. There were more than enough bedrooms, most of them empty despite Miranda's parents' best efforts to fill them all. Even after all these years, that one sunny room in the corner of the second floor stood ready to welcome a new arrival.

The house was surrounded by rolling fields and great stands of oaks, one of which afforded Peter his easy access to Miranda's bedroom. The Tolwoods lived at the edge of Majestic Oaks' grounds and Miranda and Peter had been friends from the cradle.

As Miranda turned to go inside, the sound of hooves rent the morning air. She looked up to see her father—out much earlier than usual and dressed in his finest—trotting down the drive. He must be on his way to see Mr. Rockford. She gestured frantically for him to come back, but he just waved and spurred his horse on.

Miranda slowly backed into her room and didn't stop until the back of her knees hit the edge of the bed. She collapsed onto it and covered her face with her hands. It was too late. Peter's plan had come to naught; her father would soon be offering her up to Mr. Rockford like a prize cow.

If only she'd gone downstairs earlier! She could have easily delayed his departure by taking him into the studio with some question or other about her latest painting. Then Peter would have had time to come and ask for her hand.

She pried herself off the bed and changed into a

long, dark green skirt and a white blouse embellished with lace. Sitting at the vanity and brushing her auburn hair, she tried to think of the best way to tell her parents she wouldn't marry Mr. Rockford. Peter was sweet to offer her a way out, but really, of all times, this was one where she should stand up for herself. Perhaps a confrontation with her parents wouldn't be necessary. She'd simply tell them she'd heard of their plans and wasn't interested in Mr. Rockford. They couldn't argue with that. After all, her parents couldn't *force* her to marry him.

Hopefully Miranda's mother was having one of her good days. If she was suffering from one of her headaches or felt too tired to come downstairs, Miranda wouldn't even see her today. But if she was feeling well she'd listen to Miranda and perhaps take her side. What mother wanted to send a miserable daughter to the altar?

In the parlor, Miranda found her mother lounging on the yellow chaise in front of the window, leafing through her favorite magazine, *New England Artist Monthly*.

Miranda perked up at once. One of her mother's good days. "Good morning, Mother."

"Good morning," Mrs. Harlake said, not looking up.

Miranda strolled over to stand beside her. "Any interesting articles?"

"There's to be an art exhibition in Hollingsford in August."

"Oh, good. Perhaps we could pick up supplies while we're in the city."

"Yes, I need canvas and a new flat brush."

Now was the time. Miranda glanced at the side table. No coffee cup. It wouldn't do to try to talk to her mother before she'd had breakfast. "Have you eaten yet?"

"No, I'm waiting for your father," she said and turned the page.

"Where is he?" Miranda asked.

"He had an errand in town."

Was it Miranda's imagination, or was her mother a little more pink in the cheeks than she'd been a moment ago?

"Father isn't usually out this early," Miranda said, trying to keep her voice even.

Now her mother did look up. And yes, she was pink. "He had a meeting with someone. I forget who." She turned back to the magazine, flipping through it without glancing at any pages.

"I'll wait to eat breakfast with him, too," Miranda said, settling herself on the sofa.

"There's no need for that. It could be a long time."

"I don't mind waiting." Miranda tried to recall the resolve she'd had upstairs. It was a simple matter of explaining how she felt. "This gives us time to discuss something that's been troubling me."

"I. Well." Mrs. Harlake put a hand to her forehead, rubbing her temple. "I need to go up to my room," she said, tossing the magazine aside as she stood up.

"What about your breakfast?"

"I'll have a tray brought up."

"But Mother," Miranda said, rising, "I need to talk to you. It's important."

"Talk to your father when he gets home. He's better at solving your problems than I am." Mrs. Harlake turned to go.

"I don't have a problem," Miranda said, placing a hand on her mother's arm. "It's about Ebenezer Rockford."

"What about him?" Mrs. Harlake asked, pulling out of Miranda's grasp.

Words failed Miranda for a moment as she looked into her mother's cool gray eyes. Yes, what about him? How could she admit she knew what her parents were planning without divulging that Peter had overheard their private conversation? Perhaps the best course of action was bringing the conversation around to it gradually.

"I heard he's getting married," Miranda said at last.

"If all you wanted to do was gossip, I'm going upstairs," Mrs. Harlake snapped, not meeting Miranda's eyes.

Miranda would never have a better chance than this. "As a matter of fact, Mother," she began, reaching up to brush a hair out of her face. "I—"

"Miranda! What is *that*?" Her mother grabbed her wrist just as the butler came in to announce a visitor.

Chapter Two

"Thank you, Bramwell," Mrs. Harlake said as Miranda tried to wrest out of her surprisingly strong grip. "Please show our guest in."

"It's Peter Tolwood, ma'am," he said.

Miranda's stomach dropped. Peter had missed his chance to talk to her father, and he'd only make matters worse if he mentioned the betrothal to her mother. She had to stop him.

A look of annoyance flashed across Mrs. Harlake's face. "In that case, please tell him to wait in the drawing room."

Mr. Bramwell bowed and left the room.

Miranda finally succeeded in reclaiming her hand and started backing away. "I'll take Peter out to the garden. You said you need to rest."

"I asked you what that is," her mother said, narrowing her eyes. "I know every piece of jewelry you own. Did you purchase that ring without asking your father?"

Miranda could have wept with relief. An excellent excuse she never would have thought of on her own. "Let me see to Peter and I'll come back and explain—"

"You'll explain what, darling?" Peter asked, strolling into the room with a bouquet of roses.

"Peter!" Miranda cried, shaking her head vigorously and holding her hands up as though to keep his next words from escaping.

Mrs. Harlake froze. "Darling?"

Miranda turned her back on Peter and faced her mother. "I meant to tell you. It was all so sudden. Peter and I—we've always been fond—" She held up her trembling left hand. "We're going to be married."

"Married!" Mrs. Harlake's hand flew to her chest and she grew paler than Miranda had ever seen her, even on the worst of her bad days.

"Miranda, sweetheart, you should have waited until after I spoke to your father," Peter chided gently as he thrust the roses at her. He put an arm around Mrs. Harlake's waist and guided her to the settee, where she sat down and stared mutely at Miranda.

Peter yanked the bell pull and when Mr. Bramwell arrived said, "Wine, please, and right away." He took another glance at Mrs. Harlake. "Perhaps food, too. Cake? Toast? Fruit? Anything. Right away."

After one look at Mrs. Harlake, Bramwell dashed out of the room without a word.

Miranda sat on the edge of the settee and took her mother's cold hand. "Should I call your maid, Mother?" When she didn't answer, Miranda turned to Peter. "Does your mother have any smelling salts?"

"Probably. But you'd best summon Esther," he said.

"I don't need my maid, *or* smelling salts," Mrs. Harlake said, glaring at Miranda. "I need the two of you to tell me what exactly is going on. Sit down, Peter."

Peter sat in an armchair across the room, then seemed to remember Miranda. He returned to the settee, took her hand and led her to the sofa. Once they were seated he kept her hand wrapped in his.

Miranda's heart hammered as she watched her

mother, waiting for the storm to break.

Peter cleared his throat. "Well, Mrs. Harlake, I'd planned to speak to your husband first, but it seems Miranda just couldn't wait to tell you our good news. I know it's somewhat unorthodox, me proposing to Miranda before getting permission, but I had no doubt she'd say yes."

Before Mrs. Harlake could reply, the door opened. Miranda looked up, expecting the much-needed wine, but it was her father. She set the roses down and pulled her hand out of Peter's grasp.

Mr. Harlake bounded into the room, rubbing his hands together. "It's all settled!" he said to his wife before noticing Miranda and Peter on the sofa. "Good morning, you two. Were you waiting breakfast? You could have started without me." He crossed the room and took Mrs. Harlake's hand. "Are you all right, Clara? You look pale. Should I call Esther?"

"We already rang for wine," Peter said.

Mrs. Harlake looked up at her husband. "You'd better sit down, Lucas."

He gave her a puzzled look and sat beside her. "It seems I've walked in on something. What's going on?"

Mrs. Harlake pointed toward the sofa. "These two seem to think they're engaged."

"Engaged! How preposterous," Mr. Harlake said, laughing. When nobody joined in, he looked at his wife. "Engaged?"

"Engaged," she confirmed.

Nobody spoke for a full thirty seconds. At last, Miranda stood up. "Peter and I, we've decided to get married."

Peter rose and took her hand. "Sweet pea, it wasn't

that we *decided.*" He addressed Mr. and Mrs. Harlake. "We've loved each other for quite some time. Perhaps all our lives. Lately it's been harder and harder to ignore and I finally had to ask her to be mine."

Miranda showed her parents the ring. "I said yes, happily. I love him. I do." Miranda gave Peter what she hoped was the look of a woman overcome with emotion.

Mr. Harlake loosened his collar. "When did you call for that wine?"

Within moments Bramwell returned with the wine, followed by a maid with the breakfast tray. Before the butler exited the room Mr. Harlake called, "Bramwell, perhaps something stronger."

Peter poured wine for everyone and held his glass up for a toast. Miranda touched her glass to his; her parents simply drained theirs.

The parlor clock ticked loudly as they sat in silence, eating from the tray. Mrs. Harlake's color had improved and she nibbled a slice of toast while Mr. Harlake picked at a muffin. Miranda only managed a few sips of coffee, but Peter ate a full breakfast.

At last, Miranda's father gave Mrs. Harlake a nod and rose. He stood before the sofa and, when Peter made to rise, indicated that he should stay seated.

It reminded Miranda of when they'd misbehaved as children and were about to be chastised.

Mr. Harlake put his hands behind his back. "You may not marry. You're too young, you didn't ask for permission, and the very idea is ludicrous."

"Why is it ludicrous?" Miranda asked, attempting a pout.

"I've just told you why."

Peter looked up. "I beg your pardon, sir, but we

aren't so very young, and we're in love."

"Yes," Miranda said, taking his hand. "We're in love. You know how I feel about Peter, how I've always felt about Peter." She looked at him with the warmest look she could muster. He truly was her dearest friend, so it wasn't difficult.

"Marriage is a serious undertaking," Mr. Harlake said. "What do your parents say to this, Peter?"

Peter looked away, rubbing the back of his neck. "I haven't told them yet. I'd planned to ask your permission first, but I was overcome by my feelings last night and I couldn't wait any longer to secure Miranda's hand."

"Perhaps we should summon them," Mrs. Harlake said.

Mr. Harlake shook his head. "That isn't necessary. I have an idea."

"What sort of an idea?" Miranda asked, wary of that gleam in his eye.

"I'll need to speak to your mother alone first. You two step outside."

Miranda leapt up and followed Peter out to the patio. She was so distracted she hardly noticed the perfect blue sky and the scent of flowers wafting from her mother's meticulously manicured garden. Miranda paced around the patio, biting her nails, as Peter leaned casually against a tree.

"That went well," he said.

She stopped to stare at him. "No, it didn't! I don't think they believe us. And I didn't have a chance to tell you, but my father already went to Mr. Rockford's this morning. For all we know he's already promised me to him."

"He would have mentioned it, wouldn't he?" Peter

asked, pushing away from the tree.

Miranda considered this. It did seem unlikely that her father would hold back a ready-made excuse for rejecting Peter's proposal. "Yes, you're right. Perhaps Mr. Rockford wasn't interested," she said hopefully.

"Why did you tell your mother this morning? You were supposed to wait for me."

"I planned to tell her in no uncertain terms that I wouldn't marry Mr. Rockford, but she asked me about the ring and then you strolled in with your roses and your 'darling.' I just panicked. Oh! Why didn't I leave the ring upstairs?"

Peter crossed the patio to stand beside her. "It's all right. It would have come out one way or another today. Perhaps this is better. It makes us look more like lovestruck fools."

"I wonder what they're saying in there?" Miranda asked, peering toward the house.

"Hopefully they're realizing it's too late to stop our betrothal and they'll accept it."

Miranda started pacing again. "Do you think your parents will be angry?"

"No, they've always liked you. If anything, my mother will be disappointed later when we call it off. But we have more important matters to discuss. Did I act loving enough when we were in the parlor?"

"The hand-holding was a nice touch. I'm not sure I want to be 'sweetheart,' though. It's what my aunt calls me."

"I'll think of a better name. My little rose petal?"

" 'Darling' will suit. Did I look like I'm in love?" It was hard to imagine she had, as Miranda had never been in love before. How was one supposed to act?

"No," Peter said. "You mostly looked nervous, or slightly ill. But the love declaration was almost believable."

"I'll need to practice that for when we're around other people," she said, moving to his side.

"Not necessarily. As I said last night, you don't wear your heart on your sleeve. We could be more affectionate, though. We should practice a kiss."

"A kiss!"

He shrugged. "Well, we're supposed to be in love."

"Even if we were, I doubt I'd kiss you in front of my parents."

Peter gave her a smoldering look as he ran a finger lightly down her arm. "You'd find it that easy to withstand my charms if we were in love?"

Miranda blushed, laughing. "You mustn't do such things, Peter. It's difficult to take this seriously as it is."

"I'll try not to tempt you. But it won't be easy." He took her hand and raised it to his lips.

"It will be hard for me to resist you," she said, patting him on the shoulder, "But I'll do my best."

Peter laughed and kissed her cheek just as Miranda's father called them back inside.

When they stepped into the parlor, Mr. Harlake pointed his nearly empty glass of whiskey at the sofa. "Sit down."

Miranda sat on the opposite end of the sofa from Peter, then realized she should stick to him like glue and scooted over until their legs were touching. He gave her an approving nod and took her hand.

Mr. Harlake cleared his throat and addressed Miranda, with only an occasional glance at Peter. "Do you still insist that you're engaged?"

Miranda and Peter looked at each other and nodded emphatically.

"Yes. We love each other," Miranda said.

"Your mother and I have decided we'll allow it—"

"Thank you, sir!" Peter said.

"We'll allow it on one condition," Mr. Harlake continued. "You aren't to tell anyone that you're betrothed."

"Not even your parents," Mrs. Harlake told Peter.

"Why not?" Miranda asked. She'd planned on going into town this morning to spread the word. If nobody knew they were engaged, what would stop Mr. Rockford from pursuing her if he so chose?

Peter shook his head. "I can't keep this a secret from my own parents."

"You will if you want to remain betrothed to our daughter," Mr. Harlake said, more sternly than Miranda had heard him speak in years.

Miranda wanted to ask what they'd do to break up the engagement and to insist that her father be polite to Peter. But deciding not to anger him further, again asked, "Why?"

"Because we believe your engagement won't last," Mrs. Harlake said, folding her hands in her lap. "The fewer people who know of it, the fewer we'll have to explain to when you call it off."

Peter wrapped an arm around Miranda's shoulders. "We won't change our minds. Our love is true."

"If we agree to your terms, when can we tell everyone?" Miranda asked.

Her father considered for a moment. "In a year."

"We already decided we want a long engagement," Peter said. "But won't you allow us to share this joyous news with my parents?"

"No," Mrs. Harlake said. "If you tell your mother, it won't be long before the whole town knows."

"Are you saying my mother is a gossip?" Peter asked. Miranda suspected he was acting the part of a loyal son only because it was expected. Of all people, he knew his mother's ways.

"You forget I've known Audrey since we were girls," Mrs. Harlake said. "She wouldn't be able to keep this to herself."

Peter let out a dejected sigh. "You could be right. But you'll permit me to court Miranda? We'll be able to see each other every day?"

Mr. and Mrs. Harlake shared a long look. Finally they both nodded.

"You may still visit daily," Mrs. Harlake said.

"But we'll be courting now," Miranda said and gave Peter a chaste peck on the cheek. "I can't pretend we aren't in love."

Peter laughed but managed to make it look like he was delighted by her attentions.

Mrs. Harlake leaned back, rubbing her temples.

"At home, if you must, you may express mild displays of affection," Mr. Harlake said. "*Mild*."

Peter took Miranda's hand and kissed it. "We'll agree to your wishes."

Miranda wasn't sure what to do next. Thank her parents? Squeal with joy? She settled for resting her head on Peter's shoulder and sighing happily.

They all sat looking at each other for a few minutes until Mr. Harlake said, "It's settled, then."

Peter nodded and put his hand on Miranda's knee.

Mr. Harlake gave him something resembling a glare.

"Peter, don't you have obligations at this time of day? With your father?"

"Yes, but Miranda has driven everything else from my mind," he said.

"I'm sure she'll understand that you don't want to neglect your work," Mrs. Harlake said.

Peter rose. "Yes, she's such an understanding and supportive girl. Only one of the things I love about her. I'll see you soon, darling," he said, and kissed her hand again before striding to the door, where he turned back to look at her before leaving the room.

Miranda made to follow him but her father put up a hand to stop her. "Just a moment."

"What is it now?" she asked, sinking back into the sofa.

When her parents took a seat on either side of her she knew they weren't done trying to talk her out of the engagement.

Mr. Harlake turned to her. "Now that Peter's gone, you can tell us. Why would you get betrothed without asking us first?"

"It all happened so suddenly," Miranda said, twisting the ring around her finger. She might have also pointed out that it was *her* life. Shouldn't she be the one to decide who she'd get engaged to, and when? If her parents hadn't gone behind her back she wouldn't have been driven to take part in this charade. But she held her tongue.

"You always tell us everything," Mr. Harlake said. "We had no idea you fancied Peter."

Miranda fidgeted with the buttons of her shirt. "You know how close we are."

"Yes, but we thought you were friends. Only

friends. When did things change?" her father asked.

"It's hard to say. When I look back, it's clear I've been falling in love with Peter for some time, and then it…it just overwhelmed me recently. Last week. No, a month or two ago."

Mrs. Harlake put a hand on Miranda's shoulder. "That isn't very long."

"No, not long," Miranda agreed. "But I know it's right. May I go now?"

Mr. Harlake let out a long sigh. "Well, Miranda, there's something of a problem. Besides the fact that you're too young."

"What kind of problem?"

"This morning I went to Mr. Rockford's estate to talk to him about you. He's interested in a betrothal."

Miranda did her best to look shocked. "Mr. Rockford! I hardly know him."

"You'd grow to know him," her mother said.

"You didn't actually engage me to him, did you?" Miranda asked, horrified. But no. He would have mentioned it when Peter was still here.

Mr. Harlake shifted in his seat. "Not in a manner of speaking, but as I said, he was intrigued by the idea."

This was the perfect moment to tell her parents she wasn't interested in Mr. Rockford, and furthermore that she'd make her own decisions. But she just held up her hand to show the ring. "I'm already engaged."

"For now," Mrs. Harlake said.

"Nothing could change the way I feel about Peter."

Miranda's father gave her the kind of look she'd seen a thousand times before, whenever he thought he knew better than she did. "Don't reject Mr. Rockford so quickly. He'd give you a stable home and luxurious life.

You could focus on your art exclusively until you have children."

"Peter can give me those things, too."

"Your life with Peter would hardly be luxurious," Mr. Harlake said. "He'll be an estate manager here, like his father. You'd most likely stay at Majestic Oaks all your life."

"Then I'd never have to leave home," Miranda said, attempting a light tone.

Mr. Harlake sighed heavily. "You've put me in a fix, Miranda. Now I'll need to go back and tell Mr. Rockford...I don't even know what. It's incredibly awkward. He was going to come for supper tomorrow night to get to know you better."

"If you'd spoken to me about him first—" Miranda began.

Mrs. Harlake stood up. "I can't take this bickering any longer."

Miranda looked at her mother. "I'm not—"

"Your mother's had enough talk for one day," Mr. Harlake said as he rose and put an arm protectively around his wife.

Miranda was more than happy for this conversation to end. "I'll leave you, then. I need to get outside before I lose the morning sun."

Her father glanced out the window. "Hm. Yes. I'll be along after I settle your mother and see Mr. Rockford. Will you be at the ridge?"

"I haven't decided where to go yet," Miranda said. She didn't want to spend the next three hours listening to her father singing the praises of Mr. Rockford. "I'll see you both later."

As she walked out the parlor door, her mother

called, "Take off that ring!"

Miranda removed the ring and held it gingerly in her palm as she climbed the stairs to her bedroom. It was only a tiny piece of gold, but she wanted to thank it for saving her, at least for now, from a most unwanted match.

Chapter Three

Miranda placed Peter's ring in her jewelry box and went to look out the window. The day was clear and fine; she'd have a good view of the mountains from Marigold Lake. More importantly, the lake was in the opposite direction from the ridge her father was going to.

After braiding her hair, Miranda opened the wardrobe and pulled out her favorite walking ensemble—a fitted russet jacket, matching skirt, and a pair of black trousers. Mr. Harlake had bought Miranda's first breeches years ago because they were so much easier for scrambling through the forest or going riding. When she'd been a child, nobody in town batted an eye, but as she'd grown older there'd been unpleasant whisperings. Since then, Miranda fashioned her own trousers and always wore them with skirts that swept the ground.

On her way out of the house, Miranda stopped by the art studio. Works in progress stood on easels around the room and deep cupboards held all manner of supplies. Miranda and her parents shared the space, though they weren't often here at the same time. Mr. Harlake preferred painting outside and Mrs. Harlake had her own small studio upstairs in her suite of rooms.

Miranda crossed to a corner cupboard and opened the door. Pastels or watercolors today? She knew what she'd choose if it were up to her, but her father often referred to her pastel work as "scribblings." Her pieces were certainly better than that, though she'd only been practicing with them for a few years. Watercolors, on the other hand, she'd been using since she was old enough to hold a brush.

Knowing her father would want to hear she'd completed the picture of Mount Windsor, she settled on watercolors. Miranda gathered her travel easel, paint box and the satchel holding her painting.

As she passed the stables she looked around for Peter, but he was nowhere to be seen. Though he primarily worked with Mr. Tolwood around the estate, his true love was horses.

She continued past the paddock to a well-worn forest path on the edge of the grounds and before long came to a wide lane. Tall birch, elm and maples formed a green canopy overhead and the forest floor was carpeted with lush green grass. On the edge of the lane, bushes that had been green since spring were finally sprouting strawberries and delicate wild flowers.

Walking through the forest, Miranda recalled the last twelve hours. When she'd gone to bed last night her only concern had been how to mix that certain shade of blue to finish her painting. Now she was betrothed to Peter and trying to keep at bay her parents' dreams of catching Mr. Rockford. She had the feeling they wouldn't give up on the idea quickly, given their condition of keeping the betrothal secret.

As a girl Miranda had imagined being swept off her feet one day by a dashing stranger, preferably an artist or a pirate. But as of yet she'd never fancied anyone beyond the short-lived schoolgirl crushes anyone might have. One thing she was sure of—though Peter would make someone an excellent husband, it would not be her.

Miranda continued down the lane until it split off in different directions. The right fork led to town, the left to the lake. She turned left, treading carefully over loose stones and stepping around thin gullies that ran down the center of the dirt trail. It was quiet, dark and cool under the dense trees, more like twilight than a bright summer morning. After a walk that always felt it took longer than it should, shimmering patches of blue appeared between the trees—the lake.

The path ended abruptly and Miranda stepped onto the beach, where she was instantly warmed by the sun. She set her supplies down, removed her hat, and wiped a hand across her brow. A light breeze rippled across the water and up onto the shore, ruffling her skirt as she looked at Mount Windsor in the distance. Miranda had been coming to Marigold Lake since childhood and it felt homey despite its vast size. In most places, wild vegetation ran right down to the water, save for a few small sandy beaches and scattered lakefront cottages.

She opened the easel, arranged her paints and brushes, and set the painting in place. It was nearly finished. She had only that one angle of the peak to get right, and the shadow from a low cloud.

As Miranda mixed her colors, words like "engagement," "lies," "husband" and "trouble" ran through her mind. She took a moment to clear her head before setting brush to canvas. Her eyes drifted from the mountain to the canvas and back again, and soon all other thoughts were stilled and her hand was moving as if by its own accord. Mix, brush, stroke, blend.

After a time the sun drifted too far west, taking Miranda's ideal light with it. She stood back to look at her work. Not as precise as her father would have done it, but she was pleased. Miranda made a few minor adjustments, then set about packing up her things while the paint dried. With nearly all packed, she sat down on an old tree stump and watched two loons in the middle of the lake. She reached for her paintbox and paper, intending to capture the birds' stark colors against the blue water.

But suddenly the sound of voices drifted over from somewhere close by. Men's voices. In no mood for socializing after her peculiar morning, Miranda checked her painting to see if it was dry. Not quite. She'd ruin it if she handled it too soon. She fanned the painting with her hat, hoping it would dry before the men appeared. Perhaps they weren't coming this way and would veer off into the woods.

But no. Within moments, four men emerged from a stand of trees close to the shore. They walked along, laughing and kicking water at each other. With his broad shoulders and black hair, George Rockford stood out among his companions—the last person Miranda wanted to see. Well, besides his uncle Ebenezer.

He was accompanied by Ethan Locke, Frank Jefferson, and Henry Owen. Miranda had been two grades behind them in grammar school, where the boys were well known due to their constant mischief-making. She wasn't on speaking terms with any of them, but she and Peter saw them all strutting around town often enough.

Miranda decided to pack up her work and just hope it didn't smudge. She slid the painting into its satchel, but when she turned to pick up her easel, she saw the men clustered in a group, staring at her. It wouldn't be polite to ignore them, but she didn't want to get drawn into a conversation, either.

She was considering the best course of action when Ethan nudged George and whispered something in his ear. The men watched Miranda curiously as if to gauge her reaction, and based on their expressions Ethan's comment hadn't been complimentary. Miranda was tempted to give them a truly quelling look, but instead hurried into the cool shade of the trees. She glanced down at her clothes—not remotely fashionable and now with fresh paint joining the old stains. No, not the type of elegant woman she'd frequently seen George escorting about town.

Miranda put the men out of her mind as she walked down the woodsy lane, wondering where Peter might be at this hour. She wanted to join him for lunch so they could discuss this betrothal plan more. When she arrived at home and looked all around, Peter was nowhere to be found.

Next she went to the studio to show her father the painting, but he wasn't home, either. After washing up, she changed and went to the parlor. When she asked a harried-looking Esther if she could join Mrs. Harlake for lunch, she was told her mother was resting and couldn't have company right now. And no, she hadn't seen Peter.

Since nobody was available at home, Miranda decided to go into town. She opted for Fairbanks Road instead of the forest route and half an hour later entered Darlington's, a combination mercantile and restaurant. Miranda bypassed the busy shop and stepped through a doorway on the right, where she was greeted by the scent of baking bread. She stopped by the counter to place her lunch order before sitting at a table overlooking Main

Street.

Her thoughts turned to her father. While she definitely believed her mother would hand her off to a man she barely knew, it was harder to accept that her father would betroth her to someone without considering her feelings. It would have been one matter if they'd disagreed on a suitor, it was quite another for him to choose one for her.

She leaned back in her chair just as the waitress arrived with lunch—tomato soup, a thick slice of warm bread with fresh butter and a piece of lemon cake for dessert. The soup spilled slightly as it was set down, but fortunately it didn't drip onto Miranda's clothes.

After a bashful smile the waitress turned to go.

"Wait—I did order coffee, as well," Miranda reminded her.

The waitress blushed. "How scatterbrained of me! I won't be a moment."

It proved to be more than a moment, but it was no matter. Miranda finished her lunch and had just started on the cake when her coffee arrived.

"I apologize for forgetting. Twice," the waitress said as she set a cup of coffee down in front of Miranda, being careful not to spill it.

"That's all right. It's perfect timing. I wanted it with my cake."

"Oh, good. I am sorry, though." She turned to go.

"Just a moment," Miranda said. "It's Emily, right?"

"Yes," Emily said, putting her hands in her apron pockets.

"I wanted to ask how you're settling in. You've been in Deerwood a month now?"

"Yes, already a month on Thursday. It seems only

yesterday Nathaniel and I returned from the honeymoon. Mrs. Darlington says I'm training up well in the shop, and Nathaniel's been helping 'show me the ropes,' as he calls it," she said with a giggle.

Miranda smiled. "Do you plan to attend any social functions when you have time?"

"I hadn't thought of it. I don't know much about the goings-on in town yet."

Miranda stirred her coffee, looking up at Emily. "I'd be happy to bring you to a concert or a poetry reading at the library one day."

"How kind of you. To tell the truth, I've been missing the company of my sisters back home. With one thing and another, I haven't met many people yet. Save you, since you're in here so often. Your name is Miranda, isn't it?"

"Yes, that's right. I should have introduced myself sooner."

Emily waved a hand. "There isn't usually time, with me bustling around the tables and minding the shop."

"The next time I'm here I'll tell you what events are coming up."

"Thank you. Enjoy your cake."

Miranda sipped her coffee thoughtfully as Emily walked away. She couldn't deny a twinge of envy when Emily had spoken of her sisters. She hadn't been terribly lonely as a child since she'd had Peter and his siblings, but she'd never made any close woman friends. And though Peter was her best friend, there were some things you simply can't discuss with a man, no matter how close.

Miranda's parents had been good companions when she'd been young, and their shared love of art brought them even closer. But over the years her mother had grown increasingly withdrawn due to her frail health. Miranda would have liked to help her, but Mrs. Harlake said no daughter should play nursemaid to her own mother. No matter how many times Miranda insisted it wasn't a burden, she always turned her away.

Though Miranda's father was more available, she couldn't talk to him in the same way she imagined she would her mother if they were closer. Mr. Harlake disapproved of what he called "feminine silliness," and preferred to treat Miranda almost like a son. Not, she thought with an inward groan, so much that he wouldn't try to find her a husband.

Secretly she'd love to have gowns covered in flounces and bows or embroidered with stars or silver thread, but her parents insisted dresses be "practical." So Miranda kept to her plain gowns and accessories. Though the styles were simple, Miranda couldn't resist rich colors. Her wardrobe was full of jewel tones and contained only a handful of the more neutral colors.

Miranda set her coffee cup down and glanced across the street to Easton's, the dressmaker's shop, where a gauzy pink confection hung on a lucky mannequin.

After giving Emily a little wave, Miranda crossed the street to take a better look at the gown. It was embroidered with red roses, the lace sleeves so sheer as to be almost invisible. The skirt swept the floor and ended in a short ruffled train. Perhaps one day she'd have an excuse to wear such a dress. It was almost enough to make her want to get married in truth—her parents couldn't deny her a trousseau.

Resisting the temptation to enter the shop simply to feel the sumptuous fabric, Miranda checked the watch pinned to her blouse and started down the street.

Chapter Four

A few days later Miranda was sitting on the back lawn, sketching a chestnut mare and her filly. She was so intent on her work she didn't notice Peter approaching until he sat down beside her in the grass.

"Good morning, my sweet fiancée," he said.

Miranda's pencil slipped—giving the filly a tail as long as a tree. "Peter! I didn't even hear you."

He smiled. "You never do when you're working."

She set her sketchbook aside and leaned back on her hands. "I didn't expect to see you today. Didn't you say your father wants to talk to you?"

"Yes, but I saw you from the window and I'd much rather look at you than a list of numbers. Besides, your parents are in the drawing room and have a clear view of us." He scooted a little closer.

"Do you think they're watching?"

"Definitely."

Miranda put her hand over his. "It feels wrong somehow to deceive them like this."

"There's no harm in it," he said, entwining his finger with hers. "Besides, they were deceiving you, in a way."

"That's true. Still, I don't like deceptions."

Peter glanced over his shoulder to the house. "Neither do I. I swear my mother suspects something."

"How could she?" Miranda suddenly realized that putting on this show for her own parents necessarily increased the risk of *his* parents finding out, not to mention anybody else who happened by.

He shrugged. "I don't know. I'm sure I'm imagining it."

"What's she been doing?"

"It's more the way she's been looking at me. Doe-eyed, the same way she acted when she thought me and..." Peter looked away, tugging the grass at his feet.

"Ann?" Miranda asked after a moment.

"Ann."

"Did you ever tell your mother exactly what happened with her?"

Peter gave her a disbelieving look. "How could I possibly explain it, Miranda? I'd have to tell her the woman I liked is an associate—a *friend*—of Mr. Cobbe's, the man who abandoned Mother all those years ago. The last thing I want to do is remind her of him. I don't want to hurt her."

"That's all in the past," she said, putting a hand on his shoulder. "Forgiven. Forgotten. Your parents said as much when they told you about it."

"Maybe they can forget it, but I can't," Peter said.

Mr. Cobbe, who fancied himself a gentleman because one of his ancestors was an earl, had deserted Mrs. Tolwood—Audrey Bennet at the time—after what Miranda's grandmother would have called "An indiscretion." But fate had smiled upon Audrey and she'd fallen in love with Noah Tolwood, who happily raised Peter as his own. Nobody in town suspected Mr. Tolwood wasn't Peter's true father, though he'd told Miranda his secret long ago.

"Try not to let it bother you. We'll simply pretend Mr. Cobbe doesn't exist," she said.

"That won't be easy, considering he's on every committee in town and is president of the bank."

"We'll avoid him, at least."

Peter just shrugged again and moved on to another unsuspecting tuft of grass.

"Your mother must have wondered why you broke things off with Ann so suddenly," Miranda said.

"She never knew how close we'd grown. She saw us that one night at the dance and started getting romantic fancies. Honestly, I'm glad your father forbade me from telling my parents about our engagement. I couldn't bear to see my mother's face if she thought another prospective daughter-in-law had slipped through her fingers."

"I highly doubt she thought of Ann that way. You barely knew her three weeks before she left town."

"If only I'd known who she really was. I would have steered well clear of her." He stood up and started pacing. "Just a few months ago I thought I'd found someone I could possibly love. But then I discover my— Mr. Cobbe is her guardian."

"I'm sorry, Peter. I know how much you've suffered over her."

"Yet you continually broach the subject," he said, his tone uncharacteristically harsh.

"With all this talk of love and marriage and engagements, it naturally comes up. I won't discuss it again. It never happened. Does that suffice?"

His face gradually relaxed into a smile. "It does. I'm sorry to be a beast to you."

"You're not a beast. But if you don't stop pacing and looking so upset, my parents will think we're quarreling."

"We wouldn't want that." Peter sat down and put an arm around her shoulders, all traces of agitation gone. "I thought we could go into town for lunch before I sequester myself with my father for the afternoon."

"Accounts?" she asked, leaning her head on his shoulder.

"Yes, and he's been lecturing me about the future and says it's time I shoulder more responsibility. He reminds me he won't be here forever."

"He's been saying that since you were ten years old."

"I know, but I'll humor him."

Miranda took another look at her drawing and erased the errant line on the filly's tail before closing her sketchbook.

Peter rose and helped Miranda to her feet. "Perhaps a kiss? For show? Your parents are probably still watching."

"A small one. On my cheek."

Peter gave her cheek a featherlight kiss, then offered his arm. "Shall we?"

"I need to drop my sketchbook in my bedroom," Miranda said. "Should I change my dress while I'm up there?"

"No, it's only lunch. Besides, that blue makes your eyes look pretty."

****

When they reached Main Street, Miranda took Peter over to Easton's to show him the pink gown. He agreed it was nice and suggested asking her father for it, which led to yet another of his lectures about Miranda learning to speak up for herself.

At Darlington's, Miranda and Peter claimed the last

empty table in the back of the restaurant. After a bit of a wait, Emily delivered their sandwiches, cucumber salad and a pitcher of lemonade. Peter had already finished his second sandwich by the time Miranda and Emily finished chatting and finalized their plans to meet at the library the following week.

As Miranda began her lunch, the front door was thrown open and George Rockford and his friends piled into the shop side of Darlington's. They were laughing and—again—shoving each other. She'd have thought they'd outgrown such childish behavior a decade or two ago.

Miranda and Peter's table stood next to the open doorway leading to the shop, so all through her meal she was distracted by the shenanigans of George and his friends. They wandered around picking things up, shouting, trying on hats and juggling salt water taffy they swiped from a barrel. Miranda did her best to ignore them, which was nearly impossible since they grew louder as they made their way closer.

Miranda finished her lunch and was about to ask Peter if he wanted dessert when someone crashed into their table, knocking Miranda and the crystal lemonade pitcher to the floor.

"Oh!" She landed hard on the ground as the pitcher smashed into her hand and shattered into pieces.

Peter leapt to his feet, shoving George off the table. "Watch where you're going!" he cried and immediately rushed to Miranda's side.

Miranda's face turned crimson as the entire restaurant went silent and everyone craned their necks to stare at her. She tried wiping the lemonade off her dress but it was soaked. To make matters worse, a shard from the pitcher had pierced the back of her hand, leaving a long cut.

"Are you all right?" Peter asked, helping her to her feet.

"Yes," she said, her voice trembling slightly. "But I've cut my hand and I'll need to go home at once to change."

George stood stock still, staring at Miranda as his friends chortled behind him. Finally he seemed to find his voice. "I do apologize. Someone pushed— That is, I tripped and couldn't catch myself."

"You managed to catch yourself on our table," Miranda said coldly, pressing her cut to stanch the bleeding.

"And on *her*," Peter said, handing Miranda a napkin.

Emily ran over from the counter, carrying a towel that she thrust at Miranda. "Oh, you're hurt! How can I help? Should I fetch the doctor?"

Miranda took the towel, wishing the other patrons would stop staring. She cleared her throat and answered loudly enough for everyone to hear. "I'm fine." In a quieter tone she added, "Do you have any bandages, Emily? My hand…"

Emily took one look at Miranda's wound and paled. "Bandages. Yes." She tried to push through George's friends but they wouldn't make way so she scurried around them.

"Allow me, please," George said, taking the towel from Miranda. He went down on his knees and sopped up the mess as his friends looked on, unable to control their mirth. Glaring up at them, he said, "You don't need to stay."

Ethan smirked. "We wouldn't want to miss this."

"We'll wait," Henry said, reaching for a napkin. "We'll help clean up."

George waved the towel at him. "There's no need for that."

"Yes," Peter said firmly, sliding his arm around Miranda's waist. "We have everything well in hand."

Ethan, Henry and Frank shared an amused glance. After apparently deciding nothing more interesting would happen, they said goodbye to George and went out the side door.

Peter settled Miranda in his own chair. "Now tell me what I can do for you."

"Get me a dry dress?" She suggested with a tremulous laugh. Miranda was still shaking slightly, perhaps from pain, or perhaps from the shock of being knocked over.

Peter grinned. "That's easy enough once we get you home."

George rose and carried the towel over to the counter just as Emily returned with the bandage.

Peter took it from her and gently wrapped Miranda's hand.

"I'll have Nathaniel over to clean this glass," Emily said. "Mind you don't step on it on your way out."

Miranda looked up at her. "We'll be careful. Thank you."

"I'm happy to help. I hope the wound isn't serious," she said and walked away.

George returned to the table, head slightly bowed as he wiped his hands on his jacket.

"Excuse us, we're leaving," Peter said, helping Miranda to her feet.

"I want to apologize again," George said. "I have no

excuse but that my friends and I were having some fun."

"Perhaps keep your fun outside next time," Miranda said, rubbing her now throbbing hand.

George's face turned pink. "I'm sorry. Is there anything I can do to help?"

"You've done enough already," Peter said.

George laughed. "Come now, I've said I'm sorry. It was an accident. No harm came from it but a sticky mess and a scratched hand. I didn't accost you on the street."

"No, only in my chair," Miranda said, but her voice was light.

Peter took her arm. "Let's go. I want to get you home."

"Wait," George said. "Please take my carriage."

"That isn't necessary," Miranda said.

"It's the least I can do. If you walk home, you'll truly be accosted—by honeybees."

Miranda looked at Peter.

"It's your decision," he said with a shrug.

She ran a hand over her sleeve. Sopping with lemonade and getting stickier by the moment. George might be right about the bees.

"We'll accept your carriage," Miranda said.

George looked relieved. "Meet me outside in a few moments," he said and hurried away.

"I can hardly believe that happened," Peter said as he walked Miranda to the door. "Well, we get a nice ride home out of it."

"I'd rather have avoided being knocked over and forgone the ride home. I'm afraid my dress is ruined."

He held the door open for her and they walked down the steps. "Perhaps my mother can save it."

"Perhaps." Miranda glanced around, looking for

George. "I feel odd accepting his carriage. I haven't spoken to him in years, have you?"

"It isn't as though we move in the same circles, but I've seen him at the tavern."

Within a few minutes the Rockford's carriage pulled up and George hopped out. He held the door for them to get in. "Thank you for accepting this small gesture. And again, I do apologize."

"It isn't necessary for you to apologize any more," Miranda said with a light laugh.

George glanced at her dress. "It seems I owe you a gown."

"Don't be ridiculous," she said. "As you said, it was an accident. We'll let bygones be bygones."

He smiled. "If you insist…Miranda?"

She was frankly surprised he'd remembered her name. It was years since they'd spent any time with each other. They'd never been friends but had been thrown together in that way children always are during town picnics and dances while their parents are socializing.

"Yes. Miranda. Miranda Harlake."

He nodded. "You're the artist's daughter."

"And I'm Peter Tolwood, and you're George Rockford. We should all know each other's names after going to school together."

George laughed and held out a hand to Peter, who shook it. "I, of course, remember you, Peter. I've seen you at the tavern from time to time."

"Yes, and drunk with me on occasion, too," Peter said, turning slightly pink when Miranda raised her brows at him.

"I'll let you two get on your way," George said, stepping aside so they could enter the carriage.

"But how will you get home?" Miranda asked.

"Easily." George gestured across the street to where his friends stood beside another carriage. Henry waved while Ethan and Frank guffawed about something and paid George no mind.

After Peter and Miranda climbed into the carriage, George closed the door after them. "Perhaps I'll see you at the ball next week. Goodbye." He slapped the side of the carriage and the driver clicked to the horses to set them off down Main Street.

Inside the carriage, Miranda tried in vain to arrange her skirts so none of the lemonade would soak into the velvet upholstery. "I'm such a mess."

"You really are," Peter said, laughing.

Miranda couldn't help joining in. She leaned back against the seat. "You should have heard yourself at Darlington's, Peter. It sounded like you were going to challenge George to a duel."

He wiped his eyes. "You looked like you wanted to punch him."

She laughed even harder, flinching when her hand bumped the carriage door. "Ouch."

Peter sobered at once. "Let me see it," he said, taking her left hand and unwrapping the bandages.

"It's worse than I thought," Miranda said.

"It won't interfere with your painting, will it?"

Miranda tried flexing her hand. It stung at the slightest movement. "I don't think so, since I'm right-handed. But I can think of a number of tasks that will be impossible using only one hand."

"I'll be your assistant," he said. "What are fiancés for?"

"You do make a most attentive fiancé, Peter,"

Miranda said and leaned her head on his shoulder.

They rode in silence as the bustle of town gave way to quiet, open fields. When they passed the road to Mr. Cobbe's, Miranda took Peter's hand. She felt him tense up and tried to think of something to distract him.

"It's a nice carriage," she said.

"Yes. Just think, if you married Mr. Rockford this would be yours."

"I already have a carriage."

"Not so new as this one," he said, running a hand along the deep wood of the window frame.

Not remotely interested in the finer points of the carriage, Miranda changed the subject. "What's this ball George mentioned?"

"The masked ball. You remember. The Rockfords have one every year."

"I've heard of it but I've never been."

"I've only been once. Perhaps we could go together this year."

She shook her head. "I doubt my father would allow it. He thinks balls are nonsense."

"That doesn't mean you shouldn't go. Speaking of your father, it looks like we're home."

Miranda wrapped her hand up again as they turned into the drive, wanting nothing more than to forget the whole afternoon.

Chapter Five

Despite Miranda telling her father the wound wasn't serious, he insisted on summoning the doctor.

"You can't be too careful with an injury like this," he said, peering at her hand with a magnifying glass. "You may need sutures."

Miranda, who was sitting on the sofa, blanched. "I don't think it's deep enough for that."

Mrs. Tolwood arrived with clean towels and a basin of hot water. She set them down on the table and turned to her son. "How could you let this happen, Peter?"

"I didn't let it happen, Mother. It was an accident. Somebody fell on her."

"I'd expect you to take better care of her, especially since you're her be—" Mr. Harlake pressed his lips together as though it was the only way to hold in the last word. *Betrothed.*

"Especially since he's what?" Peter's mother asked.

"Supposedly her best friend," Mr. Harlake said and began yet another examination of Miranda's hand.

"Peter, make yourself useful and go fetch some ice from the box," Mrs. Tolwood said. "It will ease the pain."

Peter, who was standing behind Miranda, put his hand on her shoulder. "I'd rather stay here. Send Jack for it."

"I'm not going to call your brother, who's probably

gallivanting around the grounds somewhere, when you're here and perfectly capable of getting it."

"It's all right, Peter," Miranda said, looking up at him. "I'll be fine."

He gave her shoulder a squeeze. "I won't be long."

Miranda fervently wished she could go upstairs and change out of her damp, sticky dress, but there was the question of how she'd manage buttons and corset laces with only one hand. She'd need to ask Esther to assist her, or perhaps Peter's sister Cassandra could help.

Just moments after Peter left, Doctor Fitz arrived. "I had an urgent message that you're injured. What happened?" he asked, looking at Miranda.

"It's her hand, Doctor," Mr. Harlake said before she could answer. "Will she be able to paint? How serious is it? Will it require sutures?"

"Let me have a look." Doctor Fitz sat next to Miranda and carefully examined her hand.

She tried to keep still and not grimace, so as not to worry her father more than necessary.

After a few silent moments, Doctor Fitz sat back and removed his glasses. "There are some glass splinters I'll need to remove, but the wound isn't serious. I'll give you some ointment for it and you should keep it bandaged until it heals."

"She'll be able to paint?" her father asked again before Miranda could thank the doctor.

"Certainly. It won't require sutures, but I advise resting it for the next few days, and keep it clean. Ice will help with the pain."

Mrs. Tolwood gave Miranda a reassuring smile. "See? Nothing to worry about."

"How long will it take to heal?" Mr. Harlake asked,

staring at the wound.

"A week or so," Dr. Fitz said. "As I said, it's not serious. There won't even be a scar." He cleaned the injury and pulled a pair of long, sharp tweezers from out of his bag.

Miranda closed her eyes and turned away.

Peter strode into the room carrying a chunk of ice wrapped in cloth. He sat beside Miranda and took her uninjured hand. "How is it?"

"The doctor says I'll be fine," Miranda said, burying her face in his shoulder. She squeezed his hand as Doctor Fitz picked out the splinters.

The doctor finished by washing her hand again and adding a foul-smelling salve before bandaging it. "There," he said. "How does it feel?"

Miranda tried moving her fingers. "Better, but still sore."

"The pain should improve now that I've removed those splinters," Doctor Fitz said. "Take aspirin if it bothers you, and ice it twice a day."

"Thank you, Doctor," Miranda said.

Mr. Harlake shook Doctor Fitz's hand and walked him to the front door.

"Can I get you anything, dear?" Mrs. Tolwood asked after they'd gone.

Miranda looked up at her. "Tea would be nice. Or coffee."

"And dessert," Peter said. "We never had any at Darlington's."

Mrs. Tolwood gave them an indulgent smile. "I'll be back in a jiffy."

As she left the room, Mr. Harlake came back in. Miranda quickly closed the small space between her and

Peter.

Mr. Harlake ran a hand over his mustache. "Peter, perhaps you should go. The doctor said Miranda needs rest."

Peter started to rise, but Miranda slipped her arm through his. "Father, Peter is such a comfort to me, and besides, Mrs. Tolwood's bringing refreshments."

"Very well," Mr. Harlake said, somewhat begrudgingly. "But after you've eaten, go to your bedroom. I'm going upstairs to tell your mother what the doctor said."

Peter patted Miranda's knee. "I'll see that she relaxes."

"Be careful of that hand," Mr. Harlake said on his way out of the parlor. Miranda wasn't sure if he was referring to her injury or Peter's hand on her leg.

As soon as the door closed behind him, Miranda sank into the sofa. "My goodness! You'd think nobody had ever cut a hand before."

"He's worried, naturally."

When they heard footsteps coming down the hall, Miranda and Peter moved to opposite ends of the sofa. Not a moment too soon, as Mrs. Tolwood came in carrying a tray holding the coffeepot, two cups, and what looked like enough cake for six people.

"How's your hand?" Mrs. Tolwood asked.

"Much better, thank you."

Mrs. Tolwood poured out coffee and handed Miranda a slice of pound cake, then turned to Peter. "Father expects you to join him in the west field this afternoon. Something about the bridge over that little brook."

"I'll go up soon," Peter said, digging a fork into his

cake.

"See that you do," she said and left the room.

Miranda set her cake down after a few bites. As she sipped her coffee and watched Peter devour two slices, she wondered about the ball George had mentioned. She'd never been to a proper ball, only the annual summer fete and the Christmas dance. Over the years, she'd avoided dancing as much as possible since it wasn't her strong suit. Truthfully, it wasn't even her weak suit.

Peter put his plate down. "I'd better go meet my father. Will you be all right?"

"Yes, I'm going upstairs to change. I think the sugar from the lemonade crystalized in my stockings."

"Get some rest. And no painting," he said as he stood up.

Pain shot through Miranda's hand. "I'm not even tempted to try today. I'm more concerned with how I'm going to get out of this gown."

"Cassandra could help you."

"No, I'll ring for Esther. I'll be able to ask her how Mother is," Miranda said, rising.

Peter took her arm as they headed for the parlor door. "Next time we go out for lunch we'll avoid Darlington's."

"The only thing we need to avoid is George and his friends."

****

The next day Miranda solved the problem of gowns by wearing her trousers and a riding coat that fit almost well enough over a haphazardly fastened corset. As long as nobody outside the family saw her, she needn't worry. She went downstairs for breakfast, where she found Mr.

Harlake at the table eating poached eggs and melon.

"Good morning," Miranda said as she sat down.

"How's your hand?"

Miranda reached for a blueberry muffin. "It feels much better today. Is Mother coming down?"

"No, she's resting."

"In that case perhaps I'll go see her after breakfast."

"I'm sure she'd enjoy that." He looked at her over his forkful of eggs. "Be sure to change first. You know she doesn't abide those pants."

"This was easier than trying to get myself into a dress."

"Ask Esther to help you, then."

Miranda sighed. "I will."

They sat in silence for a while, eating their breakfast. But her father's talk of dresses had given Miranda an idea.

"Speaking of gowns, I saw one at Easton's that would be perfect for special occasions. It's…it's pink. Mother would like it. My blue one from yesterday is ruined, so this is a good time to buy another one."

He finished off a glass of juice. "No need for a new dress, Miranda. You have plenty already."

"Not like this one."

"It's probably costly." He looked up. "You know, if you married Mr. Rockford you'd have more new gowns than you knew what to do with."

He sounded like Peter, though at least Peter had been jesting about the carriages. Miranda wasn't about to reply to that, but it did remind her of something else. "I heard the Rockfords are giving a ball soon."

"I heard that, too. I'm glad you don't go in for such things, Miranda. So crowded and loud, takes up one's entire evening. Costumes, masks..." He shivered.

"Perhaps we should go this year. There could be people who appreciate your paintings there. Someone might want to buy one."

Mr. Harlake nodded. "True, true. But it isn't as if I'd bring my paintings to the ball."

"You might enjoy yourself. We'd visit with the neighbors and perhaps make new acquaintances. I heard they invite people from the whole county."

"We have all the friends we need. Every year they invite me and every year I decline. I'm surprised they still bother. Frivolous waste of time, if you ask me." Mr. Harlake's eyes lit up suddenly. "Although if we went, you could dance with Mr. Rockford."

Miranda wanted to quash this idea at once. "It's a costume ball, so he wouldn't even know it's me. I'd be wearing a mask."

"Hm. That's true. We needn't bother, then. But I'll invite him to supper one night soon."

"Father," Miranda began, about to say the ball would be amusing even if they didn't see Mr. Rockford, but he cut her off.

"Yes, yes, I know. *Peter.*" He snapped his fingers. "That settles it. If you're already engaged, there's no need for you to attend a ball, of all things." Mr. Harlake turned back to his breakfast, looking well pleased to have found a way out of the conversation.

What would he say if Miranda told him she wanted to go? That she wanted to be ridiculously feminine and wear a frilly dress and dance with a man she'd just met? Why couldn't he see she was no longer a scrappy ten-year-old, but a young woman who wanted all the trappings that came with a certain amount of social life?

She'd never minded the trousers or traipsing across the countryside with him, but why couldn't she have that *and* girlish things?

If only she could appeal to her mother. But Mrs. Harlake had stopped showing any interest in Miranda's social life or what she wore years ago, aside from making it clear she disapproved of pants. She'd made sure Miranda knew proper etiquette so she wouldn't make a fool of herself in public, but she'd never taught her the finer things most of her friends had learned at finishing school. According to her grandmother, Miranda verged on feral.

Miranda knew what Peter would say. It wasn't for her parents to suddenly give her what she wanted, it was for her to *tell* them what she wanted. But how could she when her father refused to listen and anything that upset her mother was practically forbidden?

She rose from the table. "You're right, Father. There's no need to attend the ball. Perhaps next year."

He gave her an absentminded wave. "I'll be out at the ridge later, if you want to join me."

"I won't be able to today," she said, holding up her bandaged hand.

"Well, you'll finish your painting once you've healed."

Miranda went upstairs and, after changing with Esther's assistance, went along to her mother's suite. These rooms could have been in an entirely different house. Her mother had painted it in pale blues and yellows, unlike the dark wood of the rooms downstairs. She'd brought a number of fine furniture pieces with her when she'd moved here from her family's mansion in Hollingsford. Mrs. Harlake wasn't in the sitting area, so

Miranda passed through to her bedroom. That was empty, too.

"Mother?"

"I'm here," she called from the studio.

Miranda expected to find her lounging on the sofa, but she was standing in front of a painting she'd been working on for months. It was Majestic Oaks on a sunny day, with a young Miranda sitting in the grass.

Mrs. Harlake's arms were crossed, one hand loosely holding a paintbrush covered in green paint. "I was just adding a few last details."

"It looks nearly finished," Miranda said, moving to her side.

"Almost." Mrs. Harlake set her brush down and went to the basin to wash her hands. "I'm going to hang it in the nursery."

"Are you? Nobody will ever see it in there. Why not the drawing room?" Miranda immediately regretted her words as her mother seemed to shrink before her eyes.

Mrs. Harlake looked at the floor as she dried her hands. "That may be so."

"Oh, Mother, I didn't mean—"

"Think nothing of it. I'm going to ring for breakfast." She strode out of the room and tugged the bell pull in the sitting room.

Miranda followed and sat at the table across from her mother, who was studiously looking in the other direction. What could Miranda possibly say? She'd clearly upset her by reminding her of the empty nursery, but Mrs. Harlake might be even more upset if Miranda tried to apologize again.

"So. Your painting," Miranda said. "It's hard to believe you can remember me in such detail. How old was I?"

"I made a sketch of you that day. You must have been three or four. It's hard to believe you were ever that small," Mrs. Harlake said with a sigh.

"I'm surprised Peter isn't in it, too."

Mrs. Harlake smiled. "Peter was never far off, but he didn't make it into all of my sketches. I do have a number of you together."

"I'd like to see them one day."

Her mother just nodded, and before long a maid arrived with breakfast. Since she'd already eaten, Miranda sipped coffee and sat with her mother while she ate. After an almost silent meal, Mrs. Harlake went to rest and Miranda returned to her room.

When she opened the door to her bedroom, Miranda almost couldn't believe her eyes. A large, rectangular box sat on the bed. She wasn't expecting anything, but as she drew closer, she saw her name written clearly on the box. Her heart sped up when she read the label—Easton's.

With trembling hands, Miranda lifted the cover. Nestled inside the package were yards of pink, gauzy fabric. Her father must have ordered the gown for her as a surprise, though she had no idea how he'd gotten it so fast or why he'd changed his mind. Perhaps he'd decided to take her to the ball! Miranda ran her fingers over the delicate silk before lifting the dress gingerly out of the box. She took it over to the full-length mirror and held it up to herself, ignoring the pain in her hand.

The gown was even more beautiful up close. Her cheeks took on the rosy hue of the dress and her auburn hair stood out against the pale pink.

As Miranda fanned the skirt out to see the ruffles, a

card fell out of the folds. Smiling, she picked it up. Her face fell as she read it.

"*Dear Miss Harlake,*

I believe I owe you a gown. I apologize again for my behavior yesterday and for your injury. Mrs. Easton said this should fit you, but if it doesn't you can take it back to the shop for alterations.

Sincerely, Mr. George Rockford."

Miranda carried the gown to the bed and regretfully tucked it back into the box. She couldn't possibly keep it, and any man in his right mind would know that. Perhaps his mother had put him up to it. But no, Mrs. Rockford would know how inappropriate it was. And furthermore, Miranda doubted any young man in his right mind would tell his mother he'd knocked over a woman in Darlington's, destroyed her dress, and done her bodily harm.

Miranda ran her hand longingly over the sleeves. *Could* she keep it? She had to talk to Peter. He'd advise her on the best course of action.

Half an hour later Miranda climbed the steps of the Tolwood house and knocked. Within moments, Cassandra, Peter's twelve-year-old sister, answered the door.

"Good morning, Miranda," she said.

"Good morning. What have you got there?" Miranda asked, gesturing to something Cassandra held in her fist.

Cassandra opened her hand to show a chess piece—the king. "I'm playing with Jack, but if I leave this behind, he'll hide it and insist he won."

Miranda laughed. "You'd better get back so you can best him. Is Peter here?"

"He's in the office," she said, opening the door wider.

Miranda followed Cassandra down the hall, continuing to the office while Cassandra returned to the drawing room.

Peter was sitting at his desk, a ledger open in front of him.

"Good morning," Miranda said. "I hope I'm not disturbing you."

Peter grinned. "You aren't, my sweet—"

"Not here, Peter. Cassandra and Jack are just around the corner," she said, looking over her shoulder.

He rose and closed the door. "Fiancée," he finished in a whisper.

"You needn't say that when we're alone."

"I know. How's your hand today?"

"It still hurts, but not as much as yesterday. I'm resting it, so unfortunately I can't ride or paint for a few days."

"Is that what I owe for the pleasure of your company? You have nothing better to do?"

"No," Miranda said, laughing. "I'm in a bit of a conundrum and I want your advice. Let's sit down."

"What is it?" he asked as they sat side by side on the sofa.

Miranda explained about the gown, but before she even finished speaking she knew what Peter was going to say.

His expression grew more disapproving with each word Miranda uttered. "A gown? You know you can't keep it."

"That was my first thought. But he did spoil my other one."

"Even so, you can't accept an expensive gift from a man you barely know. Or *any* man, unless he's your husband or a relative."

"I know you're right, but I was hoping you'd talk me into keeping it?" Miranda said.

"I'm afraid not, my dear."

Miranda shifted on the sofa to face him. "It's so pretty. It's the one—the pink one—from Easton's."

He crossed his arms. "No gown would be worth being beholden to George."

"I'll send it back today," she said with a sigh. "Which is unfortunate, since it would have been perfect for the ball. Not that I'll be able to attend."

"Of course you will. Did you tell your father you want to go?"

"I tried to convince him, but he's adamant about declining the invitation."

"What about your mother?"

"She rarely attends social events."

"That doesn't mean *you* can't attend them."

She met Peter's eyes. "My father might be disappointed in me if I insisted on going to the ball. He told me he's glad I don't like such frivolous things."

"He only thinks you don't like parties and dances because you never tell him otherwise," Peter said. "You've got to tell your parents how you feel about…everything."

"I will, but they're both so busy all the time. I don't want to be a burden to them."

Her father was distracted with his work, and her mother was distracted by…Miranda wasn't even sure what. Sometimes she wondered if her mother was ill but her parents kept it a secret. Why else would she be tired so often, unable to take part in things like balls or to spend more time with Miranda?

Peter squeezed her hand. "You aren't a burden."

They sat in silence for some time. Peter looked thoughtful, but Miranda simply stared out the window, considering the best way to tell her parents what was important to her. Because Peter was right. How could her father know how much it meant for her to go to the ball—or buy a new gown or try new art techniques—if she didn't tell him? She'd hinted, but perhaps the time had come to be more direct. If only it didn't go against what she'd been trying to do all her life. Since Miranda was their only child, she'd always felt it was her place—no, her duty—to be everything to her parents and to make their lives as fulfilled and untroubled as possible. So how could she argue about simple things like the ball? She was still stewing about it when Peter suddenly broke into her thoughts with what sounded like a proclamation.

"We're going to that ball, Miranda. If you aren't ready to tell your parents what you want, so be it. But there's no reason you shouldn't *take* what you want."

Miranda sat up and met his sparkling brown eyes. "What do you mean?"

"I mean we'll go to the ball regardless. You won't ask permission, therefore you won't be disobeying your parents when we dress ourselves up and dance the night away at the Rockfords' ball."

"Peter! You mean to sneak in?"

"Let's not say sneak. It's a clandestine outing."

Miranda put a hand to her cheek. "I don't know. I don't feel right about lying."

"It isn't lying. As I said, you'll simply neglect to ask permission."

It seemed so brazen, but Miranda was desperate to go to the ball. And after all, she'd already tried to convince her father. He said he didn't want to go, but he hadn't expressly forbidden *her* from attending.

"But how will we get in?" she asked. "My father says he's invited every year, so perhaps I could intercept the invitation before he has a chance to throw it away."

"There's no need for that," Peter said. "The Rockfords send out invitations, but they don't expect anyone to reply, and you don't need to show it to enter the ball. All part of the masquerade."

"Do you really think we could manage it without my parents finding out?" Miranda asked, clasping her hands together.

He looked at her as if surprised she had to ask. "Yes, but that will be the least of it. We'll have to sneak you out of the house the night of the ball and find transportation there. And of course we'll need costumes within the next few days."

"The costumes will be easy. We can make them. I'm not sure about everything else, though."

"I can probably find some reason to ask my father for the carriage. We'll get to the ball early and blend in with the crowd, but leave before everyone takes off their masks at midnight. Nobody will even know we were there."

"It will be fabulous!" she said, but then her face fell. "There's only that one, tiny problem."

"You can't dance. But I can. We'll practice a few times before the big night."

"I can hardly wait." She rose and pretended to waltz around the room.

Peter crossed the room to take her into his arms. He

smelled homey and familiar, like a perfect summer day. Miranda smiled up at him, then trod upon his foot.

"Ow!" Peter stopped and reached down to rub his toes.

She blushed. "Sorry."

"We'll practice every day, and you'll wear slippers instead of heels."

"That sounds perfect. Luckily I won't need my hand much for dancing."

"Now that's settled, what should we do today?"

Miranda glanced at the ledgers on Peter's desk. "Aren't you working?"

"I'm finished for now. Why don't we go to Marigold Lake? I'll take you out in the boat."

"I'm not getting into a boat with you after what happened last time."

Peter clicked his tongue. "That was ten years ago, Miranda, and not my fault. How was I to know a storm would brew up?"

"I know it wasn't your fault, but it was terrible. It was much too tippy and I was queasy the entire time," Miranda said, placing her hands protectively over her stomach.

"You'll never try again, will you?"

"Probably not." Not with Peter, anyway. She'd since gone out a few times with her father.

"Then would you care to stroll along the lake?"

"I'd like nothing better."

As they left the house, Miranda's mind teemed with visions of costumes, masks and glittering ballrooms.

Chapter Six

Two days later Miranda's hand was almost back to normal. Doctor Fitz came by to check the wound and said it had healed enough to stop using the salve and bandages in a few days.

Miranda could easily hold a paint brush, but still needed her left hand for adjusting her canvas and for any number of other little tasks. In some ways she missed painting, but the break had reminded her of other favorite pastimes, like reading or lying in the grass and watching the sky. Not because light shining softly through the clouds would make a good painting, but because they were pretty.

She'd also taken the opportunity to work with her pastels. Not nearly as messy as watercolors, Miranda could easily sit on her balcony, sketchbook propped on the table, and get lost in the swirling colors of a sunset or the slope of the stable roof in the distance.

She was just admiring a sketch she'd done of a cardinal's nest when she heard the unmistakable sound of someone climbing the tree. Miranda set her sketchbook aside and walked to the edge of the balcony.

"Peter, what are you doing?"

He looked up at her through the branches, the sun bringing out coppery highlights in his hair. "I want to talk to you."

"Why didn't you come inside?"

"I don't want to be overheard," he said as he made it to the top and hopped over the railing. He pulled an envelope out of his jacket pocket. "The invitation."

"Oh! We haven't gotten ours yet, or perhaps my father already threw it away."

They stood close together as they read it.

"It's not for another week," Miranda said glumly.

Peter tucked the invitation back into his pocket. "George must have had the date wrong. That's better, because it gives us a chance to find costumes."

"Yes, and for my hand to be out of this bandage." Miranda sat at the table, flipped to another page in her sketchbook and started drawing Peter. It was somewhat difficult, as he hardly stood still for two minutes at a time while they talked.

"Do you know what your costume will be?" Peter asked.

"I have no idea. I might go through the trunks in the attic to see if there are any old gowns up there. And I'll need a mask."

"My mother's making those."

"Your mother!" Miranda exclaimed, pausing in her drawing.

"She won't tell anyone. She's helping me with my costume and I told her I'm bringing a lady, but I didn't say which one."

"Oh, good. I wouldn't want her to tell my parents. Will she be going?"

"Yes, she loves to dress up and so does my father. I'm going to be a knight."

Miranda resumed her sketching. "I'll need something worthy of you. A damsel in distress, perhaps. It's a shame I couldn't have kept that pink dress."

"You'll find something better. Speaking of which, did you send it back to George yet?"

"No, but I will today. I'm supposed to meet my father in the studio now, but I'll do it afterwards."

"I'll walk you downstairs," Peter said.

Miranda closed her sketchbook. "You can't do that. We'll be seen."

"No, we won't," he said, taking her hand. "It's only one flight of stairs."

They tiptoed down, fortunately not running into one of the maids or, worse, Peter's mother.

Before going into the studio, they put their arms around each other and Miranda tried to look as enamored as possible.

"Hello, Father," she said when they entered.

His back was to them, brush furiously working on a large canvas. He didn't answer, apparently so focused on his work he didn't hear them come in.

"Mr. Harlake?" Peter called.

Mr. Harlake started and turned, then reluctantly set his brush down. His eyes homed in on Peter's arm around Miranda's waist as if gauging how close they were to each other.

"What are you working on?" Miranda asked as she and Peter moved closer.

"A new landscape," he said, wiping his hand on a towel.

He'd managed to capture that certain moment between night and dawn; Miranda could almost feel the wind sweeping through the trees. He had such a talent— one she knew she didn't share. Her parents had watched Miranda paint since childhood, waiting for her to shift from a good artist to a prodigy. She hadn't yet had the heart to tell them it might never happen.

"Where are you two off to?" Mr. Harlake asked.

"I'm going out to the stables to see about that new gelding. He's a fine one," Peter said.

"You always have a knack for choosing the right horses," Mr. Harlake said.

"We still need to name him," Miranda said.

"He has a name. Mercury."

Miranda batted her eyelashes. "Oh, Peter! It's perfect. You're so good at naming the horses. At everything, really." She held his gaze for as long as she dared. Each second made it more and more likely that the two of them would burst out laughing.

Peter leaned in as though to kiss her, then apparently thought better of it and straightened.

At Mr. Harlake's look of disapproval, Miranda was tempted to step away from Peter but maintained the proximity for the sake of their ruse. If they were truly in love she wouldn't budge.

Mr. Harlake cleared his throat. "Perhaps you should be getting to the stables, then, Peter."

"Yes, I should," he said with a warm, sidelong glance at Miranda.

She sighed dutifully and inched even closer. "Must you go?"

He took her hand and kissed it. "As much as I hate to part, I must. But we'll be together soon."

"Later today?"

Peter kissed her hand again. "I'll count the hours until I see you again." He kept his eyes on her as he backed toward the door.

When he was gone Miranda turned back to her father, who looked a bit queasy.

"Father?"

"*Mild* displays of affection I said."

"We simply can't help it." Miranda tried to look sincere. Hopefully she and Peter weren't going too far with their deception. It was hard to imagine acting like this for a whole year.

"Please try to…to hold it in. I don't want anyone seeing you."

"Father, nobody's paying the least bit attention to us. Everyone's accustomed to seeing Peter and me together."

"Not that way. Well, he's gone now. Let me show you what I've been working on."

Miranda followed him over to his canvas and listened as he pointed out the various aspects of the painting and brushwork. He asked Miranda's opinion as he always did and at least pretended to consider her feedback. Miranda loved joining her father in the studio. He was so relaxed, and any woes he had seemed to melt away. Most importantly, he treated Miranda like a colleague instead of his daughter. They were on equal footing here, artist to artist. It was slightly different when he critiqued her work, however.

After going over a sketch for his next project, he turned to her. "Have you been able to work on anything this week?"

"I've done some pastels."

"Ah, the pastels. Nothing wrong with that until you can get back to your painting. I'd like to see you finish that watercolor of the mountain."

"It is finished," Miranda said and led him across the room to where her painting sat on an easel.

Mr. Harlake drew his head back. "Is it?" He peered

at the painting, his chin in his hand. "I suppose it could be considered finished, if that's the style you're going for."

"Father!" Miranda laughed, though his words stung. "What do you mean, *that style*? Haven't you always told me every artist is different, and I should hold my work up to nobody's standards but my own?"

"Well, yes, but…" His hand hovered over the canvas as though anxious to point out the faults. But then he let his arm drop. "You're right. It's your painting. But perhaps, if you had time, that one spot in the corner there… And the edge of the lake… I can't even tell what color it's supposed to be. Brown? Gray?"

She just shook her head at him. "Shall we have lunch?"

"I'm dining with your mother."

"I'll join you."

"Not today, Miranda. She's not having a good day."

"I see. Maybe another time." She tried not to let her disappointment show, as it would only upset him.

"Yes. Another time." He glanced at the clock. "I'd better get to Darlington's if I'm to be back in time for lunch. I need to pick up my new brushes."

"I could go for you. That way Mother won't have to wait."

"You don't mind?"

"Not at all," she said, pasting on a helpful look. "I could do with the walk."

"Just ask at the counter. They'll know what to give you. They sent me a note yesterday that they'd arrived, but with one thing and another I didn't have time to go."

"Give Mother my best," Miranda said on her way out.

As soon as she entered the shop, Mrs. Darlington gave her a wave and walked into the back room.

Miranda perused the shelves, but the only thing that tempted her was a pink hat with lacy trim and a wispy feather protruding from the top. Very impractical. Her father would never allow it. She left the bonnet and looked around for anything that could be used as a costume for the ball, but nothing here would suit.

"Here they are," Mrs. Darlington said when she returned with the brushes. "Is there anything else today?"

Behind them the door opened and closed, and Mrs. Darlington gave a smile to whoever entered.

"I do need to order some more sketchbooks. Unless you have any?"

Mrs. Darlington put a finger to her chin. "You know, I just might. Let me go check."

As Miranda waited she was startled to see there was only one other person in the shop—George. He wasn't looking at her, but she had the feeling his eyes had been on her a second before. For once, George wasn't surrounded by his friends. Miranda immediately turned back to the counter. This would be the perfect time to tell him that while she appreciated the gesture, she couldn't possibly keep the gown. How awkward, though. And what if he tried to insist she accept it, as he had with the carriage ride? It might prove too difficult to say no face to face. As she stood there debating what to do, she heard him walk into the restaurant.

Mrs. Darlington returned with two sketchbooks to choose from. Still flustered from seeing George, Miranda didn't even consider before taking the one on the right.

After paying, she peeked into the restaurant, where

George was chatting with Nathaniel.

"Good afternoon," Emily said from behind her.

Miranda turned. "Good morning. Afternoon."

"Are you here for lunch?" Emily asked.

"No, I came in to pick something up for my father. But I'd like to order some muffins to take home with me. Rhubarb, if you have them."

"We do. I made them myself. I'm just on my way home, but I'll fetch those for you before I go."

"I don't want to keep you. I'll ask Mrs. Darlington."

"Don't be silly! It won't take a moment."

Miranda paid, then sat down to wait. She kept an eye on George, her foot tapping beneath the table. This was ridiculous. What was so difficult about walking over and having a simple conversation with him?

Just then George turned around. His eyes met Miranda's for a fraction of a second before falling to her bandaged hand. He frowned and started walking in her direction.

She felt a jolt of alarm, but then she saw he was heading for the exit. Summoning her courage, Miranda opened her mouth before realizing she had no idea what to say. George paused mid-stride, but when she didn't speak the moment was lost and he continued on his way.

As soon as the door closed after him Miranda slumped in her chair. Now she'd have to go straight home and write to him. As she sat there thinking of what to say, it occurred to her that George had probably been expecting a thank you. So now he must think she was abominably rude.

Emily returned with Miranda's muffins. "Still warm," she said with a smile.

"Thank you," Miranda said, rising. "I'm going to

stop at the library on my way home. Would you like to join me?"

"Yes, let me get my coat," Emily said.

As they passed Easton's, Miranda started composing what she should write to George, then shook her head. That could wait.

"How do you like Deerwood?" she asked Emily.

"It's a nice town, and larger than the one I grew up in. There's so much to do here."

"Where do you hail from?"

"Nottingham. It's a small town in Vermont. I doubt you've heard of it."

The name struck a bell for Miranda, but she couldn't think why. "Is it well known for anything?"

"Not much besides maple farms and a famous stable," Emily said.

They waited for a milk wagon and a few carriages to pass before crossing the street. "How did you meet Nathaniel?" Miranda asked as they turned down Ashe Lane.

Emily's face took on a soft glow. "I went to a ball in Hollingsford and he asked me to dance."

"How romantic," Miranda said. Emily's dreamy expression made it nearly impossible not to ask for details but Miranda resisted. She didn't want to seem overly curious. "Are you going to the Rockford's ball?"

"Yes, and I can hardly wait! It will be my first social event in town. Are you going?"

"I might," she said evasively since it was meant to be a secret.

"I see you're carrying a sketchbook," Emily said. "You must draw?"

"Yes, and paint. If you'd like, you could come to my

house one day and I'll show you my studio," Miranda said, deciding on the spot to invite her.

"That would be lovely," Emily said and they walked into the library.

Later that day as Miranda sat at her desk pondering what to write to George, she penned a quick note to Emily inviting her for lunch the following week. That was easy. But what to say to George? She bit the end of her pen, thinking. After a few tries she settled on simple and polite.

"*Dear Mr. Rockford,*

Thank you for your kind offer of the gown. Your generosity is appreciated, but I can't possibly accept it. I've sent the gown back to Easton's on your behalf.

Sincerely,

Miss M. Harlake."

Miranda gave the gown one last regretful look before closing the box, then sealed the letter and tugged the bell pull.

When the maid arrived, Miranda handed her the box and the note. "Could you please see that this is delivered to Easton's, and send the note to the Rockfords'?"

"Yes, right away."

She watched the maid walk down the hall, fighting the urge to call her back and hide the dress in her closet. After tidying her writing desk, Miranda went down to the studio to look at her watercolor of the mountain. Finish it, indeed. She hadn't been there long when Peter arrived.

"Are you ready for your first dance lesson, darling?" he asked.

"Do we really have to do this?"

Peter took her hand. "You'll thank me later."

"Where are we going?" she asked as he led her

outside.

"Someplace we won't be seen."

They walked through the woods until they came to a small clearing out of sight of the house.

"This looks perfect," Peter said. "Take off your shoes."

She gave him a skeptical look. "Take off my shoes?"

"Yes, I don't want you to bruise my toes any more than necessary."

Miranda crossed her arms over her chest. "Really, Peter."

"*Really*, Miranda. Take them off. I'll take mine off, too." He sat down in the grass and removed his shoes. When he reached toward her feet, she stepped back, laughing.

"I'll do it," she said, shaking her head at him.

The grass tickled her toes as she waited for the lesson to begin. "Where do we start?"

"With something simple," he said.

Miranda rested her injured hand on his shoulder as he slid an arm around her waist and took her other hand in his. Peter held her close, humming a slow tune in her ear.

"What song is that?" she asked.

"It's not a song, but it has the right melody. Just listen and follow my lead."

Miranda did her best but couldn't remember the steps. More than once she was glad she'd listened to Peter and taken off her heels—his toes would have indeed been miserable. But he didn't appear to mind, just redirected her and started the song all over again. They stayed out late, dancing until the stars came out and fireflies blinked in the branches of trees in the distance.

Chapter Seven

A few days later Miranda stood beside her father on the ridge, painting the sunrise they'd risen early to capture. The world was quiet and still, waiting to awake. Behind them, their lanterns flickered in a light breeze.

Miranda didn't let go of her brush until the sky was a dusky blue. Her father kept at it, probably still envisioning the pink, orange and purple that had blanketed the horizon moments before.

She flexed her hand, pleased there was no pain or stiffness. Today was the first time she'd painted since the bandages came off. There was no mark on her hand at all, so you'd never have known she'd had even a scratch. Miranda sipped lukewarm coffee out of a flask and reached into the picnic basket for a cinnamon donut.

"Don't get crumbs on your painting. It's still wet," her father said without turning around.

Miranda took a step back. "I won't." She studied her morning's work, well satisfied.

"There." Her father stepped back from his easel. "Finished."

"A striking composition," Miranda said. "Perfect, as always."

"Thank you," Mr. Harlake said. He shifted to stand in front of Miranda's painting, nodding slowly. "You've captured the right colors just before the sun came up. Excellent work."

Miranda smiled. "Thank you."

"Next time be less heavy-handed with your brush strokes, though."

"I'll keep that in mind," she said, turning away so he wouldn't see her frown. Miranda listened to him chatter on about other improvements she could make as they packed their supplies for the trek home.

When they reached the house they put their equipment back in the studio and Miranda went upstairs to change while her father went to see Mrs. Harlake.

Miranda had hoped to see Peter on their way home, as they were supposed to have another dancing lesson today. She was becoming almost proficient, at least with Peter. It was possible she'd have no idea what to do when another man took the lead at the ball.

The ball. Miranda still needed a gown and had only two days in which to find it. If only she could ask her mother for help. It would give them a reason to spend time together, and her mother might have an idea for a costume.

Peter's mother had done an impressive job with the mask. It was shaped like a large blue butterfly and covered nearly all of Miranda's face. Nobody would ever recognize her.

Miranda hadn't found anything useful in the attic. The trunks she'd meant to look through were locked and she couldn't ask her father for the key without arousing suspicion. She'd been through her whole wardrobe, and while there were a few dresses she could use if she must, she'd rather have something special for her very first ball.

Her last hope was finding something in town. Besides Easton's, there was a secondhand shop she could try. Miranda couldn't ask her parents for money for a gown, but fortunately she had some squirreled away. After changing into a plum-colored riding habit, she went to the stable.

She heard Peter's voice as soon as she walked in, talking in that low, soft way he used with the horses.

"Good morning," she said, smiling as she moved to his side.

Peter gave Mercury's nose a pat before turning to face Miranda. "Good morning. Where are you off to?"

"I'm going to Beech's to look for a dress. I still don't have a costume."

"Are you taking Fergus?"

"Yes, if I find something, I won't want to walk home with it."

Peter carried a saddle and bridle over to Fergus's stall.

"Speaking of the ball," Miranda said, "I hope I'm not recognized. Imagine if my parents found out!"

"Nobody will have any idea who you are when you're wearing that mask," Peter said as he adjusted Fergus's bridle. He walked him outside to the mounting block and handed Miranda the reins.

She climbed into the saddle. "Would you like to come into town with me?"

"I'd love to, but I have too much to do this morning. I'm eager to see what you find."

"So am I," Miranda said and directed Fergus toward Fairbanks Road.

Two hours later Miranda was sitting in Darlington's, tired and without a costume. She'd gone to Beech's, to Easton's, and visited the seamstress. She was just wondering if she had time to make a costume herself when Emily came over with her coffee and cookies.

"Thank you," Miranda said.

Emily started walking away, then looked back. "Is everything all right?"

Miranda looked up, surprised. "Yes. Why?"

"You seem a little downcast. Never mind, I don't mean to intrude."

As Miranda watched her go, she suddenly felt compelled to call her back. There was no harm in telling one person, was there? Emily might find Miranda's confiding in her odd, as they weren't close, but somehow Miranda sensed Emily wouldn't mind and would perhaps even welcome the chance to chat. She'd told Miranda more than once that she was lonely since moving to Deerwood. After finishing her food, Miranda approached the counter and waited until Emily had a free moment.

When Emily turned and saw her waiting, she reached for the menu and held it out to Miranda. "Are you ordering something to take home?"

"No. Actually…You were right when you thought I looked upset. Do you have a moment to talk?"

Emily set the menu down. "Of course," she said, coming out from behind the counter.

"It's nothing serious," Miranda said. "A piffling little thing, really."

"What's the matter?"

Miranda leaned toward Emily and lowered her voice. "It's this ball at the Rockfords'. I'm going, but it's a secret. My parents don't want me to attend."

"I'm so glad you'll be there! But are you worried your parents will find out?"

"I am worried about that, but my main problem is

the costume." Miranda ran a hand over her forehead. "It's in two days, and I still don't have anything to wear."

Emily gasped. "I'm in the same boat!"

"You are?" Miranda asked, laughing, though it wasn't the least bit amusing.

"Yes, but just this morning I found out where I might get a costume."

"You did? Where?" Miranda asked, trying not to sound too desperate.

"There are old dresses stored in the attic above the store. I haven't had a chance to look at them yet, but Mrs. Darlington said I can take my pick. Perhaps there's one that would suit you, too."

"Do you think Mrs. Darlington would mind if I borrowed one?"

"Not at all, but I'll ask her first if you'd like."

"Please do." She paused. "But then she'll know I'm going to the ball." Keeping a secret was turning out to be more difficult than Miranda had anticipated.

"You needn't worry, she won't tell anyone," Emily said and went into the back room.

Miranda paced between the counter and the window while she waited.

A few minutes later Emily returned, smiling. "Mrs. Darlington says we can use whatever we find upstairs as long as we return it in good condition."

"How generous of her. When can we look?"

Emily glanced at her watch. "Right now, if you like."

"Yes, please," Miranda said so enthusiastically that Emily laughed.

"It's just through here," Emily said, and Miranda followed her behind the counter to the back room.

In the far corner a staircase led upstairs to a storeroom, where piles of boxes stood against the walls. They climbed another set of rickety stairs to the attic.

"Watch your step," Emily said over her shoulder. "Some of the stairs are worn."

Miranda held tightly to the railing, and when they reached the attic she caught her breath. It was full of crates, trunks, old furniture and, to her delight, mannequins draped in gowns. "Where did these come from?"

"Those are dresses people ordered from Hollingsford, but never collected," Emily said as she passed the mannequins and knelt in front of an enormous trunk.

"They're lovely," Miranda said, touching the soft velvet of a maroon dress.

"Yes, but there might be even lovelier ones in here. Years ago this was the dressmaker's shop, and she left these trunks behind when Mrs. Darlington's grandfather bought the building. Who knows what we might find?" She flashed Miranda a conspiratorial smile before lifting the lid to reveal a yellow brocade gown.

"Beautiful!" Miranda said.

"There are more underneath," Emily said excitedly as she pulled the gown free. "You can open some of the others if you like."

Miranda didn't need to be asked twice. She opened a pine chest that was almost bursting with yards upon yards of palest pink silk. "Look at this," she said, holding the gown up to herself.

Emily lit up. "That looks fit for a queen!"

Miranda marveled at the hundreds of hand-painted blue and lavender flowers dotting the wrinkled gown. "I wonder if it would fit."

"Try it on."

"Here?" Miranda asked, casting a dubious glance around the attic.

Emily pointed toward the far corner. "There's an alcove where you can change," she said and turned to unlatch the next trunk.

Smiling, Miranda gathered up the precious garment and hurried over to the alcove. Soon her riding habit was on the floor and she was wearing the gown, which had clearly been extravagant in its day. It had a bustle and a tiered, flouncy skirt trimmed with purple ribbon and silk violets. The sleeves were elbow length, with ruffled cuffs, and the bodice was decorated with fine yellowed lace. Cream-colored organza lined the low neckline of the dress. Miranda had never needed a mirror more in her life.

"Does it fit?" Emily called.

"Just a moment. I'll show you."

As soon as Miranda emerged from the alcove Emily squealed. "It's perfect!"

"Really?" Miranda spun around to see the skirt twirl, knocking over a pile of hat boxes in the process.

"It's somewhat loose in the bodice and a tiny bit tight in the waist, but otherwise it could have been made for you."

Miranda wrinkled her nose at the musty smell. "It needs to be cleaned. Did you find anything?"

"Yes, but I can't decide which I like better." Emily crossed the room to hold up an emerald green gown and a peach-colored one.

"The green would look nicest with your eyes. These gowns are incredible. I can't believe they've been sitting up here all these years."

"Me, neither. I wonder why they were left behind."

"I don't know, but I'm glad they were. We wouldn't have found anything better if we'd gone all the way to Hollingsford."

"I believe you're right. Go change and we'll take these downstairs. Mrs. Darlington might know the best way to clean them."

Miranda put a hand on Emily's arm. "I can't thank you enough. I never dreamed I'd find a costume half as nice as this."

"Neither did I. I was beginning to think I'd need to wear one of my worn-out gowns and be a milkmaid," Emily said. She gave Miranda a shy grin. "I'm glad we found a dress for you, too."

Miranda smiled at her and began stacking up the spilled hat boxes while Emily tidied the trunks before they went downstairs.

Mrs. Darlington indeed had ideas about how to freshen up the gowns. "Leave it to me, girls, they'll be good as new in no time."

After leaving the gowns with her, Miranda and Emily went to Bullard's ice cream parlor, where they discussed the ball and made plans for how and when Miranda would collect her dress.

It was evening by the time Miranda said goodbye to Emily and rode home. It had been a surprisingly delightful afternoon and Miranda could hardly believe she'd found the perfect dress in such an unlikely place. She regretted leaving it behind, but there was no way she could hide it at home. Besides, though she was good with a needle and no stranger to washing her own things, she'd never tried to make an old gown look new before.

As she rode home, she imagined how it would feel to be swept away at the ball in decidedly the most glorious gown she'd ever seen. Miranda could hardly wait to tell Peter about it.

She didn't need to wait for long. After supper with her father, Miranda went upstairs to sketch the gown. When she entered her bedroom, she wasn't entirely surprised to see Peter sitting in the chair beside her bed, his feet propped up on the nightstand.

"Peter, what are you doing here?"

He rose and crossed the room to take her hand. "It's time for another dancing lesson."

"Without music again?"

Peter shrugged. "We've done fine without it before."

Miranda removed her shoes and placed them under the chair beside Peter's.

"We'll need to be quiet," she said.

Peter took her hand and ushered her out to the balcony. "We will be."

"Which dance will I learn tonight?"

"We're done learning new dances. It's time to practice what you already know." He took Miranda into his arms and started humming a tune. Miranda was definitely improving, she only stepped on his feet three times.

After the lesson they sat together, talking quietly about their day. Miranda tried to describe the gown, but it was too unique to explain.

"What will you be? A queen?" Peter asked.

"Simply a mysterious damsel on the arm of a handsome knight."

"A knight and a fair damsel. Perfect."

"I don't know how I'll manage to change without being seen. I'd planned on dressing at your house, but that was when I thought I'd have a gown here. And I'm still not sure how I'll get out of the house without my parents knowing I'm gone."

Peter offered a number of ideas, each more ridiculous than the last, such as Miranda climbing down the tree in her gown after she'd retrieved it from Darlington's.

"Perhaps we should keep it simple," she said, envisioning her scraped knees and torn dress if she left via the balcony. "Instead of sneaking out, I'll tell my parents you're taking me out for the evening. Since we're betrothed, it wouldn't be entirely unexpected."

Peter feigned shock. "Unchaperoned?"

Miranda laughed. "We've known each other too long for them to worry about that. We'll say we're going to the new restaurant in Shrewsbury, so they'll know we won't be home early."

"Shrewsbury is two hours away. Do you think they'd allow it?"

"My father won't question it, and I doubt my mother will even notice I'm gone," Miranda said sadly.

Peter patted her arm. "She'll notice. But I think you're right that they won't mind. They trust me."

"Yes, they trust both of us," she said with a sigh. "If only I could tell them the truth."

His eyes lit up. "You could! This is the opportunity you've been waiting for. Tell your parents you want to go to the ball with your fiancé. You don't always need to take their 'no' for an answer."

Miranda's stomach squirmed at the very thought. There'd be a better time to take a stand for herself.

Besides, if she told them and they expressly forbade it, she couldn't go to the ball at all. It wasn't worth the risk.

"Not yet," she said. "But soon. For now we'll go along with this plan. Once we leave Majestic Oaks we'll go to the Darlingtons' house and I'll change there. I'll arrange it all with Emily. I only hope nobody at the ball recognizes me and tells my parents."

"Nobody will. We'll dance the night away and have a splendid time."

"What will you tell your parents?"

"The same thing you're telling yours, but I'll leave out the part about our betrothal. They'll be distracted about going to the ball, so I doubt they'll make much of a fuss."

Not long later, they said goodnight and he climbed down the tree. After Peter left, Miranda sketched for a while, then got into bed. As she lay there, she pictured her gown and imagined herself walking up the steps of the Rockfords' manor.

The next two days were interminably long. All Miranda wanted to do was go into town to see how her gown was coming along, but Emily had sent a message to say it wouldn't be ready until the evening of the ball.

Fortunately, Miranda had other things to occupy her time. Peter insisted on twice daily dancing lessons, which she enjoyed but wasn't sure how much good they were doing. He allowed her to wear heels again but soon regretted it. Luckily, he had sturdy shoes.

Miranda spent hours in the studio with her father, working on a still life. She'd been staring at the same pewter tankard, blue candy dish, brass candelabra, four apples and exactly sixteen grapes for what felt like forever. It wasn't her favorite work. She preferred painting landscapes or the horses, but Mr. Harlake insisted that still lifes were a necessary part of any good artist's repertoire.

Mrs. Harlake came down for lunch one afternoon and they all discussed the upcoming art show in Hollingsford. They'd spend the night, or maybe two, at a hotel close to the exhibition hall. The last time she'd been in Hollingsford, Miranda had spent hours gazing into storefront windows at beautiful gowns and parasols, heeled shoes and elegant shawls. Hopefully she'd be able to sneak away to do so again this time and perhaps even purchase something.

One unpleasant yet necessary task had been asking her parents' permission for the outing to "Shrewsbury." Mr. and Mrs. Harlake had been against it at first but relented after many heartbroken looks from Miranda and much cajoling from Peter. They'd stood arm in arm as though unable to be in the same room without touching, and had given each other desperately loving glances.

When Miranda reminded her parents that the ride was nothing, even in the dark, to Peter, who'd done it so many times, they agreed she couldn't be in safer hands. The fact that they didn't even suggest a chaperone proved Miranda right—her parents trusted them. She felt only a slight twinge of remorse after they'd gotten her parents' approval. But they'd never know she lied and, really, going to a ball wasn't *so* different from going out to dine. At least that's what Miranda told herself.

At long last, it was the night before the ball. Miranda could hardly sleep, even after a busy day and a final dancing lesson with Peter. She felt like a child on the night before her birthday party. Hopefully the ball would be as marvelous as she imagined. But with a gown like that and her best friend as her partner, how could it be anything short of magical? With that thought, Miranda finally drifted off to sleep.

Chapter Eight

Miranda woke with the sun and clasped her hands to her chest, smiling. Tonight! She rose and dressed in her pants and a brown dress, as she intended to spend most of the day outdoors. She'd keep busy until late afternoon, when it would be time to get ready.

She whiled away the morning on her balcony, then went downstairs to join her parents for breakfast. Miranda didn't speak or follow the conversation but went over dance steps in her mind and wondered how Peter's costume would look. He hadn't let her see it yet but had shown her his mask. His mother had fashioned it out of peacock feathers and it brought out that greenish tint in his brown eyes.

"What is the matter with you?" Mrs. Harlake asked after the third time Miranda bumped knees with her under the table. "I can't remember the last time you were so jittery."

"I'm sorry, Mother. I was thinking about tonight."

"Tonight?" her father asked as he set his coffee down.

Miranda flushed, though he couldn't know she'd been thinking of the ball. She lowered her gaze, fearing he might be able to read her deception in them. "I'm going out with Peter tonight. To Shrewsbury. Remember?"

He raised his eyes to the ceiling. "Oh, yes. The

dinner."

"That's not for hours," her mother said. "Get your head out of the clouds."

"Yes, Mother." Miranda would have liked it better if instead of chastising her for daydreaming, Mrs. Harlake had shown some interest in Miranda's date. Weren't most mothers curious about their daughter's suitors? But perhaps it was impossible for either of her parents to be excited about Miranda going out with the boy she'd been with almost every day of her life. Besides, they hoped the betrothal would be called off. At least in that Miranda would be able to please them.

After breakfast Miranda went to the lake with her father. The loons didn't have chicks yet, but it couldn't be long now. She dabbed black and white on her canvas, trying to capture their distinctive markings and the ripples they left in their wake. Painting didn't distract Miranda quite as much as usual today, and her father called her out more than once for being absent-minded. Afterwards, he offered a lengthy and meticulous critique of her work.

Miranda recalled the last time she'd been here, when George and his friends had come upon her. They were sure to be at the ball tonight. Hopefully she wouldn't inadvertently partner any of them. She assumed they'd be on their best behavior, but perhaps balls weren't as elegant as she surmised, and a bit of mischief wouldn't be frowned upon. And then there was Ebenezer. Would he seek Miranda out if he knew she was there? She shuddered at the thought.

After a picnic lunch, Miranda and her father started for home. With every step she grew more excited and nervous. How would she manage to change at Emily's and execute the whole plan without being seen or recognized? Once she was at the ball with her mask on, she needn't worry, but it was imperative that her parents didn't get wind of what she was up to.

Upon reaching the house, Miranda went straight up to her bedroom to lie down until three-thirty. Her rest lasted all of two minutes. She got up and paced the room, glancing at the clock so often her neck grew sore. When the clock finally crawled its way to one-forty-five, she stopped resisting the urge to get ready and gathered what she'd need for the evening ahead. Miranda pulled out a larger than usual purse and hid the mask in its depths, adding a matching fan in case she needed to disguise herself even more.

At three o'clock, she fixed her hair and put on her loveliest gown—teal silk with a light blue overskirt. Tiny faux forget-me-nots adorned the bodice and hem of the gown. If she were indeed going out to dinner, she would have dressed her best. Unable to settle to reading or drawing, she sat on the balcony and watched the sky, straining to hear sounds of an approaching carriage.

When the bell rang precisely at four, she knew it was Peter. Miranda grabbed her purse and rushed downstairs.

"I'll have her home safe and sound by midnight," Peter was telling Mr. Harlake as Miranda reached the parlor.

"Midnight! That's awfully late, isn't it?" her father asked.

Peter deftly avoided answering the question by crossing the room to kiss Miranda's cheek. She had to hand it to him—the way his face lit up when he stared at her, he really could pass for a man in love.

She smiled brightly at him. "Good evening, Peter."

"You're a vision," he said, taking her hand. He was wearing a long frock coat, much too warm for a night like this, and Miranda looked down to see what she assumed was his costume poking out of the bottom. It was unlike him to wear skin tight trousers trimmed with gold braid.

Mr. Harlake cleared his throat. "Enjoy yourselves tonight."

"We will," Miranda said. "Is Mother coming down?"

"She's resting, but I'll tell her you said goodbye."

"Goodnight," Miranda said.

"Goodnight, Mr. Harlake, and don't you worry. Miranda's in good hands. She'll be safe with me."

"See that she is," Mr. Harlake said, closing the door behind them.

Peter slipped an arm around Miranda's waist as they walked to the carriage. "I had some trouble with my father. He wanted me to let Walt drive."

"You convinced him otherwise, I see," Miranda said, looking at the empty seat the coachman usually occupied.

"Eventually. We couldn't have let Walt drive us to the Darlingtons', where you'll transform into a fetching damsel, and then deliver us to the ball. Your parents would know of our scheme before the orchestra finished tuning their instruments."

As they trotted down Fairbanks Road, Miranda broke into a wide smile that soon became a laugh she didn't bother trying to hold in. Peter gave her a grin and started humming one of their dancing songs. Miranda swayed along as the countryside sped by.

When they arrived at the Darlingtons' house,

Miranda was whisked away by Emily while Peter waited outside with the carriage.

Emily had donned the green gown and added a tiara and an embroidered silk shawl.

"Your dress looks incredible," Miranda said as they climbed the stairs to Emily's bedroom. "I can hardly believe it was sitting in a trunk all those years."

"Me neither. I was torn between this and the peach, but I couldn't resist this color," she said, twirling as they reached the second-floor landing.

"It was the right choice. You look beautiful," Miranda said.

Emily threw her door open. "Not as beautiful as you're going to look."

Miranda froze halfway across the room. Her gown was hanging on a mannequin, even more lovely than she remembered it. It looked brand new. The pink silk had taken on a soft luster and the flowers decorating the gown could have been real. The bodice, with its delicate lace and white organza trim, had lost its rumpled appearance.

"Oh!" Miranda said. "Oh, I've never seen anything so magnificent!"

"You'll be the belle of the ball."

They chatted easily as Miranda changed into the gown, and she idly wondered if this was the kind of experience she'd been missing all these years by having a boy for a best friend. She'd never trade Peter for anything, but there was something special about these times she'd been spending with Emily recently.

Miranda let her hair down and Emily brushed it for her until it was full and shiny. When this was done she donned the butterfly mask. Looking in the mirror, she almost didn't recognize herself. Her eyes sparkled, and Miranda wished she could have painted herself as she looked at this exact moment. It was hard to peel her eyes away and continue getting ready.

"Thank you again so much," Miranda said.

Emily smiled. "You're welcome, that gown is perfect on you. Come. Peter's waiting."

Miranda indeed felt like a queen as she slowly descended the stairs. Fortunately, she needn't worry about any of the Darlingtons seeing her, because they'd all left for the ball earlier.

Everyone but Nathaniel.

When they reached the bottom of the stairs he was just coming into the foyer, pulling on his gloves. "We'd better hurry, Em, or—"

He came to an abrupt halt when he saw Miranda.

It was a good thing she was wearing a mask, as her entire face turned red.

Frowning, Emily went to take his arm. "Nathaniel, you were supposed to wait for me in the parlor."

"I was, but you were taking an awfully long time." He didn't take his eyes off Miranda.

Miranda looked at Emily, unsure if she should speak or what she should say if she did so. Would Nathaniel even recognize her if she didn't tell him who she was?

Emily cleared her throat. "I told you I was having a friend drop by to pick up a…a—"

Miranda held up her fan.

"Yes! She needed a fan," Emily said.

Nathaniel looked at the two women, clearly no less confused by this explanation.

Miranda couldn't ask Emily to lie to her own husband. "It's me, Nathaniel," she said, removing her mask.

He looked at her for a moment as though trying to place her. "Miranda?"

"This must seem odd to you. Emily was helping me get ready for the ball."

Nathaniel still looked perplexed but laughed. "That explains why I've seen Peter drive by the house four times. I assume he's with you?"

"Yes, we're going to the ball together."

"Then we shouldn't keep him waiting any longer," Nathaniel said.

Once outside, Emily and Nathaniel bade Miranda farewell and climbed into their carriage, leaving her to wait for Peter. She'd only been standing in front of the house for a moment when he returned.

Peter pulled the horses to a stop and jumped down from the driver's seat, eyes wide as he walked toward her. He took both her hands. "Miranda! You're stunning. Glorious."

Miranda beamed. "Can you tell it's me when I'm wearing the mask?"

"Well, *I* could, but I don't think anyone else would. You should wear ridiculous gowns more often."

"It isn't ridiculous!" she said and hit his arm playfully with her fan.

"Your father would say so. Probably your mother, too."

Just the mention of her parents reminded Miranda it would be prudent to get off the street before anyone saw them. "We'd better go."

"Yes, and I want you to sit inside the carriage this time. If anyone sees me driving it wouldn't be difficult to guess who's sitting beside me, mask or no."

Miranda took his hands and gave a little hop. "I can't believe we're really doing this!"

"It's high time we did," he said and escorted her to the carriage.

Miranda fidgeted with her fan as she and Peter made their slow way up the Rockfords' torchlit drive. Ahead, costumed guests climbed the stairs and disappeared into the elegant manor.

When they at last came to a halt, Peter opened the door and helped Miranda out.

"I'll meet you inside after I settle the horses," he said.

Miranda clutched his arm. "No, we're supposed to go in together."

"I need to see to the carriage. I forgot about that when I devised this plan."

"But—"

"You'll be fine. Arriving alone will give you an even greater air of mystery."

Not seeing any other option, she reluctantly let go of his sleeve. "Don't be long."

"I won't." He jumped into the driver's seat and gave her a wave before driving away.

Miranda hesitated at the foot of the long staircase, debating about whether or not to just step onto the lawn to wait for Peter. But then she realized she was blocking the way for people behind her. Mustering her nerve, she climbed the stairs with the chattering crowd.

Once inside, she looked for a place to wait for Peter. Miranda didn't want to go too far into the house, as it would be easy to miss each other in the throng. She found an alcove off to the side of the front doors with a window affording a good view of the drive.

The entryway and sweeping staircase were marble and carved columns went all the way to the ceiling. The manor could only be described as opulent. Miranda would love to take a look at the art in this house. The Rockfords were well known for their collection. Perhaps she and Peter could sneak off at some point and find the gallery.

Miranda had just turned to look out the window again when she felt someone step into the alcove behind her. Peter had been faster than she'd thought. She turned, smiling. "Here you are, that—"

She stopped short. It wasn't Peter. It was a tall man dressed as a sea captain from perhaps a hundred years earlier. He wore a dark blue jacket decorated with gold buttons and fringe, and an arched hat topped with a feather. A black mask accentuated his blue eyes, but a white wig hid his true hair color.

He swept a low bow. "Good evening."

"Good evening," Miranda said and gave him her best, though clumsy, curtsy.

His eyes sparkled. "You were expecting someone else, I presume?"

"Yes. I'm waiting for my friend."

"The music's about to begin. Would you care to dance?" He stepped forward and took her arm.

"I... My friend..." She pointed toward the window.

"She won't mind. No doubt she'll seek you out after the dance. You'll stand out from the crowd in that lovely gown."

Miranda didn't see how she could say no. Besides, she'd gone to all this trouble to attend the ball, which naturally involved dancing with someone she'd never met. Well, perhaps she'd met him but didn't recognize him. Who knew how long Peter would be with the carriage? And she had the feeling that if he were here he'd encourage her to be more adventurous.

She looked up into the stranger's eyes. "Thank you, yes. I'd love to dance."

"This way, my lady," he said.

As they made their way through the crowd, Miranda could hardly believe the array of costumes. Kings, queens, a jockey, a fairy, a bee, another sea captain, a plethora of princesses, and countless other disguises.

Miranda caught her breath when she and her companion entered the ballroom. The walls themselves seemed to shimmer. Perhaps it was a trick of the light, or reflections from the crystal chandeliers. The room was enormous and she could hardly see to the other end of it. Doors on either side led to what must be the supper room and parlors. How would she ever find Peter? She'd never seen his full costume, only that one gold-gilded pant leg. Well, if there was one person she'd know anywhere, it was Peter. For now it was time to pay attention to her partner.

As he took her lightly into his arms, she prayed the dance lessons had paid off. At first Miranda looked around the room, but she felt the man's eyes on her and looked up at him.

"I don't recognize you," he said, searching her face.

Luckily, no matter how hard he looked, all he'd see was a butterfly.

"Isn't that the point of the masks?" she asked, smiling.

"I suppose it is, but doesn't it feel odd not knowing each other's identities?"

"Perhaps we do know each other. Deerwood isn't so

big a town. We could pass each other on the street every day."

"Now that is an intriguing thought." He gazed into her eyes. "But I feel I would have noticed someone as beautiful as you."

Miranda had to laugh. He couldn't even see her face. "If I dressed like this every day you would probably have noticed me."

"Without a doubt."

"And I'd have noticed a sea captain parading along Main Street. How did you choose your costume?"

"It was the only one I could find on short notice."

"You hadn't planned on coming?"

He looked away for a moment and shrugged, almost to himself. "I felt compelled to come, but left to my own devices I'd be out walking on a night like this."

"Out walking where?" Miranda asked as they gracefully moved through the steps. She hadn't come close to stepping on his feet thus far.

"The forest, or perhaps by Marigold Lake."

"I love Marigold Lake," Miranda said. "I go there often, to—" She shook her head and pressed her lips together. Not many other women were known to paint beside the lake. In fact, none were. She'd have given away her identity as surely as if she'd held out her hand and introduced herself.

"You what? What do you do at the lake?" he asked, grinning.

"I won't say. But tell me why you weren't planning to come. Don't you like balls?"

"I like this one," he said, holding her a little closer.

"Do you want to know a secret?" Miranda asked, wondering whatever had come over her to make her sound so coquettish.

"Certainly."

"This is the first ball I've ever been to."

The man came almost to a standstill. "It isn't."

"Yes, it is."

"So, you're what, sixteen? Not…fifteen?"

The look in his eyes tempted her to withhold her age as a jest but since he clearly thought he was dancing with practically a child, Miranda took pity on him. "I'm at least nineteen."

"Thank goodness for that. I was afraid I'd chosen a princess more than ten years younger than myself."

"You aren't thirty?"

"And if I was?" he asked, laughing.

"Well…I suppose it wouldn't matter. But you don't look that old."

"I know some thirty-year-olds who would be offended to hear themselves called *old*."

Miranda laughed. "If I had to wager, I'd say you're…twenty-five or six. But it's harder to guess since your hair is white."

"I won't tell you either way. But you haven't told me why you've never been to a ball before."

Miranda couldn't possibly explain that her father thought balls were silly, and girls who attended them even sillier. "I never had a perfect dress to wear until tonight."

"Ah, that explains it. So, if you'd found this gown earlier, we might have met years ago. How did you decide on this one?"

"It was the only thing I could find on short notice," she said, echoing his answer. They laughed together easily.

"It suits you. Though I admit I wish your mask was a tad bit smaller. Or gone." He reached for her mask, but Miranda drew her head back.

"It isn't midnight," she said, laughing.

"I'm not a patient man."

"Tonight, you'll have to be."

"If you insist, my lady."

He swept her round and round the dance floor until she was breathless. How many dances had they danced together? Two? Three? It seemed conventions were set aside as well as people's names. They talked about mundane things like the weather, the number of people at the ball, and what might be served for supper. But somehow the man—How she wished she knew his name!—made even mundane things interesting and the time flew by.

Miranda now wished more than ever that she'd come to a ball years ago. But then again, she had the feeling she was only acting this way because it was this particular ball, and this particular man. She was behaving as if she'd been acquainted with him for far longer than a few dances.

When the music ended, Miranda had a chance to look around for Peter, but there was no sign of him. She did catch a glimpse of Emily and Nathaniel, but they were so wrapped up in each other they didn't look Miranda's way.

One person Miranda easily recognized was Ebenezer. He was among only a few people not wearing a mask, or even a costume, and looked like he'd just wandered in from the parlor, complete with pipe dangling from his mouth. As he walked along the edge of the ballroom, perhaps looking for an unattended lady to dance with, Miranda took an inadvertent step closer to her partner. Ebenezer must have noticed the movement, for he looked that way and gave a slight nod. Miranda panicked for a moment but then realized he hadn't nodded at her but at her partner, who inclined his head.

"Do you know Mr. Rockford?" Miranda asked.

"Yes, I do."

"But how did he recognize you?"

The man shrugged. "We've known each other a long time."

Miranda supposed it was the same way she'd know Peter anywhere.

"Can I tempt you in another dance?" he asked, taking her hand.

"Do you think it's appropriate? I've heard you should only dance with each partner once and we've danced much more than that."

"Is that the only reason you hesitate? It isn't my abysmal company?"

Miranda laughed. "Certainly not. But I don't want to break any rules."

"Well, my lady," he said, taking her into his arms once more. "At this ball there aren't the usual rules."

"Then by all means, let us continue," she said. In the back of her mind Miranda knew she should be dancing with other men, if only to make new acquaintances. But then again, even if she did, she'd never know who they were. Identities were to be revealed at midnight, but she and Peter would be long gone by then.

As they danced, Miranda tried to get an idea of who her partner might be, or at least what he looked like. She could tell even with his mask on that he was handsome. Something about his jaw, full lips and high cheekbones suggested a very good-looking man. His eyes were blue, a dark shade she'd never seen before. The wig completely covered his hair so there was no way to guess what color it might be.

"You're studying me quite thoroughly," he said after a few moments.

"I'm trying to discern who you are."

"Any guesses?" he asked.

"Not one."

"I'm not having any luck, either," he said with a theatrical sigh. "I know many ladies with brown hair and blue eyes, but the rest of your face is a mystery to me."

"Let's not try to guess. It's more amusing this way." Miranda knew she couldn't help trying to determine his identity, but she was much safer if he stopped trying to discover hers.

"All the more surprised we'll be at midnight," he said. "But there is one thing about you that stands out."

"What's that?"

He leaned in closer. "I hope it isn't rude to say, but it's your scent."

"My scent?" she asked, surprised.

"Yes. It's a flower. Lavender? Lilacs? Something sweet and subtle. I'm still trying to determine what it is."

"Let me know when you guess, and I'll tell you if you're right." He couldn't possibly know he'd already guessed perfectly. Her perfume was lilac-scented, and she kept lavender sachets in her clothing drawers.

"In that case you'll need to dance with me all night, and at midnight reveal your identity *and* the name of your perfume."

Miranda could hardly commit to that, so she just smiled and changed the subject.

Chapter Nine

After two more dances, Miranda was in need of refreshment. "Do you know where the punch room is?" she asked her companion.

"Yes, it's on the other side of the ballroom. How remiss of me not to take you there sooner."

She took his arm, at the same time pulling out her fan. It didn't cool her at all, so she tucked it back inside her bag. Her mask had become almost unbearably hot.

When they reached the punch room Miranda looked around for Peter. She'd like to have at least one dance with him, after all he'd done to teach her. It would soon be time for supper, and they'd make their escape not long after.

"Would you like punch, lemonade, or champagne?" Miranda's escort asked her.

"Lemonade, please." She'd be far too tipsy if she had champagne, and she needed to keep her wits about her if she was going to keep her identity a secret.

"This way, then." The man kept her arm pressed close to his side as they made their way through the crowd to a counter lined with glasses of lemonade. He handed her one and lifted his glass to hers for a toast. "To your first ball," he said.

"To your…tenth?" she asked.

"More or less."

As they set their glasses down, Miranda noticed

someone coming toward her. She gulped. It was Mrs. Tolwood, dressed as an angel. Miranda considered fleeing the room, but this was a woman she'd known all her life. At any rate, Mrs. Tolwood would most likely follow her or, worse, call out her name if Miranda tried to avoid her.

When Mrs. Tolwood reached her side, she said, "Good evening, Mi—Miss."

"Good evening," Miranda said, relieved Mrs. Tolwood hadn't divulged her identity.

"I hope you'll pardon the intrusion, but I wanted to tell you how much I admire your mask," Mrs. Tolwood said with a barely contained giggle.

Miranda would have winked if she could have done so without her partner noticing. "Thank you. I like yours, too."

Mrs. Tolwood eyed Miranda's partner curiously.

"I'd introduce you if I knew who you were," Miranda said to both of them.

The man smiled and Mrs. Tolwood said, "We'll all know each other before long. Enjoy the rest of your evening." She'd only gone a few steps when she turned back. "By the way, miss, I saw a man wearing a mask very similar to yours. He must have used the same mask maker."

"How interesting. Where was he?"

"In the ballroom five minutes ago," Mrs. Tolwood said and continued on her way.

Not much to go on, since the ballroom was crowded and enormous, but at least Miranda knew where to start looking.

As Miranda and the man drank their lemonade and walked about the room, she noticed a door leading straight into a lush garden. She simply had to get outside. The mask was now not only hot but itchy. There was no way to come right out and tell her partner why she needed to go outside, so she devised a plan.

"Could you get me another drink, please?" she asked.

"I'd be happy to. What would you like?"

"Punch this time, please. I'll step outside while you get it."

"I'll be right back," he said and strode toward the other side of the room.

Miranda sprinted into the garden and down a dark path enclosed with hedges. As soon as she was clear of the house's lights she leaned against a tree and removed the mask. The cool night air on her face was heavenly. Miranda glanced up at the starry sky, smiling. Her first ball couldn't have gone much better. So far. She still needed to find Peter and was beyond curious about her partner.

She was even curious about herself tonight. Aside from not recognizing her own masked face in the mirror, she hardly recognized her personality. Miranda wasn't usually so relaxed around anyone besides Peter or her family, but her mysterious partner set her at ease. Or perhaps she was acting this way because she was free to be herself, knowing nobody would judge her. Miranda could probably even say no to his repeated invitations to dance if she had a mind to. But thus far all she'd wanted to say was yes.

Miranda wandered over to a bench overlooking a fountain and sat down. The reflection of the bright, full moon rippled on the water. She hadn't been there long when she heard the sound of someone approaching.

"My lady?" a voice called softly.

Miranda fumbled for her mask and slipped it on just as he stepped into the clearing, carrying two glasses of punch.

A smile came to his face when he saw her. "I thought you'd disappeared."

"I couldn't resist the fresh air. It's a beautiful night."

"It is," he said as he handed her a glass.

She accepted it gratefully and took a sip. "Has the dancing started again?"

"I don't think it's stopped all night. It's almost time for supper."

Miranda stood up. "Perhaps I'll finally find my friend."

"That's right, you were looking for someone. No doubt you'll see her at supper."

For some reason she didn't want to correct him and say she was looking for a man. She finished her drink, but before she could put the glass down the man took it from her and set it on the bench. Miranda expected him to escort her back into the house, but he took a step closer to her. And then a few more steps. He stopped only inches from her, looking down into her face.

"Who are you?" he whispered.

Miranda couldn't think of how to reply. Heart pounding, she shook her head slightly and gave him a warm smile.

"Only a few more hours and I'll know your name," he said and ran a hand over her hair. "Unless you want to tell me now, or take your mask off?"

She'd never wanted anything more! But what if someone else saw and word got back to her parents?

Not only that, she was enjoying the intrigue. What

sort of man was he, though? Surely even at a masked ball it was unusual to take such liberties as he was now. His hand lingered on her shoulder as he searched her eyes.

But Miranda didn't feel unsafe—quite the opposite. She trembled with delight as she returned his steady gaze and fleetingly wondered what it would feel like to kiss him. Miranda blushed and took a step back. What was she thinking? She'd never kissed a man and certainly wouldn't kiss someone she'd just met, masquerade ball or no.

"Perhaps you want to tell me who *you* are," she said playfully. His hand fell away from her shoulder as she took another step back, though the greater part of her wanted to stay as close to him as possible.

The man smiled. "I see what you're doing. But no. If you won't tell, I won't either. I'll play the game for a little while longer." He offered her his arm and they returned to the house.

The moment they entered the punch room, Miranda spotted Peter, surrounded by women. Handsome and amusing, he was always sought after at social events. But it was slightly surprising tonight since nobody knew who he was. Even more surprising was that Miranda hadn't spotted him earlier. He was wearing a bright red doublet over the gold-trimmed pants. She knew she should go over and say hello, but since he was otherwise engaged she decided on one more dance with her partner.

Just as they entered the ballroom a waltz began, and she was once more in the man's arms. They hadn't been dancing long when someone tapped on the man's shoulder. Miranda barely held back a scowl. Wasn't it customary to wait until the song was over?

She peeked around the man's arm and saw Peter

standing there. "May I cut in?" he asked.

Miranda's partner gave her a questioning look.

"Yes, of course," she said, regretfully stepping out of his arms.

The man removed his hat and gave her a slight bow. "It's been a great pleasure, Miss…? Miss."

"Yes," she said, smiling. "A pleasure."

He kissed her hand. "I'll see you at midnight," he said and strode away.

Peter pulled Miranda into his arms and whirled her around. "Here you are! I haven't caught one glimpse of you all night."

"I haven't seen you, either. I knew I should have waited for you on the lawn."

"No matter. I have you now."

She smiled and stepped on his foot. "Sorry."

"That's all right. I expected it. I hope all your other partners' feet remained intact."

Miranda didn't mention that she'd had only one partner. "Strangely, I didn't step on anyone else. Perhaps it wasn't me but my instructor that caused all the toe injuries."

"I doubt that. The women I've danced with tonight—many of them, mind you—had no cause to step on me."

Miranda giggled. "It must be something peculiar to us, then."

"It must be. It's almost time for supper, and I propose we leave immediately after. You'll need to stop at Emily's to change and I told your father I'd have you home by midnight."

"That's a good idea. We should stay together for the rest of the night. I hate to leave, though! It's been a perfect evening."

"I'm glad you're enjoying yourself. You look beautiful."

"Thank you. And you are quite dashing, Sir Peter."

"I could get used to the name," Peter said. "Have you recognized anyone tonight?"

"Only Emily and Nathaniel. Oh, I did see your mother. She almost blurted out my name."

Peter nodded. "I saw her talking to Ebenezer, but I haven't spoken to her or my father."

"I hope she won't tell my parents she saw me."

"No need to worry about that."

"I saw Ebenezer, too. I'm glad he didn't wear a costume. That made it easy to avoid him."

Peter's face suddenly clouded as he nodded across the room. "There's another who didn't deem to disguise himself, though I wish he had. I hope my mother doesn't see him."

Miranda followed Peter's gaze to Mr. Cobbe. He was surrounded by his six daughters, whose masks barely concealed their faces. Peter's half-sisters, though they didn't resemble him in the least. Fortunately, Peter took after his mother and shared the same coloring as Mr. Tolwood.

"Don't pay him any mind," Miranda said, putting a finger to his chin and turning him to face her. "If your mother does see him, she'll ignore him. As you should. Come, let me show you the enchanting garden I found earlier."

He shook his head as though trying to rid it of the frown. "No, I won't let him drive me out of the ballroom."

"But I want to show you the garden. It's too hot in

here." Miranda stopped dancing and looped her arm through his.

"A few more dances," he said, picking up the pace of the next song. "We've been waiting for this night for so long."

After three dances they went outside, venturing deeper into the garden than Miranda had before. They sat on a bench facing a small pond and removed their masks.

"This is nice," Peter said and ruffled his hair.

"Much more comfortable than inside. It's a shame the orchestra can't play in the garden."

"We can hear them well enough from here," Peter said, swaying to the music as they chatted about the ball. He told Miranda about the women he'd danced with, and they tried to guess who they might have been. His mood had vastly improved since they'd come outside. Seeing Mr. Cobbe often bothered him, and no wonder. But Miranda had the feeling lately that seeing Mr. Cobbe was more upsetting because he reminded Peter of Ann. Peter was the loyal, steadfast type and he might have fallen in love with Ann if he hadn't found out she was Mr. Cobbe's ward. Still, hearts were funny, and even though Peter didn't want to have feelings for Ann, that didn't mean those inclinations were gone.

When a gong sounded from inside, they went in for supper. The buffet featured so many dishes Miranda didn't know where to start. Fortunately Peter was up to the task and filled their plates with more than they could possibly eat in one sitting, or even two. After getting glasses of champagne, Miranda and Peter joined Emily and Nathaniel. Over the course of the meal Emily told Miranda she'd left the house unlocked and her family was staying at the ball until midnight, so Miranda could easily go in to change before going home.

Miranda had hoped to catch a glimpse of her sea captain at supper, but perhaps he'd already eaten and gone back to the ballroom, or maybe he was simply lost in the crowd.

After finishing their meal, with Peter going back to fill his plate twice with desserts, they said goodnight to Emily and Nathaniel and took their leave. As they skirted the edge of the ballroom it was all Miranda could do to resist insisting on one more dance. But one look at the clock told her that would be far too risky.

"I can't believe it's already time to leave," she said.

Peter took her arm. "The time flew by."

Miranda paused in the entryway, looking over her shoulder at the costumed dancers. "It would be fun to stay until midnight, wouldn't it?"

"Yes, but you know that's impossible. Come," he said, giving her arm a little tug. "We'll have a lovely moonlit ride home."

"I don't want tonight to end."

"It won't for a long while. Not until you fall asleep in your bed," he said as they exited through the front doors.

Miranda took her mask off. "We'll make the most of the evening, then. The moonlit ride does sound enchanting."

"You'll need to wait for me while I fetch the carriage," Peter said when they reached the head of the staircase.

Miranda started down the stairs. "I'll come with you."

"Oh, no, you won't." Peter guided her toward a small balcony overlooking the drive. "There's no way

I'm letting you anywhere near the stables in that gown."

She raised a brow, smiling. "I see I'll spend even more of my evening waiting for you."

"It makes up for all the times I wait for *you*. I won't be long," he said and hurried down the stairs, removing his mask as he went.

In truth Miranda didn't mind waiting. Perhaps she'd see her partner one last time and could say goodbye. Would he really look for Miranda at midnight? She felt sorry for the disappointment he might feel when he couldn't find her, but then shook her head. He'd been charming, but she shouldn't imagine he had any genuine feelings for her. He would have treated any other woman the same and was most likely charming someone else in the ballroom right now.

It was unfortunate Miranda had to leave before discovering his identity. What were the odds they'd ever see each other again? Even if they did meet somehow, how would she know him? Her only real clue was his dark blue eyes, but she couldn't go around town asking every tall man to let her gaze into his eyes.

Miranda strolled back and forth along the balcony, watching the sky and listening to the music through the open windows. She'd just begun to wonder what was taking Peter so long when he arrived with the carriage. Miranda fancied sitting beside him in her fairytale gown as they drove through town, but he insisted she sit inside.

They stopped at the Darlingtons' house, where Miranda ran upstairs to change. The dreamlike quality of the evening began to fade as she stepped into her teal dress. After hanging the ballgown on the mannequin, she ran her fingers along the tiny flowers, wishing she could keep it forever.

When Miranda returned to the carriage, Peter was wearing his finest suit.

"Where's your costume?" she asked as she climbed into the seat next to him.

"I changed in the carriage. Your father would be surprised if you arrived home with a knight instead of your fiancé."

"Hopefully he's gone to bed and we won't see him," she said as they trotted down the street.

Miranda had never considered Deerwood magical, but tonight it was. Lamplight cast a soft glow over the deserted streets and a gentle breeze whispered through the trees. Once they'd passed through town, the only light to accompany them was the full moon and twinkling stars.

"Did the ball live up to your expectations?" Peter asked after a time.

"Oh, yes! I wonder if I could convince my father to accept some invitations. There's only one masked ball a year, but he's invited to house parties and dances every so often."

He gave her a sideways glance. "We could sneak out again. It made the evening all the more intriguing."

Miranda shook her head. "It was worth sneaking out tonight, but I've had enough intrigue. My parents will be livid if they ever find out."

"Well, you know what you have to do," Peter said. "Tell them what you want."

"I know," she said with a sigh. "Perhaps if we receive another invitation I will, but I don't want to upset them while my mother is…whatever she is. Tired? Sick? I wish they'd stop treating me like a child and tell me what's the matter with her."

"You don't believe she's merely tired, as they say?"

"If she is, she's been 'tired' for years."

"Some people have delicate constitutions. Look at my Aunt Millie. She's never been robust, even though she isn't ill."

"That's true. But Mother was much more active when we were young. Remember? She'd play with us every day and chase us through the garden."

"She played hide-and-go-seek with us when we were small and even gave us piggyback rides." Peter smiled softly. "Yes, I remember."

"And it isn't as though she's old now."

"Not young, either."

"She liked to dance back then, too, I remember. She would have liked the ball."

"She would have loved seeing you there, Miranda. Your dancing was impressive, by the way. My toes aren't nearly as squished as they were even a few days ago."

Miranda laughed. "My only regret about tonight is that we were separated and didn't dance as much as I'd have liked."

Although if they had, maybe she never would have met her partner. It had to be close to midnight. He must be wandering through the crowd, searching for her. It probably would have been polite to tell him she was leaving early. But she had the feeling he'd have insisted she reveal her identity before she left.

She and Peter chatted about the ball until they turned into the drive at Majestic Oaks. Peter pulled the horses to a stop in front of the house, then jumped down to assist Miranda. As they approached the door he said, "Remember. We're in love."

Miranda looked up at him and batted her eyelashes. "How could I ever forget, my sweet turtledove?"

They both started laughing just as the door opened.

"Here you are, and right on time," Mr. Harlake said, looking at his pocket watch.

Peter put an arm around Miranda's shoulders and she nestled into him.

"You didn't need to wait up, Father," she said.

"I was awake anyway. I had some finishing touches on that pine tree I started earlier today. Finally mixed the right shade of green."

Miranda would have liked to ask how he'd managed it, but decided it was more important to look like a loving fiancée. "We had a grand time."

Peter brushed a hair off her forehead. "Yes, a perfect evening. Thank you for allowing me to take Miranda out."

"What did you have for dinner?" Mr. Harlake asked, not looking at them.

Miranda froze. What had they eaten? She looked at Peter.

"I had the lobster and Miranda had duck."

"That sounds delicious. Perhaps I'll take Mrs. Harlake there next week. What's the name of the restaurant?"

"I don't remember," Miranda said with a high-pitched giggle. "I was very distracted." She ran a hand up Peter's arm and kissed his cheek.

Her father glowered. "Miranda! Mild displays, I said. *Mild.* For goodness' sake! Peter, it's time you went home, I believe."

"Yes, sir." Peter took both of Miranda's hands in his. "I'll see you tomorrow. Sweet dreams."

"I'll dream of you," she said, staring into his eyes. He looked like he was on the verge of breaking out in laughter again, so she let go of his hands and took a step back.

Peter shook Mr. Harlake's hand, nodded to Miranda, and drove away in the carriage.

As Miranda and her father walked through the quiet house, he asked, "What's that?"

"What?"

He pointed to her hand. "Is that a fan?"

Miranda had forgotten she was still carrying the mask. She quickly hid it behind her back. "Yes. Yes, it's a fan Peter bought me. Isn't he sweet?"

Without waiting for an answer, she ran upstairs to her room. Miranda walked out to the moonlit balcony, where she put the mask back on and swayed to imaginary music, envisioning herself once more in the mysterious man's arms.

Chapter Ten

Miranda woke late the next day and though she'd rested well didn't get out of bed. She lay there remembering the night before... All the excitement of sneaking out, and those dances with the handsome stranger... She wondered if she'd recognize him if she ran into him in town. Maybe he was someone she encountered every day. He could even be a friend. But no. She didn't know anyone with those deep blue eyes.

After luxuriating in bed for a time, she rose and dressed for breakfast. Her father was the only one still in the dining room and most of the food had been cleared away.

"Good morning," she said to her father as she sat down, helping herself to a cup of coffee and a slice of apple cake.

He looked at her over his newspaper. "You seem pleased this morning."

"I had a fabulous time last night. With Peter. I'm so glad we're engaged." It wasn't as if she could tell him the real reason for her good mood.

"Hm. I'm glad you enjoyed yourself."

After breakfast they went into the studio.

Miranda set her still life aside and took out her pastels. Humming a tune from last night, she started a colorful ballroom scene, trying to capture the movement of the dancers and the light radiating from the chandeliers. She could almost imagine she was back there, held in unknown arms.

"That's fanciful," her father said. She'd been so engrossed in her work she hadn't heard him approach.

She took a step back from the canvas. "I was in the mood for something different."

"It definitely is that. All drawn from imagination? Or was there dancing at the restaurant last night?"

"Imagination. I remembered the Rockfords' ball was last night and it inspired me."

"It was probably hotter and more crowded than that."

"Maybe."

Returning to his own canvas, Mr. Harlake glanced over his shoulder. "You know, if you married Ebenezer you'd go to balls all the time."

She rolled her eyes. "That wouldn't induce me to marry him, and in any case I'm already betrothed to Peter."

"Talking about me, darling?" Peter asked, striding into the room.

"Peter!" Miranda cried, hurrying to his side. She kissed his cheek as he wrapped an arm around her shoulders. "I wasn't expecting you today. I thought you had plans with your father."

"I do, but not until this afternoon. I hoped to interest you in a walk into town."

Mr. Harlake cleared his throat. "You spent all last evening together, and Miranda's in the middle of working."

"I could do with a break," Miranda said. "Perhaps we could get lunch at Darlington's. I can say hi to Emily."

"Perfect," Peter said.

"Don't leave your work too long, Miranda," her father said. "You don't want to lose your inspiration. You didn't even sketch it."

"It's sketched in my mind. See you later, Father."

Mr. Harlake waved his paintbrush at her and resumed working.

Miranda held Peter's hand as they walked out the front door but released it when they were out of sight of the house. "I'm glad you suggested going into town. I want to thank Emily for her help and ask her what's become of my gown."

"It really was something," Peter said, turning to smile at her.

"Maybe I'll own a dress like that one day."

"Well, if you married Ebenezer…"

She rolled her eyes. "You sound like my father. As if I'd actually break a betrothal just to marry someone who'd buy me pretty gowns."

"To be fair, it isn't a real betrothal."

"Yes, but my father doesn't know that."

"Your parents only want what's best for you."

"I'm tired of them deciding what's best for me. They should trust me to know what's best for my own life. If I'm engaged to you, they shouldn't encourage me to break it off. And they should listen to what I say about a hundred other things."

"They won't know what you want if you don't tell them."

"I know," Miranda said, kicking at a small rock. "But it's so difficult. I'm all my parents have. All they have to plan for, dream for. I've always felt it's my place to fulfill their dreams. But Peter, it's getting harder."

"That's because now you have dreams of your own."

"I always have, but I've been so focused on my parents' I've hardly acknowledged them."

Peter took her arm. "I remember your dreams, even if you don't."

"What are they?" she asked, smiling.

He ticked them off on his fingers. "A calico kitten, a pink frock, your own art studio, a cottage in the forest, to learn glassblowing, and to find someone to live with happily ever after."

She laughed. "How do you remember all that?"

"Because you told me nearly every day."

Miranda sobered slightly. "Those are all childish dreams."

"But they're still your dreams," he said. "What do you want now, Miranda?"

"I want…"

"What?" he asked gently.

"I want to do what I want," she said simply. "And not worry that I'm hurting my parents' feelings if my plans don't coincide with theirs."

"The first thing is to decide what your new dreams are. The second is to make them come true. You had a taste of making your own choices last night at the ball. How did you like it?"

"I loved it," she said. "Maybe I should do things without telling my parents more often. It isn't really lying, as you said."

"That's a good idea. We'll have to think of some worthy things to do. A trip to Hollingsford or a dance."

"I'd be happy to start with small things, like being allowed to buy clothes I like or devote more time to my pastels."

"We'll work our way up to sneaking off to Hollingsford," he said.

They'd just turned onto Main Street when they passed the bank and a man stepped out into the street practically on top of them.

Miranda grabbed Peter's arm and pulled him out of the way just in time.

"I say! Watch where you're going!" the man shouted.

"You should—" Peter began but stopped when the man spun around to face them.

It was Mr. Cobbe.

He stared at Peter for a second before squaring his shoulders and stalking away.

Peter watched until Mr. Cobbe turned a corner and was out of sight. "Just because he owns the bank he thinks he owns the whole street," he grumbled.

"Are you all right?" Miranda asked, rubbing his back.

"Yes. Yes, of course. Let's go."

When they entered Darlington's, Miranda and Peter sat at a table overlooking Main Street. Within a few minutes Emily came over and pulled up a chair. "The ball was so exciting!"

"Just what I've always dreamed a ball would be like," Miranda said.

Emily nodded emphatically. "It's a shame you had to leave before midnight."

"It really is, but it couldn't be helped," Miranda said. "I want to know who was behind all those masks. Tell me everything you remember."

"If you two are starting in on a gossip, I'll go talk to

Nathaniel," Peter said.

Miranda batted his arm lightly. "Peter! We aren't gossiping."

"There's so much to discuss, though," Emily said, in a decidedly gossipy tone.

Peter laughed and rose. "I'll be in the shop."

Emily pulled her chair closer to Miranda's. "The mayor was wearing the peacock costume! His wife was one of the many princesses, and the librarian was dressed as a judge." She went on to list more costumes and told Miranda that at the end of the night there'd been a champagne toast and everyone had cake before departing. Emily and her family hadn't gotten home until two o'clock in the morning.

"Did you see anyone who was dressed as a sea captain?" Miranda asked, drumming her fingers on her knee as she waited for an answer.

Emily thought for a moment before replying. "There were a few."

"Who were they?" Miranda's heart sped up. Was she about to find out his identity?

"I wish I could tell you, but I haven't been introduced to everyone in town yet."

"That's all right, it doesn't matter," Miranda said, trying not to sound disappointed. "Are the gowns put away in the trunks?"

"Not yet. Mrs. Darlington's going to clean them first. I'd rather keep mine hanging in the wardrobe where I can see it every day."

"So would I," Miranda said.

"Do you want me to ask Mrs. Darlington if you can have it?"

"Oh, no," Miranda said, though she'd love to own it.

"It seems rude somehow."

"It isn't rude. That dress suited you so well. I'll tell you what. Mrs. Darlington might not have any interest in keeping it, and why shouldn't it go to you instead of sitting upstairs waiting for moths to find it?"

Perhaps this was one of those times when Miranda should ask for what she wanted instead of assuming she'd be putting Mrs. Darlington out. After all, she could say no. Peter had asked what her dreams were now, and that gown was definitely a dream come true. "You can ask her, but don't imply I was insisting on it. Do you think she might sell me the gown?"

"I don't think she'd want to do that, but I'll ask."

"Thank you. And there's no hurry."

Emily smiled. "I'll ask her if I can keep my gown, too."

They talked about the ball until Peter returned.

"It's time we went home," he said.

Miranda glanced at her watch. "Yes, I'm supposed to visit my mother this afternoon."

They rose from the table and Emily walked Miranda and Peter to the door. "Goodbye," she said. "I'm glad you stopped by."

"Would you like to meet at the park tomorrow?" Miranda asked.

"I'd love to. Noon?"

"Yes, I'll see you then." As Miranda turned to go, she nearly collided with George, who'd just entered Darlington's with his usual gaggle of friends. He swerved to avoid her, nodded to Peter, and continued on his way. Miranda frowned at his back, then followed Peter outside.

"I'm glad we were ready to leave," she said. "I

wouldn't have wanted to stay now that George and his friends are here. Who knows what they'll break this time."

Peter chuckled. "You didn't seem to mind him so much last night."

"What are you talking about?" Miranda asked as they waited for a carriage to pass.

"I'm talking about George."

"What about him?"

Peter took her arm and they started across the street. "Before I cut in, you looked like you were enjoying dancing with him. You know, the sea captain."

"That was *George*?"

He looked at her as though he thought she might be joking. "Yes."

"It wasn't him…was it?" Miranda asked, her steps slowing to a crawl.

"It absolutely was."

"But—I think you're wrong, Peter."

"I'm positive it was George. I saw him walking on the grounds when I went to get the carriage, and he'd taken his mask off. Still had the wig on, though."

"Why didn't you tell me last night?"

Peter shrugged. "I didn't think to. What does it matter anyway? You had a dance with him and that's that. You could have danced with Ethan or Henry, too, for all we know."

Miranda came to an abrupt halt when they reached the sidewalk, paying no heed to the people trying to walk around her. Her handsome, amusing partner was George? Peter obviously didn't know she'd spent the whole evening with George, and she wasn't going to tell him. But perhaps then he'd understand why she found the idea so disconcerting. One dance would have been alarming enough, but an entire evening in George's arms? She flushed when she recalled the daydreams she'd been indulging in.

"Miranda?" Peter asked, nudging her elbow.

"I simply can't believe it, but I don't know why it's such a shock. Last night I was aware he could be somebody I knew. George, though!"

"And to think you didn't recognize him after he knocked you out of your chair just a few weeks ago," he said with a teasing smile.

Miranda rubbed the back of her hand as she started walking again. "That was an accident. I wonder if he knew it was me last night."

"I doubt it. You were very well disguised."

"If he'd recognized me, he probably would have mentioned it. Last night he said—"

Miranda stopped mid-sentence, blushing. George had been outright flirtatious at the ball, but did she really want to relay all the details to Peter? She'd rather keep those memories of George as the fascinating sea captain to herself and not associate him with the boisterous, rowdy and sometimes rude man she'd known all these years.

"What did he say?" Peter asked impatiently.

"Only that he wondered who I was. He was going to look for me at midnight."

"I'm sure he said that to every woman he danced with. You know how he is with the ladies. He's a real charmer and has a new woman on his arm every week."

"Is he courting someone in particular?"

"Not than I know of. Why?"

"I'm just curious."

Peter gave her a sideways look. "Miranda, *you* haven't been charmed by George, have you?"

"Of course not! I'm truthfully disappointed it was him. I barely know George and don't hold him in very high esteem. It would have been nice if I'd been dancing with someone I admired."

"Well, you did dance with me," he said, grinning.

"That's true," she said, "and I could hardly admire anyone as much as I admire you." She linked her arm through his as they turned onto Fairbanks Road.

****

After Peter escorted Miranda home, she went upstairs. She picked the mask off her vanity and turned it over in her hands. The whole evening meant something different now that she knew her partner had been George. She fell into a chair. George Rockford!

The attentions he'd paid to her had merely been to "charm" her, as he did all ladies, according to Peter. Miranda hadn't wanted to admit, even to herself, the romantic fantasy she'd had of meeting her sea captain again one day and falling desperately in love with each other. She supposed this just went to show how naive she was when it came to men and courting. Hopefully George would never discover that she'd been his partner. It would be all too mortifying. Just as she'd never held him in high esteem, he'd never thought much of her, as far as she knew. He'd known her name that day at Darlington's, but that was to be expected since they'd grown up in the same town. She sighed and tucked her mask away in the wardrobe. It was over now, the ball and the fanciful dreams that had accompanied it.

Miranda went along to her mother's room, and when she knocked on the door it was immediately opened by

Esther.

"Your mother's resting, Miranda. Please come back later."

"We had a plan to see each other. I won't tire her."

Esther hesitated. "She's expecting you?"

"Yes, and she'll be disappointed if she thinks I forgot."

Esther said nothing but held the door open, looking as though she was taking an awful risk by letting Miranda in.

Miranda followed her into the parlor, where Mrs. Harlake was reclining on the sofa. She had a pallid look, but perhaps it was because the curtains were drawn.

"Shall I open the drapes, Mother?" she asked cheerfully. "It's a lovely, sunny day."

"If you like," Mrs. Harlake said, not looking at Miranda.

Miranda drew the curtains and opened the windows wide, letting fresh air rush in. "Have you been busy today?"

"No, I've been resting. How was your dinner with Peter last night?"

"It was perfect," Miranda said brightly as she joined her mother on the sofa.

"That's nice."

Miranda reached for a novel on the side table. "Would you like me to read to you?"

"No, thank you. Why don't we have tea?" Mrs. Harlake rang the bell beside her, and when Esther came in she ordered tea.

They sat in silence until the tea came and the silence continued while they drank it, aside from Mrs. Harlake telling Miranda the dates they'd be going to Hollingsford for the art exhibition.

Miranda hadn't intended to ask her mother what was wrong, but something about the dark circles under her eyes coupled with her wan complexion made it impossible to keep quiet today. She set her teacup down. "Mother, are you ill?"

"No," her mother said. "I'm merely tired."

"You're tired often. Are you sleeping well at night?"

"It's nothing to concern yourself over."

"I'd like to help if I could."

"Your visits are all the help I need. Tell me about this new picture Father says you started. Pastels, isn't it?"

Miranda described the ball scene and her mother made suggestions about shading methods that would make the ballgowns look more realistic. Miranda nodded along but was distracted for the rest of their visit.

Chapter Eleven

A few days later Miranda stood beside her father on the patio, watching as he demonstrated an advanced technique for color blending. As she watched him, she once again knew she'd never reach the artistic heights he had.

While she enjoyed painting, lately she'd had the strangest—uncomfortable—feeling that it wasn't for her. It felt scandalous to even allow herself the thought, but there'd been moments recently when Miranda knew she couldn't get a piece just right. A part of her didn't want to focus on the process, wanting only to lose herself in the world she'd created. But that wasn't what she'd been trained for. She'd been trained to be a master, and her parents would be disappointed if Miranda didn't reach their standards of craftsmanship. Her father's work was well renowned—people flocked to exhibitions to buy his work. Mrs. Harlake's paintings, too, had taken their place in galleries around the country and brought in their fair share of money.

Miranda had finished her picture of the ball and planned to hang it in her bedroom. She felt happy every time she looked at it, and that was what she wanted out of all her work; not slogging through still lifes trying to perfect the shadow under a pear. Perhaps her pictures would be better if she devoted her time only to subjects she truly loved.

When her mother was over this latest bout of fatigue, Miranda would consider telling her parents she wanted a change from all the technical work she'd been doing. Maybe even tell them she wanted to focus more on her pastels. But not yet.

She brought her attention back to her father's lecture, but suddenly a knock sounded on the door and Peter came out onto the patio, carrying a bouquet of red roses.

"Good afternoon," he said.

Miranda rushed to his side. She never had to pretend to be happy to see him. "Darling!"

He handed her the roses and put an arm around her waist.

"Peter," Mr. Harlake said, eyes still on his canvas.

"I didn't expect to see you this morning," Miranda said, reaching up to touch his cheek.

He unexpectedly pulled her into his arms. "I've come to tell you I'm going away for a time."

"Going away?" She studied his face, expecting to see that he was joking. But he wasn't.

Mr. Harlake turned to face Peter, not even trying to hold back a satisfied smile. "Where are you going? When?"

"I'm off to Nottingham to look at a horse for Mr. Rockford. Mr. Ebenezer Rockford, that is."

"Have a safe journey. I'll take those flowers," Mr. Harlake said and took the bouquet. Miranda knew they'd end up in his next still life.

Peter held Miranda close. "I'll miss you so much."

"I'll miss you, too. How long will you be gone?" she asked, laying her head on his shoulder.

"Long enough to pine for you every moment. Might

I have a lock of your hair?"

Mr. Harlake cleared his throat loudly.

"Let's go inside, Peter, and you can tell me all about it." Miranda took his hand and they walked down the hall to the library.

Peter collapsed onto the sofa. "How was I?"

"Very convincing." She sat down, facing him. "How did this come about?"

"I received a summons from Mr. Rockford yesterday and I called on him this morning. He's sending his groom to a horse seller up in Nottingham and wants me to go along. He said he's heard I have a good eye for horses."

"But do you really want to go?"

"I jumped at the chance. He's paying my way and giving me a salary to boot. The stables there are famous for their Morgans."

"When are you leaving?"

"Tomorrow morning."

"It will be strange not seeing you for a whole week."

He shook his head. "Nottingham's in Vermont, Miranda. More like two or three."

"That's an eternity!" Miranda said, grabbing his hand.

Peter laughed. "So you *will* miss me."

"You know I will. But can't you take the train? It would be so much faster."

"No, we'll have to ride. And I won't want to press a new horse on the journey back. Fortunately, Mr. Rockford's putting us up at inns along the way so we won't have to camp." He squeezed her hand. "Don't look so worried. I'll be home safe before you know it."

"I know you will. But I'm thinking of my parents.

What if they try to convince me to marry Mr. Rockford while you're gone?"

"I don't think they're that devious, Miranda. They know we're engaged. They've probably forgotten about wanting you to marry him."

"I hope Mr. Rockford marries someone soon. Then we can stop this charade. It's been more than a month already."

"It hasn't been that bad, has it?" Peter asked.

"Far from it. It's a bit of a lark, really, but pretending all the time does grow tiresome."

"We'll call it off as soon as Mr. Rockford's betrothed. I saw him dancing with a number of women at the ball. Maybe one of them is *the one*. Perhaps we should stage a quarrel for your parents to overhear when I return. We'll give them a hint that things aren't perfect between us."

"I can't imagine what we'd fight about. We never argue."

"We'll think of something. I could fly into a jealous rage because you looked warmly at Nathaniel Darlington."

Miranda laughed, then gasped. "Oh, I just remembered where I've heard of Nottingham before! Emily grew up there. She mentioned the stables and said Nottingham's well known for its maple candy."

"I'll bring you home a box."

She smiled. "It won't make up for you being gone so long, but I'll happily accept it."

Peter looked away and cleared his throat. "Emily isn't the only person we know who grew up there. Ann's from Nottingham."

"So *that's* where I'd heard of Nottingham when

Emily mentioned it. Is that why you're going? You're hoping to see Ann?"

He rested his clasped hands on his knees. "No, and I sincerely hope I don't. If I do see her, I'll avoid her. I'd never choose to go to her hometown, but I won't let her stand in the way of my seeing the horses."

"I doubt you'll see her. What time do you leave tomorrow?"

"First thing. But I'll come say goodbye so your parents can see what a devoted fiancé I am."

"I don't think there's any doubt of that," she said.

The next morning Peter entered the dining room as Miranda and her parents were finishing breakfast. Miranda ran to him and he gathered her into a tight embrace.

"Think of me while I'm gone?" he asked.

Miranda wiped a nonexistent tear from her eye. "Every moment. Write to me as often as you can, my love."

"If I have time. But even if I don't write, know I'm thinking of you constantly." Peter took her hand and led her over to the window. He held her close and whispered, "Should I kiss you?"

Miranda hardly knew how to respond. She'd never kissed a man before and her parents were sitting at the table, watching them. But if she was really in love with Peter, she would allow a kiss. "Yes, I think you'd better," she whispered back.

Peter closed his eyes and leaned toward her. Miranda copied him, closing her eyes, too. The kiss was over in an instant. One second his lips, pressed tightly together, were on hers and then they were gone.

"Is that all?" she asked under her breath.

He bent down as though to nuzzle her neck. "I think it should suffice."

The kiss hadn't been as exhilarating as Miranda had expected, but perhaps that's because she'd known it was coming, and it was only Peter. He may as well have shaken her hand. It had had the desired effect on her parents, though. Her father was covering his eyes while her mother stared down at her full plate.

Peter sighed loudly and wiped his dry cheek. "I need to be off. Take care of yourself, my sweet angel. I'll see you in my dreams." He kissed her hand and fled the room as though overpowered by emotion.

Miranda turned her giggle into a sort of sob and ran upstairs to her room, where she gave full vent to her laughter. Hopefully if her parents heard her they assumed she was hysterical.

A few days later Miranda sat at her vanity, twisting the diamond ring upon her finger. She missed Peter. She'd somehow never realized how often she stopped to see him in his office or the stables, or how he came to the house to visit a few times a day, especially after they'd become engaged. He'd done his best to play the part of a doting fiancé.

Miranda had to admit it was a relief to stop pretending to be in love all the time. With all this talk recently of engagements, Miranda's thoughts had turned more than once to what she'd like in a real fiancé. He had to be kind, honest, perhaps artistic. She didn't give much thought as to what he'd look like, but it wouldn't hurt if he was handsome. Miranda wanted passion, definitely, and laughter. Thus far she'd never known anyone to make her pulse jump, or someone she lost sleep over. She knew she could only marry a man she could trust. A man who could be her best friend.

Miranda didn't usually wear the engagement ring, but seeing it on her finger made Peter feel closer somehow. He'd only written her one quick note since he'd left, postmarked from a town she'd never heard of.

She slid the ring off her finger and put it back in the jewelry box, then went into town to see Emily.

As soon as Miranda walked into Darlington's, Emily ran out from behind the counter. "Mrs. Darlington says you can keep the dress!"

Miranda smiled. "Really?"

"Yes. She said it isn't doing anyone any good sitting up there in a trunk, and she wouldn't hear of you paying for it. She said I can keep mine, too."

"That's so kind of her," Miranda said, overwhelmed. It was the most beautiful thing she'd ever worn, and now it would truly be hers.

"Perhaps we could wear our dresses again sometime. To a tea party or a dance. Nathaniel told me there's a dance every summer in the town square."

"Yes, that would be a perfect occasion. I must thank Mrs. Darlington."

"She's a sweet woman. I couldn't ask for a better mother-in-law."

"You must miss your family," Miranda said. It was hard to imagine moving away from her parents.

"I do. But Nathaniel's family has been so welcoming, and now I'm making friends here." She smiled shyly and Miranda knew she meant her.

Since Emily was opening up, Miranda decided she would, too. "I haven't had many girl friends. It's always been Peter."

"I can't imagine being close friends with a boy,"

Emily said, wrinkling her nose.

"It seems natural to me, when I've known him so long. That reminds me, Peter went to Nottingham to look at some horses."

"I envy him," Emily said with a sigh. "I'd love to go up, but we won't be able to until later in the summer."

"You'll visit your sisters?"

"Yes. I miss them so much, and my parents, too. We've been writing to each other every week. I might have a photograph done of myself to send to them."

"I forgot there was a new photography studio in town. You could wear the green dress."

"That would be perfect. Perhaps you could get one, too."

"My parents have plenty of portraits of me through the years, and I have nobody else to give a photograph of myself."

"Well," Emily said, dropping her voice, "it might not be long before you have a special someone to give one to."

"Emily! What are you thinking? I don't even have a beau." For a moment Miranda thought Emily had found out about the fake engagement. She double-checked her ring finger and was relieved to find it was bare.

Emily giggled. "You're of an age, that's all. You might meet someone soon."

Miranda relaxed now that she knew Emily was only speculating. "I suppose anything is possible," she said. "Speaking of Nottingham, do you know Ann Lawton?"

"Not very well."

"Do you know anything about her background?"

"What do you mean?"

Miranda was curious about Ann's history but didn't

want Emily to think she was a gossip. She decided simple was best. "Ann was here last summer but only stayed for a few weeks. I didn't get a chance to know her."

"I don't know her well either. She only moved to Nottingham a few years ago. She mostly keeps to herself, but she was nice enough the few times I talked to her."

"That's what I thought too. She seemed kind but shy." And lied and broke Miranda's best friend's heart.

Just then Mrs. Darlington walked by and Miranda hailed her. "Thank you ever so much for the gown. I love it and can't thank you enough."

Mrs. Darlington smiled. "You're very welcome. Emily said it looked perfect on you. I didn't see you wearing it at the ball, but perhaps I will another time."

"You will," Emily cut in, taking her mother-in-law's arm. "We're going to wear the gowns to the summer dance."

"You'll look a treat, I'm sure," Mrs. Darlington said.

"I'll pick up the gown next time I'm here," Miranda said. "I walked today, but I'd rather bring it home in the carriage."

"Stop by any time that's convenient for you," Mrs. Darlington said and bustled off.

"Would you like to come to lunch next week?" Miranda asked Emily. "I can show you some of my paintings, if you'd like."

"Yes, I'd love to see them," Emily said.

Miranda bade her farewell and left the shop. On her way home she felt an unexpected pang of longing when she remembered Emily and Mrs. Darlington. They seemed so close, the way Miranda imagined mothers and daughters usually were. What would it take to form a bond like that with her own mother?

She was broken out of her thoughts by the sight of something most unusual. Three men pulling a horseless cart across a field, while one man stood precariously in the driver's seat. They all laughed uproariously when he fell to the ground with a thud. Of course, it was George. He jumped up, rubbing his backside as another man scrambled up to take his place. Miranda continued home, wondering if they would ever act their age.

Chapter Twelve

Miranda spent most of the next day in town. She went to the library for a few novels, then stopped at the milliners, where she was tempted by a purple velvet hat covered in ostrich feathers and faux flowers. But as her father would deem it too frivolous and most unnecessary, she settled on a straw boater and asked the milliner to add a sprig of artificial violets and a thin purple ribbon. Miranda strolled along the river before taking the woodland path home.

When Miranda arrived at the house she was surprised to find her mother in the studio.

"Hello, Mother," she said.

Mrs. Harlake didn't look up from the canvas.

Miranda crossed the room to see what she was working on. It was the sky; swirling, colorful, almost touchable. Miranda didn't bother complimenting it, as her mother didn't welcome critique of her work, positive or otherwise.

"Did you have a nice day? Are you feeling better?" Miranda asked.

"Yes, much better."

As her mother showed no sign of wanting to talk further, Miranda turned to go. "I'm going upstairs. I'll see you at supper."

"Be sure to change before you come down. Something nice."

"Why?" Miranda asked. They never paid much mind to what they wore for family meals, and they weren't expecting company.

Her mother let out an aggravated sigh. "Just do it, please, Miranda."

"I will." The request made no sense to Miranda, but she didn't want to argue on her mother's first time downstairs in days.

In her bedroom, Miranda put the hat box in her wardrobe then went out to the balcony with one of her new books. The next thing she knew night was falling and she was late for supper. She changed into a dress she knew her mother would approve of—a burgundy gown with flowing chiffon overskirts that had always reminded Miranda of a blooming rose. After a quick moment to fix her hair, she rushed downstairs.

As Miranda approached the drawing room she heard men's voices, and neither of them was her father's. She guessed Mr. Tolwood had stopped by and brought someone with him, but when she strode into the room she nearly gasped aloud.

George and Ebenezer Rockford stood chatting with her parents, glasses of sherry in their hands. So this was why her mother had insisted she change. Nobody looked Miranda's way when she entered the room and she wanted to tiptoe out and send Cassandra down with a message that she was ill. Very ill. She sighed. It would never work. Mentally preparing herself for an atrocious evening, she walked to her father's side.

"Ah, here she is at last!" Mr. Harlake said, taking her arm.

Miranda fixed a smile on her face as he steered her over to stand beside Ebenezer.

"You remember Mr. Rockford, don't you, Miranda?" Mr. Harlake asked, eyes twinkling.

"Yes, of course. Good evening." Miranda hadn't seen him up close in a long time. He had dark brown hair, brown eyes, and a short beard. She'd never been fond of beards.

Mr. Rockford took her hand and kissed it. "Good evening to you, Miss Harlake."

She went to pull her hand away, but he showed no sign of relinquishing it.

"Call her Miranda. So much friendlier," Mrs. Harlake said with a wide smile.

"Then she must call me Ebenezer." He motioned to George. "You know my nephew, George? Why, you two must have gone to school together."

Miranda was glad to remove her hand from Ebenezer's grip as she turned to face George. When he met her eyes Miranda blushed, sure he'd remember her from the ball. But when after a few seconds George showed no sign of recognizing her, she wasn't sure if she was relieved or disappointed.

Miranda realized that as she was searching his face for a trace of recognition, everyone else was staring at her. "Yes, we did go to school together. But Mr. Rockford was two grades ahead of me."

He smiled. "George, please."

"Miranda," she said with a little bob of her head.

"Have you met since those old school days?" Ebenezer asked.

George gave Miranda an ironic look. "We ran into each other just the other day at Darlington's."

"Yes, that was a surprise," she said, rubbing her hand.

Mrs. Harlake giggled. *Giggled.* "Miranda, you didn't tell me that!"

Certain that she had, Miranda glanced at her mother, narrowing her eyes slightly. How could her parents ambush her like this? They knew she was engaged to Peter. What she should really do was turn around and march back upstairs. But she knew she couldn't.

Mr. Harlake, possibly sensing Miranda's thoughts, said, "It must have slipped her mind to tell you, dear. Shall we go into the dining room?"

He took his wife's arm and Ebenezer took Miranda's, leaving George to follow behind.

Miranda would rather have walked alone, or at least a foot or two farther away from Ebenezer. His cologne had been put on with a heavy hand and her nose was beginning to itch.

Mr. and Mrs. Harlake took their places at the head and foot of the dining table, and Miranda sat beside Ebenezer. George winced when he sat in the chair across from Miranda and she guessed he hadn't recovered from his fall off the cart.

During the meal Miranda barely noticed what she ate. Mr. and Mrs. Harlake kept trying to draw her into the conversation and she couldn't feel more like a child whose parents were boasting about her good grades at school. Whenever Miranda spoke, Ebenezer would nod along for only a moment before turning the conversation to George, who regaled the table with his sparkling wit and anecdotes.

By the time dessert was served Miranda's cheeks hurt from all the forced smiles. She wanted nothing more than to excuse herself and retreat to her bedroom, but first she had to get through coffee in the parlor. That couldn't take more than an hour, and with any luck she'd have time for a walk in the garden to unwind before bed.

When Mrs. Harlake rose, Miranda practically leapt from her seat and led the way into the parlor instead of waiting to be escorted by one of the Rockfords. Both parents scowled at her for her lack of decorum, but at the moment she wasn't overly concerned with their anger. If anything, Miranda was raring for a chance to tell them what she thought of them for inviting Ebenezer to supper.

Miranda settled on the sofa farthest from the fire, hoping to go unnoticed. But Ebenezer joined her and drew her into a long discussion about art, mainly telling her he was hopeless at it but George had once tried drawing.

By the time her father set his coffee down and rose, Miranda was more than ready to say goodbye to their guests. But it was not to be.

"Would you care for a tour of the art gallery?" Mr. Harlake asked.

Ebenezer nodded. "Yes, indeed."

"Isn't it a getting bit late for that?" George asked, glancing at Miranda just as she tried to cover a tiny yawn.

"Heavens, no!" Mrs. Harlake said. She took George's arm, leaving Ebenezer to escort Miranda.

Miranda leaned as far away from him as possible in order to avoid being overwhelmed by his cologne again.

When they reached the gallery, Ebenezer looked in wonder at the paintings. "Stupendous. Simply stupendous. Are any of these done by Miranda?"

"Right this way," Mr. Harlake said, giving Miranda a wink.

Miranda ran a hand over her face as her father led

the group to the small, framed picture he insisted on showing everyone who visited. For the last nineteen years.

"Father, they don't want to see that one."

He laughed heartily. "She's so modest! Miranda made this before she could walk. The first time she ever held a brush!"

George and Ebenezer managed to look interested and amused at the blob of green paint surrounded by a gold gilt frame. If one looked closely enough, Miranda's smudged yellow toeprint was visible in the corner.

"How sweet," Ebenezer said.

George turned to Miranda. "What have you been working on more recently?"

Before she could answer, her father interrupted. "Why not take George and Ebenezer down to the studio?"

"I doubt they'd want to see that," she said, glaring at her father.

George, who'd apparently intercepted the look, appeared to be trying to hide a grin. "Actually, it sounds quite interesting."

"You two go ahead. I'd like to stay here," Ebenezer said, staring at a vast painting her father had done on a trip to Hollingsford. A busy street, bustling with carriages and people, bathed in the glow of lanterns at dusk.

Miranda would have liked to refuse, claiming to be too tired, but instead led George out of the gallery. They silently walked downstairs and through the house.

When they reached the studio, Miranda realized her painting of the ball was visible, so she hurried across the room and turned it to the wall.

George followed her. "What's that?"

"It's not done yet and I don't want anyone to see it," she said. For good measure she threw a clean drop cloth over the easel, then walked over to another painting. "Here's one of Mount Windsor."

He glanced at it for only a moment, then looked at Miranda. "Is this from the day we saw you at the lake?"

"I didn't know if you recognized me."

"You're the only girl from school who paints outside," George said. "This is pretty. I like the colors."

"Thank you. That day I'd gone to finish up some final details," she said, pointing to the mountain peak.

"I'd love to be able to do something so creative."

"Your uncle says you draw."

George laughed. "That's giving it more credit than it deserves. I've *tried* to draw."

"Perhaps you need more practice."

"Perhaps," he said and strolled around the studio, his hands in his jacket pockets.

Miranda had thought he might recognize her from the ball now that they were talking, just the two of them, but apparently he didn't. He was more relaxed now that his uncle wasn't in the room, and as they talked about her paintings Miranda felt herself warming to him.

She regretted that he didn't treat her the same way he had at the ball. He'd been amusing and flirtatious then, but of course the circumstances couldn't be more different. George was polite and friendly tonight, but nothing more. That would no doubt change if she told him she was the mysterious lady. Miranda suspected he'd be disappointed to find out he'd danced with her and not some irresistible siren.

Having completed a tour of the studio, George said,

"I'm sorry if we intruded on you tonight."

She frowned. "What?"

"You didn't look particularly happy to see me and my uncle."

Miranda could have sunk straight into the floor. It was one thing to be annoyed with her parents, but quite another to be inhospitable to guests. Although, truthfully, she'd thought she'd hidden it from them.

"I was surprised," Miranda said, knowing she sounded flustered. "I didn't know we were having company."

He nodded, not looking entirely convinced. "What do you do besides paint?"

The comment came across as almost an insult, as though painting couldn't possibly be a fulfilling occupation. But Miranda wasn't about to discuss the details of her life with George. "This and that. What do you do?"

"This and that."

Miranda didn't glare but it must have been obvious that she wanted to because he laughed.

"I'm sorry. I couldn't resist." He cleared his throat, maybe waiting for her to laugh, but when she didn't he went on. "I help my father and uncle on the estate."

"That must be interesting."

"Parts of it are. I like working on the accounting."

Miranda couldn't hold back a grimace. Math.

George laughed again. "Not your favorite subject?"

"Not at all," she said.

"Perhaps you need to practice," he said, cocking a brow, and this time she did laugh.

"Perhaps," she said.

Just then Ebenezer walked into the room. "What's

funny?" he asked.

"Nothing," George said. "Just chatting."

Ebenezer looked like he wanted to insist on hearing the joke, but let it go. "It's time we took our leave."

"Thank you for showing me the studio," George said before leaving the room.

Ebenezer kissed Miranda's hand. "Until we meet again."

"Goodbye," she said, pulling out of his grip.

He followed George, and soon Miranda heard her parents saying goodbye to them in the hall.

Her good mood disappeared at once to be replaced by irritation. No. By anger. She simply must talk to her parents about what they'd done tonight. There was no need to be subtle about it, as her mother was obviously feeling healthy. Miranda heard them climbing the stairs and rushed out to the hall.

"Mother? Father?" she said, hands on her hips.

They stopped to look down at her, both clearly pleased with their evening.

"Yes?" Mrs. Harlake asked.

Now that Miranda was faced with it, she didn't know if she should say anything. She didn't want to upset her parents. But no. If she didn't confront them, they might do this again. Peter would be gone for weeks yet.

Miranda raised her chin. "Why did you invite the Rockfords over?"

"To show Ebenezer the gallery," Mr. Harlake said. "He brought George with him at the last minute."

"So it wasn't anything to do with me?" Miranda asked, feeling rather foolish.

Her parents exchanged a glance and came back

down the stairs.

Mrs. Harlake sighed. "There's no reason you shouldn't get to know Ebenezer a little better."

Miranda gasped. "I knew it!"

"Don't be so sure you don't like him," Mr. Harlake said. "He's interesting and intelligent, and with—"

"I'm engaged!" she said, her voice rising to a high pitch. "I'm marrying Peter!"

Her parents looked shocked and Miranda wondered if, like her, they couldn't recall the last time she'd raised her voice to them.

"There's no need to yell," her mother said, rubbing her temple.

Mr. Harlake put an arm around his wife. "No, indeed. We agreed to this engagement, but that doesn't mean we consider the matter settled."

"But it *is* settled! I know my own heart and I won't change my mind." Miranda hoped she sounded convincing, but it was difficult when she knew she was lying and would break off the engagement within a year.

"I know you feel that way now, but feelings change. You're so young," her father said.

Mrs. Harlake crossed her arms. "You aren't marrying Peter for months, and before you do, your father and I will entertain whatever guests we see fit. My head is throbbing. I'm going to bed." She turned on her heel and marched up the stairs.

Miranda was at once sorry she'd given her mother a headache and alarmed by her statement. Would they invite Ebenezer here regularly? Were they going to parade other men in front of her in hopes she would fall in love with one of them?

"Mother, I'm sorry, I…"

But her mother just waved a hand without turning around.

"Was that really necessary, Miranda?" Mr. Harlake asked tiredly before following his wife.

Miranda stood at the bottom of the staircase until the upstairs light flickered out, then trudged up the stairs as if she were climbing a mountain.

Chapter Thirteen

Miranda's parents didn't mention the incident the next day at breakfast. They'd either forgiven her or decided to pretend it hadn't happened. She suspected the latter.

After eating, Mrs. Harlake even went so far as to invite Miranda for a walk in the garden. As this was unusual, Miranda took it as a gesture of forgiveness. They didn't talk about Ebenezer or Peter, but discussed plans for their trip to Hollingsford.

When her mother went upstairs to rest, Miranda made her way to the gazebo. She hadn't been sitting there long when her father jogged across the lawn, waving a piece of paper above his head. Miranda rose, expecting a telegram or other important news.

Mr. Harlake ran up the steps and before Miranda could even ask blurted out, "We're invited to the Rockfords' country estate!" He sat on a bench and caught his breath.

"What on earth for?" Miranda asked, sitting beside him.

"Ebenezer wants me to look over the gallery and see if any paintings are in need of restoration."

"I'm sure you'll have an interesting time."

"*We* will. You're invited, too."

"Me?" She narrowed her eyes at her father. "I told you last night, I'm marrying Peter. I'm not interested in

Ebenezer."

Mr. Harlake looked insulted. "Don't be so suspicious. I didn't invite myself. Ebenezer sent the invitation, and furthermore I told him weeks ago that you're seeing someone."

"Then why are you still trying to throw me at him?"

"There's no *throwing*. Besides, you aren't married yet."

Miranda crossed her arms and legs tightly. "I'm not going." She didn't know where the words had come from, but apparently she'd uttered them. After the ball she'd decided to stand up for herself more and this was a perfect place to start. Peter would be proud.

Mr. Harlake fanned himself with what Miranda could now see was a letter. "Don't be foolish, Miranda."

"I'm not foolish. I don't want to be in an uncomfortable situation again like I was last night."

Her father cocked his eyebrow. "You'd give up a chance to see their extensive art collection merely to avoid Ebenezer?"

"Yes." She set her feet back on the ground.

"You don't even need to see him," he said, stroking his mustache. "I'll deal with him. You can simply enjoy their hospitality and look over their art. They have a collection of antique silver and at least two marble statues from Rome. Then there are the paintings and tapestries…"

She uncrossed her arms. "How old are the tapestries?"

"At least three hundred years. And," he said, with an air of someone who'd already won their argument, "they have original pastel drawings from the sixteen hundreds."

Miranda groaned and collapsed against the back of the bench. "Fine. I'll come. But I'm not talking to Ebenezer any more than necessary."

"I knew you wouldn't want to miss this."

"Is mother eager to see the statues? I know how much she loves Roman art."

Mr. Harlake stood up. "She isn't up for traveling right now."

"Shouldn't we stay home with her if she isn't feeling well?"

"She'll have Esther. She won't mind."

"If you're sure," Miranda said, following him down the gazebo steps. "When are we leaving?"

"Monday."

"Then I'd better go into town and tell Emily I can't have lunch with her next week."

"I'll ask Bramwell to get the trunks down," Mr. Harlake said, folding the letter and tucking it into his pocket.

As they walked across the lawn Miranda realized the visit might mean seeing George again. If he was there she'd be on edge all the time, worrying he'd realize she'd been his partner at the ball. Miranda wasn't sure why it mattered if he did. Maybe because it would be hard to explain why she hadn't identified herself since that night, or because it was embarrassing that she'd been so forgettable George hadn't figured it out himself. She'd have thought her voice or her eyes would have given her away. At any rate, she had the feeling she'd never feel truly relaxed around George until the truth came out.

****

When Miranda walked into Darlington's, Emily waved her over to the counter. As soon as she saw

Miranda's face, she frowned. "What's wrong?"

"Nothing too serious," Miranda said, leaning against the counter. "But I've come to tell you I can't make our lunch next week after all. I'm sorry I have to cancel, but my father just told me we're going to the Rockfords' country house for a visit."

Emily set a dish of black licorice beside the cash register. "I've driven by there with Nathaniel. It's a beautiful house and I daresay you'll have a good time."

Miranda propped her chin in her hand and shrugged.

"Won't you?" Emily asked.

Miranda tried to smile, not wanting to take her sour mood out on her friend. "I'd better go. I just wanted to tell you we'll have to reschedule our lunch."

Emily came out from behind the counter. "I'll tell you what. Why don't we have lunch now? We can stay here or go over to Lamberton's for a change."

"Let's go to Lamberton's."

"I'll get my bag and tell Nathaniel I'm stepping out."

As they walked down the street, Miranda and Emily talked about goings-on around town. Miranda sensed that Emily was waiting until they reached Lamberton's to delve further into her problem. It was sweet, really, and she appreciated it more than she'd have thought. Miranda wasn't accustomed to sharing her problems with anyone but Peter. She was glad she'd taken the time to get to know Emily. Since the ball Miranda had ceased to see her as only an acquaintance—she felt like a true friend now.

At Lamberton's they were seated at a table toward the back, perfect for a private conversation. After ordering lunch and getting their drinks from the waitress,

Emily looked at Miranda expectantly.

Miranda had to laugh. "I feel as if you're trying to read my mind, Emily."

"Only your face. What's wrong?"

Miranda leaned back in her chair, drumming her fingers on the table. "It isn't much of a problem, as problems go. I don't want to go to the Rockfords'."

"Can't you tell your parents you want to stay home?" Emily asked and sipped her lemonade.

"I did, but my father insists. I do want to see their art collection."

"Then you'll enjoy yourself, I imagine."

"Yes, but that's not the main issue. It's—" Miranda stopped talking when the waitress returned with their food.

Once she was out of earshot, Emily said, "Go on," and dipped a spoon into her soup.

"It's George." Miranda leaned closer. "The truth is, I don't especially like him. He was obnoxious when we were children and doesn't seem much better now. But this is where it gets complicated." She sipped her iced tea and took a few bites of her club sandwich, while Emily looked like she was going to prod her physically to get her to continue her story. Miranda dabbed her mouth with a napkin and went on. "At the masked ball, I danced with one man half the night. He was sweet and flirtatious and quite good-looking. I've since found out it was George."

Emily's eyes widened. "You're certain?"

"Yes, Peter told me the next day."

"Does George know you were his partner?"

"No, he came to supper last night and didn't give even a hint that he recognized me. You remember my mask—it covered almost my entire face."

Emily looked at her thoughtfully for a moment. "Perhaps you *do* like George. I don't mean romantically, but you said you got along well at the ball. How was he last night?"

"Friendly, but not flirtatious. I have the feeling he doesn't like me, either."

Emily laughed. "That's nonsense, Miranda. George not flirting doesn't mean he doesn't like you. Maybe you need to look past what you thought of him as a child and get to know him better now before you write him off."

"But Emily," she said, "he still acts ridiculous. He knocked me over that day at the restaurant, and just recently I saw him cavorting with his friends. Almost every time I see him he's acting like a ten-year-old."

"He and his friends do get up to their share of skylarking. But when George comes into the shop alone or with a young woman, he's always polite."

As they finished lunch, Miranda considered Emily's words. Maybe she was right and it wasn't fair to judge George based on his more indiscreet moments. He'd been absolutely captivating at the ball, and not remotely offensive when he'd come to supper.

Miranda and Emily spent the rest of their lunch discussing Emily's plans to improve the bedroom she and Nathaniel had at home.

As they walked back to Darlington's, Miranda realized this was a perfect opportunity to find out if Peter was right about George's dating habits. "Do you ever see George at the restaurant with women?" she asked.

"Yes, about once a week."

"Who is he walking out with?"

Emily squinted up at the sky as though trying to

remember. "I don't know all of their names, but it's someone different every week. He usually brings them in on Saturday afternoon."

"Anyone in particular?"

"No, he never brings the same woman twice. Why?"

"I was just wondering about something Peter said. But it doesn't matter. Come, let's go peek in at Easton's." She took Emily's arm and they crossed the street to look at gowns in the shop window.

****

Sooner than she would have liked, Miranda was sitting in the carriage with her father, the Rockfords' house getting closer by the minute. The ride hadn't been long, as their country estate was in the neighboring town of Middleton.

The Rockfords' sprawling, three-storied white house was enclosed by a wraparound porch, and multiple outbuildings were scattered around the acres of green lawns and woodlands.

As the carriage came to a halt, the front doors opened and Ebenezer, accompanied by Mr. and Mrs. Rockford, stepped outside. Mr. Rockford and his brother Ebenezer could have been twins, right down to their well-trimmed beards. Mrs. Rockford had a kind face, and it seemed George had inherited his blue eyes from her.

Mr. Harlake exited the carriage first, then helped Miranda out. He looked so happy Miranda thought he might break into a jig. She took his arm as they approached the house.

"Good afternoon, we're so happy to have you," Mrs. Rockford said, smiling.

Mr. Harlake brought Miranda forward. "This is my daughter, Miranda. I daresay you've met at one point or another over the years."

Mr. Rockford nodded at Miranda. "Yes, we have."

"Not for quite some time, though," Mrs. Rockford said, with what Miranda felt was a rather appraising look.

"Hello," Miranda said, smiling at the group.

Ebenezer stepped forward. "Splendid to see you again."

"And you." Miranda put her hands behind her back as nonchalantly as she could. She didn't want a repeat of the hand-kissing from the other night.

"You have little ones of your own, don't you?" Mr. Harlake asked the Rockfords.

"Not so little anymore," Mrs. Rockford said. "But yes, they're off with George somewhere."

So George was here. Miranda had hoped that since he wasn't there to welcome them that meant he'd stayed back in Deerwood.

"Shall we go in?" Mr. Rockford asked, gesturing to the door.

"I'll have Sally show you to your rooms," Mrs. Rockford said as they walked into the house. "Lunch will be in an hour."

"Thank you," Miranda said, looking around as subtly as she could. The rooms she could see were elegantly furnished and comfortable. Whoever had decorated this house had an artistic eye and she was anxious to see the rest of it.

Sally, a maid, soon arrived and escorted Miranda and Mr. Harlake to their connecting rooms on the second floor. After seeing her father settled, Miranda went into her bedroom. It was good sized, with two windows overlooking the back of the property. Woods surrounded the house and grounds, and in the distance a blue lake glistened in the sunshine. Miranda was glad she'd brought her trousers, because as soon as she had time she'd walk to the lake with her sketchbook. She removed her hat and set it on the desk, deciding to make the most of this visit. The room was comfortable enough, and the Rockfords had greeted them warmly. Perhaps staying here wouldn't be so bad. She only hoped Ebenezer wouldn't be a nuisance.

Miranda unpacked and had just finished a sketch of her view when there was a knock on the door and her father came in.

"It's a pretty room," he said. "Old house. Good bones. I'm eager to see the rest of it."

"Yes, and the gallery," Miranda said.

"I'd like to go out and paint the lake."

"I had the same idea," Miranda said, holding her sketch up for him to see.

Mr. Harlake looked at it for a moment and Miranda expected a critique, but instead he checked his pocket watch. "It's time for lunch. Let's go down."

They walked downstairs and while searching for the dining room found a small parlor overlooking the gardens. Lilac bushes crowded the edge of the patio, almost obscuring a winding path that disappeared into a deep grove of maple trees. Three wooden swings hung from a towering oak and Miranda was just wondering if they could hold an adult when she heard children's voices coming from the next room, followed by what sounded like a reprimand.

"Could that be the dining room?" Miranda asked, pointing to a door on the far side of the room.

"Perhaps," Mr. Harlake said and strode across the

parlor.

Miranda hesitated, not wanting to disturb anyone's privacy. "Should we knock?"

In answer her father opened the door and walked in without even a backward glance at her.

They had indeed found the dining room. They also found Mr. and Mrs. Rockford, three children, and George, who was holding a pile of broken crockery.

"Who was responsible for it, then, Sybil?" Mr. Rockford asked, peering down at the oldest girl.

Sybil glanced at George, who gave her what looked like an encouraging nod.

Miranda felt they should make themselves known, but before she could speak a little boy said, "It wasn't me."

"No?" Mrs. Rockford asked, looking like she was trying to hold back a smile.

The boy shook his head.

"It seems we have a mystery on our hands," Mr. Rockford said, stroking his beard.

The other little girl suddenly looked up and pointed at Miranda and her father. "Who are they?"

All the Rockfords turned at once to look at them. They didn't look embarrassed to be overheard, and in fact Mr. Rockford laughed. "Come in, we're just having a little discussion. It can wait, though." He nodded to a footman, who took the porcelain pieces from George and carried them out of the room. The children visibly relaxed when the evidence of their apparent misdeed was gone.

George arranged the children in a line in front of him. "Time for introductions." He put his hand on each child's head in turn. "This is Sybil, Harriet, and

Nicholas."

"Nice to meet you," Miranda said.

Harriet was a carbon copy of George, but the other two children were fair. It was hard to discern their ages, but Sybil didn't look older than twelve. Miranda had seen them from time to time with their parents in town but had never spoken to them.

"Are you the painters?" the middle child, Harriet, asked.

"Yes, we are," Mr. Harlake said, getting that soft look on his face he always did when speaking to children. He knelt down to the girl's level. "Do you like to paint?"

"I don't really know how," Harriet admitted.

"Perhaps you'd like to learn," Miranda said.

Harriet's eyes lit up. "Yes, I would! Could you teach me?"

"Miss Harlake is probably busy," George said.

When Miranda looked up, she saw him gazing proudly at Harriet, as though it had taken great nerve to speak to strangers.

"I might have time to teach you," Miranda said, smiling at Harriet.

"Me, too!" Nicholas said, running over and taking Miranda's hand.

Miranda looked into his eager face as Mr. Harlake laughed, probably imagining two more burgeoning artists to take under his wing.

"Perhaps later in the week, Nicholas," George said. "Come along."

Nicholas kept his hand in Miranda's and guided her over to the table, where he took the seat beside her.

Ebenezer strolled in and sat on Miranda's other side.

"All settled in?"

"Not yet, but the room is lovely, as is the house," she said, including Mr. and Mrs. Rockford in her compliment.

"I'm pleased you like it," Ebenezer said before Sybil started interrogating Miranda about painting.

Lunch was long, with conversation coming at Miranda from almost all sides. Everyone but George seemed interested in her. He ate his lunch without commenting on much but cast benevolent smiles on the children and occasionally addressed the butler or the footmen as though he was in charge of the meal and not his mother.

After dessert, Miranda set her fork down and was about to excuse herself when Ebenezer addressed George. She paid no attention to their conversation until she heard her name.

"George, will you give Miranda a tour of the house? She should have some idea of where she's going so she doesn't get lost," he said.

George's brow creased for a second, but then he smiled. "I'll be happy to take Miranda and her father on a tour."

"Not necessary to take Lucas," Ebenezer said. "We're going up to the gallery."

Miranda wanted to protest that she'd much rather go to the gallery than look over the house, but her father and the other adults were staring at her as though they expected her to jump at the chance for a tour. "A tour would be helpful," she said, trying to sound enthusiastic.

"We'll help with the tour," Nicholas said, pushing his chair back. "The tree house first."

Sybil rose. "You'll want to see the stables. I'll show

you my pony."

"No, no," Mr. Rockford said. "Miranda and George will be fine on their own. Besides, you have lessons this afternoon."

"That's right," Nicholas said, frowning. His sisters obviously shared his disappointment.

"Never mind," George told the children in a consoling voice. "You'll be able to see Miss Harlake later. And it isn't as though *you* need a tour of the house." He paused and put a hand to his chin, a concerned look on his face. "Wait—do you? Have you forgotten where your bedrooms are?"

"No!" Harriet said, laughing.

All three children giggled as if it was the silliest thing they'd ever heard, then got up and followed their mother out of the room.

As soon as they were gone, Mr. Harlake, Mr. Rockford and Ebenezer practically sprinted out the door.

Miranda avoided looking at George for as long as she could, but at last she took one more sip of coffee and looked up to find him watching her intently. She wondered if he recognized her from the ball, but if he wasn't sure it was her, Miranda certainly wasn't going to tell him.

He shook his head slightly and rose, setting his folded napkin on the table. "Shall we?"

As they left the dining room it was hard to tell whose steps were more reluctant.

Chapter Fourteen

For the first ten minutes George gave Miranda a detailed description of the grounds she'd yet to see, after which he took to pointing at doors and saying, "Drawing room," or "Library," but not letting Miranda look inside. She supposed it didn't matter very much, but if she was getting a tour it might be nice to actually see the rooms. Hopefully the gallery would be included in the tour. If it was, perhaps Miranda could insist that George go back to whatever it was he'd rather be doing and she could peruse the art alone.

Miranda considered starting a conversation, but about what? If she asked him about himself, that might seem nosy. Besides, she'd known all about him for years. Although, after the ball, she must admit a slight uptick in her interest in him. She wondered what Peter would do if he were here. Probably feign interest in the ceiling moldings or ask for a lecture about cornices. She laughed softly, thinking of it.

"What's funny?" George asked, turning to look at her.

Miranda covered her mouth, shaking her head slightly to indicate it was nothing of consequence. She could hardly tell him she was imagining her best friend mocking him.

George shrugged and pointed at another door as they continued down the hall. "Billiard room."

Miranda held back a sigh. As they climbed the stairs to the third floor, she finally saw something of interest—a stained glass window depicting an intricate floral design. She couldn't walk by without trying to get a better look. Miranda stood on tiptoes, watching the colors dance when sunlight shone through the window.

George continued up the stairs and it was some moments before he seemed to realize he'd lost his companion. He came back down and Miranda didn't turn to him until he spoke.

"Lovely, isn't it?" he said.

"Yes. Where did it come from? Not Deerwood, surely."

"No, it was imported from out of the country long ago when the house was built. It was a gift from my great-great-grandfather to his wife. Her name was Lily. See the flowers?"

"How sweet." Miranda stepped back a few paces, trying to get a better look, and nearly went over the banister.

George quickly put out a hand to keep her from falling over, and Miranda somehow ended up in his arms.

"Oh! I'm all right now," she said. "Thank you." Miranda felt more comfortable than she should have, most likely because being in his arms was familiar to her. He smelled the same as he had that night. A foreign sort of cologne, like it was made of exotic flowers from a distant land.

George looked perplexed as he stared into her face. Finally, he let his arms fall away from her. "I can see you're easily distracted by art."

"Not usually enough to topple down the stairs," she

said with a light laugh.

He surveyed her for a moment, then looked up at the stairs, obviously debating something. "I think you've seen enough of the house for today. I'd rather show you something you'll enjoy more." George started back down the stairs, the rest of the tour apparently forgotten.

"Where are we going?" she asked, trying to keep up with him.

"It's outside. Well, partially. You'll see."

Miranda followed along, glad George's less stoic side had returned. When they reached the first floor, George strode down a long hallway, then turned and went down another hall. At length they came to a door.

"Here it is," he said, and stepped aside so she could enter first.

Miranda walked into the room but stopped after a few paces. Behind her, George laughed and she had the feeling she'd reacted as he'd expected her to. Probably the way everyone who saw this room reacted.

They were in a round room that looked like a small library or perhaps a study. The far side of the chamber was made up entirely of stained-glass windows that extended up to the ceiling, where they formed a domed roof.

Miranda slowly walked toward the windows, trying to take in all the colors and images. "It's spectacular!" She stepped right up to the glass. "I've never seen anything like it."

"Yes, it's quite special," he said. "My great-great-grandparents had a tradition of gifting each other pieces of stained glass. Over the years they had it installed in here. I never met them, but my father remembers them from when he was a small boy. He said Lily called this her rainbow room, and she'd sit in here during sunrise and sunset, when the colors are their brightest."

"That makes me love it even more," Miranda said, running her hands over the image of an ocean scene. "I wonder why they picked each panel? They're so unique."

"I always wondered that, too. Maybe they were special to them for some reason, or perhaps they simply liked the design."

They stood in silence, looking at the glass. After a time Miranda glanced at George, who was watching her. His face had taken on a hue of the rich colors, like a sunset was playing across his features.

"Would you like to see the gallery?" he asked.

"Oh, yes," she said, going for the door.

George laughed. "Eager, are you?"

"I admit it's what I wanted to see most when my father told me we were coming here to see if any of your paintings need restoration."

"Do they?" George asked.

"Your uncle thought they might."

"Hm," he said. "I had no idea. Well, I'll be curious to see what your father thinks." He crossed the room and disappeared into a little nook, then called her over.

"Aren't we going upstairs?" she asked, pointing to the door they'd entered through.

He peeked around the corner. "Yes, but since I'm meant to be giving you a tour, we'll go this way."

Curious, Miranda followed him down a short hallway. He pushed open a door featuring another stained-glass window, all blues and purples, and they were in a lush garden full of fragrant flowers. Between two enormous rhododendrons was a rose-covered arch that led to a winding, cobbled path. They followed this and before long came to the oak tree Miranda had seen earlier. The swings were empty but still swinging as if they'd recently been vacated.

"The children must have just been here," Miranda said, speaking her thoughts aloud.

"Probably," George agreed, looking at his pocket watch. "They'll be done with their lessons by now. After I show you the gallery, I'll find them and take them for a walk."

"Doesn't their nanny do that?" Miranda asked.

"They don't have one. Now that they're older they have a tutor, but they don't need a nanny with me and my parents and my uncle to look after them."

"I suppose not," Miranda said, though she knew this was unusual. Mrs. Tolwood, with her five children, had employed a nanny when the children were small. Since Miranda had been young at the time, too, she could attest to the fact that Mrs. Tolwood had needed all the help she could get with five, sometimes six, children underfoot.

They entered the house through the parlor and went down so many hallways Miranda lost track. As they mounted the stairs to the third floor, she wondered if they'd encounter her father and Ebenezer. She'd love to get her father's opinion about the art but didn't want to deal with Ebenezer at the moment.

When they reached the top of the stairs, George threw open a set of decorative double doors and stepped aside so Miranda could enter first. Her shoes echoed lightly on the tiled floor as she walked about the chamber, too overcome with wonder to speak.

The Rockfords did indeed have a fantastic collection that must have taken years to build. So many paintings, so many styles. Miranda took as much time as she liked observing each painting, but it was never quite long enough because she was anxious to move on to the next piece.

As engrossing as the paintings were, she wanted to ask George where she could find the pastels. George. She'd almost forgotten he was with her. Miranda looked behind her and saw him lounging on a sofa, hands folded over his stomach, eyes closed.

"Are you exhausted from showing me your house?" she asked lightly.

"No," he said, opening his eyes. "But not many places in the house are as quiet as the gallery. It's one of the only places the children don't barge in and break one's repose."

"They seemed interested in art when I spoke to them at lunch."

George rose and walked toward her. "They're interested in creating it, but not so much in appreciating the finer works." He met her eyes. "Do you have a favorite?"

"Not yet. I haven't had time to look at them all, Do you?"

"A few. I'll show you." He brought Miranda over to a large painting of a sunny meadow covered in bluebells, then a snowy, barren landscape with moonlight reflected on the drifts, and finally to a portrait of a young woman with rosy cheeks.

Miranda moved in closer to look. "Who is she?"

"We don't know. There's no name on the back, or even a date. But she must be a relative. Why else would she be here?"

"The work is exquisite, and so is she."

"I've always liked the way the colors blend."

"Yes, the artist used pastels," she said, trying to hide her excitement.

"How can you tell?" he asked, a slight grin coming to his face.

She wondered for a moment if he was teasing her, but answered nonetheless. "I use pastels, too, so I recognized it."

"Do you? How interesting. I wish I could do something like that."

"Well, as we discussed the other night, maybe you need to practice."

"Maybe. I'll need to learn to draw before I can start with colors."

Miranda was tempted to ask him why he hadn't practiced more, and what else he did with his time, but it seemed too personal. "My father said you have other pastels. Are they in here?" She'd looked around but hadn't seen any others.

"I don't know the difference between pastels and anything else, but we have another room with some of our older paintings."

Miranda's heart beat a little faster. The pastels from the sixteen-hundreds. Masters must have made them. "Where are they?"

Not seeming to notice her agitation, he checked his watch. "It's getting close to supper time, but we can look for a few minutes."

"Where?"

As he guided her to the end of the gallery, Miranda promised herself she'd return to study the rest of the paintings again soon. Other doors led off the gallery, too. Apparently the Rockfords had their own private museum. Just before they reached the staircase, George led Miranda into a room lit by tall windows.

There they were. A few portraits and a number of landscapes. Each one was extraordinary. Miranda could have spent hours staring at them. She almost laughed when her eyes fell on a still life of grapes and apples. Her father was right. They really could be beautiful. In the midst of admiring a picture of a sailboat drifting on a calm lake, Miranda had a distinct feeling that she'd never match this type of artistry.

"What sort of pictures do you make?" George asked, breaking her out of her reverie.

"I like drawing our horses and painting landscapes or flowers. I'd like to do more portraits. But I doubt if I'll ever be as good as these artists."

"Perhaps you will, if you *practice*," he said, cocking an eyebrow. Again she wondered if he was mocking her.

"Perhaps," she said, and left him standing there as she strolled about the room.

Before long it was time for supper. They didn't speak as they made their way downstairs, and Miranda was glad when they entered the busy dining room. The children leapt at George, demanding to know where he'd been all afternoon. Ebenezer had an oddly smug look on his face when George told the children he'd been with Miranda. She didn't pay him any mind, but took a seat beside her father. They tried to chat about the gallery, but there were too many other conversations to follow.

After supper Miranda and her father went back to the gallery and stayed until the light failed. Mr. Harlake said he didn't think any of the paintings needed work, but he'd examine them all more closely in the morning.

On the way out, her father asked, "So what do you

think of the place?"

"It's beautiful, and we haven't even seen all of it yet."

"You didn't see the whole house on your tour?"

"No, but I don't know if I really need to. I'll find my way around in due course. Anyway, it isn't as if we'll be here long."

"Did you see Ebenezer at all this afternoon?" he asked in a would-be nonchalant tone.

An exasperated groan slipped out before Miranda could stop it. "You said I needn't spend time with him if I came along."

"I only wondered. It wouldn't be unusual to meet up with him in his own house."

Miranda looked at him, shaking her head. "I should have known. I'm off to bed."

"It's not *that* late," her father said. "If it makes you feel better, I'll stop talking about Ebenezer."

"No, I'm going to my room. I think I'll write to Peter."

He chuckled. "Miranda…"

"Goodnight," she said, giving him a wave. She had no intention of writing to Peter, and furthermore she wouldn't even have minded seeing the Rockfords again. But it had been a long day and she needed time to settle before she tried to sleep in a new place.

On the way to her room Miranda heard a high-pitched giggle, and upon looking out the window she saw George pushing Sybil on the swing. The other children stood by, waiting their turn. One of these days, Miranda would sneak down there and use the swing herself.

****

The next day Miranda didn't spend time with

George, but he seemed to always be in the thick of things around the house. Talking to the cook, walking about the grounds with his father, cutting flowers with his mother in the garden, and especially playing with the children.

Miranda and her father went up to the gallery immediately after breakfast and, even though it meant more time with Ebenezer, she couldn't resist the chance to linger. She took her time over the pastels and afterwards peeked into a few other rooms, where she found the antique silver and Roman statues. Miranda stayed in the gallery until it was time for lunch. On her way downstairs she stopped by her bedroom to fetch her sketchbook and change into her walking clothes.

The dining room was deserted, but food was set out on the sideboard. After eating, Miranda left through the patio and made her way to the arch in the hedge, guessing it led to the forest path. It did, and she was soon surrounded by tall, leafy trees. It was so invigorating she picked up her pace and reached the lake twenty minutes later. She'd expected to have it to herself, but there was already somebody there—George and his siblings were sitting on the shore with their feet in the water.

Not wanting to intrude, Miranda settled herself close to the trees and pulled out her sketchbook. It was peaceful by the lake. The sun sparkled on the water, and every so often the sound of children's voices, mingled with George's deeper one, reached her on the light breeze. Suddenly inspired, Miranda flipped to the next page and started sketching George and the children. She'd just finished Sybil's skirt when George rose and started chasing the children around. They ran in all directions, laughing. George looked relaxed and happy, a far cry from the man she'd thought obnoxious and had wanted to avoid. A few minutes later, Mrs. Rockford walked over from the other direction and gathered up the children. Miranda couldn't hear what they were saying, but they'd clearly rather have stayed with George.

He watched as they walked away, waving now and then when they looked back at him. Once they'd rounded the bend and were out of sight, George ran a hand through his hair and turned around. It was inevitable that he saw Miranda. He looked embarrassed, maybe from being caught playing, or maybe because he hadn't known he was observed.

Miranda rose to go, but George waved, indicating that she should join him. She gathered her things and walked down to the shore.

"Hi," he said, blue eyes shining. His top two buttons were undone and his hair was unkempt, which only accentuated his good looks.

"Hello."

"Care to join me?" he asked, sitting down in the sand and resting his hands on his knees.

"For a little while." Miranda sat down and stretched her legs out in front of her. "I hope you don't mind that I was drawing you and the children. I came down to sketch the lake and didn't think anyone else would be here. I didn't say hello because I didn't want to disturb you."

"You wouldn't have been disturbing us. May I see the drawing?"

Miranda handed him the sketchbook. He smiled when he saw the drawing and, after a questioning look and her nod, flipped through the book. While he leafed through it Miranda tapped the toes of her shoes together, looking over his shoulder.

"These are very good," he said, handing it back.

"Thank you. Perhaps one day you could show me some of your drawings."

He picked up a small rock and skipped it across the water. "No, I'd be embarrassed to show you."

"There's no need for that," she said. "Everyone has to start out somewhere."

"Maybe you could give me some advice on how to improve my work."

"What do you like to draw?"

"I've been practicing drawing fruit. You know, it can't move."

Miranda broke into laughter before she could stop herself.

"What's so funny?" he asked, squinting against the sun as he looked at her.

"My father's always trying to convince me to draw still lifes."

George skipped another rock. "Did he teach you to draw?"

"Yes, and my mother. They hired tutors, too." Miranda wanted to change the subject, but George asked question after question about her art experience and education. When she was finally able to switch topics, Miranda asked, "How old are your siblings?"

"Sybil's twelve, Harriet is eleven, and Nicholas just turned nine."

"They're all so close together. At first I thought the girls were twins."

"Most people do, but they're just very close in age. Do you have brothers or sisters?"

"No, but when I was younger I wished I did. I always hoped my mother would bring home a baby. I practically had a sibling, though, because my best friend lived at Majestic Oaks. Well, in a house on the grounds."

"Who is she? Did she go to our school?"

"Peter Tolwood," Miranda said.

George looked surprised. "Peter's your best friend?"

"Yes. He has brothers and sisters that I played with, too, so I wasn't lonely growing up. But it was a long time before I stopped hoping for a baby." She didn't elaborate any further, already surprised at herself for sharing so much with George. He didn't need to know about her childhood dreams.

The conversation lapsed as they both looked out over the water, sitting in silence until the sky hinted at sunset.

"Time to go in. It will be time for supper soon," George said after a time and put his shoes back on.

Miranda drew her knees up and wrapped her arms around them. "It's so pretty here."

"It's one of my favorite spots. My mother has a cottage on Marigold Lake. It's even more secluded than this." He rose and offered Miranda his hand.

She took it and stood up. "That sounds lovely."

As Miranda bent to brush the sand off her skirt, she noticed George staring at her feet and realized the cuffs of her trousers were showing. She blushed, not sure if she should explain. George just met her eyes and smiled. If he wasn't going to mention it, she wouldn't either.

Miranda had only been at George's house for three days, but she was seeing a whole other side of him. He hadn't done anything rude, and he was so sweet with his siblings. George was more like the man from the ball and almost nothing like the boy who'd acted foolish in their school days or the young man who had knocked her over at Darlington's. From what she'd seen, he was helpful and kind, and as they walked back to the house Miranda began to wonder if she'd ever really known George at all.

Chapter Fifteen

The next day Miranda spent the morning with her father, then took a stroll to the lake. She returned in time for lunch, which was a loud affair with all the children in attendance. They hadn't yet tired of talking to Miranda and Mr. Harlake about art, but had taken to asking just as many questions about Miranda's life. They wanted to know all about her home, as well as her favorite color, flower and dessert. (Teal, bluets and apple pie.) Once they learned she'd gone to school with George, they had even more questions, most of which Miranda couldn't answer for fear of insulting him.

After lunch Mr. Harlake took Ebenezer to the gallery, but Miranda declined his offer to accompany them. She had an afternoon of drawing in mind and headed for her bedroom to get her sketchbook. As she passed through the drawing room she noticed a sunlit courtyard and couldn't resist stepping outside for a moment.

Miranda raised her face to the sky, and from a corner of her mind came the song Peter often hummed in her ear when they practiced dancing. She closed her eyes and tried to remember all the steps. Her skirt swished on the courtyard flags and she put her arms out as if Peter were really there.

She hadn't been dancing long when she was shocked to find herself taken into real arms, and a deep voice said, "It's easier with a partner."

"Oh!" Miranda's eyes snapped open and she came to an abrupt halt, stomping on George's foot.

George smiled as he bent down to rub his toes. "Ouch."

"What are you doing?" she asked, retreating a few steps.

"I'm sorry. You looked so happy, dancing in the sunshine, and I never could resist a good partner. Won't you continue?" He held his arms out and looked at her in such a way that Miranda knew she couldn't resist his invitation. Surprisingly, she didn't even want to try.

"There's no music," she said, not quite holding back a smile.

"Give me a moment," George said and walked into the house. A few minutes later he returned, carrying a phonograph.

He set it down on the courtyard floor. "Fast or slow?"

"We can't dance outside!" Miranda said.

"Why not?"

She glanced at the windows. "What if someone sees us?"

"Nobody would mind," he said with a small smile, as if amused it even crossed her mind that anyone would care.

With every moment George became less the man Miranda thought she knew. Well, what was the harm in a dance? She knew Peter would tell her to try something new.

"Slow," she said. "I'm not a very good dancer. I only learned how recently."

He went about setting up the phonograph, and

before long a tinkly tune came through the bell-shaped horn.

George made a little bow to Miranda. "Would you care to dance?"

"Why yes, I would," she said, dipping a curtsy.

George put an arm lightly around her waist and took her hand in his. They didn't speak, but looked at each other as they floated around the courtyard. The afternoon sun trickled through the trees to dapple the floor, and branches from the hydrangea bushes caught at their clothes.

"I believe we need a bigger dance floor," George said.

Miranda smiled. "Or perhaps a ballroom."

George laughed, then his brows furrowed as he met Miranda's eyes. He slowed to a stop and looked hard at Miranda's face, not releasing her from his arms. "It's you, isn't it?"

Miranda flushed. "What do you mean?" she asked, though she knew perfectly well what he meant. She should have known he'd discover the truth eventually, but she couldn't imagine worse timing. What if he told her father?

"You're the one from the ball," George said, and it was clear there was no doubt in his mind.

Miranda wanted to deny it, but there was no point. She took a deep breath and let it out slowly as she nodded.

George gazed at her for a long moment then said, "But how extraordinary. Why didn't you tell me?"

"It was a masked ball. It was supposed to be a secret."

"I meant later. The next day. Last week. Today."

It would be easier to gather her thoughts if Miranda weren't still held in his arms, the phonograph singing behind them. She couldn't tell George she'd kept the secret to herself because she didn't like him. Besides, that didn't seem to be true anymore. Miranda looked into his kind blue eyes. No, it wasn't true at all.

She might as well tell him the truth. "I wasn't supposed to be there, and I was afraid if I told you word might get back to my parents. Also, I thought you might be disappointed if you knew your partner was just Miranda, whom you've known for years, and not a mysterious new woman in town."

"I wouldn't have been disappointed, and I'm not sure I do know Miranda. I thought I did, but now I think I haven't been paying attention to her at all." His eyes took on that warm look they'd had at the ball.

"How did you know it was me?" Miranda asked as they started dancing again.

"I don't know. Perhaps the scent you're wearing, or the way you feel in my arms." He looked self-conscious as soon as he said it. "I'm surprised I didn't guess sooner. I looked for you at midnight. I was so disappointed when I couldn't find you."

Miranda glowed inside. "I had to leave early. My presence there wouldn't have been much of a secret once the mask came off."

"But why was it secret?" he asked, holding her a trifle closer.

"My father doesn't approve of balls. He thinks they're a waste of time and always tells me he's glad I don't like those sorts of things. I've tried to tell him I do, but he just won't listen."

"That sounds frustrating."

"It is," she said, frowning. "But it feels wrong to disagree with him. Since I'm my parents' only child, I've always felt it's somehow my…duty, I suppose you could say, to do what they want. That probably doesn't make sense."

"It does make sense. Sometimes I feel the same way." He paused and glanced at the house, then gave her a playful grin. "So even though your parents don't always let you do what you want, you find ways around their rules?"

"Oh, no," Miranda said. "It's highly unlike me to do anything like sneak out of the house. That was the first time I've ever done it. But for once I wanted to see what it was like. Dancing, music, meeting new people."

"I do remember you telling me it was your first ball." He raised his brows. "Wait…how did you guess it was me?"

"I didn't, but I found out later."

"How?" he asked as they passed by the phonograph.

"Peter told me the next day."

"Peter?" he asked. "How did he know? I didn't even see him that night."

"He saw you outside and you'd taken your mask off," she said.

"Were you disappointed it was me, and not a mysterious gentleman?"

"No, but I was surprised I didn't recognize you."

"I'm not. We haven't spent much time together since grammar school."

"That's true. But it isn't as if we haven't seen each other at all," she said.

"No, there was that time at Darlington's." He suddenly looked concerned. "Is your hand better?"

Miranda was surprised he remembered it had happened. "Yes, the cut wasn't deep."

"I'm glad. I was worried I'd affected your ability to paint."

"I was, too, at first. I did take a couple of days off from painting, but that was nice because I had time for other pursuits." She almost told him it was because she'd started questioning not only her talent but her passion for art, but she held back. She'd already told George too much about herself today. Funny, the George she'd thought she knew couldn't have drawn even a hello from her, but now she felt an unusual pull to share things with him she'd never told anyone, except maybe for Peter. Oh…perhaps that explained it. With Peter gone, she didn't have anyone to talk to. George was a convenient stand-in.

The music came to a stop. "Another?" George asked.

"Yes, please."

He restarted the phonograph, this time playing the faster tune. This didn't leave much opportunity for talking, but Miranda enjoyed herself nonetheless. George was even more attractive up close. Every feature seemed perfect, but it was the look in his eyes that was most alluring. Open, warm, welcoming. He'd always been handsome, of course, but Miranda had never allowed herself to appreciate it because he was usually acting like a mischievous fool. But she appreciated it now.

When the song ended, she stepped out of his arms, breathless.

"I'd say you're a very good dancer," George said as he picked up the phonograph to carry it into the house.

"Thank you. It's probably due to all the practice Peter insisted on."

"Peter taught you?"

"Yes, and he took his job as tutor seriously. But he always hummed while we practiced because we don't have a phonograph at home."

"That was kind of him," George said, and Miranda couldn't quite understand the look on his face. It bordered on disapproval, but hopefully she was wrong. Then again, he wouldn't be the first person to think it odd that her best friend was a man.

Miranda followed George into the parlor, where he set the phonograph on a table.

"Since we're clearing the air," he said, "I want to apologize for sending you that gown. It didn't occur to me that it was inappropriate."

"It was a kind thought," Miranda said. "I did appreciate it." If only he knew how much she'd wanted to keep it!

"Yes, but it seems I only caused you more discomfort. So again, I apologize."

"Thank you," she said.

As they stood facing each other in the quiet parlor Miranda wasn't sure what to say next.

"I think I'll go upstairs," she finally said, at the same moment he asked, "What are your plans for the afternoon?"

They both laughed and George gestured for her to speak first.

"I was on my way upstairs to get my sketchbook before I went out to the patio."

George seemed to consider for a moment, then asked, "Would it be all right if the children watched you draw?"

"It isn't very exciting."

"As you've seen, they're interested in art, but there isn't much I can teach them."

"I'd be happy to let them watch. Where should we go?"

"There are some interesting statues in the garden."

"That sounds perfect. I'll get my things and meet you there. If the children have any art supplies, you could bring those along."

"Excellent," George said. "We'll see you soon."

In her room, Miranda marveled at her strange afternoon. Dancing with George in the middle of the day! She gathered her sketchbook and pencils and went to the garden, where she found George, Sybil, Harriet and Nicholas sitting around a fountain, all with sketchbooks on their laps. Apparently Miranda had been promoted to professor. When she looked at the sketchbook in George's lap he shrugged and gave her a small smile.

"Will you teach me to draw a person?" Harriet asked at once.

"Or a duck," Nicholas suggested.

"Miranda may only want us to watch her," George said. "She might not want to instruct us."

"I don't mind," she said, though she'd never given lessons before. "You can stand behind me while I draw and I'll describe what I'm doing."

She sat in the grass and they clustered behind her as she sketched the fountain. It was simple enough. A round, marble pool with a pedestal in the center holding up a seashell-shaped basin. She explained how to get the right perspective and how to shade the drawing to look three-dimensional. Miranda had the feeling it was too complicated for Nicholas, who had simply drawn a duck, but the girls did well enough, and George made a realistic rendition of the fountain.

"You've practiced, I see?" Miranda asked when she looked at his drawing.

He glanced at Miranda's paper. "Not as much as I should."

Afterwards the children wanted to show Miranda the milkweed and butterflies, so she left her sketchbook beside the fountain and allowed them to lead her through the extensive gardens. After a time, they reached the outskirts of the forest and the children ran ahead.

"Do they know where they're going?" Miranda asked once they'd disappeared into the trees.

"Yes, we walk here regularly. They love spending time outside, especially if it means they're missing lessons."

"Does that happen often?"

"More than it should."

Miranda grinned. "And are you the instigator of these little jaunts?"

"Perhaps," he said, plucking at the tall grass as they walked.

"I'll take that as a yes."

George laughed. "I can't help it. It's so nice here during the summer, and Sybil will be going away to school soon. I want her to enjoy her free time while she can."

"Boarding school?" Miranda asked, surprised.

"No, she's going to the grammar school in town. The same one you and I went to. Now that she's older, it's important for her to meet more children her own age. Harriet will go next year."

Miranda couldn't help noticing the sad tone in his voice. "You'll miss having them around?"

"Yes, but it's not like I won't see them anymore, and Nicholas will still be at the house with his tutor." He paused and looked toward where the children had gone. "My mother will have more free time now. She'll enjoy that."

Miranda was about to ask what George would do with his free time when he had fewer children to look after, but Sybil ran out of the woods, urging them to hurry.

Miranda and George quickened their pace. They passed through a thick stand of white birch trees and came out in a field full of wildflowers. Nicholas scampered through the tall grass, chasing a butterfly, while the girls stood beside a patch of milkweed. Monarch butterflies flitted in and out among the plants.

Sybil walked over to stand beside Miranda. "Aren't they pretty?" she asked.

"Yes, they are," Miranda said, wishing she'd brought her sketchbook.

"We come here every year to see them, and in the fall we open the milkweeds so they can float through the forest," Harriet said. "I can't wait for that."

George ruffled her hair. "A few more months. We'd better get back to the house."

"We just got here," Harriet said.

"Just a little while longer," George said. "Why don't you go round up Nicholas? He's almost on the other side of the meadow."

The girls ran off to fetch their brother, leaving Miranda once more alone with George. She couldn't understand how she'd been so wrong about him. But maybe that was because she'd never spent much time with him before. This easygoing, charismatic side of George explained why he took a different woman to lunch at Darlington's every Saturday.

"Can I ask you something?" Miranda said, not having planned to speak at all.

"Of course."

"How are you so…different here?"

"What do you mean?" George asked, his smile fading.

"Never mind," she said, regretting she'd asked such a question. How could he possibly answer that? She turned to go back to the house.

George caught her elbow. "How am I different?"

Miranda couldn't tell him what she really meant. Her true question was, *How are you so much kinder than I thought? Why are you so irksome when I see you around town?* But there was no way she was going to ask him that. "Really, it's nothing. I think I know the answer to my own question," she said and tried to laugh. "I'm going back to the house. Goodbye."

"Wait, Miranda," he said, but she just smiled and went on her way. She'd come too close to offending him and embarrassing herself. She walked back to the garden and collected her sketchbook before returning to her bedroom.

****

Miranda didn't sit beside George during supper but observed him throughout the meal. Again he was helpful and friendly. He chatted with her father and Ebenezer, expressing great interest in the art gallery.

Mr. Harlake hadn't found much that needed restoration, which led Miranda to wonder if the very idea had simply been a ruse to get them to come here. But that seemed unlikely. Why would Ebenezer do that? It wasn't as though he still held any romantic notion, if you could even call it that, about marrying her. And it was just as unlikely that her father had contrived it somehow.

Miranda spoke with Mrs. Rockford during the meal and it passed pleasantly. After supper George took the children to the lake. He invited Miranda but she declined, having already spent too much time with him today.

She did accept her father's invitation to visit the gallery.

"Not much restoration needed?" Miranda asked as they stood in front of a five-foot-long canvas depicting rolling hills covered in glorious fall foliage. She'd wanted to look at the pastels, but her father said he'd seen enough of them. She would have gone to look alone but sensed he wanted her company after not seeing her all day. It crossed her mind that she could insist on him accompanying *her*, but it was simpler to go along with him to see the oil paintings.

Mr. Harlake ran a hand over his mustache. "There were a few minor issues, but nothing urgent. I arranged to come back in a few months and do some work. It will be a good chance for you to get some restoration experience."

"I don't have the skills for a project like that," Miranda said, shaking her head. "I'm sure they want you to do it."

"Nonsense. They'd never know."

"I wouldn't feel right working on such important pieces. Perhaps Mother could come with you."

"She doesn't need practice, but you do. But never mind that for now. How do you like this watercolor?" he asked and pointed out a painting of a flock of mallards nesting in a marsh.

They discussed the merits of the picture before going into another room to examine the tapestries until it was time to retire.

Miranda bade her father goodnight and went to her room to change for bed. She slipped into her favorite nightgown and pulled on a peacock blue robe. Though it was late, she wasn't sleepy. Miranda missed her balcony at home, as she often went out to look at the sky before bed. Suddenly an idea occurred to her. The children were in bed and the adults were most likely in their own bedrooms. Why not go down to the swings? She could sit for a time and would possibly even have a view of the stars. Miranda picked up her lantern but left it behind when she stepped out into the hall and saw the lamps were still lit.

On the first floor, however, most of the rooms were in complete darkness. Luckily the parlor light was on and she could easily make her way outside to the swings.

The night was clear and crisp. Miranda took hold of the thick ropes and hopped onto the swing. Her nightgown billowed around her as she swung higher and higher, the wind ruffling her hair. From her vantage point she could see lights on in some of the second-floor rooms. She soared through the air, unable to stop the joyful laugh that bubbled up. Miranda was just wondering if she had enough space to jump off when the door opened and a long shadow fell across the grass.

Chapter Sixteen

Miranda wanted to skid to a halt, but her feet didn't quite touch the ground. She attempted to slow herself, at the same time trying to see who was on the patio. At best it would be her father, at worst, Ebenezer. When the swing finally stopped, Miranda somehow wasn't surprised to see that it was George.

"Good evening," he said.

Miranda slid off the swing, drawing her robe closer and tightening the sash. "I haven't done that in years. I couldn't resist," she said, brushing a hair away from her face.

"I come out here myself from time to time. Do you mind if I join you?"

"I was about to go inside," she said.

George took a seat on a swing. "Just a few minutes?" he asked.

"Have you been picking habits up from the children? You sound like Nicholas," she said, getting back on her swing.

"Maybe," he said, grinning. "He doesn't often take no for an answer."

Miranda thought she could do with taking a page out of Nicholas's book. It was too late now, but what if when she'd been a child she'd always told her parents what was on her mind and didn't relent when they refused her requests? Her life might be different now. Perhaps she'd be able to do what she liked without going behind their backs.

"What are you thinking about?" George asked, breaking into her thoughts.

Miranda swung her feet gently. "I was thinking children have the right idea about some things. And that I should install a swing at my house."

"It's relaxing, isn't it?" he asked, leaning back in his swing. "In the winter, when the leaves are gone, you can see through the trees and watch the stars. It's cold out here at that time of year, but the children are impervious to weather and insist on coming out anyway."

"Do you join them?"

"When it isn't *too* cold," he said. "They've been known to come out here in the snow."

"I like the sunshine," Miranda said. "Besides, it's easier to take long walks when it isn't snowing."

They fell into a silence that was more comfortable than Miranda would have imagined just a few days ago.

After a time, George cleared his throat. "Miranda...I'm glad you snuck into the ball," he said, not meeting her eyes. "And I'm glad it was you. When I couldn't find you at midnight, I thought I'd never know who you were. I liked talking to you that night."

Miranda smiled. "I liked talking to you, too. You made my first ball quite special."

"That's good to hear. Maybe next time you can stay for the whole ball."

"If I ever dare sneak out again," she said.

"Or you could tell your father you want to attend. I imagine he'd be understanding and allow you to," he said.

"I don't think so."

"Maybe if you explain to him how much you want to go—"

"It's more complicated than that," Miranda said, pulling her eyes away from his. It was one thing for Peter to admonish her for not speaking her mind, but George had no right to. She didn't want to talk about it anymore but didn't know how to change the subject without being rude. She hopped off her swing. "It's time I went in."

"I hope I didn't upset you," George said, rising.

"No, not at all," she lied. "I'm tired."

"All right," he said, but didn't look convinced. "Would you care to join me for a ride tomorrow?"

"Yes, thank you. Goodnight."

"Goodnight."

She went through the parlor but paused in the doorway to look back. George was sitting on a swing, watching the sky.

****

The next morning Miranda dressed in her habit, assuming she and George would take their ride right after breakfast. She wondered if it was wise to go out with him alone again. But he was interesting to talk to, especially now that he knew they'd gone to the ball together. Perhaps today she could somehow make up for her abrupt departure from the swings last night.

On her way to breakfast, Miranda stopped by the stained-glass room to see what the colors looked like in the morning light. As soon as she walked into the room, she wished she hadn't.

Ebenezer was sitting in a brown arm chair, smoking a pipe. "Well! This is a surprise," he said, getting to his feet. "Where did you leave my nephew?"

"I haven't seen George this morning," Miranda said.

"I wanted to see the glass, but I'll come back later. I'm sorry to disturb you."

Ebenezer waved his pipe in the air. "You didn't disturb me. Come, I'll show you George's favorite pane."

Miranda followed him over to the wall, where he pointed out a pane depicting two people walking beside a river.

"He's always liked this one. Sweet, isn't it? He's a romantic, George is," Ebenezer said. "Not all fellows are like that. But you must know that about him, eh?"

"Um, no, I don't. I hardly know him," Miranda managed to get out.

Ebenezer nudged her with his elbow. "You seemed cozy enough dancing with him on the patio."

It was a moment before Miranda was composed enough to speak. "I didn't realize you'd seen us," she finally said coldly.

Ebenezer blew out a long stream of smoke, chuckling. "Now, now, don't look so offended. I passed through the drawing room and saw you. Don't worry, I won't tell anyone what you two were up to."

Miranda bristled. "We weren't 'up to' anything."

"Never mind. So kind of him to drag the phonograph out for you. Not every young man would think of it."

"Yes, it was a thoughtful gesture." Miranda tried to think of an excuse to escape him without being outright rude, not that he deserved such consideration after his familiarity and insinuations.

Ebenezer tapped the ash out of his pipe and onto the floor. "That describes George to a T—thoughtful."

"I think I'll go find my father before breakfast," Miranda said before he could start extolling George's virtues anymore. She heard Ebenezer calling to her as she hurried down the hall, but ignored him.

Fuming over the unpleasant conversation, Miranda wandered aimlessly through the house until it was past time for breakfast. She considered going back to her bedroom, as it was hard to imagine facing Ebenezer after that encounter, but she knew her father would wonder where she was.

When she entered the dining room, George gave her a bright smile, Ebenezer a knowing smirk. Miranda gave a halfhearted nod to both of them and took a seat beside her father.

"Good morning," Miranda said to the table at large.

George, who was dressed for riding, said, "We'll have a fine day for our ride. I thought we'd go out toward the lake, then up into the hills."

"That's a lovely trail," Mrs. Rockford said to Miranda. "There's a nice view from the peak."

"I'm looking forward to it," Miranda said and started on her omelet.

Mr. Harlake suddenly seemed to realize what they were talking about and stared at Miranda for a moment. "Don't you need a chaperone? Ebenezer and I could join you."

Ebenezer set his juice down, shaking his head as if in disbelief. "Chaperone! Don't be ridiculous, Lucas. They're only going up the hill."

"But I haven't seen the lake yet," Mr. Harlake pressed. "I'd like a look at it."

"Never mind the lake," Ebenezer said. "I want to show you some fifteenth-century miniatures. They're not in the gallery."

Mr. Harlake swallowed. "Miniatures?"

"Just a small collection, but you'll enjoy them. I think one of them has flaking paint."

Miranda and her father winced.

"How disastrous," Mr. Harlake said.

"I hope the miniature isn't too damaged," Miranda said.

"They looked fine to me," Mr. Rockford said. "But I'm no expert."

George set his coffee aside and looked at Miranda. "Are you ready to go?"

"Oh. Yes." She would have liked to see the miniatures, but perhaps there'd be time tomorrow.

Suddenly the dining room door opened and the butler, looking agitated, hurried to Mr. Rockford's side.

"This just arrived, sir," he said, holding out a silver tray. "They said it's urgent."

"Thank you." Mr. Rockford picked a letter up off the tray and read the name. "It's for you," he said, and handed the letter to Mr. Harlake.

Everyone at the table sat in silence, watching him. Miranda rose and stood behind her father as he opened the message. What urgent matter could possibly involve her father?

After a moment Mr. Harlake pushed his chair back, nearly knocking Miranda over. The expression on his face chilled her bones. Something was wrong. Very wrong.

"What is it?" she whispered.

Mr. Harlake took her hand and addressed the table. "Miranda and I need to leave at once. This very moment."

"What does it say?" Miranda pressed.

Mr. Harlake met her eyes. "It's from Esther."

If there was a problem with the house, Mr. or Mrs. Tolwood would have sent the message. But if it was from her mother's personal maid…

"Is Mother ill? Hurt?" Miranda asked and put a hand over her mouth as fear coursed through her.

"The message only says we're needed at home," Mr. Harlake said shakily.

George leapt to his feet. "I'll have your trunks brought up and send maids to help you pack." He ran into the next room.

"I'm sorry, I—" Mr. Harlake began, addressing the Rockfords.

Mrs. Rockford rose and put a hand on his arm. "Think nothing of it."

"Don't let us keep you," Mr. Rockford said.

Mr. Harlake gave them half a nod and hurried away.

Miranda suddenly felt a warm hand on the small of her back. She looked over her shoulder and saw George.

"Is there anything I can help you with?" he asked gently.

"No, thank you," she said. "I'm going right upstairs to pack."

"You've had a shock. At least let me escort you." He took her arm, which she hadn't realized was shaking.

Miranda nodded, her lips pressed tight.

George walked her to her bedroom, and Miranda regained her senses when he opened the door and started to follow her in.

She stood in the doorway, facing him. "I'll be all right now."

"Please do ring if you need anything."

"I will," she said, just as a footman arrived with her trunk, followed by two maids. "Thank you. I have to go."

"We'll have you on your way as soon as we can," he said reassuringly and strode away after a quick word with the footman.

Miranda barely remembered packing, but within an hour of the message's arrival she and her father were in the carriage, speeding home.

She watched the Rockfords' house disappear into the distance, but she couldn't say she regretted leaving. Her only regret was that she hadn't stayed home with her mother. Miranda recalled all those instances when Mrs. Harlake had been tired, and how very pale she looked sometimes. Perhaps it wasn't about that at all…perhaps her mother had been hurt. Miranda bit her thumbnail, her heel tapping the floor of the carriage. She'd like to talk to her father, but he was oddly quiet and she sensed he couldn't or wouldn't speak. Miranda crossed the carriage to sit beside him and took his hand. He gave her a wan smile and she rested her head on his shoulder, willing the horses to fly.

Chapter Seventeen

When Miranda and her father arrived at Majestic Oaks, Mr. Harlake jumped out of the carriage the moment it stopped and ran into the house.

Mrs. Tolwood was waiting on the porch. She didn't appear upset but oddly expectant.

"What's going on, Mrs. Tolwood?" Miranda asked in a trembling voice when she reached the top of the steps.

The woman patted Miranda's arm. "Nothing for you to worry about, dear. Now come along inside."

"But we had a message. An urgent message."

Mrs. Tolwood shook her head, her lip curled. "I told Esther not to send it. But when does she ever listen to me?"

Miranda gripped Mrs. Tolwood's hands. "Please tell me what's wrong."

"All that's wrong is you've been worried for no good reason, most likely. Come with me and we'll get you cleaned up. The coffee is waiting, and I'm sure you'd like a bite."

"I can't possibly eat! What's the matter with Mother?" It was all Miranda could do not to break into sobs right there on the front porch.

Mrs. Tolwood put an arm around her shoulders. "I'm not the one to tell you. But trust me when I say nothing is wrong and your mother is right as rain."

"Truly?" She clutched at the words like a lifeline.

"Yes. I do wish Peter was here. He's always such a comfort to you," Mrs. Tolwood said as they walked across the porch.

Miranda's steps faltered. "Why do I need comforting? Something *is* amiss."

Mrs. Tolwood actually laughed. "Oh, Miranda. No, no. I only meant he'd help you calm down. There's no need to worry. Now come inside."

Miranda followed her into the house. Bramwell didn't look in the least perturbed, nor did the men carrying the trunks inside. She began to relax but would only be satisfied once she'd seen her mother.

"Will you wash up first, or have something to eat?" Mrs. Tolwood asked.

Miranda made for the stairs. "I'll see Mother before anything else."

"She's with your father just now. There's no need for you to go up."

"I know there isn't a need, but I have to see for myself that she's all right."

Mrs. Tolwood gave her arm a gentle squeeze. "They need to talk things through. No doubt they'll send for you when there's something to tell. Probably."

"Mrs. Tolwood, how can you insist nothing's wrong, yet be so mysterious? I'm about to go to pieces."

"I know. But how long have you known me? All your life. Have I ever lied to you? No. Now go along and freshen up, and then come to the parlor. Perhaps your father will be down by then."

"Fine." Miranda tried not to sound churlish, but this was one of the most maddening things ever to happen to her.

In her bedroom, Miranda removed her jacket and draped it over a chair, then went out to the balcony. She walked right to the edge and gripped the railing. How dearly she wished Peter were here! He'd no doubt climb up to her room and tell her all he knew, which was bound to be everything.

There was a knock on the door and Cassandra came in, carrying Miranda's purse and gloves that she'd left in the carriage.

"I'm glad you're back," Cassandra said. "It's been too quiet here with both you *and* Peter gone."

"It's always too quiet without Peter," Miranda said as she walked back into her bedroom.

"It's a pity you had to rush home. Esther really does overreact at times," Cassandra said. She pursed her lips, looking exactly like her mother. "Did you enjoy your stay at the Rockfords'?"

"Yes. Do you know if my father's downstairs yet?"

"I didn't see him on my way up."

"Thank you for bringing my things. I'll come down soon."

"My mother will keep the coffee warm," Cassandra said on her way out.

After changing, Miranda went downstairs, where to her immense relief and surprise she found her parents sitting in the parlor.

"Mother!" she cried. "How are you? We were so worried." She kissed her mother's cheek and stood beside her.

Mrs. Harlake smiled. "I'm sorry Esther worried you. I was under the weather this morning and she sent the message without me knowing."

Miranda sank into a chair. "So you *are* ill."

Mr. and Mrs. Harlake exchanged a glance, and then Mrs. Harlake reached over and took Miranda's hand. "You mustn't worry, Miranda. I was sick today, and will be from time to time for a few weeks. But after that I'll be fine. You see…" Tears sprang to her mother's eyes. "I'm going to have a baby."

Miranda gasped. "A baby!"

"Yes!" Mrs. Harlake started to cry, smiling all the while. Mr. Harlake looked barely able to contain his joy.

"But—but how? No, don't answer that. I understand *how,* but I didn't think you could have more children."

"I didn't think I could, either, but here we are," her mother said, wiping her eyes.

Miranda's father smiled on them both. "We'll need to be very gentle with your mother and take good care not to upset her or cause her any distress."

Mrs. Harlake laughed gaily, a sound Miranda barely recognized. "I'm not breakable, Lucas."

"So that's why you've been tired," Miranda said. Though it didn't explain the months—years—of her mother's fatigue. But Miranda wouldn't delve into that just now.

"Yes, but I didn't want to tell you until things were a little further along," Mrs. Harlake said.

Miranda felt giddy with relief. "When will the baby be born?"

"In about six months," Mrs. Harlake said dreamily. "We have so much to do! The layette to buy, the nursery to prepare. Oh! We'll need to think of a name."

"That's easy," Mr. Harlake said. "Lucas."

Mrs. Harlake wiped her eyes again. "What if we have a girl? I'd love Miranda to have a sister."

"We have some time to think of a name," Miranda

said. "But in the meantime, what can I do to help, Mother? You must tell me if there's anything at all you need."

"There's nothing you can do, only be patient with me needing rest, and try not to worry."

Mr. Harlake took his wife's hand. "On that note, I think it's time you went back to your room."

"You're probably right. I don't want to overdo." Mrs. Harlake rose and allowed Mr. Harlake to take her back upstairs.

Miranda served herself from the tray Mrs. Tolwood had provided, ravenous now that she knew her mother wasn't in danger. A baby! It was almost too much to believe. What would it be like having a sister or brother? She couldn't imagine, given their age difference. Why, she was old enough to be the baby's mother. But she'd try her best to have a close relationship with the child.

For now, Miranda couldn't help worrying about her mother. She was no longer young. But some women had babies even later, and Mrs. Harlake was in seemingly good health. Miranda was sure her father would have the best doctors in to see that her mother was well looked after. She hoped for her father's sake that her mother would give birth to a boy. It was common knowledge every man wanted a son. For herself, she didn't mind as long as the child and her mother were healthy.

A little while later, Mr. Harlake came downstairs. He poured himself a cup of coffee and sat beside Miranda.

"I'm glad Esther sent that message," he said. "Now you know what's been happening with your mother."

Miranda set her cup down. "Why didn't you tell me sooner?"

He looked as if he'd rather not answer, but after a sip of coffee he met her eyes. "These things don't always…pan out. We didn't want you to be disappointed if that happened."

Miranda frowned. "But everything should be fine now, right? Otherwise, you wouldn't have told me."

"That's right. Your mother will rest and take care, and you and I will see that she doesn't have anything to worry about." He ran a hand across his forehead.

"Are you worried, Father?"

"No. Somewhat. Well, there are always risks, aren't there? But I'm not going to say so in front of your mother. Not that I need to. She isn't naive. But we'll all assume the best outcome, and this time next year we'll have a healthy little one in the house. I'm glad I can tell you of my worries, Miranda. I don't want to burden your mother with it, but it isn't the kind of thing one likes to keep to themselves."

"No, it isn't," she said, wishing she had someone to talk to about her own worries. Of all times for Peter to be gone! She could tell her father was doing his best to reassure her, but it was hard to believe when he didn't seem confident himself. Perhaps once her mother was further along they'd all breathe easier.

"I should send a message to the Rockfords," Mr. Harlake said.

"Why?"

"We left in such a hurry, they'll be wondering what happened. But I don't think your mother would want me to tell them about her condition."

"Perhaps you could tell them it was a false alarm? Or simply say she was under the weather?"

"Yes, I'll tell them she was ill, as it isn't far from the

truth. Everyone in town will know sooner or later, but there's no need to spread it around just yet."

"Would you like me to write to them?"

"No," her father said, rising from his chair. "I'll go along and do it now." He started toward the door, then stopped to smile at her. Beamed, really. He looked twenty years younger. "This is good news, Miranda. Wonderful news. Your mother will be fine, and we'll finally have the family we've always wanted."

After he left, Miranda finished eating and went upstairs. But instead of turning into her bedroom she continued down the hall to that sunny room in the corner. She opened the door and went in. The nursery wasn't dusty, nor did it have that abandoned, neglected air of most unused rooms. A crib stood between two windows, and a rocking chair sat beside it. As Miranda walked in and put her hands on the crib railing, she noticed a book and a pair of her mother's glasses on the chair. It brought a tiny ache to her heart. How often had her mother come up here over the years? Or had she only come recently, now that she knew a baby was coming?

Miranda strolled about the room. It was a nice size, with three large windows overlooking the back woods. As she stood in the center of the room, Miranda had a sudden inspiration to paint a mural on the far wall. It would give her something to do to distract her from worrying, and it would be a gift from her to her new brother or sister. Smiling, she walked to her room to sketch ideas for the baby's mural.

Two days later, while Miranda ate breakfast with her parents, she realized she hadn't mentioned Peter in days. The news of the baby had driven everything else from her mind. When there was a lull in the conversation, she rested her chin in her hand and let out a loud, heavy sigh. As expected, both parents looked up at her.

"What's wrong?" her father asked.

Miranda looked up as though surprised they'd noticed her. "I was just wondering when Peter will be home. I miss him so much."

Her father rolled his eyes. "Hasn't he written to you?"

"Only once," she said, sighing again. "I'm sure he's been busy."

"Maybe his father knows when he'll be back," Mrs. Harlake said.

"Maybe. I'll go ask him." As she left the room Miranda realized that talking about the engagement might be stressful for her mother, so in future she'd only put on these little acts for her father. After getting the answer she'd expected from Mr. Tolwood—he had no idea when Peter would be back—Miranda walked into town.

She stopped by Easton's to see if the pink dress was still there. It was. One day soon she'd muster the courage to ask her father about it again. Miranda started toward Darlington's but hadn't gone half a block when she crossed the street to avoid Mr. Cobbe, who was chastising a young boy for leaving a pile of newspapers too close to the bank's front doors.

When she entered Darlington's, Miranda saw George sitting at a table, deep in conversation with a pretty woman she didn't recognize. When the door closed behind Miranda, George looked up. Miranda smiled at him and he gave her an almost imperceptible nod before turning back to his date.

At the counter, Emily was jotting something down

on a pad of paper.

"Hi," Miranda said as she approached.

Emily looked up. "What a nice surprise. I didn't expect to see you today." She sent a glance in George's direction, and Miranda knew she had some explaining to do.

"I came back early. Do you have time for a walk? I can tell you all about it."

"I'm afraid I can't leave the store because nobody else is here, but you could come to the back room with me." Emily opened the lift-up counter for Miranda to walk through.

They went into a storage room just behind the counter, and Emily positioned herself so she could still see the cash register. "What happened?" she asked. "I thought you were staying at the Rockfords' for a while yet."

Miranda told her they'd been called home early because her mother was sick, then briefly described what had happened at the Rockfords'. She left out the dancing and the swinging at midnight.

"It sounds like you had a nice visit. It's a shame you had to cut it short," Emily said.

"Yes, it was better than I thought it would be. How have you been? How's Nathaniel?" Miranda asked to change the subject.

Emily talked about her renovations to their room and said Nathaniel was taking her to dinner in Shrewsbury next week.

"That sounds delightful."

"I can hardly wait. But tell me more about—" Emily glanced out into the dining room and lowered her voice. "George. Did you spend much time with him?"

"Yes, quite a bit," Miranda said. She didn't mention that she felt closer to him than she had before and found him more intriguing than ever.

"Do you still think he's obnoxious?"

Miranda shook her head. "I shouldn't have called him that. He was very helpful last week, and I have a better understanding of him now. I'd almost consider him a friend." She glanced over at George. He was staring at his date, who looked slightly dazed.

"See? He isn't as bad as you thought," Emily said. "Speaking of friends, is Peter home yet?"

She sighed. "No, and I don't expect him for at least a week."

"He'll be here before you know it. I'd better get back out to the counter. Stop by again soon."

"I will. By the way, could you come over for lunch next week?"

Emily glanced at a calendar on the wall. "I'm free on Tuesday."

"Perfect," Miranda said.

Before leaving Darlington's she bought some of her mother's favorite butterscotch candies and peanut butter fudge. As she walked down Main Street, Miranda noticed a display of toys in the front window of Burford's. She hesitated for a moment before going inside. A cozy corner of the shop was filled with stuffed animals, soft blankets, rattles, silver cups and impossibly tiny clothes. She chose a silver baby rattle and a soft, light brown bear.

Miranda lightly swung her parcels by their strings as she strolled down the woodland path, thinking of baby names. She recalled her father's assumption that any boy would be named after him. That was natural, but it brought to mind something else he'd said the other day: *We'll have the family we've always wanted.* The family they'd always wanted? Miranda hadn't realized how unsatisfied her parents were with just one child—her. But no, she couldn't believe that was how they truly felt. It was amazing that her parents' dreams were finally coming to fruition, but she couldn't help wondering if all these years they'd felt something was missing. Why? What else could she possibly have done to fill in that gap where a son or another daughter should have been?

Miranda had just passed the turnoff to Marigold Lake when she heard someone coming up behind her. She moved to the edge of the lane so whoever it was could pass her more easily. But they didn't. Instead, he called her name.

Chapter Eighteen

Miranda looked over her shoulder and saw George jogging up the path. She turned back and went to meet him.

"George," she said as she approached. "What are you doing here? Isn't your house across town?"

He took his hat off. "Yes, but I need to talk to you."

For some reason this statement made Miranda's pulse jump. Or maybe it wasn't what George said but the way he was looking at her. Tenderly? Warmly? She blinked and remembered she should reply instead of staring at him. "What do you want to talk to me about?"

"Your mother. We had a message that she's ill."

"How kind of you to ask. She's much better. It's nothing to worry about," she said and started back up the path.

"I'm glad to hear it. May I walk with you?"

"If you like, but you'll have a long walk home."

George matched his stride to hers. "I don't mind. I'll take Fairbanks Road and that will be quicker."

So, Miranda found herself alone with George again, trying to think of something to talk about. She supposed it would be rude to ask why he'd ended his date early. Or maybe he hadn't. Maybe they'd been sitting in Darlington's for hours before she'd come along.

"How are the children?" Miranda asked after a few minutes.

"They're doing well. Sybil's been trying to draw the fountain."

"Her drawing the other day was quite good for a beginner. Have you tried it again?"

"Not yet, but I will." He gestured to Miranda's parcels. "May I carry those for you?"

"There's no need," she said.

He grinned. "I know, but I'd like to."

"Thank you."

When George went to take the packages from Miranda, the strings came loose and the items from Burford's fell to the ground.

"Oh, no!" Miranda scrambled to pick the bear up before it got dirty, but George was quicker.

He held up the bear and rattle, giving her a questioning look.

Miranda took them and hastily wrapped them up again. "They're a gift," she said.

"For someone in town?" he asked, taking the packages from her and tying the strings with a double knot.

Miranda had an inexplicable urge to tell him the truth. She didn't understand why he was so easy to confide in, but for some reason she trusted George.

"If I tell you something, will you promise not to tell anyone?"

"Yes, of course," he said, looking concerned. "Is anything wrong?"

"I hope not." She took a deep breath. "Those things, the bear and the rattle—they're for my mother. Well, not exactly my mother."

"They're for your mother but they *aren't* for your mother?" he asked, and Miranda wasn't surprised he sounded confused.

She nodded. "Yes, she's—"

"Wait. I think I understand. When you say your mother's ill, you mean she's ill for say, nine months?"

"Yes, and she just told me. We aren't announcing it yet."

"Congratulations! That's happy news."

"Yes…" Miranda said and stared at the ground.

"But?"

"I'm worried about her. She isn't young."

"She can't be more than forty. Try not to worry. I'm sure she and the baby will be in good health."

Miranda looked up at him. "I'm trying not to be anxious, but it's difficult."

"I do understand, Miranda. My mother…she wasn't young when she had Sybil, never mind when she had Harriet and Nathaniel. I worried every time she was expecting—I couldn't help it. I didn't think she should have more babies, but what did I know? I was a child myself. She was frail for a time after Nathaniel was born, but now she's back to her old self."

"Why did she become frail?" Miranda asked, fear creeping back to the surface.

"I didn't have much time with her after the babies were born, so I can't say for certain. Perhaps she was tired? She had three babies in the span of five years. That would take a toll on any woman. But your mother's only having one. All I'm saying is, I do understand the worry—you're her daughter, so you can't help it. But try not to. Enjoy this time with her before she's busy with the baby all the time."

Miranda was surprised to detect something is his tone…resentment? Sadness?

"What's it like?" Miranda asked. "Having siblings, a baby?"

George smiled. "It's wonderful, and it's hard work at times. I adore them, but when I was young it was difficult. I didn't understand why my mother couldn't play with me anymore, why I was sent off with my nanny more often. It will be different for you. You're an adult and even if your mother is busy you'll understand why. If anything, you'll be able to help out. That's what I did. Once I got over my pouting, I made myself useful. I admit that didn't happen right away," he said and looked sad for a moment. "But once I realized I'd have more time with my mother if I made myself somewhat indispensable, things were better."

Miranda remembered all the times at the Rockfords' when George seemed to be in charge of things, the ways he helped with the children or dealt with the staff.

"Oh, I see," Miranda said.

"What do you see?" George asked.

"I noticed at your house how you're in the thick of things all the time. Helping out, playing with the children. Was it a habit you developed when you were young?"

His brows drew together. "I like doing those things."

"I didn't mean to imply you don't," she hurried to clarify. "I only meant I noticed you're helpful at home. It wasn't a criticism."

The expression on his face cleared. "I'm sorry for being defensive," he said. "You told me a secret, now will you allow me to tell you one?"

Miranda nodded.

"It was exhausting then, and it still is now. I tried to be everything for my mother so she'd notice me. Don't misunderstand—I know she loved me, but she was busy all the time. I was ten when Sybil was born, so if any child had to go without attention, it was me. I'm sure I sound pathetic, but there were days my mother seemed to have forgotten I existed. You'd think my parents would have gotten a nurse for the babies, but my mother wanted to care for them herself. Maybe I made myself *too* useful. Perhaps if I hadn't, they would have brought in more help and I'd have gotten more time with my parents."

"George, really?" Miranda asked, unable to stop herself. "That sounds so lonely."

"It was. But that was years ago. Don't pay me any mind. I'm just complaining." He laughed suddenly. "Of all people, I shouldn't be telling *you* all of this. Your situation won't be like mine. You'll enjoy all the special moments…like the baby's first smile, first steps, watching them sleep. You'll love being a big sister. Your parents must be ecstatic."

"Yes, they are," she said, but her voice was quiet. Miranda walked over to a fallen tree on the side of the path and sat down.

"Aren't they?" George asked and sat beside her. "Or are they too worried to be happy?"

"They're only a little worried. But my father said something odd."

"What was that?"

She shifted so she was facing George. "He said now they'll have the family they always wanted. As if I wasn't enough for them." It hurt to say it out loud, but she continued. "I've tried to be everything for my parents. Absolutely everything. But it hasn't been enough. The whole time they wished they had more children, or perhaps wished I was someone else entirely. I've spent my life trying to be perfect, amiable, artistic. For goodness' sake, I don't even know how to say no to them or tell them what I like, or...or who I really am. And it's all been for nothing. They weren't satisfied, no matter what I did."

"I've seen you with your parents. You're clearly everything to them."

"But I won't be next year," Miranda said, though she knew this sounded both unrealistic and childish. "At least I'll finally be free to do whatever I want because they'll be so distracted by the baby," she said, trying to make it sound like a joke.

"That isn't true," he said, and gave her shoulder an awkward pat.

"I know. Why am I telling you this? Please don't think I'm ridiculous. I never act this way."

"I don't usually tell people about my bygone days of being a petulant child, either," he said and smiled. "But sometimes you need to share your thoughts, no matter how unpleasant. I won't hold it against you, and I promise I won't tell anyone."

"I won't, either," she said and felt a warm glow of friendship.

After a moment, George said, "It seems to me we have the same problem."

"How so?"

"Trying to be everything for our parents, in one way or another." He gave her a quick glance. "If you ever repeat this to anyone, I'll deny it, but...it's hard having everyone expect you to be helpful and perfect all the time."

"I agree. I'm so accustomed to trying to keep my

parents happy that I'm not honest about what I want—or don't want. Especially now. How can I say no to them about anything if it would distress my mother?"

George looked at Miranda thoughtfully for a moment, stroking his chin. "Since we've already told each other our secrets, why don't we make a pact?"

"What do you mean?" she asked, a smile coming to her face.

"We won't lie to each other. I'll be the person you can always tell the truth to."

Miranda raised a brow. "And what is it you demand from me in return?"

"In return, I'll always be honest with you, and…and I'd like to be able to say no on occasion. Whenever I'm asked to do anything, I agree. But sometimes I don't want to give piggyback rides all day or talk to the cook or fetch the horses."

"I promise you, George, I will not ask you for a piggyback ride."

Their eyes held for a moment before they broke into laughter.

"Let's start now," George said. "What's something you've always wanted to tell your parents but couldn't?"

Miranda had intended to say something flippant, like she didn't like lettuce on her sandwiches, but what came out was much different. "I don't think I'm meant to be an artist." Miranda covered her mouth with her hands, shocked she'd uttered her deepest doubts about herself.

"Do you mean that?" he asked softly.

She lowered her hands. "Yes."

"Why not?"

"I can't explain it. My parents hope I'll be a great

artist one day, like them. But I enjoy art more for the process, not the end result. I do like painting, but sometimes I feel like I could never pick up a brush again and be happy."

"You've got to listen to that. It's your life. You should do what you like with it."

Miranda stood up. "Can I really be honest with you?" she asked.

"Yes. We have a pact," he said with a small grin.

"It's easy enough to say I should tell them, but my parents have put all of their dreams and plans onto me. I just can't disappoint them, especially now. How can I tell them I don't want to paint, and I don't want to hike out to the ridge before the sun is up, and I never want to see my mother's mushroom casserole recipe again?"

"And that you wear pants under your dress?" he asked.

Miranda's face went pink. "I hoped you didn't notice!"

"I didn't say anything because I didn't want to embarrass you. Not to mention I shouldn't have been looking at the hem of your gown."

"Do you think it's odd?" she asked as they started walking down the path.

"Honestly?"

She nodded.

"I'd say…unusual. I don't think it's wrong, but I've never met a woman who does that before."

"It's so much easier to go riding or to trek through the woods with trousers on. I'm so embarrassed that you saw them."

"You don't need to be embarrassed with me," he said.

Miranda glanced at him. "I'm not. I don't know why, but I'm not."

"Maybe because, even though we've known each other for years, we're strangers in a way."

"Maybe. Or maybe because I don't believe you'll tell anyone my secrets."

"I won't. And I know you won't tell anyone that I was jealous of my baby siblings when I was young, and that I don't like dates with women I barely know, and that if I had the choice, I wouldn't take the children anywhere near the lake again because no matter how I try to avoid it, I end up soaked."

"I won't tell anyone," she said, grinning. "I have another secret."

"Yes?"

"I didn't want to show you the studio the night you came to my house."

He nodded. "I didn't want to go, but it seemed rude not to. Ebenezer practically shoved me out of the parlor to accompany you." George got a funny, quizzical look on his face, then shook his head.

"Thinking of more secrets?" she asked.

It took him a moment to answer. "I didn't want to give you a tour of my house. I had paperwork waiting in the study."

"I wasn't interested at all in the tour. But I did enjoy it once we saw the stained glass and the gallery."

"It's unfortunate you had to go home early."

"Yes, I enjoyed my time at your house more than I thought I would."

"Let me guess…you didn't want to come but couldn't say no?"

Miranda laughed. "Yes, but in the end I went

because I wanted to see the art collection."

"So it wasn't a total loss."

"Not at all. I'm glad I told you about my mother. I feel better about the baby now, and I think I'll like being a sister."

"You will. There's nothing like it."

"Would you like to come in?" Miranda asked as they approached the gates of Majestic Oaks.

George hesitated. "Well…no."

"That's all right," she said. "Thank you for being honest."

"Thank you for letting me." George bowed deeply and said again in a faux serious tone, "No, thank you, I would rather not come in."

Miranda laughed. "Have a good walk home. I suppose I'll see you around town."

He handed her the parcels. "That you will. Goodbye." He tipped his hat to her and walked down the drive and out onto the street.

Miranda stood watching him for a few moments, then went into the house. She went upstairs to her mother's room, expecting to find her resting, but she was sitting in a chair beside the window.

"Good afternoon, Mother," Miranda said.

Mrs. Harlake looked up and smiled. "Hello."

Her mother's color was much better today, as was her mood. Perhaps now that she'd told Miranda about the baby she'd lose that somewhat aloof air she'd had much of the time. Maybe this would bring them closer. Miranda crossed the room and handed her mother the packages from Darlington's and Burford's. "I bought you some things while I was in town."

"How sweet," her mother said, pulling out the toys.

Tears came to her eyes. "These will be the baby's first gifts, and how appropriate that they're from you." She shook the rattle, smiling at the tinkly sound, then set it and the bear on her lap while she opened the bag from Darlington's. "My favorites. Thank you."

"You're welcome. How are you feeling today?"

"Better. I think the illness will pass soon. How was town?"

"Nice. I saw Emily and then ran into George Rockford on my way home. He wanted to ask me how you are."

"That was kind of him." Her mother set the gifts aside, keeping the bear in her lap. "I wanted to talk to you about Hollingsford. I don't know if I'll be able to go now, considering."

Miranda tried not to look disappointed. "We can always go next year."

"I don't want you to miss it."

"Perhaps Father and I could go, or if he doesn't want to leave you alone for that long, Peter could accompany me."

Her mother's soft glow disappeared. "You are not going alone to Hollingsford with Peter."

Miranda realized she was causing her distress, which she'd vowed not to do. "Never mind, Mother. If Father can't come, I'll stay home."

Her mother just nodded. "I think I'll get some rest. Thank you again for the gifts."

"You're welcome. See you at supper?"

Mrs. Harlake put a hand to her temple. "Perhaps."

Miranda went upstairs and took her sketchbook out to the balcony. She was flipping to a blank page when she came across the drawing of George and the children.

It was only a week ago but felt longer when she considered how much better she knew him now. Had she been missing out on a friend all these years, simply because he sometimes acted boisterous when she saw him around town?

Miranda could hardly wait to see Peter so she could tell him they'd been wrong about George. Perhaps they could all go riding one day, or have lunch. Miranda considered other things they might do together as she began a new sketch for the nursery mural.

The next day Miranda went to Marigold Lake, forgetting that the warmer weather would bring crowds to the beach. She considered leaving, but the refreshing breeze, the sunshine, and the sparkling lake drew her down to the water's edge. Miranda removed her shoes and walked along the shore for a while, watching tiny minnows dart away from her feet.

After a time she sat down and pulled out her sketchbook, burying her toes in the cool sand. The loons were far out in the middle of the lake and, as expected, there were now two tiny chicks swimming beside the parents.

Miranda had been drawing for an hour or so when she heard a familiar voice. She looked up to see George and his friends walking down the beach. As usual, they were making a racket and not paying much attention to those around them. She tried to catch George's eye, but he was laughing with Henry and didn't notice her.

She went back to her work, but within moments let out a shriek as cold water doused her hair, clothes and, worst of all, her sketchbook. Miranda sprang to her feet, looking for the source of the commotion. George and his friends had taken it into their minds to run pell-mell along the shore, and from the looks of it she wasn't the only one they'd disturbed. A little way down the beach two children stood crying beside the remains of their crushed sandcastle, and someone's blanket and picnic basket had been swept out into the lake.

Not even thinking of what she was doing, Miranda called after the men, "You should watch where you're going!"

She shook the droplets off her sketchbook, but the drawing of the loons was ruined. Hopefully some of the pages inside were still dry, but it was doubtful. Miranda put her shoes back on and was turning to go when she saw Ethan, glowering, striding toward her. Henry and Frank walked behind him, but George had a hand on Ethan's arm as if trying to pull him back.

"What business is it of yours what we do?" Ethan demanded when he reached Miranda.

Miranda took a step back. She hadn't expected to be confronted like this, though she probably shouldn't have been surprised. Drawing herself up, she looked Ethan in the eyes. "You destroyed my sketchbook and drenched my clothes."

"Next time you should sit farther up the beach," Ethan said with a sneer. "You may not have realized, but the shore tends to be wet, what with the *water*."

Miranda briefly caught George's eye, expecting some support or at least a friendly face. But looking half concerned, half embarrassed he turned away and went to stand out of sight, behind Henry.

"Well?" Ethan said, crossing his arms. "Move along, Miss Harlake. Don't let your precious book get even wetter." He kicked water at Miranda and she gasped, hugging the book to her chest. All the men laughed, even George.

Miranda shot them a glare, mustering what she could of her dignity. "Next time you should confine your antics to your own home, where you won't bother anyone else. People here are trying to relax and enjoy the day. They don't need to be subject to your buffoonery!"

She turned on her heel but had barely gone three paces when Frank began mimicking her. The men broke down in hysterical laughter, and Miranda's heart clenched when George's laugh rang out with all the rest.

As she made her way up the beach, Miranda saw a few adults nodding their approval. The woman with the upset children gave her a small smile. Though she appreciated it, Miranda's mood could not be restored.

She stomped all the way home, burning with regret for having bared her soul to George. This was the man she'd told her secrets to! Miranda should have listened to Peter and to her own better judgment and stayed away from him. Well, from now on she wouldn't delude herself that George was a better man than she'd always thought. She'd taken his measure years ago and her only mistake had been giving him another chance.

Chapter Nineteen

Two days later, Miranda went along to see Mrs. Tolwood to ask if she'd heard from Peter. He'd already been gone for more than two weeks and Miranda was ready for him to come home. True, once he returned they'd need to keep up their betrothal charade, but at the moment that seemed a small price to pay for having her best friend back. Besides, the more she thought of it, Miranda knew she had to tell her parents the engagement was fake. She'd wait until her mother was further along to tell them the truth. Or maybe after the baby was born, just to be safe.

Miranda couldn't find Mrs. Tolwood, but spoke to Mr. Tolwood in the office. He hadn't had any messages from Peter but agreed with Miranda that it was high time he came home.

With no other plans for the afternoon, Miranda went into town to buy a new sketchbook to replace the one that had been ruined at the lake. On her way home she passed through the park in the center of town and on a whim climbed the steps of the gazebo. It was peaceful and quiet, somewhat removed from the carriages and people on bustling Main Street.

Bluebirds flitting amongst the branches of a nearby tree gave her an idea for the nursery mural, so Miranda sat on the bench and pulled out her sketchbook. She'd just finished her drawing when footsteps alerted her to someone coming up the stairs.

It was George. He gave her an odd sort of wince mixed with half a smile, then removed his hat and held it in his hands.

Miranda couldn't decide if he looked more embarrassed, sheepish, or just plain awkward. Whatever it was, it definitely wasn't the confident George she'd known for years. As Miranda rose to her feet she considered giving him a nod, but thought better of it. She held the sketchbook to her chest and brushed past him.

"Wait, Miranda. Please," he said as she started down the stairs.

Remembering their supposed honesty pact, she didn't slow her steps, but said over her shoulder, "To be quite honest, I don't want to talk to you. Goodbye."

Miranda heard him give an exasperated groan as she strode away.

"I know I deserve your anger," he called. "But I want to apologize. Please."

She kept walking and had just reached the sidewalk when he yelled, surely loud enough for everyone in the vicinity to hear, "I was a colossal fool—an idiot! I'm sorry!"

Miranda and several other people stopped and stared at George. He was sitting on the gazebo steps, his head in his hands. After some curious looks in her direction, the townsfolk continued on their way.

Miranda started to walk away but hesitated.

George did look contrite. What harm was there in hearing him out? Though what he could possibly say to explain his behavior she had no idea. As she turned back and slowly crossed the park, George rose to his feet and met her halfway.

"Will you sit with me for a time? I'd like to talk to you," he said.

"Yes, but I must tell you, since we don't lie to each other, that I don't see what good will come of it. You were dreadful to me the other day." There, she'd said it. It felt good not to hold back her feelings.

"Just listen, please."

Miranda picked up her pace, reaching the gazebo before he did. She sat on the bench and set her things down, then looked at him expectantly as he took a seat beside her.

"Were your drawings damaged?" he asked.

"Yes, they were. Is that all you wanted to ask me?" She started to rise.

George put a hand on her arm. "No, it isn't."

"Where are your friends?" Miranda asked, pulling out of his grip. "Shouldn't you be out taunting a flock of geese or some such thing?"

"I know you're upset, but there's no need to be spiteful."

She just looked at him. Who was he to judge her behavior when he'd stood by while his friend insulted her and kicked water on her? Worst of all, George had joined in laughing at her humiliation.

"What is it you want to say?" she asked tiredly.

George was silent for so long that Miranda thought he'd decided not to tell her. When he finally did speak, his voice was quiet. "I want to say I'm sorry. I shouldn't have gone along with my friends when they were storming around the beach, and especially when Ethan was so rude to you. I don't know what I was thinking when I joined in with them laughing at you." George paused and ran a hand over his brow. "The last couple of days I haven't been able to get the expression on your face out of my mind. You looked to me for help, and I turned away. I'll never forgive myself for that. It isn't who I want to be, or who I want everyone to think I am."

The knot in Miranda's chest began to soften. "Then why did you act like that? Why were you so cruel to me?"

"I don't know." He shook his head. "No, I do know. My friends don't bring out the best in me." George laughed harshly. "I wouldn't even call those men my friends. I've known them since we were children, but they don't truly *know* me. They know a version of me that only comes out when I'm with them. But I can hardly blame them for my behavior. I'm an adult. Do you remember how I told you I tried to be indispensable to my parents when I was a child?"

Miranda nodded.

"You were right when you said it was a habit I developed when I was young. I behave how the people I'm with expect me to behave. My parents needed me to be responsible, helpful, available all the time. So I was. With my teachers I was a model student, with women I'm charming, with my siblings I'm the perfect older brother, and with my friends I'm…"

"A buffoon?" she offered, a slight smile coming to her face.

George nodded. "A buffoon. But I promise, Miranda, I'll never treat you so poorly again."

From the look in his eyes and the tone of his voice, Miranda knew he meant it.

"But what if your friends get up to their shenanigans?" she asked. "How will you say no to them?"

George let out a long sigh. "I don't know. It's hard to refuse, even when their ideas are ridiculous."

"When I see you with them, you look like you're enjoying yourself."

He grinned. "I admit I do enjoy some of our escapades. But knocking over sandcastles and causing a ruckus at the theater is unacceptable. I'm probably better off without those particular people in my life, but I already feel lonely sometimes, and if I cut them off I won't have any friends."

"Yes, you will," Miranda said. "You've always been popular."

George snorted. "Superficial relationships with many people, but nobody I'm truly close to."

Miranda looked at him thoughtfully for a moment. "When you aren't trying to please other people, what do you like to do? Who are you really, George?"

"I don't know."

"Oh, you must," she said, laughing. "When do you feel most like the person you want to be? When you're alone? With the children?"

"I suppose when I'm with my uncle. When I'm by myself I can do whatever I please, but it does get lonely. Also—"

"Yes?"

He looked at her out of the corner of his eye. "I think one of the only people who sees the real me is you."

"Perhaps because you aren't allowed to lie to me," she said, grinning.

George laughed. "I felt that way before our pact. Since the ball, really."

"When you didn't even know who I was!"

"And you didn't know who *I* was. I think it was

freeing somehow. Can I be honest?"

"I'd expect nothing less."

"I loved every moment of that ball. Dancing with you was a pleasure, and it was refreshing to be with someone who didn't expect anything of me at all. You saw me as I was, so I could be myself. I thought you were delightful." He met her gaze. "I still do."

Miranda's heart did an odd little flip as she met his eyes. "I had a wonderful time at the ball, too. I think you're a nice man, and..."

George leaned his shoulder into hers. "What? You have to be honest, remember?"

Could she really tell him she hadn't *liked* him before the ball? No, but she could come close. "You weren't what I expected once I got to know you. I thought you were like your friends, but after spending time with you I know you're not. And I'm glad."

"So am I. I enjoyed making mischief when I was younger, but not anymore."

"You'll simply need to practice saying no, as I am. Perhaps we could help each other."

"That's a good idea. Maybe it's time I started acting like myself around my friends and not who they want me to be. If I can convince them I don't like taunting geese or destroying public property, I wouldn't need to drop them altogether. They're fine men on their own. Except perhaps Ethan."

"Maybe you could have a pact with them."

He drew his head back. "Certainly not."

"Why?"

"I think having one person I need to be completely honest with is enough, don't you?" he asked, smiling.

"All right," she said. "But you can tell them when

225

you don't want to do anything too outlandish."

"I'll keep that in mind for next time. I'm sorry you've taken the brunt of my recent hijinks with them. First your poor hand and now your sketchbook. I feel I owe you something to make up for it all. Besides trying to send you the dress, that is."

"Your apology is enough."

"I have an idea. I'll show you my mother's cottage one day soon. You'd like it there. We'll take the boat out or sit on the dock."

"I don't know about the boat. Once I went out with Peter and, well, let's just say I'm not fond of sailing since then," she said with a laugh.

He studied her face for a moment. "You mention Peter often."

"Well, yes. He's my best friend," she said.

"Isn't that unusual for a young lady?"

"Perhaps, but we've always been close."

"People might talk. They might think you're courting."

Though it was really none of his concern, Miranda said, "If they do, I haven't heard of it. I think most people in town are accustomed to seeing us together."

"Perhaps you're right. So...no boats. But you should still come to the cottage. It's right on the water."

"I'd like that." She glanced at her watch. "For now, it's time I went home. My parents are probably wondering where I am."

"Thank you for taking the time to listen to me. I know I didn't deserve it."

An hour ago Miranda would have agreed with him. But not now. It seemed as if she and George grew closer every time they met. "I'm glad we talked," she said.

"And...I'm glad we're friends," she added with a shy smile.

"So am I. Thank you for forgiving me for the other day. I do apologize again."

"There's no need to apologize anymore. You're forgiven. *Honestly.*"

George laughed, and they stood up at the same time.

"I'll see you over the course of the next few days, I dare say," Miranda said.

"Where?" George asked as they started down the stairs.

"I don't know, but I always seem to run into you."

"Let's make a plan. What are you doing tomorrow?"

"Going out with my father. I'm working on a new painting."

They walked down Main Street to the intersection that sent them in different directions.

"Would you like to meet somewhere afterwards? The lake?" George asked.

Miranda wondered if it was wise to meet him there alone. Would it seem like *they* were courting? She set that thought aside for now. "What time?"

"In the evening. I'll have tucked the children in, and the lake won't be so crowded then."

"All right. I'll see you tomorrow." Miranda went on her way, only looking back once. George was still standing there, watching her walk away. He gave her a small wave and started down Ashe Lane.

Miranda replayed their conversation in her mind as she walked home. This time a few days ago she'd never have imagined there was anything George could say to make up for what had happened at the lake. Not that his explanation excused his behavior, but now she understood why he'd done it and knew it wasn't personal. She believed him when he said he wouldn't act like that again.

It was hard to believe how close they'd become in so short a time, although it had really started at the ball. Now that George had confided in her about his friends, maybe she could help him stand up to them. Miranda laughed to herself. She still needed to learn to stand up to her own parents.

Maybe she could start out with something simple. It probably wouldn't distress her mother to hear that Miranda didn't want to miss the trip to Hollingsford. She promised herself that the next time she had a chance to stand up for herself, she would.

The next afternoon Miranda had the perfect opportunity to test her resolve. She and her father were out in the west field, standing on the bridge Peter had recently repaired. Her father's brush glided over his canvas, painting the myriad of colorful wildflowers.

Miranda's brush had been still for quite some time. She'd been trying to recreate the color of a patch of bluets, but it just wasn't working. Furthermore, the tiny painted petals kept running together, making her flowers look more like a blob than a cluster of delicate blooms. Sighing, she set her brush down and stood back from the easel.

A few minutes later her father stepped away from his work and wiped his brush on his jacket. His painting looked perfect, as usual. He came over to stand beside Miranda.

"What happened here?" he asked, pointing to a smudged area.

"The colors are running together."

He glanced down at her palette. "Your paint is too thin. Should have mixed it better."

"It would have been better with pastels."

He scoffed. "Those colors would be too bold for this." He went on to critique her painting, ending with a suggestion that she start all over with a fresh canvas.

Miranda took a deep breath. She had to say it sometime. "Father, I don't know if I'm meant to be an artist."

Mr. Harlake gasped. "What a thing to say! One bad painting doesn't mean you should give up your craft."

Bad?

"But it isn't only this one," she said. "I don't always feel that passion that I did in the past."

"You can't work only when the mood strikes you, Miranda. You know that. Yes, there can be dull moments. There are technical aspects that aren't the most inspiring. But that doesn't mean you should give it up. Maybe you need different subjects. But you must persevere. Your mother and I are proud of your work, and you should be, too."

Miranda let it drop. She knew Peter would shake his head at her, but she'd tried and her father just wouldn't listen. Anyway, it was a first step. Perhaps next time she'd come right out and say she didn't want to be an artist anymore. If that was true. It was confusing, really, because sometimes she felt so happy when she was deeply engaged in a piece, but at others it felt boring and a waste of time. Maybe the first thing to do was decide how she felt before making any proclamations.

She transformed the patch of bluets into a pond and made an imaginary scene. It wasn't the best she'd ever done, but it made her happy, and she managed to lose herself in the project until it was time to go home for supper.

Mrs. Harlake didn't come down, so Miranda chatted with her father and listened to him critique her work some more. Finally, she excused herself and went upstairs. She changed into a violet-colored dress but didn't bother removing her trousers since George knew about them already. It crossed her mind that she should tell her father where she was going, but she feared he might say no since Ebenezer wasn't involved in the scheme.

When Miranda arrived at the lake, George wasn't there. She paced slowly up and down the empty shore, expecting him to emerge from out of the trees or around the bend at any moment. After a time she worried she'd missed him. Perhaps he'd already come and gone.

Miranda had just come back from checking the forest path again when she heard oars on the water. Turning, she saw a boat approaching. When she reached the shore, she quickly realized it was George.

When he was within earshot he called, "Good evening!"

Miranda waved as she watched him maneuver the boat closer to the beach.

"I was at my mother's cottage and fancied rowing over," George said as he clambered out of the boat and pulled it ashore.

"Wait a moment," Miranda said, stepping forward. "Will you take me out on the lake?"

He pushed his sleeves up to his elbows. "I thought you didn't like boats."

"It's been a long time since I went out in one. The water looks calm tonight and there's hardly any wind.

But if you want to stay on the beach that's fine."

"I'd be happy to take you out," George said. "Shall I carry you to the boat so you don't get your dress wet?"

"Carry me! No, I'm not worried about it getting wet." She lifted her skirt over her ankles so he could see the trousers, and he laughed.

"Come along, then," he said, reaching out his hand. When Miranda took it she was immediately aware of his strength and warmth.

She sat in the stern while George settled in the bow and took up the oars. As the boat drifted away from shore, Miranda gripped the seat and closed her eyes, bracing for the rocking and jostling. But she almost couldn't tell they were moving. She opened her eyes after a few moments to find George watching her.

"Do you want to go back?" he asked. "Be honest."

"No." Miranda leaned back and let her hand trail in the water. "The water is so smooth, not at all like that other time. Do you come out often?"

"From time to time. The children like it when I row them."

"Do you like it?" Miranda asked.

"Most of the time, but I do it even when I don't want to. They love it."

"I wonder if I'll be like that with my brother or sister," she asked as they moved into deeper waters.

"Probably," he said. "It's hard to say no to things that make them happy."

"I understand. It's difficult saying no to my parents, and I imagine even more so with the children," Miranda said. "Today I told my father I might not want to paint anymore and he didn't believe me. But I didn't press it."

"It's good you tried. Maybe we need to start out by

refusing small things. For instance, I could tell my parents I don't want to accompany them to dinner at someone's house."

"Such as an artist's house?" Miranda asked, eyes shining.

George laughed. "Yes, something like that."

"Oh! Do you remember I hid a picture from you that night?" she asked.

Pulling hard on the oars, George shook his head.

"I made a picture of the ball. But I was afraid if you saw it you'd somehow realize that I was your partner."

"Was it a portrait of my unmasked fair lady?"

"No," Miranda said, blushing. "It's more of a general scene. You'll have to see it for yourself."

"May I take that as an invitation to come to your house and see it?"

"Yes, you may," she said, and it felt more like a commitment than a teasing invitation.

When they reached the middle of the lake, George pulled the oars in and they drifted slowly in the current. Waves lapped the sides of the boat and the low cry of loons drifted over the water. Miranda lay back in the boat to look up at the twilight sky, where stars were just beginning to emerge.

After a time Miranda sat up and looked at George. He was watching the sky, too, but he must have felt her gaze on him. His eyes met and held Miranda's and she felt an unexpected warmth in her chest as her heart gave a flutter.

They gazed at each other in silence for a few moments, and then George set the oars to water and headed back.

By the time they reached the shore, it was nearly

dark.

"Will you be able to find your way back?" Miranda asked as she stepped out of the boat.

George jumped out and walked her up the beach. "It isn't full dark, and I left a lantern burning on the cottage's dock. Will you be all right walking home alone?"

"Oh, yes, I've done this walk hundreds of times, even in the dark. Besides, the moon will give me some light."

George hesitated, as though unsure about letting her go alone. "You'd tell me if you wanted me to escort you?"

The affectionate tone in his voice, combined with his sweet, protective air and the sudden thumping of Miranda's heart, convinced her she should *not* walk home alone with him under a moonlit sky. "I'll be fine, and you know I'd have to tell you if I thought otherwise."

"That's good enough for me," he said. "Thank you for meeting me. I enjoyed our evening."

"So did I," Miranda said. They looked at each other for a moment, and then she turned to go.

"Wait," George said. "Will I see you again soon?"

"Tomorrow?" Miranda asked at once, wondering what had gotten into her. It was one thing to be amenable to the idea, quite another to seem overly eager. But George didn't seem to mind.

"I'll call at your house. Will you show me the painting of the ball?"

Miranda hesitated, unsure of what her parents would think. But she wanted him to come, and perhaps this could be more honesty practice. "Yes, I will. Come in the afternoon."

"See you tomorrow." George climbed into the boat, picked up the oars, and disappeared into the night.

As Miranda strolled home, her mind swirled with sweet, new ideas about George.

Chapter Twenty

Miranda spent most of the next few days with George. He came as planned to see the painting, complimenting it though admitting he'd like it better if Miranda had painted herself into it. After visiting the studio Miranda considered a tour of the house but didn't want to encounter her parents, so she took George on a long walk around the grounds and he didn't go home until suppertime.

On Friday, Miranda went to the Rockfords' to give the children an art lesson. Only Sybil drew anything, but Harriet wrote Miranda's name in calligraphy and Nicholas demonstrated his newfound cartwheeling skills. George sat by Miranda's side the whole time, talking to her whenever there was a break in the children's antics. The drawing lesson took only an hour but when Miranda suggested leaving, George and the children implored her to stay longer. She was happy enough to comply and spent the rest of the day with George. The children accompanied them for much of the time, but Miranda and George managed to have a few pleasant hours all to themselves. They ate lunch in the stained-glass room and afterwards sat on the swings, talking until dusk.

If Miranda's parents noticed her spending time with George, they didn't mention it. Mrs. Harlake spent most days in her room and Miranda didn't talk about George when she went up to see her. Miranda suspected her father would be glad of her friendship with George because it meant she might bump into Ebenezer.

The more Miranda knew of George, the more she liked him. They were always honest, at least about most things, laughing over refusing certain foods or not wanting to take a walk or simply saying no about any little thing. He was almost as easy to talk to as Peter.

On Saturday afternoon, George picked Miranda up in his buggy to take her to Darlington's. When she and George walked in, Emily looked up from her work at the counter. She waved at Miranda and opened her mouth to speak, but promptly closed it again when she saw George. Emily gave Miranda a meaningful look that said with no doubt she'd want an explanation the next time they saw each other.

George escorted Miranda to the very chair he'd knocked her out of all those weeks ago. After ordering lunch he told her all about the new automobile Ebenezer was buying—the first in town. Miranda tried to pay attention as he spoke of engines and horsepower and leather seats, but she was too distracted to pay much attention. She wondered how many other ladies had sat across from him on innumerable other Saturdays. A small part of her wondered if coming here with him was some kind of jinx. According to Emily, George only ever took women to Darlington's once—and then what happened? Did a trip to Darlington's mark the end of their acquaintance? Miranda somehow doubted that but reached under the table to knock on wood, just in case.

After lunch they walked around Main Street, looking in shop windows, then stopped for ice cream at Bullard's before heading for home. Though they'd talked all day, they were both quiet once they climbed into the buggy. While George kept his eyes on the road, Miranda's eyes were on him. She noticed tiny things she never had before in all the years they'd known each other. A tiny birthmark on the edge of his jaw, the way his eyebrows lifted slightly as if he was always ready to be surprised. There was a barely noticeable scar above the right brow. Perhaps he'd acquired it during some kind of ruckus with his friends. Miranda was about to ask him about it but he suddenly turned to look at her.

There was something in George's eyes that Miranda had never seen before. She held his gaze for a few moments, trying to discern what it was, until he turned away.

"Let me help you," he said and jumped down from his seat.

Miranda hadn't even noticed they'd come to a stop at the end of Majestic Oaks's drive. So soon?

George took her hand as she climbed out of the buggy. She didn't need help but wouldn't say no to handholding.

"Thank you for another nice day," she said.

"It was my pleasure."

Miranda was about to invite him in when she noticed a new horse grazing in the pasture. *A new horse.* That could only mean one thing.

"Well, thank you again. Goodbye," Miranda said and shook his hand firmly as though they'd just sealed a business deal.

"Oh. Goodbye. I'll see you soon, I hope."

She started backing away, wondering if Peter was watching from the house. "Yes, soon. We'll see each other soon." Miranda folded her hands in front of her and waited impatiently for him to leave.

"Goodbye," he said again, looking slightly bemused as he climbed into the buggy.

Miranda waved, bouncing on her heels until George rounded the corner and was out of sight.

She ran up the drive but hadn't gotten anywhere near the house when the front door burst open and Peter flew down the steps.

"Miranda!" he cried, running to meet her.

They ran straight into each other's arms.

"Peter!" Miranda said, holding him close.

They pulled away just enough to look into each other's faces, unable to stop smiling.

"When did you get back?" she asked.

"Not too long ago, and I arrive to find my fiancée out of the house, not pining for me in the front window as expected."

She placed her hands on Peter's shoulders. "If I'd known you were coming I would have been waiting in the drive, or I would have run up the road to catch the first glimpse of you. But you hardly wrote. Some betrothed you are," she said playfully.

Peter put an arm around her shoulders and they started toward the house. "I did write a few times. Didn't you get my letters?"

"Hm. That's odd. I got one soon after you left. Perhaps they're in the house but nobody thought to bring them to my room." Miranda realized he wouldn't have heard about her mother. "We've had some excitement here that distracted everyone for a time."

"What happened? No, wait. Let me look at you." He turned her to face him and gave her another hug. "I missed you."

"I missed you, too. You were gone for far too long. Did you see Ann?"

"Not exactly. I'll explain, but tell me your news first."

As they walked into the house Miranda told him about her mother and he was just as shocked as Miranda had been.

"Congratulations! Big sister Miranda, at last. I'm happy for your parents."

"So am I. Now tell me about Ann."

"I saw her but I didn't speak to her."

She rubbed his arm. "That must have been difficult. What happened?"

"It was the day I arrived in town. I'd just gotten my room at the inn and was heading out for the horse farm. There she was, getting into a coach to Hollingsford. I didn't see her again during my visit, so she must not have returned to Nottingham."

"Hollingsford? I wonder what business she has there?"

"I don't know, or care. It's so good to see you. Did I miss any other news?"

"A bit," she said as they entered the drawing room and sat on the sofa. "Right after you left, my parents invited Ebenezer here for dinner, and he brought George."

"They didn't!"

"Unfortunately, they did. And then Ebenezer invited us to their country house and we went there for a few days."

Peter shook his head. "You were worried your parents would pressure you about Ebenezer and I didn't believe you. Was it terrible at the Rockfords'?"

"At first. But then I spent some time with George and his sisters and brother. That was enjoyable."

Peter looked surprised. "Was it? I'd have thought you'd avoid him."

"I did, in the beginning. But you know, Peter, he isn't as bad as we thought. Next time he comes over—"

"Next time?" Peter asked, knitting his brows. "He's been coming here?"

"Well, yes. Or sometimes we meet at the lake, or in town."

Peter leaned back against the sofa. "It appears I have missed some things."

"He's so much nicer than we thought."

He surveyed her for a moment, almost smirking. "Miranda, you haven't fallen for *George*, have you?"

"Of course not," she said, blushing. "But we've become friends."

"Be careful," he said, shaking his head slowly. "You remember what I told you about him. He's a charmer, but it doesn't necessarily mean…well."

"Well what?"

"Don't go falling in love with him, will you?" he said gently, taking her hand. "I don't want to see you get hurt."

"Just because I've decided he isn't the most odious man on earth, you're worried I'll fall in love with him?"

"He is handsome. And rich."

"I don't care about either of those things. Speaking of George—well, his family—Emily told me she's seen Ebenezer in town a few times with Miss Jenkins. They might be courting. Maybe they'll get engaged and we can stop pretending to be betrothed."

"Do you think we should stage a quarrel to prepare

your parents for us breaking up?"

Miranda snuggled into Peter's side. "Not yet, you just got back. Maybe in a few days we can argue over who gets the last slice of angel cake."

Peter kissed her hair. "It's good to be home."

Miranda stayed with Peter all afternoon and through the evening. They told each other all the things they'd been saving up until they were together again. Finally, around midnight, Peter left and Miranda went up to her room.

She couldn't stop smiling. Being with Peter was like a breath of fresh air. Miranda didn't have to think about how she acted or what she said. She'd almost forgotten how easy it was to be with someone who knew her so well.

As she prepared for bed Miranda recalled Peter's comments about George. He was worried she'd be taken in by his charms, or even fall in love with him. What a ridiculous notion! But as she drifted off to sleep Miranda remembered watching the stars as she and George sat in the boat in the middle of the lake. And that warm feeling she'd had lately when their eyes met. Love? No. But suddenly the idea didn't seem so ridiculous after all.

****

Miranda met Peter for breakfast and would have liked to spend the day with him, but he had to deliver Ebenezer's horse. As they rose from the table, he asked Miranda if she wanted to come along in case George was there, but the question was in such a teasing manner that she said no.

"You should talk to him, though, Peter. He really is nicer than we thought."

"I don't need to talk to George to know what he's

like. You forget I've seen him at the tavern and other places over the years. Places you wouldn't have gone."

"You might be surprised if you try to get to know him better. Anyway, give him my regards if you do see him."

"I will. I wish you could come with me, my precious dove. It's impossible to part from you so soon. We were only reunited last night." Peter took her hands and gave her a syrupy look. Miranda eyed him quizzically before realizing her father had just walked into the room.

She took a few steps closer to Peter. "I'll miss you, my darling. Must you go?"

Her father cleared his throat loudly but said nothing.

"I'm afraid I must, sweetheart," Peter said. "Mr. Rockford will want his horse. But I'll come home to you as soon as I possibly I can."

"And then we won't be parted for the rest of the day," she said.

Peter kissed her hand. "I'll see you soon, poppet."

"Be careful!" Miranda called as he walked out the door.

"Still betrothed?" Mr. Harlake asked.

"Yes, why wouldn't we be?"

"He was gone for so long, and you seemed to be getting friendly with George Rockford."

So, her parents *had* noticed. "Peter was only gone for a few weeks, and it only made me love him more. Absence really does make the heart grow fonder!" she said with a giggle. "As for George, we've become friends of a sort."

Mr. Harlake sat at the table. "Peter will be missing you again soon. We're going to Hollingsford next week."

"Are we? Will Mother come?"

"The doctor said it's safe as long as we take the carriage. He said riding is out of the question."

"I'm glad she'll be able to see the exhibition."

"Yes, nothing like it to inspire you," he said and picked up his fork.

Miranda started for the door. "Perhaps I'll go talk to Mother about the trip."

"No," he said after swallowing a bite of eggs. "She's resting. Would you like to come out into the woods with me? I'm looking for lady slippers to paint."

The last thing Miranda wanted to do was traipse around looking for the elusive blooms and try to recreate their perfect color and shape. "No, I'm going to see Emily. I just can't wait to tell her Peter's home," she said with the biggest, brightest smile she could manage.

Her father just grunted and turned back to his breakfast.

Perhaps Miranda shouldn't have been surprised to see George with his friends at Darlington's, but she was. Oh, well. Old habits died hard, and it wasn't as though George had set himself a deadline for when he'd stop associating with them. They were getting up to some kind of tomfoolery involving a tower of empty glasses, a salt shaker and a fork, but at least they were at a table this time and couldn't knock anyone over. Still, Miranda made sure to give them a wide berth.

She made her way over to Emily, who was organizing a glove display. "Hi, Emily. I wanted to stop by and find out how your dinner with Nathaniel was."

Emily glanced toward the back storeroom dreamily. "It was perfect. The dinner was delicious, and then we went dancing. Nathaniel told me he wanted to take me out because it was the anniversary of when we'd met. I didn't even remember!"

"How sweet," Miranda said. She'd had no idea men thought of such things.

"It was so romantic. Afterwards he gave me this," she said and pointed to a silver bracelet on her wrist. "He's such a good man." Just then Nathaniel walked by and the glowing looks on his and Emily's faces as they smiled at each other brought Peter's words from last night to mind. His talk of falling in love. Or rather, his warning that Miranda should take care not to fall for George.

Miranda looked over her shoulder to where George and his friends were. There was no way he could hear her, but she lowered her voice anyway. "Emily, how did you know you loved Nathaniel?"

She tilted her head slightly. "It's hard to describe. Haven't you ever been in love?"

"I don't think so," Miranda said. Surely, if she had, she would have noticed.

"It's just the way I feel when I'm with him," Emily said, leaning in closer. "It's as if a little part of me isn't settled when we're apart, and when we're together I feel like I'm home."

"So you love everything about him?"

Emily laughed. "I wouldn't say that. He sometimes talks over me and he leaves his dirty clothes on the floor. He can be so stubborn he puts the mule to shame. But I don't love him for the things he does or doesn't do. I love him because of who he is. It's this feeling that everything is all right as long as I have him in my life. Does that make sense?"

"Yes. I'm so happy for you."

"Thank you. But why do you ask? Have you met

someone?" Emily asked, eyes shining.

"No, I only wondered. It's hard to imagine feeling that way about anyone."

"What about Peter? You two are so close."

Miranda recalled her joy at his return and how everything about Peter felt so right. But no. Their relationship had never been romantic. Whatever their bond was, something was missing that would have made it the all-encompassing emotion she'd heard of. Truthfully, when she'd asked Emily the question she'd been thinking about George. But Emily's description of love didn't fit him, either. Miranda did like George, and sometimes there was a certain feeling, a spark, she felt when they were together that made her wonder about love. But he wasn't crucial to her happiness, which seemed to be how Emily described being in love. George wasn't "home."

"Miranda?" Emily prodded.

"Sorry, I was lost in thought. Peter and I are only friends."

Emily grinned. "Up until now, but perhaps something more in the future?"

"No," Miranda said, laughing. "It's never been that way between us and it never will be."

"Oh, well," Emily said and sighed. "Someday you're bound to meet a man who catches your fancy."

"Yes, someday..." Miranda said and her eyes flickered over to George's table. She shook her head and turned back to Emily. "Speaking of Peter, he came home yesterday and I want to get back to the house to see if he's free for lunch."

"Have a good walk home. I'm going to find Nathaniel," Emily said and gave her a wink.

Miranda laughed and made her way out of the shop. It would be lovely to find someone to care so deeply about one day. She walked down Main Street but hadn't gotten as far as Beech's when someone called her name and she turned to see George running up behind her.

When he reached her side he stopped to catch his breath. "I hoped to catch you before you left Darlington's," he said. "Why didn't you stop by the table and say hello?"

"I didn't want to disturb you with your friends." And she didn't want to get within ten feet of them, or George, when they were up to their foolishness.

"You wouldn't have been disturbing us."

"Honestly?" she asked with a grin.

"Not me, anyway," George said and smiled. "Speaking of disturbing things—cows, actually—I told my friends I wouldn't go with them to let Farmer Thomas's herd out tonight, so that's progress."

"Indeed it is. I told my father I didn't want to go paint lady slippers this morning."

George offered his arm and Miranda took it. "It seems we're getting better at standing up for ourselves already," he said. "Where are you going now?"

"Home."

"Would you like to come see my mother's cottage?" he asked.

Miranda was sorely tempted but didn't want to miss seeing Peter, although she wasn't certain what time he'd be coming home from the Rockfords'. He could be there for hours for all she knew. She looked up at George, who was watching her with an adorably hopeful look on his face. "Yes, I'll come. It's quite a walk, though, isn't it?"

"Yes, but I have the buggy. It's over by Darlington's," George said, and turned them around.

Chapter Twenty-One

As they trotted down the road George described his mother's cottage, but it didn't really register with Miranda, as she was more focused on the sound of his voice and the way his hands deftly handled the reins.

They'd driven for half an hour or so when George turned onto a wide drive and, after cresting a short hill, pulled the buggy to a stop. "We walk from here," he said, jumping down from the driver's seat. He came over to help Miranda, but she'd already climbed down on her own. George unhitched the horse and left him in a shady spot close to a babbling brook.

"Is it far to walk?" Miranda asked.

"No, not really. It's this way."

They started down the hill and, after a few twists and turns, emerged into a clearing. A white clapboard cottage sat on the very edge of the lake. It was two-storied and its foundation matched the stone wall surrounding the yard. A gravel path led down to the front door, which George unlocked and held open for Miranda to enter first.

The main floor had a comfortable sitting room and a kitchen, but the main feature was the three-season porch. It was made up entirely of windows and gave the impression of floating on the lake. George escorted Miranda through the porch and onto the dock. As it swayed under their feet, he took her arm.

Miranda looked up at him, smiling. "This is lovely."

"I had a feeling you'd like it."

They strolled out to the end of the dock, where Miranda saw the rowboat they'd taken out the other night, bobbing on the waves. In the distance she could just make out the beach she usually went to. The water looked dark today and, based on the clouds overhead, rain was likely.

"I wish I'd brought my pastels," Miranda said.

"You'll need to come back one day."

"Thank you, I'd love that."

"Maybe once I conquer drawing you could teach me to use pastels," George said, shifting so he was standing in front of her.

She nodded, already thinking of what they'd need. "I'd be happy to. We could set the easels up right here on the dock."

George didn't answer but held her gaze for so long that Miranda felt her cheeks growing warm. She turned to look out over the water, suddenly nervous, though there was no reason to be. Or perhaps it wasn't nervousness, but a new emotion she'd never known before.

Miranda sat down on the end of the dock and started removing her shoes before realizing it was somewhat inappropriate. She looked up at George, who was still standing. "Do you mind if I dip my toes in the water?"

"Not at all. I'll join you." He sat beside her and removed his boots.

Miranda shivered slightly as she slipped her feet into the water. "Do you ever swim here?" she asked.

"Not much anymore, but I came often when I was young. I'd run down the dock and dive in, or use the rope swing." He looked above, into the trees. "It's still there. I'm not sure I'd trust it now, though. I'll put a new one up. The children would love it."

"You might not be able to keep them off it," she said, swirling the water with her feet.

George was quiet for a few moments, looking out over the lake. When he spoke again, his voice was softer. "My mother would bring me here when I was young, and it was always a special place for just the two of us. That changed once the babies came."

"Perhaps she'll be able to come here again once the children are older," Miranda said.

"Maybe. They keep her busy for now. But it's all right. I like having somewhere quiet to come by myself. Not that I mind being at the house with the family." He swayed his feet in the water, raising tiny bubbles.

"So this is your private hideaway?" she asked, grinning.

"You could say that." He looked into her eyes. "I've never brought anyone else here before."

Miranda sensed this was meant to be a compliment and indicated that she was special to George in a way. "Thank you for bringing me."

George held her eyes and for the second time that day Miranda was tempted to look away. But this time she didn't. Curious feelings stirred inside her as she and George looked at each other, and though she'd never kissed a man—save a fake kiss from her fake fiancé— her eyes were drawn to George's mouth. How easy it would be to lean toward him, a mere few inches, and press her lips to his. What would it feel like? A reckless part of her told her to do it, but a deeper, probably wiser, part told her it wasn't time. Listening to that wiser voice, she reluctantly broke their gaze and looked up at the gathering clouds.

Miranda was about to tell him about her plans for the nursery mural when George unexpectedly took her hand. She didn't look at him but entwined her fingers with his, her heart beating wildly for such a simple gesture. Miranda leaned her head on his shoulder and George let out what sounded like a deep sigh of contentment. They sat on the dock, holding hands and talking, until nearly sunset. Though neither one acknowledged it, something had changed between them today.

"I'd better be getting home," Miranda said when the first plump raindrops splattered the dock.

"So should I. I was supposed to take the children to see the milkweed today."

"Tell them I said hello," Miranda said as she pulled her chilled feet out of the lake and put her shoes back on.

George laced up his boots. "I will."

They took a moment to look out over the lake before walking through the house and back to the buggy.

"The children would like it if you came to visit soon," he said. "You're a favorite of theirs now."

Miranda smiled. "That's sweet."

"Could you come by tomorrow?" George asked as he hitched the horse to the buggy.

"I'm afraid I can't. I'm going to Hollingsford with my parents the day after tomorrow, and I'll need to pack."

"Oh. Why?" he asked, disappointment evident in his tone.

"We're going to an art exhibition."

George and Miranda climbed into the buggy and

started back down the road. Light rain sprinkled their clothes and hair, but Miranda didn't mind. It was fresh and sweet, somehow perfect for today.

"That sounds like an interesting trip," he said.

"Yes, but it feels odd leaving so soon after Peter's return. We've hardly seen each other."

"He'll be here when you get back, though," George said, giving her a strange look. "He lives at your house."

"Yes, and we'll have caught up on each other's news by then." She didn't elaborate any further on Peter, since she suspected George was once again thinking it unusual that he was her best friend. As they drove back to town, a deeply unsettling thought occurred to Miranda. Though their pact had started as a joke, she was supposed to be honest with George. Which meant that at some point she'd need to tell him about her betrothal to Peter. The closer they grew, the more she genuinely wanted to be open with him. George believed she and Peter were only friends, but would he feel the same way if he knew Miranda had an engagement ring from Peter tucked away in her jewelry box? To make things even more awkward, she'd have to explain it had all started because she'd been desperate to avoid getting engaged to George's uncle. On that note, she decided there was no harm in putting it off just a little while longer. Perhaps when she returned from Hollingsford she'd take George on a walk to the ridge and explain everything.

When they came to a halt in front of Majestic Oaks, George walked over to Miranda's side to help her out of the buggy.

"Thank you for an enjoyable afternoon," she said as they stood in the drive, heedless of the rain.

"Thank you for coming."

Their eyes met and Miranda again felt that strong urge to lean toward him. Perhaps George saw something in her eyes, because he took a step closer.

Suddenly the front door opened and Miranda stepped away from George. Peter, standing on the porch, gave them a little wave and a grin.

"Well. Goodbye," Miranda said, folding her arms over her chest. "I'll see you when I get home from Hollingsford."

"Not before?" George asked, wiping his wet bangs out of his eyes.

"No, I'll be busy getting ready."

He reached over and took her hand. "Have a safe trip."

Fiercely conscious of Peter watching, Miranda reluctantly pulled her hand out of his warm grip. After tipping his hat to her, George climbed into the buggy and drove away.

Miranda watched until he was out of sight, then turned and ran up the porch steps. When she reached the top, Peter was shaking his head at her, arms crossed.

"Miranda," Peter said in a mocking voice.

"Peter," she replied in the same tone.

He took her elbow and walked her over to a wooden porch swing, out of the rain. "What are you doing, Miranda?"

"I don't know what you mean," she said as they sat down in the swing.

"Come now. This is *me* you're talking to. You've gone soft over George, even after I warned you. It looked like he was about to kiss you right in front of the house, with who knows who watching."

"Do you really think he was going to kiss me?" she

asked before realizing it was the very last thing she should have said.

Peter looked at her almost pityingly. "George isn't what you think. He's known for amusing himself with women and then casting them aside."

"You don't know that he casts them aside. Maybe…maybe *they* break it off with *him*." An irksome doubt formed in the back of her mind when she remembered his habit of bringing a different woman to Darlington's every week.

"You shouldn't see him anymore. I can tell it's already gone too far. *Has* he kissed you?"

"Peter! That's none of your concern," she said, color flooding her cheeks.

"Everything about you is my concern. I'm your best friend and I want what's best for you. And George isn't it."

Miranda didn't say anything but lowered her head, her eyes filling with tears. As if she weren't confused enough already! She would have liked to tell Peter they'd *almost* kissed, but now probably wasn't the time.

"Miranda," Peter said gently and put an arm around her shoulders. "I don't want you to get your heart broken, that's all."

She leaned against him and wiped her eyes. "He isn't as bad as we thought, Peter. I told you. He's kind and funny and thoughtful. I think you'd like him if you got to know him better."

Miranda felt his shrug.

"Maybe," Peter said. "I'll ask around town. Perhaps I'm wrong about him. But…"

She looked up at him. "But what?"

"Is it too late? Are you already in love with

George?"

She settled back against his shoulder. It seemed like it should be an easy question to answer, but it wasn't. "I just don't know."

Peter rubbed her arm and they sat together watching the rain until it was time to go in for supper.

****

Since Miranda hadn't seen Peter much over the last few weeks and would be parting from him again soon, she spent most of the next two days with him. When her parents were close by, the two pretended to be in love, but by this point they'd had so much practice it wasn't difficult. They'd become quite adept at casting loving glances at each other and holding hands any time they came within five feet of one another.

The morning they left for Hollingsford, Miranda and Peter put on a good show of forlorn lovers facing an unbearable separation. Mrs. Harlake became a little teary, which Miranda took as a good sign, but Mr. Harlake snapped at them to finish getting ready and stop carrying on so, since Peter was driving them to the city anyway.

Miranda asked to be allowed to sit in the driver's seat with Peter, but her parents refused. When they arrived at the hotel in Hollingsford, Peter helped unload the luggage and Miranda bade him farewell, blowing him a kiss when she knew her parents were looking. She stayed on the street until the carriage was out of sight, then joined her parents in their suite of rooms.

As Miranda unpacked she recalled Peter's comments about George and his worries that Miranda would end up with a broken heart. She'd like to think Peter was only being protective, but what if he was right?

George himself had told Miranda he was "charming" with women because that's what they expected of him. It hadn't crossed her mind to ask him why he only took women to Darlington's once and, for that matter, why he took so many women. But perhaps that was one question he wouldn't have answered, pact or no.

George was always attentive and engaging—he had a way of making Miranda feel she was the only person in the world. But was she fooling herself to think they had a special connection? Was she just another Saturday date? Somehow, though well aware this could be only wishful thinking, she didn't think so.

Remembering that day on the dock, Miranda wished she'd kissed him. Well, at least made it clear she'd wanted to be kissed. She wasn't brazen enough to come right out and kiss a man. Perhaps if George had kissed her they'd be courting right now. Hopefully a moment like that would come again. If it did, she knew just what she'd do.

****

The exhibition was all Miranda had dreamed it would be, with more mediums and styles than she'd ever seen in one place. She walked about in a daze, going from room to room, floor to floor, soaking it all in. The art had the dual effect of inspiring Miranda to practice, yet filling her with doubt that her work would ever be good enough. What was the use of continuing with something she couldn't master and wasn't even sure she liked, just to please her parents?

But as she wandered the exhibition halls, she realized it wasn't so much her art she didn't like but the pressure of trying to live up to her parents' expectations. It was only when she tried to use *their* mediums or match *their* styles that her projects felt cumbersome and difficult. Using pastels was almost effortless, and when she sketched she barely need think at all.

It was time to tell her parents she was giving up painting. After her mother had safely given birth, or perhaps when the baby was a few months old, she'd tell them. Miranda felt stronger now that she'd made the decision, and from now on she'd do her best to follow her heart.

The day after the exhibition Miranda went shopping on her own. She'd only intended to buy art supplies but was drawn to a display of fashionable dresses in the shop next door. Her father had given her permission to purchase "anything that strikes your fancy" while they were in town, and though he hadn't specifically mentioned what type of dress she could buy, Miranda took the opportunity to choose a few beautifully impractical gowns. Afterwards she popped into the art store for a new box of pastels. Next she found a quaint little shop where she bought a green scarf for Emily and a horse-shaped tie pin for Peter.

Hurrying back to the hotel to meet her parents for lunch, Miranda was startled to hear someone call her name as she passed the train depot. Who here could possibly know her? She glanced around and, much to her surprise, saw Ann Lawton standing beside a bench.

After what Ann had done to Peter, Miranda was tempted to act as if she hadn't heard her. But they'd already made eye contact and it would be beyond rude to turn her back on Ann now. Still, she need only stop for a quick greeting before making an excuse to get away.

Ann looked pale and tired. Her brown hair was escaping the low bun she'd pulled it into, and that rosy glow she'd had when Miranda first met her was gone. She approached Miranda slowly, as if unsure of her reception. "Good afternoon, Miss Harlake," she said.

Miranda kept her tone polite and civil, but not warm. "Good afternoon."

"I thought I saw you at the art exhibition. And here it is. You." Ann looked over Miranda's shoulder. "Are you alone?"

"At the moment, but I'm in town with my family."

"How nice." Ann pointed to Miranda's bags. "Oh. You've been shopping?"

"Yes." Miranda wondered how long decorum dictated she stay and talk with Ann. "Are you waiting for the train, or did you just arrive?"

"I'm on my way to Peabody to start a job," Ann said, glancing at the empty tracks. In the distance, a cloud of gray smoke announced the train's imminent arrival.

"A job?" Miranda asked. Why would Mr. Cobbe's ward need employment?

Ann walked back to the bench and stiffly sat down. "Yes, I'm going to be a companion to a Mrs. Carleton. She's my great aunt's friend."

"I didn't realize you were looking for a position, but that seems like a good one," Miranda said, sitting beside her.

"Yes," Ann said absentmindedly. She hesitated for a moment as if steeling herself to speak. "Will you tell Mr. Tolwood…that is—How is he? How's Mr. Tolwood?"

"Excellent the last time I saw him. Peter drove me and my parents to town a few days ago."

"Peter's here?" Ann's face flushed as she half rose, staring intently at Miranda.

"Not anymore," Miranda said. "He dropped us off and went home."

Ann sagged against the back of the bench. "Oh. Oh, I see."

Miranda peered at Ann, who was now tying little knots in her handkerchief. Something was wrong, but it didn't seem Miranda's place to ask. She was about to take her leave, but instead pressed Ann's hand with hers.

"Ann, are you all right?"

Ann looked up at her with teary eyes. "It's nothing."

Miranda couldn't leave someone in this miserable state, even someone who'd broken her best friend's heart. "What's wrong? Is your train late? Are you sad to leave Hollingsford? Are you ill?"

"No. No, nothing like that." Ann looked up at her as though deciding how much she should tell. Finally she gave Miranda a half smile and let out a shaky sigh. "Mr. Cobbe isn't going to adopt me after all. I'm going back to being packed off from distant relation to distant relation, as I have all my life. I was so happy when he wanted to adopt me. I thought I finally had a home to call my own."

"But where are your parents? Aunts? Uncles?"

"My parents died when I was a baby. I've been shuffled around from place to place since then. Within the extended family but on the fringes of it, you could say."

"But what happened with Mr. Cobbe?" Miranda asked gently. "I thought he was your guardian."

"He isn't anymore," Ann said, sniffling. "He says he thought I'd marry Mr. Tolwood, but when he didn't propose Mr. Cobbe said he couldn't take on another unmarried girl who needs a dowry because he already has six daughters of his own."

"Why on earth would he think Peter was going to marry you?" Miranda hoped it didn't sound insulting but, really, it wasn't as though they'd officially courted. They'd only seen each other a handful of times.

"I don't know, but he was furious when he found out Peter stopped calling on me. He sent me away then, but a few weeks ago I got the letter saying he's…he's done with me."

Something didn't feel right about this, but Miranda couldn't put her finger on it. Ann had arrived in Deerwood, seemingly with no connections. She didn't stay with Mr. Cobbe, but at the boarding house. When Mr. Cobbe found out Peter was no longer interested in Ann, he sent her away. Looking at Ann now, so bereft and lost, it occurred to Miranda that Ann might not have been aware of Mr. Cobbe's schemes, whatever they were.

"Ann, do you know about Peter? Who he is?"

"I don't know everything about him, but of course I know who he is," Ann said somewhat irritably. "Peter Tolwood of Majestic Oaks. He manages your estate with his father. And he lives with you."

"But do you know who his father *is*?" Miranda pressed.

"Noah Tolwood," Ann said, looking at Miranda as though she was daft.

A shrill whistle announced the arrival of the train just as Miranda realized Ann was completely blameless in all of this. She hadn't sought Peter out intentionally for whatever Mr. Cobbe had planned. Ann didn't even know they were related. She'd genuinely cared for Peter when they met and, based on the way she was acting, she still did.

"Ann, there's something you—" Miranda began.

"I have to go, this is my train," Ann said, rising and wiping her eyes

She put a hand on Ann's arm. "Do you have a moment?"

"I'm sorry, but no. I can't miss my train. Please give Peter my best, and I hope the two of you will be very happy together. Goodbye."

"Goodbye. Have a safe journey."

Ann dragged her suitcase over to the train and handed it to the porter, then climbed aboard.

Miranda watched Ann shuffle down the aisle and take a window seat, dabbing her eyes with a handkerchief as she stared straight ahead.

It was only then Miranda comprehended Ann's last words. Wishing her happiness with Peter? *Oh, no.* She was under the impression they were romantically involved.

"Ann!" Miranda cried, but the train pulled away and it was far too late for an explanation.

Chapter Twenty-Two

When Peter arrived in Hollingsford the next day, Miranda wasted no time in telling him she'd seen Ann. As soon as the carriage pulled to a stop in front of the hotel she rushed outside to greet him.

Peter pulled her into a tight hug. "Miranda."

"I have so much to tell you," she said, pulling away to look into his face.

"I have news for you, too. First let me see to the horses."

As Peter settled the team, Miranda told him about her meeting with Ann.

He shrugged the information off. "I'm sorry things didn't work out for her, but it makes no difference. I can't be involved with anyone who's that close to Mr. Cobbe."

"But she isn't anymore," Miranda said. "She looked so sad."

"What does it even matter?"

"It matters because you liked her. It would be ridiculous to let a misunderstanding get in the way of that."

Peter offered his arm and they walked into the hotel. "This isn't about a misunderstanding. I stopped seeing her because she's Mr. Cobbe's ward."

"I told you, she isn't. What if you visited her in Peabody?"

"I've been down that road before. Even if she isn't

his ward, she's still connected to him." They were about to enter the elevator when he stopped her. "Now I want to tell you something about George."

"What?" she asked. An accident? Was he seeing someone? "What do you want to tell me?"

"Don't look so worried," he said.

After a few moments she put her hands on her hips. "Well?"

"You might be right about George. About him not being as bad as we've always thought."

She grinned. "I told you you'd like him! What changed your mind?"

"I've been thinking about my encounters with him over the years, and I remembered he's nice enough when he's on his own. It's his friends who seem to bring out the worst in him."

"Yes, that's what I thought, too."

"But ideally a man—anyone, really—stands up to their friends and doesn't simply go along with whatever they do. I still think he's the type you should guard your heart from." He gave Miranda a penetrating look. "Is it too late?"

She looked away, sighing. "I still don't know."

"Oh, Miranda. What happened between you two while I was away?" he asked.

Knowing her parents were waiting for them, Miranda was reluctant to tell Peter the whole story. But she had to. She took him to the empty billiard room down the hall. There she told him all the details she'd held back about her trip to the Rockfords'. Though it was embarrassing, she described the visit to the cottage and the near-kiss. Miranda even told him about the unpleasant incident at the lake, though she knew Peter would be angry.

He was. More than angry.

"That Ethan is a menace! George should have stood up for you."

"He apologized afterwards," she said. "He said he won't act like that again."

Peter paced about the room. After a few minutes he turned back to Miranda. "What happens with you two now? Are you courting?"

"No, and I don't know if we will."

He looked stunned. "After all that? After almost kissing you? After taking you around town unchaperoned?"

She laughed. "Unchaperoned! It isn't as if we needed one. He's friendly with all the women he steps out with and hasn't said he wants to be anything more than friends."

"That's probably for the best." Peter put a hand on her shoulder. "That was the other thing I wanted to tell you. I've seen him with Ms. Hodgkins a few times in the last week or so."

Miranda tried to hide her surprise and disappointment. "Well," she said as if it didn't matter, "We didn't make any declarations or the like. He's free to do what he wants."

"Are you free to do what *you* want?" Peter asked.

She gave him a puzzled look. "What do you mean?"

"We're still engaged, aren't we?"

They had to be until Miranda told her parents the truth, which wouldn't be for months. Though her mother hadn't been pleased about the engagement, discovering it had all been a sham would definitely distress her. And that must be avoided at all costs. "Yes, but my parents are hoping we'll call it off," Miranda said.

"Still?"

"Yes, and my mother's joined in with Father's daily comments about how perfect it would be if I married Ebenezer."

"I thought they'd have given up on that by now."

"You know how they press and press me until I relent. Without you, I'd already be engaged to Ebenezer."

"This has to be the one time you *don't* relent, no matter what they say."

"They can be very persuasive. But I'll do my best not to discuss engagements or weddings with them at all. Perhaps with Mother expecting they'll forget about it."

"Yes, and hopefully Ebenezer will get engaged soon and it won't be an issue."

"I hope so." Miranda glanced at the clock. "We'd better get upstairs. My parents are waiting for us."

Not long later they were on their way back to Deerwood. Halfway home Miranda started thinking about George…or rather, worrying about George taking up with Ms. Hodgkins. Just the thought hurt, but there was really no reason why it should. As she'd told Peter, it wasn't as though she and George had a formal attachment. Or even an informal one. But Miranda would be lying if she didn't admit she'd been hoping he'd ask to court her. She couldn't bear the idea of being cast off after all they'd been through together.

Miranda closed her eyes, resting her head against the carriage window. It would be impossible if he did ask, because her parents thought she was engaged to Peter. If, as she dearly hoped, George cared for her, would it be possible to hold him off for a time? Would he wait for her even if she couldn't give him a good reason why?

Most importantly, there was the question of how she felt about George. Miranda still couldn't decide if she loved him. But perhaps that was her answer—love seemed like something you just knew, not something you decided. She enjoyed spending time with him, and she liked their honesty pact. But there should be more to love than that. As these thoughts whirled around in her mind, all Miranda knew for sure was she couldn't wait to see George when she got home.

When they reached Majestic Oaks, Peter stayed for supper. Miranda moved her chair as close to him as possible without sitting in his lap. After the main course, Mrs. Harlake bade them all goodnight and Mr. Harlake helped her upstairs. When he returned to the dining room, he averted his eyes from Miranda and Peter's hands clasped tightly together on the table.

During the rest of the meal they talked first about the visit to Hollingsford, but then Peter told Mr. Harlake one of his mares had delivered a foal while they were away. Mr. Harlake wanted all the details about the foal and afterwards rapturously described the art exhibition to Peter.

"It was so inspiring," Mr. Harlake said over lemon meringue pie. "Seeing all those magnificent pieces makes you want to work even harder to perfect your own work, doesn't it, Miranda?"

"Oh, yes. Or perhaps learn something new."

"Might as well be well rounded, eh?" Mr. Harlake said with a wink.

Peter looked at Miranda. "Oh, you mean you'd like to stop painting?" he asked as though it was the best idea he'd ever heard.

Miranda's mouth dropped.

"So it's you, Peter!" Mr. Harlake cried, throwing his napkin down as he stood up. "Miranda never talked about giving up her art before you two became engaged. Of all people, you should know how much it means to her."

"No, Father, Peter didn't mean anything by his remark!"

Mr. Harlake's voice trembled as he pointed at Peter. "He doesn't appreciate art, not like Ebenezer."

"This isn't about Ebenezer," Miranda said.

Peter met her eyes. "You should tell him."

"Tell me what?" Mr. Harlake demanded.

"Nothing! Peter misunderstood. He wasn't suggesting I give up my art, he was just asking a question. Weren't you, darling?" She widened her eyes at him, imploring him to go along with her explanation.

Peter gave a small nod and crossed his arms. "Just asking a question, sir."

Mr. Harlake looked in no way convinced as he turned on Peter. "We've put up with this betrothal of yours, but you should know—as much as we all like you, we won't allow Miranda to marry someone who doesn't support her art." With that he marched away.

When the front door slammed, Miranda rounded on Peter. "What do you think you're doing?"

"I'm sorry. I was only trying to help."

"By antagonizing my father?"

"I thought it was an opportune moment. You've got to tell your parents how you feel. This is your life we're talking about. Why waste it on things that don't make you happy?"

"Painting does make me happy sometimes. Just not

267

as happy as they want it to make me." She sighed. "You're right. I know you're right. But I can't talk to them about it until after my mother's had the baby."

"I won't bring it up again. Not to your parents, anyway," he said, nudging her arm.

Miranda's nudge back bordered on a shove. "Speaking of wasting your life… You're being silly about Ann. I know you liked her."

Peter groaned and fell back against his chair. "I don't want anything to do with Mr. Cobbe's family."

Miranda just raised her brows at him.

"You know what I mean," he said testily. "How about I don't interfere with your life, and you don't interfere with mine?"

Miranda laughed. "As if we could help ourselves." She took his hand and his defensive posture melted away.

"We'll at least be a bit more subtle about our interference. How does that suit you?" Peter asked.

"It suits me just fine," she said.

"I should warn you, though, before I stop interfering, that everyone in town is saying Ebenezer's bought a diamond ring at the jeweler's. They say he's going to propose to a girl he's known for quite some time."

Miranda clicked her tongue. "How would 'everyone' know that?"

"The servants up at the house, I expect. They say he already has her parents' consent," he said, giving Miranda a meaningful look.

"They can't be talking about me! I'm engaged." She held up her left hand, though it didn't have the desired effect since she wasn't wearing her ring.

"Just be careful," Peter said in a serious tone.

She smiled and put a hand on his arm. "I doubt Ebenezer's going to storm the house and drag me away by force."

"No," he conceded, "but he and your parents might convince you he's the better match. The wealth and art and all that. They don't want me for a son-in-law."

"It isn't for them to decide, is it?" she asked, standing up. "Let's take a walk and see the new foal."

Peter rose and gave her a solemn look. "Remember what I said. They aren't through trying to convince you to cast me off."

Miranda didn't answer but led him through the house and out to the stables. Peter might not believe her, but there was no way she was breaking their engagement. Not yet.

****

The next day Miranda walked into town to deliver Emily's gift. Before entering Darlington's, she checked her reflection in the window pane and smoothed down a wayward lock of hair. She needn't have bothered. Most of the tables were empty and there was no sign of George. Miranda considered stopping by his house on the way home but decided it would be too forward. She'd been there before but never uninvited. Perhaps she'd send him a note tomorrow just to make sure he knew she was back in town.

Emily didn't have time for a long visit, but came out from behind the counter to admire Miranda's new dress. It was ivory, with a square neckline, and the skirt was embroidered with sprigs of blue flowers that matched the wide waistband. Miranda knew it wasn't practical for a walk through the woods but had worn it in case she saw

George. Now she wished she'd ridden into town.

After giving Emily her gift, which she loved, Miranda sat at a table near the window and had a glass of lemonade and a slice of butter cake. Emily stopped by from time to time to chat whenever she had a free moment.

A little while later, as Miranda was exiting Darlington's, she found herself face to face with George in the doorway. Their eyes met and he smiled down at her in a way that set her heart galloping.

"George!" she cried happily before she could stop herself.

"*Oh, George*," Ethan, standing behind him, said in a simpering tone. Frank guffawed, but Henry glanced toward Miranda and didn't laugh.

Miranda wanted to go right back into the store but she seemed rooted to the spot, face burning.

George looked over his shoulder as his hand reached out to claim Miranda's. His hand was warm, solid and protective.

"Apologize, Ethan," he said.

"What for?" Ethan asked, barely containing his laughter.

George bristled. "You know what for. Being so rude to Miranda. I told you before—you need to treat her with respect."

Ethan's brows shot up as he noticed George's hand entwined with Miranda's. "So that's the way it is," he said. "Miranda now, is it? I'll be polite until you move on to the next one."

George just glared at him while Miranda stood there wishing she could think of a scathing retort.

Ethan gave Miranda a low, mock bow. "My

apologies, Miss Harlake."

She didn't bother with a response.

Grumbling, Ethan and Frank pushed past Miranda and George into the shop.

Henry paused and gave Miranda an apologetic look, then turned to George. "Are you coming?"

"No, you go on," he said, tightening his grip on Miranda's hand. "Perhaps I'll see you later."

"I doubt it," Henry said. He gave Miranda a friendly smile and tipped his hat to her before continuing inside.

George turned back to Miranda. "Are you on your way home?"

"Yes," she said, grappling with a raft of conflicting emotions…overjoyed to see him again yet disturbed by Ethan's comment about "the next one," grateful that George had stood up for her but mortified that Ethan had treated her that way in public. Hopefully nobody else had heard.

"May I escort you?" George asked.

"Yes, I'd like that. And thank you for standing up for me," she said as they walked down the steps and onto Main Street.

George grimaced. "I'm sorry I couldn't have stopped him to begin with."

"It's not as if we can control our friends," Miranda said, recalling Peter's escapades.

"No. It would be like trying to control the children," he said. "But I've been making more of an effort to remove myself from the situation when they get too rowdy."

They turned onto the woodland path. "How's that been?" Miranda asked.

"I've had fewer injuries the last week or so," he said,

laughing. "It feels good to behave in a way I don't regret later. Henry's been following my lead somewhat, but there's no holding Ethan and Frank back from their fun."

"That's great, George." She'd never noticed before how delightful it felt to say his name. She wanted to repeat it over and over.

"How was your trip?" George asked, guiding her around a fallen tree in the middle of the trail.

"Going into the city is always interesting, and the exhibition was amazing."

George looked down at her. "I see you have a new frock. It's pretty."

"Thank you," Miranda said, surprised he'd noticed.

She was acutely aware of George's warm hand on her arm, and how he seemed to be holding her closer than usual. She felt inexplicably nervous and tried to think of something to say, but her mind was oddly blank. All she could think of was George.

Miranda turned her head slightly to look at him and their eyes caught and held. Without a word they stopped in the middle of the trail and fell into each other's arms as George bent to kiss her. His lips were soft, yet their touch bolted through her like lightning. It was a slow and gentle kiss, hesitant as if he too could hardly believe it was happening. Miranda gave herself over to him. She was dazed, her senses full of him. His scent, the feel of his body against hers, the sound of his voice whispering her name between leisurely, sensuous kisses.

They pulled apart just enough to look into each other's faces and George's eyes were shining just as Miranda guessed hers must be. She put her head on his chest, wrapped tightly in his arms as she listened to his racing heart.

After a time she looked up at him, and George brushed a hair away from her forehead.

"Can I be honest?" he asked.

Miranda was unable to hold back her grin. "Naturally."

"I've wanted to do that for weeks." He bent down and kissed her again.

Miranda smiled. "So have I."

"There's something else," George said in a more serious tone.

Miranda tried not to look too worried as she replied, "What's that?"

"I know we said we wouldn't keep secrets, but there's one I've been too afraid to tell you." He took a tremulous breath but his voice was steady. "I like you, Miranda. I like you very much."

Her heart soared. "I like you too, George."

"Of all secrets to keep! I would have liked to hear that one more than all the others."

"I don't think it's a secret anymore." She put her hand on the back of his head and drew him down for another kiss.

George wrapped an arm around her waist and they started walking again, though Miranda would have liked to linger in the woods all day.

"I missed you when you were gone," he said, rubbing her shoulder.

"I thought of you when I was in Hollingsford."

George smiled at her. "What did you think?"

"That I wanted to get home to see you, and I wondered what you were doing." She cleared her throat, unsure if she even wanted to ask, especially at a moment like this. But remembering Peter's words, she had to know. "Did you take anyone to Darlington's on Saturday?"

"Yes. Miss Hodgkins."

Miranda couldn't find her voice but nodded, trying to appear indifferent.

They were silent for a few paces, but then understanding dawned on George's face. "Not like I *usually* take women to Darlington's. Miss Hodgkins might be coming to teach Sybil how to ride, and I've met with her a few times to discuss lessons and her experience with children."

Miranda let out a light laugh as relief flooded through her. "Oh. I'm sure Sybil will enjoy that." Perhaps she should have let it rest, but after asking one awkward question, she might as well ask the one that had been troubling her for weeks. "George?"

"Yes?" he asked, smiling down at her in a way that almost made her forget the question.

"Why do you only take women to Darlington's once?"

His eyes clouded and Miranda immediately regretted asking.

"Never mind," she said.

"No, it's all right. I don't want to have any secrets from you. Not that this is a secret, exactly." He let out a heavy sigh. "People in town think I'm some kind of rogue. You've heard that rumor, haven't you?"

Miranda wanted to deny it, but how many times had she heard Peter say it, or thought it herself before she truly knew George? "Well, yes, I suppose you do have a bit of a reputation."

George laughed mirthlessly. "Only because I go out with so many different women, and never more than once. But I didn't do that because I'm a cad. It's because I never wanted to get close enough to any of them that they could break my heart. I was looking for someone I could trust. Someone I knew I could be myself with, someone who wanted to be with me for *me*."

"Didn't the women ever ask you why you didn't take them out again? Were they offended?"

"No, I think it's a well-known fact about me." He paused, blushing. "I never wanted to go out with any woman more than once before I met you."

George stared into Miranda's eyes for a heartbeat, then his lips were on hers and she lost all track of time. They continued home, stopping every so often to fall into a passionate embrace. It was a long time before they reached Majestic Oaks.

George walked Miranda up to the front door and promised to call the next day. Since they couldn't kiss goodnight on her front porch Miranda tried to convey with her eyes how much she wanted to. George held her hands for a moment before turning to go. At the end of the drive he looked back and waved.

Miranda walked into the house and leaned against the door, sighing happily as she placed her hands over her heart. She could hardly believe she hadn't dreamed the last few hours. But her lips still remembered George's kisses, his sweet words rang in her ears, and his cologne lingered on her clothes. There was no question now of how they felt about each other. All that remained was to officially begin courting.

Suddenly she heard footsteps coming through the house.

"Miranda?" her father called.

She straightened at once and had just managed to get

the blissful look off her face when Mr. Harlake strolled into the foyer.

"Where were you?" he asked.

"I was in the woods. Walking in the woods."

"At this hour? You missed supper. Peter just left, and your mother went to bed over an hour ago."

For once Miranda was glad she'd missed Peter, because he'd have taken one look at her and known she was hiding something. Something marvelous. "I lost track of time." On impulse she added, "I was looking for interesting trees I might paint."

"Ah," he said, nodding in approval. "It's easy to lose track of time when you're inspired. Only, next time, I'd suggest your trousers instead of a dress like that. That's why we don't bother buying them. Just look at the hem."

Miranda glanced down at the hem of her dress, which was indeed dirty and somewhat frayed. It was the least of her concerns at the moment, but she put on a regretful expression. "Yes, I will next time."

"Do you want something to eat?" her father asked as they walked into the parlor. "I could ring the kitchen."

"No, I'm not hungry." All she wanted was to be alone and go over every second of her time with George.

"Hm. If you're sure. Not good to go to sleep on an empty stomach."

"I had something at Darlington's." Only a slice of cake, and that hours ago, but still, she *had* eaten.

"Oh, in that case."

"Goodnight," she said and kissed his cheek.

Miranda practically floated upstairs to her room, taking each step slowly as her hand trailed along the banister. One thought was foremost in her mind. George liked her. He really did. They'd been honest with each other up to now, and she'd hold to their pact and tell him her last secret—she'd tell him about the fake betrothal.

Tomorrow she'd tell Peter they didn't need to continue with their ruse, and perhaps they could stage the quarrel he'd mentioned. Miranda had planned to wait until after the baby was born to break off the engagement, but the situation was different now. George would want to call on her more often, and Miranda could hardly have two men courting her, especially when her parents thought she was betrothed to Peter.

Miranda considered seeking Peter out tonight to tell him about George, but she wanted one night where the kiss was her secret and hers alone. It was too precious to share, even with her best friend. Miranda put her nightgown on and climbed into bed, but it was a long time before she could fall asleep. She felt lit up inside, full somehow. Miranda no longer wondered how she felt about George. She loved him. There was no need to justify it, or understand why. She loved him, and it was as simple as that. And Miranda had the most wonderful feeling that he loved her, too.

Chapter Twenty-Three

The following day was much too long. Before breakfast, Miranda received a note from George telling her he couldn't come to her house until later that evening, when he'd be accompanying his uncle on some business. In his note George said he'd be counting the minutes until he saw her again, which did somewhat make up for the delay.

Since she was too fidgety for much else, Miranda spent the day with Peter. She followed him around the stable as he cared for the horses. Then they walked out to the north field to check on a fence repair. During lunch she told him they could stage an argument in front of her parents whenever a good opportunity presented itself, and they had fun debating what would be the best thing to fight about. Miranda thought a disagreement about which house they should live in after the wedding would be believable, but Peter was convinced a quarrel about her art would anger her parents even more. Miranda really couldn't argue with that.

Peter was under the impression this was all in anticipation of calling off their betrothal once Ebenezer got engaged, and Miranda didn't correct him. She didn't know how he'd react if she told him it was because she wanted to be available for George. Miranda tried telling him about the kiss, but the moment she mentioned George's name Peter began a lecture about how he was practically a rogue and reminded Miranda of all the juvenile things he'd done with his friends, and how he'd hurt Miranda's feelings. She regretted telling him about that. Apparently, even though Peter had decided George wasn't as bad as they'd always thought, he still didn't trust him with Miranda's heart.

When Peter returned home for dinner, Miranda went up to her room and changed into another new gown, this one lilac with a narrow skirt and elbow-length sleeves. A single pink rosette sat in the center of the lacy neckline.

Miranda had just left her bedroom when she heard the sounds of arrival. She picked up her pace, smiling to herself as she remembered that night months ago when she'd been so shocked and disappointed to discover George and Ebenezer downstairs. Now nothing could make her happier. Well, perhaps if George had come alone…and if he'd arrived with her parents' permission to take her away somewhere else…somewhere quiet and secluded.

In the drawing room, Miranda's father talked to Ebenezer and George while Mrs. Harlake sat on the sofa.

George looked up the moment Miranda entered the room, and she had the feeling he'd been waiting for her. Her heart swelled at the way George lit up when their eyes met.

"Ah, here's Miranda," her father said as she moved to his side.

"Good evening," Miranda said.

Ebenezer took her hand and kissed it. "Ravishing as always."

"Thank you," she said, taking her hand back and looking at George. "How are you, George?"

"Excellent, thank you." He took a few steps closer

to her and seemed to be having a hard time holding back a smile. Miranda guessed she looked the same way and could hardly wait until they were alone.

"Shall we go in for dinner?" Mrs. Harlake asked, rising.

Ebenezer cleared his throat. "Actually, I was about to make an announcement," he said, drawing all eyes to him.

"Oh, what's that?" Mr. Harlake asked.

Ebenezer looked around the room with the air of someone who knew he was about to astonish everyone. "I'm getting married."

"You're what!" George exclaimed.

"Married, dear boy," Ebenezer said. "It's high time, I think."

"Married to whom?" George asked.

Ebenezer nudged him. "As if you didn't know! You've spent enough time with her, so you know what a treasure she is."

"Oh, how sweet," Miranda said and laughed. Finally, someone had caught Ebenezer's eye!

"You'll want to start planning the wedding right away, I imagine," Mrs. Harlake said.

Miranda nodded. "A summer wedding would be perfect."

"Yes, as soon as possible. I don't want to wait any longer than necessary," Ebenezer said.

"When it's right, it's right, eh?" Mr. Harlake said, chuckling. "We couldn't be happier for you."

"Thank you, thank you," Ebenezer said. "Now there's only the matter of proposing."

"How can you say you're getting married when you haven't even asked her yet?" George asked incredulously.

"I know she'll say yes. It's all settled as far as we're concerned."

"Well, that—" Miranda began, but just then the door flew open and Peter burst in.

"Miranda, here you are," he cried. He strode across the room, eyes blazing in a way she didn't understand at first. But then she recognized that determined look on his face. In a flash she understood what he was doing and in the same instant knew she was powerless to stop him. Miranda stole a glance at George, who was watching Peter but clearly didn't know what his intentions were. How could he? How could anyone besides Miranda?

She started to call Peter's name, not even knowing what she'd say, but it was too late. Before she knew what was happening she was in Peter's arms and his lips were on hers. The kiss was chaste and quick, but she knew how it must look to everyone else. Peter kept his arms tight around her, smiling in that beloved way as though he knew he'd just come to her rescue. He all but winked at Miranda as he spoke. "I know we're supposed to meet later, darling, but I couldn't wait to see you. I hope I'm not interrupting anything."

Fainting dead away seemed the best course of action, but Miranda just put her hands on his shoulders and pushed him away gently. Peter kissed her cheek and slid an arm around her waist.

The room was utterly silent. Her parents stared in horror, even Ebenezer seemed shocked. Miranda didn't want to look at George, but she had to. She slowly turned to face him.

George seemed like a man who thought he was dreaming. His face had drained of all color and he looked slightly ill as he shook his head slowly and backed away from Miranda, arms outstretched as though to guard himself from her.

Miranda reached for his hand but he snatched it away.

"No, George, wait!" she cried. "It's pretend. It's all pretend!"

George glared at her, his blue eyes hard and cold. "I trusted you," he said in a harsh whisper and fled the room, slamming the door behind him.

Ebenezer scowled at Miranda and followed his nephew.

"What in heaven's name is going on, Miranda?" her mother asked, gripping the back of a chair.

Mr. Harlake stared at Miranda as though she was a harlot. "Kissing Peter in front of our guests!"

Miranda didn't care what her parents thought. All she wanted was to find George and tell him the truth about everything, then beg his forgiveness. She didn't want to remember that devastated look in his eyes.

"I need to go, I need to explain!" Miranda said, but her father caught her arm before she could leave the room.

"No! You need to stay here and tell us what's happening," he said.

Miranda's head swam as she stood there on trembling legs, staring at the door that had just shut her off from the only man she had ever loved. The man who would never come back. And she had no one to blame but herself. If she'd told George the truth, he would have known Peter's outrageous behavior was all an act. But now it was too late.

Peter guided her to the sofa, where she sat stiffly on

the edge of the cushions. He hurried over to the liquor cabinet and poured out a glass of sherry. "Here, drink this," he said gently as he sat beside her.

She pushed it away, not wanting any more "help" from Peter at the moment.

He clicked his tongue. "Miranda…" he said and she looked into his eyes, which were full of regret. "I'm so sorry."

Miranda took the glass, cradling it in her hands as her eyes filled with tears.

Mr. and Mrs. Harlake both stood before them, arms crossed.

"Well?" Mr. Harlake said.

"It's as simple as this—" Peter began, but Miranda held up a hand.

"Don't, Peter. I've let you clean up my messes for long enough."

He nodded and gave her an encouraging smile.

Miranda downed her sherry and set the glass on the floor, then rose to face her parents. "Peter and I have only been pretending to be engaged."

"What!" Mrs. Harlake exclaimed. "Why would you do such a thing?"

Mr. Harlake looked utterly bewildered. "Pretending?"

Miranda took a steadying breath. "Peter found out you were going to offer me to Ebenezer. I was too afraid to tell you that's the last thing I'd ever want, so Peter and I concocted this plan to keep me from marrying someone I didn't like."

"You've been lying to us all this time?" Mr. Harlake asked in a tone that broke Miranda's heart.

"Yes, I've been lying," she said. "And not only

about this, not only recently. I've been lying to you about who I truly am for years. I've—I've hidden myself from you."

"That doesn't make any sense," her father said. "We *do* know you. We probably know you better than you know yourself."

"No, you don't!" she shouted, then took a moment to calm herself. "You only see me as you want to see me. You want me to be the perfect artist, the perfect daughter, the perfect wife of some pompous ass, the—"

"Miranda!" her mother said with a gasp, her hand flying to her chest. "There is no need for that kind of talk. Your father and I have never said we want you to be the perfect *anything*."

"You don't need to say it. It's the way you push me toward what you want and don't listen when I tell you my own thoughts and plans and dreams. You won't even let me pick my own clothes, for goodness' sake!"

Mr. Harlake put on a patient expression as though trying to reason with a cranky toddler. "We've always supported you, so what precisely is it that you think you aren't getting from us?"

Somehow the question blindsided Miranda and she needed a few seconds to think about it. More than anything she wanted to tell her parents to forget she'd brought this up, and to go on as before. But the cat was out of the bag now. She looked at Peter, who rose to his feet and motioned for her to go on.

Miranda faced her parents. "I want to make my own decisions about my life, but whenever I try, you don't let me. You don't listen to me and I'm always afraid to say no to you. I can't go on this way any longer. I just can't. I want to be with whomever I like, and I don't want to be a painter, and I want to make my own choices and go to parties and wear pretty clothes. I want to be who I *am*, not who you think I should be."

For a few moments Mr. and Mrs. Harlake stared at each other with matching expressions Miranda didn't think she'd ever seen on their faces before. A combination of sorrow, regret, and perhaps... understanding.

Her mother was the first to speak, looking at Miranda with teary eyes. "Why didn't you tell us this before?"

"I didn't want to disappoint you. I've tried so hard to be everything to you, all these years, because I'm all you had," Miranda said as the tears began to flow.

"You could never be a disappointment to us!" her father said, seemingly shocked at the very idea.

"You *are* everything to us," Mrs. Harlake said. "Not because you're our only child, but because we love you so very much. All we've ever wanted is for you to be happy."

"Miranda," her father said, his eyes glinting with tears. "I'm sorry you felt that way. If we'd only known..."

She started crying even harder, and Peter stepped aside as Mr. and Mrs. Harlake moved in to embrace her. The three of them stood together until Miranda's tears finally ceased. "I'm sorry I didn't try harder to tell you the truth."

"No, no. We should have listened to you," Mr. Harlake said. "You tried to tell me you don't enjoy painting, and I didn't listen. I love it so much, and I suppose I wanted to share it with you."

Mrs. Harlake rubbed Miranda's shoulder. "I'm sorry

I haven't been here enough for you. I've been so distracted. Well, not only distracted. I felt ill, too. It was to do with trying to have another baby. But it's no excuse, I should have put you first."

"Why did you keep trying if it made you ill?" Miranda asked.

"It didn't make me sick, exactly, but every time I failed it made me so depressed. I couldn't bear to be with anyone at those times, save your father, because he understood the disappointment, too."

Miranda lowered her head. Her mother had tried year after year to have another baby because Miranda wasn't enough for her. If only she could have been the perfect daughter and saved her the anguish of trying!

Mrs. Harlake seemed to read Miranda's thoughts. "The reason I wanted another baby was because I wanted you to have a sibling. I love my sisters and I couldn't fathom my own child growing up alone."

"I wasn't alone. I had you and Father."

"Yes, but it isn't the same," Mrs. Harlake said.

"I couldn't have been happier," Miranda said. "I had Peter and the Tolwoods, and now we *will* have a baby."

"This is what I've been waiting for," Mrs. Harlake said through happy tears. "But it isn't because you weren't enough, Miranda. You've been the joy of my life. I'm sorry for those times when I was neglectful. If I could do it all over, I'd be a better mother."

"You're a wonderful mother. You're both wonderful," Miranda said, taking her parents' hands. "It was for me to find the courage to tell you how I feel."

"No, no. You shouldn't need courage to talk to your own parents," Mr. Harlake said with a heavy sigh. "But the air's cleared now. You can tell us everything, and we promise to listen."

Beside him, Mrs. Harlake nodded emphatically and wiped her eyes.

"From now on I'll try to be honest all the time," Miranda said, feeling lighter, free now that she'd finally told them how she felt.

"Try?" her father asked, a lilt in his voice.

"It might take some practice," Miranda said and they all laughed.

Mrs. Harlake gave Peter a stern look. "And what do you have to say for yourself?"

He flushed slightly. "I'm sorry I lied to you. I was only trying to help Miranda. But I promise I won't do anything like that again."

"I don't think there'll be a need for us to get engaged again," Miranda said.

"No, I'm sure there won't," Peter said. "Oh! I'll need that ring back. It was my grandmother's."

Before Miranda could reply, Mrs. Harlake cut in, "I won't tell your parents about all this mischief, Peter, though I think you'd deserve it if I did."

Peter clasped his hands in front of him as if in prayer. "Please don't. They'd be so angry." He grimaced. "I don't want to even think of what my father would say."

Mrs. Harlake gave him a wry grin. "I know how they'd feel."

"You're a fine actor, my lad," Mr. Harlake said. "At least now I won't have to watch you pawing at Miranda anymore."

"There wasn't any *pawing*," Peter said as Miranda giggled.

Mrs. Harlake looked at them both thoughtfully. "So

it was all fake?"

"Yes," Miranda said. "All of it."

"I have to hand it to you two," her mother said. "I was convinced Peter would be our son-in-law."

"But the whole time you were hoping I'd change my mind and marry Ebenezer!" Miranda said.

Mr. Harlake shrugged. "It would have been a grand match. But I suppose he's marrying someone else now. I wonder who?"

"Miss Jenkins, I heard," Peter said.

Mr. Harlake was watching Miranda closely. "But wait. George looked so upset when Peter…when he kissed you. Why? Was there something between the two of you?"

Miranda's tears began anew. "There might have been. But there won't be now," she managed to get out between sobs.

"But how? When—" her mother began, but Miranda just cried harder.

Peter pulled Miranda into his arms. "I'll look after her," he said, stroking her hair.

"I need to rest," Mrs. Harlake said wearily. "Lucas, let's leave these two alone. But Miranda, I'm upstairs if you need me. Always."

"As am I," her father added and they left the room.

Peter led Miranda to the sofa, where she cried for what felt like years as he held her in his arms.

"I was going to tell him," she said at last, sniffling. "Even though I never dreamed he'd find out about us."

"I'm so, so sorry. I thought Ebenezer was about to propose right here in the drawing room, and it sounded like you'd been persuaded to accept him. I shouldn't have done anything without finding out what was happening first. I meant to be your knight in shining armor, not the villain in your story."

"You're not a villain, Peter. It's my fault. Yesterday I was going to tell you our engagement was over because George kissed me. But I know you don't like him so I let you believe it was because of Ebenezer. If I'd told you the truth, you would have acted differently. Ugh. I am never lying again. To anyone." She leaned back against the sofa cushions and covered her face with her hands.

"George kissed you?" he asked in surprise.

Miranda peeked between her fingers and nodded.

"How was it?" Peter asked with a sly grin.

She sat up and wiped her eyes. "It was the best thing that's ever happened to me. It won't happen again, though. Did you see how angry he was?"

"I think he was more hurt."

"That's even worse. He'll never come back," she said in a small voice.

"He might," Peter said and stood up. "I'm going to talk to him."

Miranda jumped to her feet. "No! You can't. Besides, I need to clean up my own messes now, like I said."

Peter put his hands on her shoulders. "This is my mess. Please, let me do this for you. I'll explain everything and hopefully bring George back with me."

"How can we tell him it was all because I'd have done anything to avoid marrying his uncle?"

He considered that for a moment. "No, it was because you wanted to make your own choice. And now you have. Right?"

"I have. But it's too late." She sank back onto the sofa.

"We'll see," Peter said and kissed the top of her head.

****

The emotional toll of the day caught up to Miranda and she fell asleep in the drawing room as soon as Peter left. A few hours later, he shook her awake and she sat up, rubbing her eyes. One look at his face told her all she needed to know. Her heart sank.

"I'm sorry," Peter said, sitting beside her. "George wouldn't come to the door, and Ebenezer refused to let me in."

"Thank you for trying. I'll ride over first thing in the morning. Perhaps he'll be ready to talk by then. You should go home and get some sleep."

"Will you be all right alone?" Peter asked, looking into her puffy eyes.

"Yes. I'm sad about George, but I'm glad I finally told my parents the truth. It's like a weight has been lifted off me. And we don't have to be engaged anymore."

"I didn't mind it so much," Peter said, smiling.

"Neither did I, aside from the lying." Miranda rose and stretched. "I'm going to bed."

Peter stood up. "So am I. I'll see you in the morning."

Miranda walked him to the front door and went upstairs. She'd expected to fall asleep the moment her head hit the pillow, not anticipating the tears that began as soon as she blew out her bedside candle. There were hours of worry and regret before she at last fell into a fitful sleep in the small hours of the morning.

Chapter Twenty-Four

When Miranda woke at ten o'clock the next morning, she cursed herself and threw back the covers. She'd intended to get to the Rockfords' as early as possible. She ran to her wardrobe and threw on her riding habit, then headed to the stables. Peter was already there, holding Fergus by his bridle.

"I hope George will see you," he said. "Do you want me to come with you?"

It was tempting to have his support, but Miranda shook her head. "No, I need to do this on my own."

Peter gave her a leg up. "I'll be here when you get home. We'll talk then."

She nodded and clicked to Fergus, who trotted out of the stable yard. Miranda urged him to a gallop when they reached Fairbanks Road. Her mind was filled with George's words last night—and that look on his face.

The Rockfords' finest carriage was just pulling up to the house when Miranda arrived. She slowed Fergus to a walk and they continued to the end of the long drive, where she dismounted and secured his reins to a hitching post.

Miranda mounted the stairs, smoothing her windswept hair as she looked up at the house. When she reached the landing, she took a deep breath and raised a hand to ring the bell. But there was no need.

The door opened and George stepped out, suitcase

in hand. He started when he saw her.

"Miranda." He said her name with no warmth whatsoever. It came out like a curse.

She tried to catch his eye but he sidestepped her.

"George, please, I need to talk to you."

"I don't have time, I'm leaving town," he said and walked down the porch steps.

Miranda's stomach plummeted. "Where are you going?" she asked, following him.

He didn't answer but handed his bag to a footman, who carried it to the carriage.

"George!" She quickened her steps, trying to keep up with him.

Miranda felt a glimmer of hope when he paused, head bowed. She moved to stand in front of him but he refused to look at her.

"There's nothing between Peter and me," she said after she'd caught her breath. "It was all a misunderstanding."

George finally met her gaze, but she wished he hadn't. His eyes were distant, his jaw set. "My carriage is waiting."

He swept past her and Miranda chased after him, knowing she was humiliating herself. "Please, George. You have to believe me!"

George spun around so fast Miranda had to step aside to avoid crashing into him. "Believe you? After last night? You promised me there was nothing between you and Tolwood, but then he calls you 'darling' and kisses you?" He pinched the bridge of his nose and let his arms drop to his sides. "Look, I don't care what you do with Peter. That doesn't even matter anymore. What matters is I opened up to you in a way I haven't with anyone for years. Maybe ever. I know our honesty pact was a joke at first, but it meant something to me."

"It meant something to me, too." She put a hand on his arm but he jerked away.

He narrowed his eyes at her. "You didn't act like it. I don't know what to believe anymore, or who you are. I thought I could trust you."

"You *can* trust me. George—wait, please!"

He strode to the carriage, climbed inside and was driven away without looking back.

She watched until the carriage disappeared out of sight. When it was gone, she mounted Fergus and rode slowly home, haunted by the look on George's face. It was hard to imagine a worse outcome of last night. But she couldn't blame Peter. It was her own fault for not telling George about the fake engagement. She could only hope that when he returned from wherever he was going he'd be willing to give her another chance.

****

Miranda's melancholy only grew as the days dragged on and George still hadn't returned. Where could he have gone? Would he ever be back? She felt sure she would have heard, somehow, if he'd moved away permanently. The Harlakes weren't communicating with the Rockfords anymore, so she would only hear such news through town gossip.

One bit of gossip Miranda did hear was that Ebenezer was indeed getting married. News had spread that Ebenezer was marrying not Miss Jenkins but Miss Hodgkins, the riding instructor.

Before George left, Miranda hadn't really noticed how much her days had come to revolve around him. She'd always been visiting him, expecting him, or just hoping to run into him in town. Now that he was gone she tried to remember what she'd done before they started spending so much time together. Her painting, of course, but she was currently taking a break from that. Some people found inspiration in their sorrow, but not Miranda. The few times she'd tried starting a new piece, she'd stared blankly at the canvas, holding the brush—which felt like it weighed a hundred pounds—until she simply gave up and left the studio.

One new way she'd found to occupy her time was visiting her mother. After the discussion the other night, it was as if a floodgate had been opened. Well, perhaps not a floodgate. Her mother was more social but not exactly verbose. Still, Miranda cherished their time together in her mother's rooms or, more often than not, in the nursery. Miranda was now able to talk to her about things she wouldn't have dreamed of mentioning before. Like the fact that she wanted to dress in the current fashions and attend social events in town. Mrs. Harlake was pleased to hear it and promised that once she was up and around after the baby was born they'd do whatever Miranda liked. It was as if she was trying to make up for all the times Miranda hadn't felt heard.

Mr. Harlake was another story. Though he claimed to support her in her own endeavors, he couldn't resist pointing out how much Miranda loved painting and always had. He was still pressuring her to paint, but it felt good to have discussions with him rather than to automatically agree with everything he said.

When Miranda wasn't with her parents she was with Peter or Emily. Usually Peter. To his dismay, most of Miranda's talk centered around him giving Ann another chance.

"Miranda," he said one day as they strolled through the woods, "just stop. I've already told you I'm not interested in her anymore."

"But you liked her. I know you did."

He quickened his pace. "She's gone. There are other fish in the sea."

"But you aren't looking for the other fish," Miranda said, catching his sleeve.

Peter stopped and threw his hands up. "I will at some point. What does it matter? I'm young, I have time."

"But what if she marries somebody else?"

"Then I will wish her well," he said, but a shadow passed over his face.

"Peter, be serious."

"I am. There was nothing between me and Ann, and there never will be."

Miranda took his hand in both of hers. "Don't make the same mistake I did with George. I should have told him sooner that I liked him. I should have been honest with him. You don't like Ann because of Mr. Cobbe. I understand that. But wouldn't it be worse to let him rob you of a chance to love somebody just because she happened to be his ward? I'm telling you, when I spoke to her she didn't even know you're…well. She doesn't know how you're connected to Mr. Cobbe."

Peter kicked at a rock at his feet, sending it careening off a tree trunk. "I'm not connected to him."

"Just don't let resentment of him get in the way of your chance at happiness. That's all I'm saying. If you don't like Ann, then by all means forget about her. Plenty of girls in town would love a chance to be with you."

Peter didn't say any more but looked thoughtful as they walked back to the house.

They parted in the front yard, and Miranda went upstairs to change, but when she went to fetch a clean dress she noticed her watercolors sitting on the bottom of the closet. She picked them up and wiped dust off the cover. How had so much accumulated in just a few weeks?

Miranda glanced outside, where the leaves of the big oak tree were flirting with changing color. With her watercolors in one hand and a pad of paper in the other, she went out to the balcony. Before she knew it, an hour had disappeared and she had made a painting different from anything she'd ever done before. Smiling, it occurred to her that her art didn't have to be perfect. It didn't even have to be good, or seen by anyone but her. All that mattered was that she liked it.

She'd just set the painting aside and was going inside for her pastels when Peter suddenly appeared on the balcony.

"What are you doing here?" she asked, giving him a hand over.

"I want to talk to you."

"About what?"

"Two things. I'm inviting you to the town dance, and I was thinking we should take a few days off and go away somewhere, just the two of us. I know you've been sad about George, and it might do you some good to leave Deerwood for a while."

Miranda walked into her room and climbed onto the bed. Peter sat beside her.

"I'd still be sad if I went away," she said.

"Yes, but you could be sad at a concert or a fair or the beach. That has to be better than being sad here." He took her hand. "Say you'll come."

Miranda considered it. Every day, she hoped George would not only come back to Deerwood but also come to her house and say he forgave her. In her daydreams, this was followed by him sweeping her into his arms and kissing her senseless. But that was just a dream. In truth there was no way of knowing when George would return, and it was highly doubtful he'd come straight to her house to apologize. He'd probably never come here again. It was hard to imagine she'd feel better anywhere else, but Peter had a point. Maybe a change of scene would do her good.

"Where would we go?" she asked, folding her hands in her lap.

"You just went to the city, so maybe that country fair near Ellingsworth? It's only half a day's ride and close to my Uncle Jonathan's, so we could stay with him and his family. We needn't worry our parents by going off alone. We can even have Walt drive us if that would please your parents."

"I'd love to. Thank you for being here for me, Peter. Standing up for myself is much easier with my best friend at my side."

"That's what I'm here for," he said. "Now about the dance. What time should I pick you up?"

"I don't think I'd be very amusing at the dance. Perhaps you should take someone else."

"No, I want to go with you. We should put all our dance practice to good use. Please come?" he said with a pleading look.

She fell back onto the bed, hands folded over her stomach. "Why?"

"Because you're wallowing."

"No, I'm not!" she said, laughing.

He lay down beside her. "Prove it. Come to the dance."

"Fine. I'll go. But only because I feel I owe you for being so good to me."

"What better reason could you have?" he said, grinning.

She looked over at him. "I'll need to decide what to wear."

"You can wear your new frock, or the one you wore to the masked ball."

"No, that one would make me even sadder. I'll look through my wardrobe. I'm sure I have something suitable. Oh, I keep forgetting…" Miranda rose and crossed the room to her jewelry box, where she pulled out the engagement ring.

Peter stood up and took it from her. "Well, it did keep you from marrying Ebenezer," he said as he slipped it into his pocket.

"Thank goodness for that." Miranda looked at the clock. "It's time for supper. Will you stay?"

"Yes, but I'll go down and ring the doorbell. Your parents are already mad at me for our betrothal and wouldn't be pleased to know I've been in your bedroom."

"Good idea," she said.

Peter climbed back down the balcony, and Miranda walked down the stairs.

****

In the end, Miranda was glad she went to the dance. It was a yearly event that almost everyone in town attended, so she had no lack of partners. Miranda's favorite part of the dance was her dress. She'd decided to test her new communication skills with her parents and asked them if she could buy the pink dress from Easton's that George had gifted her all those months ago. Her father hesitated, but Mrs. Harlake insisted Miranda should have it. Her only stipulation was that Miranda not wear it with pants.

Miranda had a desperate hope that George would return in time for the dance, but he wasn't there. She did catch glimpses of his friends but stayed as far away from them as possible. Things were still strained between Miranda and the Rockfords, but that didn't include the children. They all wanted to talk to her and gave her an update on the monarch butterflies.

Halfway through the dance, Emily approached Miranda to compliment her on her dress. Emily had worn her green ballgown, and just looking at it transported Miranda right back to the masked ball and those sweet first hours with George. Tears started in her eyes, but she didn't let them fall. With great effort she kept her feelings to herself, smiling and talking with Emily until Nathaniel and Peter came to escort them to supper.

They shared a table with Mr. and Mrs. Harlake, the Tolwoods and Peter's siblings, who'd been allowed to attend. The talk and laughter managed to help Miranda forget her sadness for a time, and after their parents left, she and Peter danced under the stars until well past midnight.

After spending most of the following day working on the nursery mural, Miranda rode into town to see Emily. When she walked into Darlington's, she saw Henry sitting alone, finishing a slice of pie. They exchanged smiles as she walked by his table and Miranda considered asking him if he'd heard from George but decided against it. He might tell Ethan and

Frank, which could lead to more teasing. On top of that, if George heard about it, he'd probably be annoyed that Miranda had been pestering his friend.

Miranda approached the counter, where Emily was setting out a new scarf display. "Hi, Emily."

"Hi," she said, smiling. "Did you enjoy yourself last night?"

"Yes, very much." Miranda set her purse on the counter and climbed onto a stool.

"So did I. I wish it had lasted even longer."

As they chatted about the dance, Miranda's mind repeatedly drifted over to George and her issues at home. She did her utmost to be polite and listen to Emily, but at the next break in the conversation she blurted out, "Oh, Emily. I have the worst problem."

Emily dropped the scarves she'd been holding onto the counter. "What? What's the matter?"

Without even planning to, Miranda told her everything. The truth about the fake engagement, her mother's unexpected pregnancy, and finally what had happened with George.

"No wonder you're upset," Emily said when Miranda finally finished talking. "Perhaps the engagement wasn't the wisest choice, but we all make mistakes. You didn't do it on purpose to hurt anyone's feelings. When George comes home you'll be able to explain."

"I tried to, the day after it happened. He was so angry," Miranda said, wrapping her arms around her middle. "He barely looked at me. I don't think I'll get another chance with him."

"He should at least hear you out and let you apologize."

"I broke his trust, and I don't think I could have done anything worse."

"Maybe he'll come around."

"Maybe," she said with no real conviction.

Miranda felt better after sharing her troubles with Emily. They whiled away the rest of the evening talking and before long they were the only two people left in the shop.

"I can lock the door in fifteen minutes," Emily said, glancing at the clock. "I'll start cleaning up."

Miranda scooped up some empty scarf boxes. "I'll help you," she said, and followed her into the back room.

It was five minutes to six when the bell over the front door jingled.

"Somebody always comes in when I'm about to close up," Emily said with a weary sigh. "I'll go see what they want. Hopefully not food, since the cooks already went home."

Emily went out to the shop and Miranda heard her ask, "Hello, is there anything I can help you find?"

"Yes, I'm looking for gloves," a woman said.

"I have a display right over here," Emily said, and Miranda heard footsteps as they walked to the counter.

A man cleared his throat, obviously irritated. "Imelda, must you do this now? I don't want to go home to a cold dinner. Besides, the girls are anxious to see you."

"The gloves are *for* the girls. I didn't have time to shop before I caught the train here this morning."

"Just be quick about it."

"Don't rush me, Jeremy."

Miranda peeked into the shop. It was Mr. Cobbe and a woman who had to be his sister. Miranda quickly moved to the wall opposite the open door, the better to stay out of sight until he left.

After less than a minute Mr. Cobbe started pacing. "Aren't you done yet?"

"No. Be patient," Imelda said, then addressed Emily. "Excuse me, miss. Do you have any other colors?"

"I'll go check," Emily said. She returned to the back room and started rummaging through the shelves.

Miranda was about to ask if she needed help when she heard something too intriguing to ignore.

"I'd love to see Ann while I'm in town," Imelda said. "I wonder what color gloves she'd like."

"No need to buy her any. She left. For good," Mr. Cobbe said.

"What?" his sister exclaimed. "But aren't you adopting her?"

"Not anymore."

"Whyever not? She's a sweet child."

"Indeed, but I already have six sweet children."

Imelda lowered her voice. "Is this because Mr. Tolwood wouldn't marry her?"

"Would you be quiet?" he hissed.

"Calm down, Jeremy. Nobody can hear us. That girl is puttering around somewhere in back."

"Well, then, yes," he said, his voice barely audible. "There's no reason to adopt her if she doesn't bring my son back to me."

Miranda had to cover her mouth to keep from gasping. She looked at Emily, who stood wide-eyed.

Imelda tutted. "The poor thing. Where is she now?"

"I have no idea."

"Well!" Imelda said. "Well, it isn't as though she's

actually family. Your sister-in-law's niece, wasn't she?"

"Second cousin? Third? It was a stretch to consider her a connection. She isn't a true Cobbe. I only took her on because she seemed a suitable bride for the boy."

Imelda's tone hardened. "I'm surprised at you. It was cruel to let her think she'd become part of the family and then cast her off again."

"Ah, well. She's gone now, along with any chance of making the boy my heir." He drummed his fingers on the counter. "Where's that blasted shopgirl?"

After a frightened look at Miranda, Emily grabbed a stack of gloves and hurried out to the shop.

It seemed an age before Imelda chose her six pairs of gloves, but at last she and Mr. Cobbe left. Emily locked the door after them and returned to the back room.

"I can't believe it," Emily said, putting a hand to her cheek.

Miranda realized at once the significance of another person now knowing Peter's biggest secret.

"Please don't tell anyone, Emily," she implored. "Peter's kept this quiet for so long. Only his parents and the people in the shop just now know the truth."

"I wouldn't dream of telling! I promise I'll never tell a soul, not even Nathaniel," she said fervently. Miranda knew Emily well enough now to know she'd remain true to her word.

"I always knew Mr. Cobbe was cruel, but what a thing to do to poor Ann. I have to go," Miranda said. "I have to tell Peter."

They both gathered their things and rushed outside, where Miranda jumped onto Fergus and galloped home.

Chapter Twenty-Five

Peter was irate by the time Miranda finished telling him what she'd overheard.

"How could he do such a thing?" he cried. "No son to pass his estate on to so he tries to hoodwink poor Ann into marrying me so *I* can be his heir? Of all the nerve!"

"What will you do now?" Miranda asked, watching him pace in circles around his mother's parlor. "Peter?" she asked again when he didn't answer.

He collapsed beside her on the sofa and leaned his head back, covering his face with his hands. "I don't know. I think telling Ann is the right thing to do. But would it only make matters worse?"

"No, it would help her understand why she was sent away. And it would give you a chance to see her again. You do care for her, don't you?"

"I do. We barely had a chance to get to know each other before she left, but there was something about her."

"If she hadn't been Mr. Cobbe's ward would you have courted her?"

"Yes, but who knows what would have happened?"

Miranda tried not to sound too excited. "Are you going to Peabody?"

"Maybe, but there's someone I need to speak to first."

"Who?"

"My mother," he said. "I can't even consider seeing

Ann unless I have my mother's approval."

Miranda rose and took his hand. "What are we waiting for?"

They found Mrs. Tolwood on the back porch, drinking iced tea with her husband.

"Mother?" Peter asked in a slightly trembling voice.

Both of his parents looked up at once.

"What's wrong?" Mr. Tolwood asked.

"Nothing's wrong, exactly. It's difficult to explain," Peter said.

"Maybe we should sit down," Miranda suggested and led Peter over to two chairs facing his parents.

"What's troubling you?" his mother asked.

Peter shifted in his chair and glanced at Miranda, who gave him a reassuring smile.

"It's like this," Peter said. "There's a girl I knew last year. Ann. I liked her and took her to the dance, but I found out she was—" He closed his eyes for a moment as though bracing himself. "She was Mr. Cobbe's ward. I cut all ties with her. But Miranda saw her in Hollingsford recently and discovered Ann isn't his ward anymore. I might try to find her, but I don't see how I can associate with Ann without offending the two of you, or reminding you of things you'd rather forget. Things about—about the past."

Mr. and Mrs. Tolwood shared a long look before Mrs. Tolwood addressed her son. "Peter, we don't want our past to get in the way of your future."

"It's all over and done," his father said. "A lifetime ago."

"But how can it be?" Peter asked in exasperation. "After everything he did? And how can I bring Ann into our lives without also bringing him in?"

Mrs. Tolwood brightened. "What do you mean 'bring her into our lives'?"

Peter put a hand up. "All I mean is, if I go and talk to her, there's a chance we might become friends." He turned to Miranda. "Perhaps you should tell them what you heard."

Miranda proceeded to relay all she'd overheard, and the Tolwoods' countenances grew darker by the minute.

"How could he!" Mrs. Tolwood said when Miranda finished.

Peter's father looked appalled. "That's despicable."

"It's horrible," Peter said. "Miranda and I think I should tell Ann, so she understands why Mr. Cobbe doesn't want to adopt her anymore."

"And so she can steer clear of him in future," Miranda added.

"But this all comes down to how you feel about it," Peter said to his parents. "You must still be angry with him, and the last thing I want to do is stir up old grievances."

"You wouldn't be," Mrs. Tolwood said. "We aren't angry anymore."

"But perhaps it would be difficult for you. We know seeing Mr. Cobbe upsets you, Peter," his father said.

Peter sighed. "I'd hoped you hadn't noticed. It's confusing. I would never want him in my life, and it's odd being angry with someone I've barely ever spoken to. But I can't forgive what he did to Mother. I don't understand how you two can sit there and act like it was all nothing."

"It was far from nothing," Mr. Tolwood said. "But time does have a way of putting things into perspective." He turned to his wife. "Perhaps it's time, Audrey."

Mrs. Tolwood nodded and addressed Peter. "We didn't tell you the whole story because we didn't think you'd want to hear the details. But it's obviously been bothering you all these years. Perhaps if you knew what happened it would help you to move on."

"I don't know," Peter said, crossing his arms. "It could make it worse."

Miranda rubbed Peter's shoulder. "The truth might help you see things more clearly. I think it will help."

"Maybe," Peter said. "All right. Go on, Mother."

Mrs. Tolwood was about to speak, but her husband interrupted. "Wait," he said and looked at Peter. "I want to make it absolutely clear that I fancied your mother before any of this happened. There was never a question of my love for her."

Mrs. Tolwood smiled and took his hand.

Peter looked slightly confused but nodded. "I understand."

Mrs. Tolwood gazed across the room as though seeing into the past. "I was sixteen when I met Jeremy Cobbe. He was a dashing young romantic back then, not the curmudgeon he became later. We grew friendly. I want you to know that though I made a mistake, it was only because at the time I thought he loved me. I believed him when he said we would be married. I wasn't a...a wanton. His parents refused to approve the match. Jeremy told me he'd be happy to set me up in a little place in Hollingsford and he'd visit me whenever he could. Me and the baby. I, of course, refused. This more than anything showed me the type of man he really was. A spineless wretch. It was what I needed to break whatever spell I'd been under. I hadn't really loved him."

"You could have been ruined!" Peter said.

"Yes, I could have been. But your grandparents weren't the type to cast me out. We made a plan to move across the country. I'd be introduced as their widowed daughter, and when I had my baby, my parents would help raise you. But that plan never came to fruition," she said, looking at Mr. Tolwood, who took up the tale.

"When your mother came to Majestic Oaks to hand in her notice, I begged her not to leave. We'd gone to a few dances together in the past, and I never saw a finer girl than Audrey Bennet. I wanted to marry her and take care of you both. She refused, thinking I was a romantic fool and that someday I'd come to resent her and the baby. I somehow convinced her to stay in town for two more months and let me court her. To this she agreed."

Mrs. Tolwood smiled. "I'd already liked Noah before I took up with Jeremy, and it took me far less than two months to realize I loved him. And that he truly did love me. So we were married. You were born a little early, but all people thought was that your father and I had—"

"I understand," Peter cut in, blushing. "So nobody ever suspected?"

"Perhaps the servants at the Cobbes'. And apparently his sister knows," Mrs. Tolwood said. "That's why we told you when you were younger. If you were ever going to hear whispers, we wanted the information to come from us. We didn't want you to hear from anyone else who your father was."

"I've always known who my father is," Peter said, and rose to embrace Mr. Tolwood. They broke apart some minutes later, both wiping away tears.

"Did Mr. Cobbe ever talk to you about Peter?" Miranda asked.

Mrs. Tolwood shook her head. "I've never spoken to Jeremy since the day I broke things off with him. Not out of spite, but there's nothing to say."

"You see, son," Mr. Tolwood said to Peter, "it really did end all those years ago. And your mother and I wouldn't have it any other way. We love you so much and we're very proud of you."

"I wouldn't change a thing about what happened. Not one," his mother said.

Miranda felt she should slip out of the room as all the Tolwoods embraced again, but Peter held fast to her hand.

Afterwards, Mr. and Mrs. Tolwood went back into the house, leaving Peter and Miranda alone.

"How do you feel?" she asked.

Peter smiled. "Light. I had no idea how much that's been weighing on me all these years."

"I did," Miranda said. "I'm sorry it's been so difficult. But now you can move on."

"Yes, though now I know far too much about my parents' courtship," he said with a laugh.

"I thought it was romantic."

He looked at her fondly. "I'd expect nothing less from you."

"What will you do now? Will you try to find Ann?"

"Yes, there's nothing to stop me." He stood up as though ready to leave that very moment. "I'll tell her what you found out. Would you like to come? It wouldn't be the vacation we'd planned, but you could get out of town."

"No," she said. "It's probably better if you go alone. We'll take our trip in a few weeks."

"I don't know how to find her once I get there," he

said, running a hand through his hair.

"Peabody isn't very big. She said she's working for a Mrs. Carleton, so you can ask at an inn or the post office when you get there. Somebody's bound to know who she is."

"I'd better pack my things. Thank you for helping me through this."

"That's what I'm here for," she said and looped her arm through his as they went inside.

****

Over the next few days Miranda spent hours in the nursery, completing the mural. It took up one entire wall of the room and depicted a field of wildflowers on a sunny day. Birds flitted among the tree branches and sunshine sparkled on the lake. The room was almost ready. All Miranda wanted for it now were some new, whimsical curtains. Since no shops in town carried what she had in mind, she decided to go into Shrewsbury.

After a leisurely lunch with her parents, Miranda went to the stables, which seemed oddly empty without the chance of running into Peter. She saddled Fergus herself and headed out, wondering if Peter had seen Ann yet and when he'd be home.

Hours later Miranda was on her way back to Deerwood with no fabric. The shop she'd wanted to visit was closed. Since she was already in town, Miranda visited other stores and bought baby shoes, wind chimes for the nursery window and a new shawl for her mother. At the last minute, she popped into a store to buy her father a tin of his favorite root beer candies.

Not long into the journey home, a chipmunk suddenly darted into the road, startling Fergus. He reared and came down hard. Once Miranda calmed him down, they set out again but within a few strides it was clear he was limping. She immediately jumped off to examine him and found that his front left leg was tender. Miranda couldn't tell if he'd injured his fetlock or perhaps bruised his foot. Fortunately Fergus didn't appear to be in too much pain, but it would be safer not to ride him. Sighing, she took him by the reins and started walking down the road.

Miranda had tarried longer than she should have in Shrewsbury, assuming she'd be home well before dark with Fergus galloping part of the way. Now they'd need to walk, and slowly at that. She wasn't concerned about walking but knew her parents would worry if she was out much later than expected. Hopefully Mrs. Harlake would fall asleep before she realized Miranda wasn't home. Her father had been in the studio when Miranda left, so he wasn't likely to notice either way.

Miranda and Fergus hadn't gone far when a carriage came up behind them. She guided the horse to the side of the road so it could pass. But it didn't. Miranda heard someone give a strange half sigh, half groan, and turned to see George looking out the carriage window.

"George," she whispered.

"What are you doing?" he asked sharply, not meeting her eyes.

"Fergus hurt his leg. We're walking home."

He looked at her like she was mad. "Walking? That will take hours, and it's almost dark."

"I know, but I don't want to add my weight to his injured leg. I don't mind the walk. But perhaps—I hate to ask it—could you send a message to my parents when you get home? They might worry if I'm out after nightfall."

George sighed heavily. "No, I won't, because I'll be arriving home at the same time you do." He climbed out of the carriage and walked over to examine Fergus.

"What do you mean?" she asked, her heart thundering at being so close to him again.

"We'll tie Fergus to the back of the carriage, and you'll ride with me."

Miranda flushed. "You don't need to do that."

"Yes, I do. I'm not going to leave a woman to walk home alone in the dark. Get in," he said as he snatched Fergus's reins from her, still avoiding her gaze.

Miranda drew herself up. Yes, she needed help, but she wasn't quite desperate enough to accept it from someone who apparently could barely stand the sight of her.

"I'll be fine," she said. "I don't mind walking. The best thing you could do to help me is to give my parents the message." She tried to take Fergus's reins back but George held them fast.

"Please get into the carriage. If you don't, we'll follow behind you to be sure you make it home safely. So you might as well ride instead of walk."

"Then I must say thank you," she said in as dignified voice as she could manage, though she felt she should have offered an apology.

George secured Fergus's reins to the back of the carriage and, after a word with the driver, held the door open for Miranda. She'd planned to sit across from him, but the carriage had only one bench. She climbed in and sat as close to the window as possible.

When George got in and closed the door, the quarters were very cramped indeed. He smelled the same and being in his presence *felt* the same. The only difference was his eyes. If he looked at Miranda at all, it was as though he looked at a stranger.

George tapped the roof and the driver set off at a slow pace.

Miranda looked out the back window at Fergus, who didn't seem to have any trouble walking.

"Are you on your way home?" Miranda asked, simply for something to say.

George nodded curtly but didn't reply.

A few minutes later she made another attempt at conversation. "Where did you go?"

He hesitated for a moment as though weighing whether she deserved an answer. "The coast," he said and pivoted in his seat to stare out the window, his back to her.

Over the course of what had to be the longest three hours of Miranda's life, George never said another word.

She spent her time checking on Fergus, fiddling with her coat sleeves, and taking surreptitious glances at George. At one point when she looked at him, he was watching her and opened his mouth as though to speak. Miranda held her breath, willing him to say something, but he just closed his eyes and turned away.

It was odd being with him like this. It felt warm and familiar in a way, yet the waves of discomfort rolling off him seemed to form an invisible wall. A hundred times Miranda was on the verge of apologizing again, or trying to explain about the fake betrothal and the secret she'd kept. But she was too afraid of how George would respond, although it was hard to imagine anything that could be worse than this cold—freezing—shoulder.

At long last, they pulled up to Majestic Oaks and George leapt out of the carriage. He held the door open for Miranda, then went to untie Fergus.

One of the stable hands appeared and Miranda explained what had happened. She told him to see to Fergus's leg and call the veterinarian if necessary. As he walked the horse away, Miranda turned back to George, who was already in the carriage.

"Goodnight, and tha—" she began.

George slammed the door and faced forward as if she wasn't there.

"George, really!" Miranda said, surprised by her own vehemence. "I know we've had our…our differences, but you could at least be civil. I didn't ask for your help tonight and would have gladly spared you my company, but as you were good enough to come to my rescue, please once again accept my gratitude and my deepest apologies for encroaching on your time. In future I'll do my utmost not to require anything of the sort from you."

George leaned out the window as though he was going to speak, and Miranda's heart leapt. Perhaps he was going to finally hear her out about Peter, or apologize for ignoring her all the way home. At this point she'd be glad just to hear his voice, no matter what he said. When he met Miranda's gaze there was an anguished look in his eyes that she couldn't comprehend. Whatever it was, it pierced her heart to see it.

She took a step closer to the carriage. "George?"

"I… Goodbye." He closed his eyes and rapped the side of the carriage. As it drove away Miranda saw him slink down into his seat.

"So much for a reconciliation," she said aloud once the carriage was out of sight. Miranda gathered her parcels and went inside. The lights were on but the house was quiet. She left her parents' gifts on the dining room table and tiptoed upstairs.

As Miranda undressed and prepared for bed, she went over her words to George. Perhaps she could have put things a bit more delicately, but she was proud of herself for expressing her feelings. Maybe now that she'd learned how to stand up for herself it was impossible not to when she felt slighted.

The weeks since George left she'd spent overwhelmed with remorse, which seemed only natural under the circumstances. Yes, she owed him an apology and could apparently never make up for breaking his trust. But could George really forget all of their special times together and treat her as worse than a stranger?

Given all that George had done to help her practice being honest, it was bitterly ironic if expressing her feelings tonight cost her whatever slim chance she'd had of regaining his friendship. Well, there was nothing to be done about it now. She blew out the candles and climbed into bed.

Miranda lay there for a long time, staring at the ceiling. Since George hadn't replied to her comments or taken the opportunity to suddenly declare forgiveness, she had to assume things were truly over between them. Over before they'd even begun. At least now Miranda knew what it felt like to be in love. Unfortunately, she also now knew what it was to have a shattered heart. Doubtful it would ever mend, she turned over and cried herself to sleep.

Miranda was still in bed the next morning when somebody knocked on her door. She didn't answer, as she intended to sleep late and it was not yet six o'clock. Hopefully, whoever it was would go away.

A few minutes later the knock came again. "Miranda?" her father called.

"Come in," she said through a huge yawn and eased herself into a sitting position.

Mr. Harlake sat on the edge of the bed. "I fell asleep before you got home last night. When did you get back?"

"Late. Fergus hurt his leg so I started walking home, but—"

He looked alarmed. "You *walked* from Shrewsbury?"

"No, George happened by and gave me a ride. Fergus walked behind the carriage."

Her father's eyes grew sympathetic and a bit too understanding for Miranda's liking. "I see," he said. "He's a nice lad, isn't he?"

Miranda just nodded, as her tears were perilously close to starting up again.

Mr. Harlake patted her arm. "Can I get you anything? Breakfast?"

"No, I'm not hungry. I'd like to rest more, I barely slept last night."

"I'll send Cassandra up with a tray," he said, going to the door. "You'll feel better after you've eaten."

"Thank you," she said, not bothering to repeat that she didn't want anything since he was obviously sending food up whether she wanted it or not.

Miranda lay back against her pillows, thinking about George. After last night, it was abundantly clear he truly was lost to her. She wasn't sure she could blame him. When she considered how much they'd shared with each other and how close they'd grown, she could only imagine how she'd feel if she found out George had hidden something so important. Not only that, he'd been curious about her relationship with Peter the whole time, and she'd assured him there was nothing romantic between them. Then he saw them kissing. Though it was a misunderstanding, it made sense that he felt hurt, even betrayed.

But Miranda would have hoped the bond they'd formed would warrant George at least hearing her out and being open to forgiving her. It seemed she was now lumped in with all the other people who'd disappointed George, and perhaps that was what he couldn't bear. He'd said he enjoyed being with Miranda because he could be himself with her. But that was only true if he trusted her.

Not long later, Cassandra arrived with breakfast. Miranda was surprisingly hungry and finished almost everything on the tray. Afterwards she snuggled back into the blankets, staring at the ceiling while she tried to envision George in happier times.

Miranda had just drifted off to sleep when she was awakened by the welcome sound of someone climbing onto her balcony. She sat bolt upright and threw back the covers.

"Peter!" she cried, running outside. Hot tears started as soon as she saw his face. Miranda wrapped her arms around him and sobbed into his shoulder.

He rubbed her back, laughing. "I wasn't gone *that* long."

She pulled away to look at him, wiping her eyes. He looked so happy she didn't want to burden him with her troubles at the moment. "How did it go with Ann?"

His failing to press her on why she was crying was proof enough that he had good news.

"It went well." Peter smiled widely. "Here, let's sit

down," he said and led her to a chair, then sat in the one beside her.

"What did she say?" Miranda asked, wishing she'd put her robe on against the morning chill.

"She was shocked to see me and confused about why I'd come, so I had to tell her the whole story. My story, from the beginning. But she didn't mind at all. She doesn't think any less of me. And when I told her what you overheard, she was very angry. But hurt, too. Ann had a feeling she'd done something to offend Mr. Cobbe but had no idea what."

"So I was right. She didn't know anything about his plans concerning you."

"No, she didn't, and she told me how he came to be her guardian in the first place. It was very recently, and she'd never heard of him before he contacted her last year. She's somehow connected to Mr. Cobbe's wife and he invited her to stay with them and promised to adopt her."

"But she wasn't even staying with him, she was at the boarding house."

"Mr. Cobbe told her she couldn't stay at the manor because he hadn't told his daughters about the adoption yet."

"Has he ever told his daughters about *you*?" Miranda asked though she knew it was a difficult subject.

"I have the feeling that if he'd told his wife and daughters, it would have all come out years ago. Besides, my mother told me that during their very last conversation he promised to keep the secret. So apparently that's one promise he kept."

"It must be one of the only good things he's ever done."

"Yes, but I think it was also in his own best interest not to tell anyone. What would people in town have said? Anyway, it's all over now. Really over, now that I know Ann wasn't involved with his lies."

"I'm so glad it's settled now. What happened next with Ann? Did you see her again after that first day?"

Peter couldn't stop grinning. "I saw her every day I was in Peabody."

"And...?"

"*And* she's delightful. I know you'll like each other when you get to know one another better."

"Is she coming back?"

"She'd like to visit, perhaps next summer. In the meantime, we're going to write."

"I'm so happy you went to see her!"

"I am, too. I'm glad you wouldn't let it rest," he said. They sat in silence for a moment, then he peered into Miranda's face as if just seeing her for the first time. "But what about you? Why were you crying? You look like you've hardly slept at all."

She waved a hand. "It's nothing. Just that yesterday I went to Shrewsbury, and Fergus was hurt on our ride home, and then a carriage came along and George was in it. He didn't talk to me during our three-hour ride back here, and when he dropped me off I called him out on it. Now I know he hates me and we'll probably never see each other again."

Peter blinked. "I wouldn't call that nothing. I'm so sorry. This is all my fault."

"No, don't blame yourself."

He started to speak, but Miranda cut him off. She couldn't bear to go over it all again. "Would you like to come in for breakfast?" she asked.

Peter seemed to consider her for moment, then shook his head. "I should go say hello to my family."

Miranda stood and stretched her arms over her head, yawning. "Then I'm going back to bed. But come back later. Oh, and please stop by the stables to check on Fergus."

"I saw him when I arrived. His foot's bruised, but he'll be fine in a week or two. I'll come by later when you're rested and we can talk. It's good to see you," he said and disappeared over the railing.

Miranda crawled back into bed and was asleep within minutes. A few hours later, she groaned as she was awakened yet again. The next time she needed to sleep in, she'd draw her bolt first. But this sound came not from the door but her balcony. A thump followed by a moan.

"Go away, Peter! I told you I need to sleep." She pulled the blankets over her head.

"No," he said. "I want to talk to you."

But it wasn't Peter's voice.

Chapter Twenty-Six

Miranda could almost believe she was still asleep. The vision of George standing on her balcony with windswept hair, a soft smile, and tender eyes was certainly something she would have seen in her dreams. But it was the tone of George's voice that made the moment seem more like a dream. He didn't sound cold or distant, as he had last night. He sounded caring. Even affectionate.

"George," she said, hopping out of bed. "What are you doing here?"

Before he had time to answer, Miranda remembered she was wearing only her white nightgown. "Oh!" she exclaimed, and rushed to draw the curtains over the balcony doors. Blushing furiously, she crossed the room to her wardrobe and hastily changed into a forest-green dress. When Miranda caught a glimpse of herself in the mirror, she wanted to go right back to bed. Her hair was a tangled mess, her eyes puffy and red. But at least the embarrassment put some color into her cheeks.

She stepped out to the balcony where George stood waiting. "What are you doing here?" she asked again as she attempted to smooth down her hair. "Why didn't you go to the front door?"

George gave her a little shrug, grinning. "Peter thought this would be more romantic. He told me how to get in."

Miranda gasped. "Peter!"

"He came to my house this morning."

Miranda put a hand to her forehead and sank into a chair. "I'm sorry he bothered you. What did he want?"

"He wanted to explain about the betrothal," George said, sitting next to her. "And he told me I should forgive you."

"What did you tell him?" Afraid to meet his eyes, Miranda stared at the horses grazing in the meadow.

George reached over and wrapped her hand in his. "I told him he needn't have made the journey, because I was already on my way to your house this morning to apologize to you."

She met his eyes then, hope stirring in her chest. "You were?"

"Yes. After I left here last night I couldn't forgive myself for the way I acted during our ride home from Shrewsbury. I promise that will be the last time I behave in such a reprehensible manner."

Miranda wanted to merely bask in his presence and his apology. But somehow, she couldn't. "You've made that promise before, and broken it," she said, holding back tears she hadn't realized were so near.

George took both her hands in his. "I know. But…but I understand myself better now. Last night was an ideal chance to be honest, and I failed. Miserably. I can't say I'm perfect, but I can promise to do my best. I would never hurt you intentionally, Miranda. Last night in the carriage—"

Guessing what he was about to say, Miranda interrupted. "I'm not surprised you didn't want to talk to me. It was kind of you to stop and help, but it's no wonder the ride was awkward, after what happened with

Peter."

"No, it wasn't that. When we were in the carriage I wanted to talk to you, but I didn't know what to say. But I do now. I'm sorry I left town after that night. I was hurt and angry, and—"

"You were right to be! I'm so sorry I didn't tell you the truth."

George's fingers tightened around hers. "I know you are. But let me get this out. I was blindsided when I saw you with Peter, and I was scared I'd been all wrong about you. Worst of all, I thought I'd lost you to him."

"No, it wasn't like that at all," Miranda said.

"I know that now, but at the time all I could think about was how hurt I was. So I left. I realized later that I'd made a terrible mistake in not listening to you, but I was too scared to come back. Too scared of the rejection I've always dreaded. But now all I fear is that I've completely broken your faith in me. Do you think you can ever trust me again?"

Miranda stared into his eyes for a long moment and found what she was looking for, what she'd known all along she'd find. "I do trust you, George. Now I have a question for you. Can you forgive me for not telling you about Peter?"

"I've already forgiven you. When I found you on the road last night, I could hardly believe my luck at seeing you before I even reached town. But it was also a shock. I had no time to decide what I wanted to say, or how. I lost all courage and couldn't tell you how I felt, so I remained silent." He laughed lightly. "Even though I was an unsociable boor, I hoped you'd know I still cared because I stopped to help."

"So...so you weren't acting cold because you were

angry? I thought you were so upset over what happened that you never wanted to talk to me again."

"I was a number of things, but not angry. Not with you. With myself, perhaps. I didn't know how you were going to respond to me and I was afraid to ask. What if I told you how I felt right there in the carriage and I was too late? What if I'd already lost my chance with you? Not because you loved Peter. Once I calmed down I knew in my heart you weren't lying about him, but it was obvious I'd hurt you by the way I reacted. Hopefully you can forgive me for my behavior last night and for abandoning you after Peter kissed you."

"I do forgive you. I've replayed it in my mind over and over, and of course you were hurt by what happened. I wanted to tell you so many times about Peter, but I was afraid you'd take it the wrong way. I've never lied about anything so important in my life, and I promise I'll never lie to you again. Can we go back to the beginning and start over?"

George took her hands and pulled her to her feet. "No. I don't want to start over. I didn't know you then. I want to start now. While I was away I thought about you every moment, and it's been clear to me for quite some time that you're the perfect—the only—woman for me." He paused and took a shuddering breath. "I'm so in love with you, Miranda."

Miranda's heart nearly stopped, and if she hadn't been touching him she truly would have believed it was a dream.

"Oh, George," she said. "I've been in love with you for so long I don't even know when it started. Probably the ball, when I didn't know who you were, but I *knew* you."

As they stood staring into each other's eyes, George's expression shifted from tender to a look that turned her knees to water. She knew what was coming a second before it happened, but before she even had time to wrap her arms around George, his lips were on hers. He lifted her off her feet in a passionate embrace, kissing her in a way she'd never imagined possible. She gave herself to him completely, running her hands over his strong shoulders and wishing she never had to take another breath again if it meant their kiss had to end.

Their first kiss in the forest had been slow, easy, exploratory. This kiss was demanding, fiery, and perfect. This kiss was an oath.

When at last they broke apart, chests heaving, Miranda threw her arms around George's waist and rested her head against his heart. "I'm so happy."

She heard a deep rumble in his chest when he laughed.

He held her even closer. "That night in your drawing room I already knew I loved you, and seeing you with Peter was like watching my future disappear in a cloud of smoke. I think that's why I reacted so rashly. I'd grown to believe you cared about me, too, but that night threw me into terrible doubt."

"There was no need for that."

"I know that now, thank goodness. But there's one more thing we need to discuss."

"What's that?" she asked, looking into his eyes. She was worried until she saw how they sparkled.

"Will you come with me to Ebenezer's wedding?"

She laughed. "If he'll have me. He must be angry after what happened with Peter."

"I'll explain it all to him later. Besides, he'll be

pleased as punch that we're together."

"Would he? Why?"

"It's a long story. Let's sit down."

Miranda led him into her room, where they sat side by side on the bed.

"When I returned home last night, I was beyond distraught," George said, taking Miranda's hand. "Ebenezer came upon me in the gallery, and after I told him what was wrong, he basically told me I was a fool for letting you slip away."

Miranda gasped. "He didn't!"

"He did. Apparently he's been doing his best to get us together all summer."

"Has he really?" That would be news to Miranda's parents, who'd been doing their best to pair her off with Ebenezer.

George nodded. "He saw us at the masked ball and he could tell I liked you. But he thinks I'm too insecure or obtuse to court 'the right woman,' as he said, so he tried to find ways to throw us together."

"So that's why he invited me and my father to the country house?"

"Yes, and"—here George raised his eyes to the sky—"he sent Peter off to Nottingham so he wouldn't be in the way. He saw the two of you dancing and thought you might have feelings for each other."

"But how did he know it was me at the ball?"

"He asked Mrs. Tolwood who you were. He must have seen us talking to her in the punch room. I assume she told him Peter's identity, too."

"I had no idea your uncle was such a meddler!"

"Me neither, but I should have. But it didn't matter if he meddled or not, because I liked you from the moment we danced at the ball."

"But you didn't even know who I was," she reminded him.

He looked at her seriously. "I would have found you. I'll give Ebenezer a little credit for making it easier, but I was already making inquiries around town. I would have discovered your identity sooner or later."

Miranda lit up inside. "If only I'd told you I was your partner when I found out who you were the next day. We could have gotten to know each other even sooner."

"But you didn't like me."

Miranda covered her face with her hands, but George pulled them away.

"I didn't know you. As soon I truly knew you, I loved you," she said.

George kissed her softly. "I think we need a new pact."

"What is it?" she asked, smiling.

"A pact not to be perfect but to always do our best by each other and to be honest."

"And to love each other, support each other and trust each other," Miranda added.

"For the rest of our lives." George went down on one knee and pulled a diamond ring out of his pocket. "Will you marry me, Miranda?"

Miranda sank down onto the floor beside him and took his hand. "Yes. Yes, I'll marry you," she said, barely able to speak through her smile.

George rose and helped her to her feet. She held her breath as he slipped the ring onto her trembling finger. A perfect fit. As they fell into each other's arms, Miranda laughed with pure joy.

Suddenly there was a loud knock on the door.

"Miranda?" her father called. "Are you all right?"

She clapped a hand over her mouth, trying to control her mirth. George only made matters worse, as his panicked expression while he looked for places to hide made her laugh even harder.

Miranda composed herself as well as she could and went to open the door as George dropped to the floor behind her bed.

She opened the door a crack. "Yes, Father?" she said, wiping her eyes.

"Still crying, eh?" he asked, voice full of concern.

"Only a little." Why deny it, when her face was covered in happy tears? "But I'm much better than I was earlier."

"Are you? You sounded a trifle hysterical, to be honest."

"I'm fine, really."

He looked skeptical but nodded. "Glad to hear it. Care to join me in the studio? I'm starting with some new pastels."

"Perhaps later, Father. I'm still tired. I didn't sleep much last night."

He patted her shoulder. "Better get back to bed, then."

After giving him a smile she closed—and bolted—the door.

When Miranda turned around, there was George standing beside the bed. With not a moment to lose, she ran across the room and threw herself into his arms, where she stayed for quite a long, glorious time.

Chapter Twenty-Seven

A few hours later, Miranda sat up to check the clock. "It's nearly one."

"Early yet," George said, pulling her back onto the bed and kissing her neck.

"I'll be expected downstairs for lunch," she said, snuggling into his arms as if she had no intention of leaving them. And she didn't.

"My family is probably wondering where I am."

Miranda toyed with his waistcoat buttons. "Didn't you tell anyone where you were going?"

"No," he said, "but Ebenezer probably has a good idea."

She shook her head. "I can't believe he was trying to get us together all that time."

"I can. Like you said, he's a meddler. Hopefully your parents won't be disappointed that you chose me." He smiled when he spoke, as if he couldn't believe his good fortune.

"How could they be disappointed? You're perfect. Even if they were, I don't care. I adore you and we're going to spend our lives together," she said and kissed him.

Miranda lost all track of time, lunch, and even wedding plans as they lay entwined in each other's arms. George's hands wandered to her shoulder, her hips, her waist. Miranda ran her hands over his strong arms and lingered on his chest, for the first time in her life realizing just how much a thin layer of cotton could stand between her and what she wanted most. She settled for touching whatever of George's skin she could. His cheek, his throat, his beloved face. After a time they paused to look into each other's eyes and then she rested her head against his heart.

"I can't wait to get married," she said dreamily.

"Neither can I. When shall it be?"

"Tomorrow?" she asked lightly.

"Perhaps the day after," he said. "We'll need to get your ballgown ready."

She raised herself up on her elbows to look into his face. "Oh! I would love to wear that. I don't suppose you'd dress as a sea captain? But without the wig and mask."

He smiled. "No, but I'll look as dashing as I can for my beautiful bride."

"You're always dashing." Miranda kissed him, then glanced at her wall calendar and sighed. "I suppose we should plan the wedding for after my mother has the baby."

"Yes, but that's only a few months away."

"In the meantime we'll see each other every day."

George ran a hand over her hair. "We'll take walks and visit the lake and you can teach me to draw."

"And you can show me around your estate. But my favorite thing to do with you is talk. I want to hear all there is to know about you."

"I want to know everything about you, too. And perhaps when we aren't talking…" he said and brought his lips to hers.

A little while later Miranda looked at the clock. "I

really should get downstairs, though I'd rather stay here with you all day. If I don't make an appearance soon, my father will come back to check on me. He was so worried about me earlier."

"I'm sorry there was need of that," George said. "It was my fault you were so miserable."

"None of that talk," she said. "We both made mistakes and both apologized, and now we're starting afresh."

"You're right. Our new life starts today, with no regrets." George climbed out of bed and held a hand out for Miranda.

She took it and wrapped her arms around him for a few more precious seconds.

George kissed the top of her head. "I'll go home and change, but I'll come back later today to talk to your father."

"You'll need to tell your family, too. Do you think they'll approve?"

"Oh, yes," he said, taking her hand and walking out to the balcony. "They all like you. The children will be over the moon." He started for the railing, but Miranda didn't release his hand.

"What are you doing?" she asked.

He pointed to the tree. "Leaving."

"Not that way! It's far too dangerous."

George laughed. "I came up that way. Peter does it all the time," he said. "I'll be fine."

He turned to go but she clung to his arm.

"Peter's been doing it for years," she said. "He could do it blindfolded. But you've only done it once, and I think it's harder going down. I simply won't allow it." Miranda put her hands on her hips and tried to look stern.

331

"How am I supposed to get out? Wait until nightfall and leave when everyone's asleep?"

Miranda couldn't deny the idea was tempting. Hiding in her bedroom all day long with George? If she thought they could get away with it, she would.

"No," she said. "We'll be very quiet going downstairs. My mother's bound to be resting right now, and my father is probably outside painting on a day like this."

"If you're certain. I don't want to get you into trouble or anger your parents when I'm about to beg for your hand."

"You won't have to *beg*," she said, laughing. "Don't worry. Nobody will see us."

"All right. Let's go."

Miranda took his hand and walked to the door. She opened it a crack. "All clear," she said.

They tiptoed halfway down the staircase, and just when Miranda thought they were safe, Peter rounded the corner. She shrieked and Peter cried out, "What the blazes!" but fortunately George kept his head and didn't yell.

They all stood on the landing, staring at each other for a good ten seconds before Peter, looking angrier than Miranda had ever seen him, hissed, "Just what is going on here?"

Miranda had the distinct feeling the only thing keeping him from punching George in the nose was the heavily laden lunch tray he carried.

"Nothing's going on!" she whispered. "George just… He just… He's just visiting." Miranda realized too late that she and George both looked decidedly rumpled. Tousled hair, wrinkled clothes, and probably red lips from all the sublime kissing.

Peter rounded on George. "I only told you how to get in so you could *talk* to her. And that was hours ago!"

"We did talk," George said. "I apologized, and then I proposed and Miranda said yes." He turned to look at her, eyes shining with love.

"You proposed?" Peter asked. "Already?"

"I should have done it sooner," George said.

Peter turned to Miranda, lowering his voice even more. "You said yes? You're sure? Do you know him well enough?"

It was a simple question, but Miranda didn't know how to answer. Would it be naive to say she just knew George was the one? That something in her soul settled into place when she'd professed her love for him? All Miranda knew was that any future without George in it would be bare and empty. She gave Peter the plainest answer she could, the only one that really mattered. "I love him."

Peter's scowl relaxed into a smile. "Then I'm thrilled for you. Truly. As we've discussed many, *many* times, you need to do what makes you happy."

"After all your badgering, I'm finally taking your advice, Peter," Miranda said and he laughed, then turned to George.

"I told you the balcony was the more romantic way to go," Peter said. "Still, you arrived hours ago. *Hours.* What have you two been doing?"

"Talking," Miranda and George said simultaneously, blushing in tandem.

Peter looked at Miranda, shaking his head. "Here I was thinking you were crying and miserable all day, and finally I couldn't take it anymore. I had to check on you and bring your lunch. But it seems I needn't have worried."

"Do you want me to carry that?" George asked Peter, motioning to the tray.

Suddenly Mr. Harlake's voice boomed up the staircase. "Peter! What are you doing up there? You know you aren't allowed in Miranda's bedroom."

"Oh, no," Miranda said. She fell back against George, who put an arm around her.

Peter turned to go back down the stairs, but Miranda caught his arm. "What are you going to say?"

"I have to go down," he whispered, then cleared his throat and called, "I was bringing Miranda her lunch, Mr. Harlake!"

"Cassandra can do that. Get down here!"

"What do we do?" Miranda asked nobody in particular.

"George could go through the window," Peter said.

Miranda shook her head. "No!"

"I'll deal with this," George said, meeting Miranda's eyes. "This isn't how I would have preferred talking to your father, but there's nothing to be done about it now. It's best to be honest, right?" he asked and gave her a smile.

Miranda nodded but still couldn't see how this would turn out well.

"Peter!" Mr. Harlake bellowed.

"You two should, um, straighten up a bit, if you can," Peter said and hurried down the stairs.

Miranda heard her father chastising Peter but couldn't make out the words. She only knew the tone, all too well.

"How do I look?" George asked.

Miranda looked up at him. He'd attempted to smooth his clothes and fix his hair, but it hadn't really worked. "Wrinkled," she said. "Me?"

"Like you spent the morning in bed."

George gathered her into a tight embrace as they were overcome with silent laughter.

She pulled away after a moment. "Are you sure you want to do this? Maybe you *should* take the balcony."

He shook his head. "I'm not going to skulk away. I'll do whatever it takes to marry you, including facing your father's wrath."

"Should I go talk to him first?"

"No, we'll go together. That's what this is all about, after all," he said and kissed the engagement ring on her finger.

As they started down the stairs, Miranda thought she should be nervous, but somehow, with George's hand wrapped around hers, all she felt was strong and happy, as if she could take on anything.

That feeling altered slightly when they reached the bottom step. Mr. Harlake was still yelling at Peter, who stood there holding the lunch tray.

Miranda's father must have caught a movement out of the corner of his eye, because he turned to look at her. He froze when he saw George. The fistful of pastels he was holding clattered to the floor as he backed into the doorframe and nearly fell over. "What? What? How… What?" he spluttered.

"Father, it's nothing, really," Miranda said, putting her hands up as if to calm a wild animal.

"Nothing?" he spat, white as a sheet. "He was in your bedroom!"

Miranda considered denying it, but her burning

335

cheeks instantly confirmed her father's suspicions.

Peter put the tray on the floor and rushed over to take Mr. Harlake's arm. "Let's go into the parlor and we can talk," he said.

"Yes. Talk!" Mr. Harlake said, pointing at George. "And then get the hell out!"

"Father!" Miranda cried, taking George's arm.

George gently pushed her hand away and rose to his full height. He took a step toward Mr. Harlake. "I know how this looks, sir, but—"

"Don't you *sir* me!"

"Let's go into the parlor," Peter said again, tugging on Mr. Harlake's arm. "I'll get you a brandy. Or whiskey. Rum? Come, let's sit down."

Mr. Harlake finally allowed Peter to lead him into the parlor but shrugged out of his grip and strode to the sideboard, where he poured out an extremely generous measure of whiskey. He downed it in one gulp, then spun back to face them. He pointed at George and Miranda. "Sit. Talk."

Miranda kept George's hand in hers as they moved across the room and sat on the sofa. Peter sat on Miranda's other side and went to take her hand, then noticed it was already taken. He shrugged to himself and folded his hands in his lap, watching everyone else as though a play was about to begin.

"Well?" Mr. Harlake asked Miranda. "After all your talk the other day about not keeping secrets from your mother and me!"

"Father, please don't sound so angry. George and I were in my room, yes. Talking. But nothing untoward happened. You know me better than that."

He glared at her. "Do I?"

"Father!" Miranda cried, stung.

George stood up. "I must ask you not to insult my fiancée," he said.

Mr. Harlake's brow grew even stormier. "Fiancée!"

"Yes," Miranda said. "We're engaged." She managed a smile that was wasted on her father.

"But…but… How?" Mr. Harlake asked, though slightly less vehemently.

"Please, if you'd allow me to explain," George said. "Won't you sit down?"

If Mr. Harlake was offended by being offered a seat in his own home, he didn't show it. He went back to the sideboard for another drink, then sat on the settee across the room and crossed his legs tightly.

George remained standing and put his hands behind his back, positioning himself in the middle of the room where he could see both Miranda and her father.

"I know how it must look to you, sir, me coming down from Miranda's bedroom. But as a man of honor I swear to you nothing scandalous happened. I came over this morning to talk to Miranda because we had some things we needed to iron out. I admit there was a kiss." He cleared his throat. "Or two, after she accepted my proposal."

Mr. Harlake looked like he might explode again, but then took a deep drink and said, "I didn't hear the doorbell and I've been in the studio all morning. When did you arrive?"

"He climbed the tree up to Miranda's balcony. I told him how," Peter said, sounding rather pleased with himself.

"Well, thank you for that, *Peter*," Mr. Harlake grumbled. "I knew I should have chopped that tree down."

Miranda gasped. "You knew about that?"

"Of course. You two weren't especially quiet, nor is Peter invisible. But he must have grown stealthier over time because I foolishly thought you'd stopped letting him into your bedroom years ago. The tree goes tomorrow. Never mind that now. Go on, Mr. Rockford."

"George, please," George said.

Mr. Harlake just shrugged.

George cleared his throat. "I want you first to know that I have nothing but honorable intentions. As you know, Miranda accepted my marriage proposal and made me the happiest man on earth. This may come as a surprise to you because you haven't seen us together often, but I've loved your daughter for a long time and I know I can make her happy. I can provide for her and support whatever she wants to do with her life. Art, a family, both, or something else. Anything she wants I'll be sure she gets. Miranda is the most amazing woman I've ever met, and I only wish I'd realized it sooner. I can't express to you how much I love and cherish her, and I hope you'll allow me to make her my wife." With that he went back to the sofa and took Miranda's hand.

Miranda had never heard anything more wonderful in her life and could barely keep the tears at bay, never mind resisting the urge to throw herself into George's arms and kissing him.

"Congratulations!" Peter said, jumping up to wring George's hand and kiss Miranda's cheek. "I'm going to fetch the champagne." He practically skipped out of the room.

Miranda thought this was a bit premature, as her father hadn't given his approval or spoken at all in the last few minutes. Looking dazed, he'd opened his mouth to speak a few times, then closed it again.

Miranda was about to make her own feelings known when Mrs. Harlake walked into the room, a handkerchief held to her face as tears ran down her cheeks.

"Clara!" Mr. Harlake cried and ran to her side. "What's wrong?" He placed a hand on her round stomach.

"Oh, Lucas!" she hugged him, then turned to Miranda. "Miranda, I'm so happy for you!"

"You heard all of that?" Miranda asked, standing up to take her arm.

"Yes, I was in the next room. It's so sweet!" She kissed Miranda's cheek and turned to George. "We'd love to have you as our son-in-law," she said and held a hand out to him.

Smiling, George went to her side. Mrs. Harlake had to stand on tiptoes to kiss his cheek, and then started crying again.

Peter walked into the room with a tray full of overflowing champagne glasses. "Good to see you up and about, Mrs. Harlake," he said. "Did I miss anything?"

Miranda went over and took two glasses off the tray. "Only the moment I found out all my dreams are coming true, but I'll tell you about it later."

Peter carried the tray over to Mr. Harlake, who took two glasses. He drained one and slid an arm around his wife's shoulders.

Miranda handed George a glass and he held it up high. "To Miranda," he said. "The most beautiful, talented, extraordinary woman in the world."

"And the best friend," Peter added.

Mrs. Harlake wiped her eyes. "The perfect daughter."

"A most beloved daughter and a talented artist," Mr. Harlake said.

Miranda hardly knew what to say as she held up her own glass. "To the people I love most in the world." She turned to George. "And to George, my beloved fiancé. I love you beyond words."

They all drank, and after much hugging, congratulations and handshakes, Mr. Harlake collapsed onto the sofa. He wiped his brow and looked at his daughter. "Miranda, I sincerely hope this is the last time you surprise me with a fiancé out of the clear blue sky."

Miranda and George's eyes met as they said together, "It will be."

She wrapped her arms around him and their lips met in a sealing, binding, perfect kiss.

Epilogue
A year or so later
Miranda climbed into the carriage, once again on her way to what she was certain would be a magical evening at the Rockfords'. The ball was the same and her gown was the same but, instead of Peter, George sat beside her.

George was more wonderful than she had ever dreamed, and every day brought new depth to their relationship and more reasons to love him. He was sweet, kind, funny, supportive. In short, everything she ever could have wanted in a husband. The strong, loving connection they shared hadn't faded at all; it had only grown stronger. It was difficult at this point to remember a time when George hadn't been in her life, by her side, every day.

Miranda leaned her head against his shoulder. "It's a shame you couldn't dress as a captain again."

"It was frightfully uncomfortable. Especially the wig. Besides," George said, pulling a royal blue mask out of his jacket pocket. "I have a costume."

"That is *not* a costume."

"It's enough of one. But I have more important things on my mind than costumes." He dropped the mask onto the carriage floor and wrapped his arms tightly around her, holding her close.

Six months of marriage had yet to quell the intoxicating effect George had upon Miranda, and her pulse seemed to triple its pace as he stared into her eyes.

She held her breath as his fingers traced the edge of her bodice and he bent to give her a long, luxurious kiss.

After a few blissful moments, he rested his chin on the top of her head. "It's a shame we needed to leave the house tonight."

Miranda laughed. "I must agree with you. But we'll be home before long, and we'll be able to…well…do whatever we like."

"We have a bedroom at my parents' house," George said, pulling away to look at her with a twinkle in his eye. "Nobody would notice if we slipped away for a time."

Though the very idea filled Miranda with yearning, she shook her head. "We can't possibly leave the ball and go to our room. We'd be missed."

"No, we wouldn't. Nobody would notice if we slipped up the back stairs," he said and nuzzled her ear.

"I can name a number of people who would notice, starting with your siblings, not to mention Peter and Ann. Your parents, Emily—"

George laughed. "You're right as usual, my love. But I'll have you alone before the night is through."

"That you will," she said, and gave him a deep, lingering kiss that only ended when they pulled up to the Rockford home.

Miranda stepped out of the carriage and looked up at the house, which glowed with the light of hundreds of candles. Though it was a second home to her now, the beauty of the place never ceased to amaze her. She'd been slightly disappointed when George wanted to settle into the cozy guesthouse on the grounds of the Rockfords' Middleton estate instead of here in town, but it hadn't taken her long to realize nothing could be better than having a home of their own. Besides, now she could use the swings any time she wished and linger in the gallery for hours at a time. George had gone to great lengths to turn the old three-season porch into a small art studio, where he often joined her to practice his drawing.

"Ready?" George asked as he took her hand.

Miranda smiled at him and put her butterfly mask on. "Yes, let's go."

As soon as they reached the ballroom, she spotted Peter and Ann. He was dressed as a shepherd this year, while Ann wore a shepherdess costume. They weren't dancing but stood close to one another at the edge of the dance floor.

"Peter!" Miranda called as they drew closer.

He whirled. "Shh, you'll give away my disguise."

"I do apologize," she said. "I didn't realize we're hiding again this year."

"There's no way you'll go unrecognized, Mrs. Rockford. Aside from wearing the same gown as last year, your husband's identity makes it easy to guess yours." He turned to George. "No costume, George?"

"As I've told my wife, this *is* a costume. I don't normally wear a mask in public." He looked around the room for a moment. "Please excuse me, I need to find my parents."

"I'll come with you," Miranda said.

"No, darling, you stay here. If you don't dance with Peter now, you won't have another chance tonight."

"I won't?" she asked.

George kissed her hand. "When I return, I don't intend to let you out of my sight—or arms—for the rest of the night."

She felt her cheeks turning pink. "Hurry back," she said.

"I will." He kissed her forehead and disappeared into the crowd.

When she turned back to Peter, he was watching her with a smirk. She sensed a sarcastic remark coming but didn't give him a chance to utter it. "We don't need to dance, Peter. I wouldn't want you to leave Ann alone."

"I don't mind," Ann said.

"Tired of me already?" Peter asked, feigning a distraught look.

Ann turned to Miranda. "He never stops teasing, does he?"

"No, but you'll grow accustomed to it," she said.

Peter's prediction about the two women liking each other had been correct and, next to Emily, Ann was one of Miranda's closest friends and confidantes.

"Only three weeks until the wedding," Peter said, taking Ann's arm. "You still have time to bring out my serious side."

"I wouldn't want to, nor do I think it's possible," Ann said with a grin. "Escort me to the punch room and I'll have a drink while you two dance."

Miranda followed behind them as they made their way through the ballroom. She kept an eye out for George but didn't see him or his parents.

After seeing Ann to a comfortable seat and fetching her three glasses of lemonade, Peter took Miranda's hand and escorted her to the dance floor, where he swept her into his arms.

He smiled down into her face. "Quite a change from last year, isn't it?"

"Quite," she said. "I'm married and you're about to be."

"All thanks to me."

"You! I think George had something to do with it."

"If I hadn't sent you in alone last year, you two would never have danced with each other," he said and nodded at his parents as they passed them on the dance floor.

"If you're taking credit for my marriage, I'll take responsibility for yours. If I hadn't encouraged—"

"*Badgered.*"

"*Encouraged* you to go find Ann, you wouldn't be about to marry her."

"The wedding is so soon," Peter said and twirled her. "I have to admit I'm a bit nervous."

"About Ann?"

Peter's face took on a lovestruck look that he would have teased Miranda for. "No. No doubts about Ann. It's standing up in front of everyone that has me rattled."

"Peter," Miranda said, shaking her head. "You never mind making a spectacle of yourself, so I don't see why you'd object to having people watch you at your own wedding."

"It's only that it's so personal. I feel it should be a private moment, and not one that ends with people pelting us with rice."

"Once you're in the front of the church, you won't think of anything besides Ann. And I'll be right there with you. Your matron of honor, remember?"

"I prefer 'best matron,' " Peter said. "The wedding wouldn't feel right without you by my side."

"My wedding wouldn't have been complete without you as gentleman of honor, and I'm happy to stand up at yours."

"Did you tell your parents yet that you'll be my best matron?"

"Yes. I thought they might object, but since Flora was born nothing I do seems to upset them. They have other things to worry about now." Adorable things, such as when Flora would say her first word or learn to walk. Having a sister was sweeter than Miranda could have imagined, and it brought her closer than ever to her parents. They shared a common interest in the little girl and spent hours fawning over her.

"Are they coming tonight?"

"They never have before, so I doubt they'd come now when they have a baby at home. They can't tear themselves away from her. I envy you seeing Flora every day. How is she?"

"She seems happy. She doesn't do much besides babble, but the other day she crawled into the studio."

"My father must have been delighted. He bought paint brushes for her before she was born," Miranda said.

"I'm sure he already knows where he'll put her first painting."

"Or pastel. I convinced him to buy those, too. And I—"

Someone tapped on Miranda's shoulder and she looked behind her.

"George!"

"My lady," he said with a deep bow. He was wearing his full sea captain costume, save the wig.

Miranda covered her mouth, laughing.

Peter squeezed her shoulder lightly. "Try not to step on his toes," he said, then turned to George. "I leave her in your capable hands." He gave them both a smile and strode away toward the punch room.

Miranda stared at George. "How?"

"I brought it over when I visited the children last

346

week," he said and pulled her into his arms.

"I'm so glad," she said. "Now I feel as if we've gone back in time to last year."

"Would you care to step into the garden?" he asked, eyes shining.

"We haven't even danced yet!"

"We have all the time in the world for that."

"Then by all means, let's visit the garden," she said and took his hand.

George guided her behind a blue curtain and down a short corridor. They exited through a side door and emerged into the dark, quiet garden.

"I've never seen this part of the garden," she said, turning to face him.

"There's much you still need to learn about the estate."

She took a step closer to him. "Will you show me?"

"I'll show you everything," he said before bringing his lips to hers for a soft, searching kiss. "But first there's something I want to do."

"And what might that be?" she asked, running a hand over his chest.

He surprised her by taking a few steps back. She'd expected quite the opposite.

"Wait here a moment," he said and she could hear the smile in his voice.

"Where are you going?" she called, but he'd already disappeared into the night. She wandered among the rose bushes as the rising moon cast its delicate light over the grounds. Before long she heard the sound of someone approaching.

"My lady?" George called before emerging from behind a tree, carrying two glasses of punch.

Miranda went to meet him.

"Good evening," he said, a smile lighting up his face. "I thought you'd disappeared."

She suddenly realized what he was doing and had to stifle her laughter. She cleared her throat and tried to recall how she'd replied to his words last year. "I couldn't resist the fresh air. It's a lovely night."

"It is," he said, holding her gaze as he handed her a glass.

"Thank you, I didn't realize how thirsty I am."

She kept her eyes on his as she finished her drink. Before she could set it aside, he took it from her, put it on the grass, and took a step closer to her. And then a few more steps. He stopped a hair's breadth away from her.

"Who are you?" he whispered in that sweet tone she'd come to know and love so well. "Do you want to tell me who you are, or take your mask off?"

Miranda reached up to untie her mask and let it fall to the ground. "And now you," she said.

George removed his mask and took her into his arms. He kissed her with a wild abandon that had her wondering if they could indeed sneak upstairs to their room.

"I wanted to do that last year," he said, cupping her face in his hands. "I fantasized about it for days after the ball, and I never dreamed I'd have the chance to reveal my lady's true identity, and to make you my wife."

"It seems impossible we didn't know each other then."

"I always knew you," he said and kissed her. "I love you, Miranda."

Her heart sang. So much had happened in the last

year. Her life had changed in unexpected, amazing ways and was full of new people to love. Most importantly, she knew herself better than she ever had before. She now understood what it meant to love and be loved, to ask for what she wanted, to be honest with everyone, especially herself, and to say yes to the incredible future stretching before her.

"I love you, too, George. This has been the best year of my life, all thanks to you."

"Has it?" he asked softy, caressing her cheek.

"Yes. Honestly," Miranda said and drew him down for another kiss.

A word about the author...

Kate Ellington grew up in a small, woodsy town not far from the New England seacoast. She read her first historical romance at age eleven when a teacher challenged her to find a book in the library written by an author she'd never heard of. Thus began a lifelong love of love stories.

She currently resides in the Pacific Northwest with her delightful family and three cats. When not writing she can be found reading, baking, traveling and spending time outdoors.

Thank you for purchasing
this publication of The Wild Rose Press, Inc.

For questions or more information
contact us at
info@thewildrosepress.com.

The Wild Rose Press, Inc.
www.thewildrosepress.com